Loans are up to 28 days. Fines are charged if items are
not returned by the due date. Items can be renewed
at the Library, via the internet or by telephone up to
3 times. Items in demand will not be renewed.
Please use a bookmark

Check out our online catalogue to see what's in stock,
or to renew or reserve books.
www.birmingham.gov.uk/libcat
www.birmingham.bov.uk/libraries

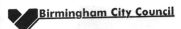
Birmingham City Council

Birmingham Libraries

50706

RETURN TO JARROW

RETURN TO JARROW

Janet MacLeod Trotter

headline

First published in 2004
by HEADLINE BOOK PUBLISHING

10 9 8 7 6 5 4 3 2 1

RETURN TO JARROW is a work of fiction based on (and inspired by)
the extraordinary lives of the historical figures in this publication.

Cataloguing in Publication Data is available from the British Library

ISBN 0 7553 0848 4

Typeset in Times by Avon DataSet Ltd,
Bidford-on-Avon, Warwickshire

Printed and bound in Great Britain by
Mackays of Chatham plc, Chatham, Kent

HEADLINE BOOK PUBLISHING
A division of Hodder Headline
338 Euston Road
London NW1 3BH

www.headline.co.uk
www.hodderheadline.com

In memory of Mum – always with me.
To Dad – for laughter and encouragement
– with love and thanks.

Chapter 1

1923 – Jarrow

Catherine stood in the stark ante-room of the registry office, seething with anger. Her mother was about to get married. She dug her nails into the palms of her hands to stop herself from shouting out, *Don't do it! Don't do it! How can you marry Davie McDermott? He's just a common stoker who spends all his wages on drink. He can hardly string a sentence together. And now he's going to be family. And where am I supposed to sleep once he's moved into your bed?*

She glared across at her mother – the woman she could never bring herself to call Mam. Kate smiled back, as if there was nothing the matter, as if they had not had one of their blazing rows just that morning.

'You'll not spoil me wedding day with your twisty face,' Kate had snapped, half stripped in the scullery, washing herself. 'I've waited for this long enough.'

'Why can't you get married by the priest in church?' Catherine had protested for the umpteenth time. 'It won't be a proper marriage.'

'It's all the marriage I need. Davie doesn't want any fuss and neither do I.'

Catherine glanced away from her mother's thick muscly arms and large breasts. It made her think about what Kate and Davie would be doing in the large feather bed by nightfall, the bed that she had shared with her mother for years. Tonight there would be no protective arm slung carelessly over her body, no sound of her mother's heavy breathing next to hers. For too long she had resented the snoring and reek of whisky on Kate's breath, but now, for the first time, Catherine was afraid of not having her there. Not that she could tell her mother in a million years.

'And where am I supposed to sleep, the night?' she asked. 'I'm not ganin' in the parlour with Grandda. It wouldn't be right – and he snores worse than you do.'

'You can kip on the settle – it'll be snug in the kitchen. Don't you remember how we used to sleep there when the house was full of lodgers – before the war when Uncle Jack was alive?'

Kate stopped and Catherine tensed. Any mention of Jack usually reduced her mother to tears. It was nearly five years since Kate's young half-brother had been killed in the war, but her mother still cried about it, especially when she'd had a drink or two.

'I'll stop over at Lily's,' Catherine declared, handing her mother a threadbare towel from a nail on the back of the door. 'At least I'm welcome there.'

Kate rolled her eyes. 'It'll not be for long,' she promised. 'Davie'll be joining his ship in a week, then things'll be the same as before.'

'No they won't, they'll never be the same! You'll be Mrs McDermott, and I'll still be Kitty McMullen.' *Your bastard daughter*. Catherine felt sick anger at the thought.

'There's nothing to stop you taking his name an' all,' Kate pointed out.

'Never!'

'Why not? You should be grateful that I'm giving you a da at last. It's what you've always wanted, isn't it?'

'Not a da like him.'

Kate took her by the shoulders and shook her. 'Don't you stick your nose in the air at the likes of Davie McDermott. He's a good man and you're lucky he wants to take us on. I've waited years to have a ring on me finger – made respectable – to hold me head up high round here. By the saints, I have, and you're not ganin' to spoil it!'

'Well, I'll not bother coming if you don't want me there,' Catherine pouted.

Kate immediately changed tack. 'Hinny, don't be daft, course I want you there. We both do. Now haway and get dressed, and we'll say no more about it.'

That was so typical of her mother, Catherine thought with resentment: one minute scolding her like a child, the next brushing aside her concerns as if they were of no importance. But she was a child no longer; she was seventeen, with a young woman's body and feelings.

She watched Kate now, her face flushed under a large hat that Aunt

Mary had lent her, her blue eyes lively. At forty-one, she often looked ten years older, but today her mother looked pretty in a lilac dress, her mood skittish as a girl's.

They had already had a drink at the house before leaving; Kate, Grandda John, Davie and cousin Maisie. There would be plenty more drinking afterwards at the Penny Whistle where Kate sometimes worked. How many times had she been sent there as a child, to fill up that hateful jug with whisky for her mother and grandfather? Catherine shuddered at the memory.

'Just fill the "grey hen" for me, Kitty.' Kate would slip her the money. 'I'll make it worth your while – a twist of sweets from Aflecks. I've had a hard day, hinny, don't give me that look.'

And she would go, in the slim hope that it would sweeten tempers in the warring household at Number Ten, William Black Street. More often, it fuelled her grandfather's violent drunkenness and Kate's morose self-pity. A jug of whisky meant smashed crockery and Grandda chasing Kate with filthy words and the fire poker. It meant black eyes and pictures off the walls. And later it meant Grandda wetting himself and Catherine being woken by Kate to placate him and coax him to bed, the smell of urine making her retch.

Well, she would not be setting foot inside any pub today, Catherine determined. As soon as the dismal little ceremony was over, she was going to get out of this dress and escape to Lily's for the rest of the weekend.

The next moment, the clerk called them.

'But our Mary's not here yet,' Kate said, suddenly flustered, staring past the outer door for her younger sister.

'Doesn't surprise me,' John McMullen grunted. 'She'll want to make a grand entry and keep everyone waiting.'

'Well, we can't wait,' Kate said in annoyance.

Catherine was not going to be the one to tell her mother that Mary had no intention of coming. She thought nothing of Davie McDermott either. Aunt Mary saw the marriage as further proof of Kate's poor judgement.

'If she thinks I'm going to wish her well, she can think again. I've better things to do than watch the pair of them getting drunk and making a spectacle of themselves. And I'll never forgive her for calling my Alec a conchie and a yellow-belly, just 'cos he failed his medical during the war. Well, he's twice the man that David McDermott will ever be.'

3

'Come on Kate,' Davie chivvied, 'we don't need your sister. Maisie and Kitty can be our witnesses.'

He helped old John to his feet and into the inner room where the registrar was eager to get on with the proceedings.

As Catherine listened to the short address, the curt questions and hasty answers, she felt a stab of guilt. Davie was not a bad man. He was gruff and shy, and had never been unkind towards her. He was one of the first lodgers she could remember, swaggering through the door of their home with her Uncle Jack and another seaman, Jock Stoddart, noisy with drink and laughter, the smell of the sea on their kitbags. She had preferred Stoddie, but he had married someone else, and Kate had been left with the choice of Davie or endless years at the beck and call of her boorish stepfather, John McMullen.

Why shouldn't her mother marry Davie? Didn't she deserve a bit of happiness after all the years of being bullied and vilified for her one mistake, bearing a child out of wedlock?

A familiar wave of shame engulfed Catherine. She was that mistake. Her mother's life had been ruined because of her. Kate was the laughing stock of the New Buildings in East Jarrow where they lived. Kate the drinker, Kate the slut. 'Thought she could pull the wool over our eyes and pass that bairn off as her little sister. As if old Rose could still be bearing babies at her age! Mark my words, the lass will go the way of her mother, see if she doesn't. Blood will out. She's too big for her boots already, that Kitty McMullen.'

How often she had overheard the gossips' hurtful words about the two of them. They were seared into her soul as if from a branding iron. Better if she'd never been born.

Catherine's eyes smarted with tears. Her feelings were so confused. She was wicked and bad to wish ill of her mother's marriage to Davie.

After the brief ceremony, she kissed her mother and Davie.

'Good luck,' she smiled, forcing an act of being pleased. 'I'm glad for you.'

'Thanks, hinny,' Kate beamed tearfully. 'This is the happiest day of me life.'

Catherine's heart twisted. What about the day you met my real father? What about the day you fell in love with him? The day you gave birth to me and first held me in your arms? There was so much she yearned to know but could never ask.

'Haway, let's get on with the celebratin'!' John stamped his stick with impatience. 'Give me your arm, Kitty.'

4

Catherine helped him round to the pub, then said, 'I'm not stoppin', Grandda.'

'It's your mam's weddin' day, lass. Let your hair down! You cannot gan to confession with nowt to confess.'

'How would you know?' Catherine teased.

'Don't give me your lip,' he growled. But she knew he would not take offence. For all the trouble her illegitimacy had caused the family, her grandfather had always been fair to her. He and Grandma Rose had brought her up as their own daughter until the truth had leaked out, and he had shown her a rough love and protection that she had never seen him give his stepdaughters, Kate and Aunt Mary, or Aunt Sarah in Birtley.

'I promised to see Lily.'

'Keep out of trouble, the pair of ye,' he grunted.

'Father O'Neill's youth club is all the trouble we'll see.' She pecked him on the cheek. 'Tell Kate I'll be back the morra after Mass.'

'Away you gan, Saint Catherine, and save us from a sermon!'

She hurried away before her mother reappeared and dragged her inside. Within half an hour, she was changed into a skirt and jumper, and riding her bicycle down the hill from East Jarrow, under the dank railway arches of Tyne Dock and into South Shields.

Catherine knew its streets well. Ever since she could walk, she had wandered far from home, exploring its shops and gazing at the street sellers: organ-grinders with monkeys, medicine men with potions, strolling players, rag-and-bone men, carpet sellers and fishwives. This river town meant the excitement of the noisy, stuffy picture houses on Saturdays, as well as the humiliation of carrying a heavy bundle to the pawnshops on Mondays. She loved and hated it.

Lily lived on a terraced street, similar to hers on the outside, but a world apart inside. Lily's mother filled the neat kitchen with flowers from her husband's allotment, which added to the comforting smell of furniture polish and starched linen. Kate's kitchen smelt of other people's wet washing, stale beer and the soot of an unswept chimney.

Lily's home was flooded with light from sparkling windows, while Catherine's was dingy from the grime that blew from the docks and ironworks. Not that she and Kate did not try hard to keep the place clean. But with John around all day long, demanding attention, and Kate too tired after working odd jobs and taking in washing, the housework never quite got finished.

Lily's father worked on the trams, polished all the shoes and never took a drink. Her mother made the best stottie cake and scones on Tyneside. Good food, flowers and sunshine, that's what Lily Hearn's parents offered, and Catherine longed for all of these on this strange day.

Lily was waiting with a parcel of sandwiches in her saddlebag and a bottle of lemonade.

'Wasn't sure if you'd come,' she smiled cautiously. 'Everything gan all right?'

Catherine nodded. 'Let's cycle out to Cleadon – it's too hot in the town.'

Lily agreed and they were soon on their way, the breeze off the river pushing them up hill and out of Shields. They stopped in a cornfield above the solid mansions of Cleadon. In the distance, a hazy smoke lay over the docks and factories of Tyneside and beyond that, the pearly shimmer of the North Sea.

Catherine lay back among the green wheat and closed her eyes in the warm sun.

'Is it all right if I stay at yours the night?'

'Aye,' Lily agreed with a nudge. 'Giving the bride and groom a bit time to themselves, eh?'

Catherine sat up. 'It's not like that. Kate's just gettin' wed so she can call herself Mrs McDermott, nothing more. It's not as if they're in love – they're too old for all that.'

Lily arched her eyebrows. 'Your mam's not so old. You could have a baby brother or sister by this time next year. That'd be canny, wouldn't it?'

'No! It'd be terrible. Don't say that, Lily. I don't even like to think of them – you know – doing it.'

Lily giggled. 'Do you ever think of what it must be like?'

'What?'

'Going with a lad.'

Catherine gasped. 'Course not! I mean, not until after I'm wed.'

Lily gave her a shove. 'Eeh, your face – what a picture!'

Catherine abruptly laughed. 'We shouldn't be talking of such things. Imagine what the priest would say if he heard us.'

'It's only natural to be curious,' Lily said, playing with tendrils of her dark hair.

Catherine watched her friend running slim fingers through her springy fringe.

'Doesn't it frighten you – the thought of having a bairn?' Catherine asked quietly.

Lily pursed her lips. 'Not really. Mam says giving birth is like going three rounds with the poss tub. It leaves you all done in – but the results are worth it.'

The two friends burst out laughing.

'I could never talk about such things with Kate,' Catherine said in admiration. 'I wish I had your mam and dad.'

'Well, at least you've got a da now.'

Catherine felt quick resentment. 'Kate has a husband,' she said sharply. 'It's not the same as me having a da.'

Lily shrugged. 'You'll get used to him in time.'

'I don't want to get used to him,' Catherine said with passion. 'I want . . .'

Lily regarded her with puzzled dark eyes. 'What do you want, Kitty?'

Catherine felt gripped by a deep longing. Lily was the only one in the world she could possibly tell.

'I want me real da. I feel like only half a person, not knowing him. He must've been someone really special for Kate to take such a risk.' Her green eyes shone with intense yearning. 'I want to see what he looks like, hear how he speaks – know everything about him. I feel like a square peg in a round hole – always have done. I don't feel like Kate's daughter. I feel like *his* daughter, whoever he is.'

Lily frowned. 'Didn't know it meant that much to you, Kitty.'

'It does! Ever since Kate said she was going to wed Davie, I've thought of me real da more and more. I can't think of owt else.' Catherine seized her friend by the hand. 'Will you help me look for him?'

'What, your real da?' Lily looked startled.

Catherine nodded vigorously. 'Say you will, Lily. I'll never be happy till I find him.'

Lily's look was dubious. Only reluctantly did she agree. 'Aye, if it means that much to you, Kitty.'

Chapter 2

Catherine made an effort to be nice to Davie that week. She had the tea ready for her mother coming in after her cleaning jobs, and made herself scarce afterwards.

'I've a parcel to deliver down Jarrow,' Catherine announced one evening, wrapping up a set of finished cushion covers that she had been working on all day. She was proud of her small business of hand-painted furnishings. The next evening she said, 'I'm off over to Lily's. Be back before dark.'

But the McMullen house was too cramped for comfort: three rooms and a scullery, yet Davie and her grandda had to lounge around in the kitchen, getting under her feet while she tried to work. It got on her nerves the way Davie watched her painting the delicate flowers and birds on to the cushion covers and mantelpiece borders. She needed peace and quiet, but he never stopped whistling. She tried to tell Kate.

'I need the table for me painting, you know that. But he spreads his newspaper all over it – and his baccy. Bits get in me paints.'

'It's his home an' all,' Kate pointed out.

'And I've a business to run,' Catherine said in exasperation. 'I thought you were proud of me making me own way?'

'I am, hinny.'

'Then speak to him,' Catherine pleaded.

'I will. But you'll have to get used to sharing,' Kate warned.

Catherine bit back many a retort when Davie snorted brown snuff off the back of his gnarled hand and sneezed over her work.

'Canny day for a walk,' she suggested pointedly the next day.

Davie nodded in agreement. 'Aye, you spend too long cooped up in here with your painting. Can't be good for your eyes. You get yourself out and I'll keep an eye on old John for a bit.'

Catherine got up in annoyance and cleared her work into a box. She could not stand another day of him peering over her shoulder with his tobacco smell.

'And if you're passing Aflecks, will you get me a bit of baccy, pet?'

She felt like telling him to get it himself, but didn't. Just three more days and he'd be gone. Maybe then Kate would show her an ounce of attention, help her sew in the evenings instead of getting drunk and loud with her seaman husband. She longed for those rare quiet times when she and Kate worked on the cushion covers together and there was no extra money for whisky.

Catherine wandered aimlessly down the street and stood at the end looking down at the River Tyne. The tide was out. A raw smell of effluent, mud and timber wafted up from Jarrow Slake, the tidal inlet below. She had played there as a child, defying her mother and grandmother. The game had been to run along the bobbing planks of timber stored in the Slake, daring each other to go further and deeper. Then there had been the day when a young boy had nearly drowned and she had never gone there again. Billy. Catherine had not thought of him for years. She felt a chill shiver go down her back. No, she could not think about it. There were memories locked inside her head that were too painful to probe. Best to forget.

She turned on her heels and away from the breezy riverside. A few minutes later she was at the top of the dusty street and knocking on Aunt Mary's door. An upstairs window flew open.

'Come on up,' Mary called out. 'Remember to wipe your feet.'

Catherine smiled to herself, recalling Kate's comment: 'When her house burns doon, our Mary'll be tellin' the firemen to wipe their feet before they come an inch further.'

The upstairs flat was stifling, the windows closed against the swirling black dust from outside. Her aunt was ironing in the kitchen. It looked so much bigger than theirs, uncluttered with the large mismatched furniture that Kate and Grandda collected.

'Had enough of the drunken sailor already?' Mary snorted.

Catherine felt disloyal as she nodded.

'Pour us both a cup of tea,' her aunt ordered, 'and you can tell me all about it. How was the wedding? Young Alec wasn't at all well and I couldn't leave him.'

Catherine saw no sign of her younger cousin. 'Is he still ill?'

Mary flapped a hand. 'No, no, he's out with his father – gone down to Shields fishing.'

How Catherine wished she could be in the company of her gentle

Uncle Alec and cheerful cousin on the pier at South Shields at that moment. Father and son fishing in the sunshine. She pushed the thought away quickly.

'Did our Kate make a spectacle of herself?' Mary asked eagerly.

'No,' Catherine defended her mother. 'It was quiet and quick, and they both looked happy. Kate looked grand in your hat, Aunt Mary.'

Mary sniffed. 'Well, tell her I want it back. She's never thanked me for it.'

'You've never been to see her yet,' Catherine dared to say.

Mary gave her a sharp look and Catherine knew to be cautious. Her aunt took offence at the slightest remark. That was why Kate, who always spoke her mind, was constantly in trouble with her younger sister. All through her growing up, Catherine could remember spectacular rows between the sisters and threats of never speaking to each other again that could last for months. She quickly poured the tea from the pot on the stove into delicate china cups.

'Anyway, I didn't stay for the weddin' party,' Catherine confessed.

Mary gave a tight smile of satisfaction. 'I can't blame you. What would a good devout Catholic lass like you be doing in the sort of place Kate chooses? No, you're more like me – too much breeding to be seen inside a public house. That's the Fawcett stock showing through. My father was a respectable steelman, you know, and a brethren of St Bede's. It's a crying shame he died of consumption so young, and me just a baby. Life would have been very different for us if he'd lived. We'd have stayed Fawcetts instead of coming down in the world as Irish McMullens.'

She blew out her flushed cheeks and sipped the strong tea. Catherine loved it when her aunt talked about the family history. Kate hardly ever did. Only once did she remember her mother mention William Fawcett, Grandma Rose's first husband. With tears in her eyes, Kate had spoken of a loving father who had delighted in grabbing his daughter by the hand and running down the street, chasing the moon.

Kate had seemed so soft and tender in that moment that Catherine had dared ask her about her own father. Immediately Kate had clammed up and been cross, telling her that her mysterious father was dead and not to ask about him again. But Kate's alarm had been so great that Catherine doubted she was telling the truth. She just did not want her to find her missing father. Catherine was sure he must still be alive somewhere, living a more interesting life than theirs.

10

'I don't want to be a McDermott, any more than you wanted to be a McMullen,' Catherine said quietly.

'Poor Kitty,' Mary said indulgently, 'of course you don't. Davie's just a common stoker – rough as they come. I don't know what Kate was thinking of. Course, a bad husband is better than no husband in some lasses' opinion – specially those with as little reputation left as your mother.'

Catherine winced. 'I don't blame Kate for what she's done, it's just – I hate the way she thinks I should see him as me da. I could never think of Davie like that.'

'Course you can't. Davie McDermott is a world away from your real father—' Mary stopped herself. Catherine's heart began to thud.

'You knew me real father?' she whispered.

Mary was flustered. 'Shouldn't talk about it. It's all long in the past. Your mam wouldn't thank me.'

'Please, Aunt Mary, just tell me some'at about him – anything. All Kate ever said was I've got his eyes and hair.'

'Aye, you have his good looks,' Mary mused. 'Beautiful chestnut hair and bonny eyes.'

'Tell me a bit more,' Catherine pleaded.

Her aunt relented. 'He used to call at the inn where we worked,' Mary said cautiously.

'What inn?'

'The Ravensworth Arms – on the Ravensworth estate – you know, where your Great-Aunt Lizzie lives.'

Catherine nodded. When she had been alive, Grandma Rose had spoken fondly of a special place in the country where her sister lived. Since the war and Rose's death, Lizzie had lost touch with the Jarrow relations.

'I didn't know you'd worked away,' Catherine marvelled. 'Thought you'd always lived on Tyneside.'

'No, I worked at the Ravensworth – a respectable place – a coaching inn where men of business and folk from the castle came to sup. Got your mam her job there – I had a good reputation as a hard worker, you see, so they agreed to take Kate on too.'

Catherine kept to herself the thought that her mother, for all her faults, could work twice as hard as Mary any day of the week.

'Mind you, it would've been better if I hadn't put in a word for her, with all the trouble she got into.'

Catherine flushed. 'So that's where she met me da?'

Mary nodded.

'Was he a lad from the castle?'

'No, not exactly.'

'Then who?' Catherine held her breath.

'He was a real gentleman, your father. Oh yes, with his silver-topped cane and his beautiful black coat with an astrakhan collar. Quite the gent. They say he was distantly related to the Liddells themselves.'

'The Liddells?'

'The gentry at Ravensworth Castle.'

'Never!' Catherine caught her breath.

Mary nodded, her eyes bright with the telling of the long-kept secret.

'Well, he used to come on business to the estate—'

'What sort of business?'

Mary shrugged. 'I don't know, but it must've been important. He always seemed to be visiting the estate – and he always found time to call at the inn.'

'And that's how he fell in love with Kate?'

'Fell in love?' Mary snorted. 'Men of his standing don't fall for barmaids! No, they're only after one thing. Bold as brass he was – calling on her days off and taking her out in his carriage. Thought nobody knew what they were up to, but she was the laughing stock of the inn. "Look at Lady Kate," they'd say, and, "There goes the Duchess of Jarrow with her fancy man!" '

Catherine swallowed. 'So they were courtin' – it wasn't just . . .?'

'If you can call it courtin' when a gentleman takes a fancy to a working maid.' Mary was scathing. 'But, yes, he came visiting regular – over two years or more, it must've been.'

'Maybes Kate thought he would marry her, then? To have courted for so long,' Catherine said quietly.

'The more fool her! The number of times I warned your mam not to lose her head over him. Oh, I could see she was daft for him – and what lass wouldn't be? He was tall and handsome, with that posh voice – and such a way with words. But he would never have married her in a month of Sundays.'

'I suppose not,' Catherine said wistfully.

'No, never. Besides, he was promised to another. That's what he came to tell her when – well, when, you know, she made her big mistake. Just the once she went with him, I'm sure of that. But once is all it takes,' Mary declared.

Catherine blushed. Perhaps Kate had lain with him in the desperate

12

hope he would choose her? She rubbed her clammy hands on her skirts.

'What happened to him?'

'Disappeared into thin air,' Mary said in disapproval, 'and left Kate to face the music with old John. By the saints, he would've skinned her alive if our Jack hadn't got between them!'

'Maybes me da would've stood by Kate if he'd known about me?' Catherine said with a hopeful glance.

Mary shook her head. 'He did know. Came back months later asking for Kate. Well, I gave him a piece of me mind; told him good and proper she'd gone back to Jarrow in disgrace, carrying his bairn. Even told him where to find her.'

Catherine gulped down tears. 'But he never bothered?'

'That's the odd thing,' Mary mused. 'I could've sworn he was going to fetch her there and then – left the inn like a dog off the leash. But I would've heard if he'd gone to see her – Kate and Mam never said a thing about any visit. So I kept me mouth shut an' all. Kate was in a bad enough state without me giving her a shock about his lordship turning up looking for her. Eeh, she was like a lass in mourning all the time she was carrying you.'

Catherine sat stunned and speechless. Could it be true? Her father had been a gentleman, a man of wealth, just as she had always daydreamed? As a child she had created a fantasy world in which her father would come and whisk her away from Jarrow's backstreets to a country mansion bathed in never-ending sunshine. Now it seemed, the reality was not so far removed from her dream world. Perhaps if he knew about his long-lost daughter, he would claim her as his own? The thought made Catherine sick with longing. She had to find him and know for herself what kind of man her father was. He had rejected Kate, not her!

'What was he called?' Catherine whispered.

Mary frowned. 'Alexander something.'

'Please try and remember.'

'It was that long ago,' Mary protested. 'Double-barrelled. Alexander . . . Pringle-Davies! Yes, that's it.'

'Alexander Pringle-Davies,' Catherine repeated in a dreamy voice.

Mary glanced at her in alarm. 'Don't you go telling any of this to Kate. I shouldn't have said so much. She'll go light with me if she finds out! You never heard anything of this from me, do you hear?'

'Aye, Aunt Mary,' Catherine agreed.

'It's just our secret, then?'

Catherine nodded. She could never imagine asking Kate about such intimate things. Her mother had made it plain years ago that the shameful past was never ever to be mentioned. Catherine knew she would get no help from Kate in tracking down her father. But now she was armed with these new revelations, she felt even more determined to discover her father. Just being able to talk about him – a real flesh-and-blood person with a name and a position in society – gave her a thrill.

All the way home, Catherine hugged this new knowledge to herself. It gave her strength to face Davie, the impostor in their household who dared to be a father to her. She passed Aflecks, but did not go in for tobacco. Davie could fetch his own. She was the daughter of Alexander Pringle-Davies and did not belong round here. She was born to something far better than the sooty lanes of a shipyard town. Catherine held her head high.

Chapter 3

It was Lily who persuaded Catherine not to go chasing after her unknown father.

'And when you get to Lamesley, what you ganin' to do? Knock on the castle door and ask if he's in? What will you say to folk, Kitty? They'll wonder why you're asking for him. Who will you say you are?'

Catherine had not thought of that. It might lead to awkward questions. *I'm Kate's bastard daughter.* She felt nauseous at the thought of being exposed. Once people knew, they changed towards her, gave her that look. She had seen it so often in the eyes of neighbours: pity mixed with contempt. Even among her friends she had endured the casually cruel jibes of children, the arbitrary exclusion from games. That time at Bella's party . . . no, she would not think about it. The memory lay like an unhealed wound.

'No,' Lily was adamant, 'you'll open up a can of worms with your questions. Leave it be.'

Catherine felt frustrated, but what could she do? Lily would not go with her and she did not feel brave enough to go on her own. She would have to abandon her plan.

Through the summer, Catherine threw herself into other activities. With Davie gone back to sea, she kept busy at her painting during the day, and in the long evenings went to Lily's. On Saturday afternoons, when Lily was off duty from her job at the workhouse laundry, they cycled far and wide. Twice a week, they attended the Catholic youth club run by Father O'Neill.

The elderly priest kept a strict eye on proceedings at the club dances, but Catherine loved them. She took little persuading to get up and sing a song or recite a poem in front of the others during breaks in the dancing. She was never one to sit out the dances either. Catherine was light on her feet, quick to laugh and banter with the boys and was never short of a partner. Lily may have been prettier, with her dark looks, but

Catherine was equally popular. She was vivacious and could tell a joke and was always the centre of a laughing, chattering crowd.

Catherine lived for such moments when she could be with her friends, away from her demanding mother and grandfather, playing the clown. Underneath, she might feel anxious or unsure of herself, but she hid it under a carefree mask.

'Dance with me, Kitty,' Tommy Gallon grinned, pulling her to her feet.

'Father O'Neill will have some'at to say,' Catherine teased. 'That's twice in one evening.'

'And it'll be twice more, if I get me way,' Tommy declared.

Catherine laughed. 'That's an hour in confession for you this week.'

'It'll be worth it for you, Kitty.'

Catherine blushed as he led her in the dance. Tommy was a miner, a couple of years older than she, and she felt his wiry strength under his best suit. He had boyish good looks, but she could imagine the fuss Grandda would make if she brought him home.

'Pitmen – nowt but trouble. They're half animals digging under the earth for a living. Dirty troublemakers, that's what they are.'

It did not matter that his stepdaughter Sarah had married one. Or maybe he said it to goad her. Some of Catherine's cousins were now working down the mine, but her grandfather blamed everything from the slump in the iron trade to bad weather on the luckless miners.

So when Tommy asked if he could walk her home, Catherine refused. 'I'm stopping at Lily's the night.'

'I'll walk you there, then,' Tommy persisted.

Catherine hesitated, but Lily intervened. 'You can walk the pair of us. You in the middle, so we can keep an eye on you.'

Tommy walked them home and they chatted all the way, but Catherine slipped quickly inside before he could kiss her good night.

Lying in bed next to Lily that night she thought of Tommy and her pulse quickened. She was attracted to him and knew he liked her. But where would a kiss lead? She was terrified that she might be over-whelmed by passion like Kate, and not be able to control herself. Catherine flushed all over. She should not even be thinking of such things. Once, at confession, she had spoken of having sexual thoughts and the priest had threatened her with the flames of Hell. She was bad for thinking them.

'Are you ganin' to kiss Tommy next week?' Lily asked, startling her.

'No, never!' Catherine said, flustered.

16

'Why not? I think he's canny.'

'It wouldn't be right.'

'No harm in a bit kiss and cuddle,' Lily said.

'Yes there is,' Catherine protested. 'It can lead to bairns.'

'I don't think it's in the kissing,' Lily said doubtfully.

'Well, I'm not taking any risks. Anyway, Tommy Gallon's only a pitman – I'm ganin' to marry someone better.'

Lily snorted. 'Don't you be so fussy. Tommy's in work and earning canny wages compared to some round here. Lads at the steel mills haven't worked for six months. You should see the poor souls who turn up at the workhouse desperate for anything.'

Catherine felt uneasy. If Rose and John had not stuck by Kate, she and her mother might have ended up in the workhouse too. According to Lily, there were many unmarried mothers and their babies locked away there, until their children were of working age.

'Well, I'm not looking for a lad,' Catherine said.

She curled up tight in the bed, trying to banish thoughts of Tommy's strong arms around her and the smell of soap and coal-dust on his skin. Maybe one kiss wouldn't do any harm.

Just as she was drifting into sleep, Lily murmured, 'Wonder what they look like underneath?'

'Who?' Catherine yawned.

'Lads. I've never seen a lad with nowt on – not even me da. Have you?'

Catherine's heart pounded. For a moment she could not breathe. A terrifying image came barging into her mind, unbidden.

'Course not,' she gasped.

But in a deep part of her, she knew she was lying. She must be lying, or from where did this picture in her head come? She could never speak of it, not even to Lily, not even the priest.

Catherine lay sweating and shivering, engulfed by anxiety, the joy of the evening gone. Was it her imagination? If so she must truly be wicked. If not . . . She clenched her fists and screwed her eyes tight shut, trying to forget. Just as she had as a child, she pushed her thoughts into an imaginary box and locked them away.

Chapter 4

All through the autumn, Catherine went to the dances with Lily, and Tommy vied with his friend Peter to walk her home. She was baffled by their attention. What was it about her that they could possibly find alluring? Lily was far the prettier. It was just that she gave as good as she got, answered them back instead of blushing and being tongue-tied like some of the other girls. Or maybe they had heard the rumours about her having no da and thought she would be an easy conquest? Well, she wasn't. They could walk her home till they were drawing their pensions, she wouldn't give in to either of them without a ring on her finger and the priest's blessing.

As the days shortened, the light for Catherine's painting went early. One evening in early December, the family was enjoying a quiet evening around the fireside, Grandda John dozing in his chair, Catherine at his feet, perched on the fender, stitching a cushion cover. Kate was making bread at the kitchen table, flour rising in a yellow cloud in the lamplight.

Catherine's eyes were aching from the dim light. She rubbed them and looked up. Kate was watching her, hands plunged in a ball of dough.

'Don't strain your eyes, hinny. Haven't you done enough the night?'

'I've a big order for Christmas,' Catherine yawned.

'I'll help you the morra,' Kate promised. They smiled at each other. 'Now shift yoursel' while I put the bread to rise.'

Catherine stood up and stretched her tired limbs. As Kate dumped the tin of bread on the hearth, the latch on the kitchen door clicked and heavy boots stamped into the scullery. Kate whipped round.

'Is that you, Davie?'

'Aye!'

Kate darted towards the door, flinging her arms out as her husband bowled into the room. He caught her in a bear hug and she planted a kiss on his mouth. They laughed like young lovers. Catherine looked away, her stomach clenching. Lily's words went through her head. *You could have a baby brother or sister by this time next year.* Heaven forbid! She'd be the one with the burden of helping to bring up a child, stuck here for ever.

'Hello, Kitty,' Davie said amiably.

Catherine nodded and sat back down on the fender.

'Well, don't just sit there!' Kate cried. 'Fetch our Davie a cup of tea from the pot – and there's a piece of cheese pie left in the pantry. Go on, our Kitty!'

Catherine scowled as she picked up her sewing. 'I've this to finish.'

Kate looked furious, but Davie held her back. 'Let the lass be. I'm past eating.' He pulled a half-bottle of whisky out of his duffel coat.

Kate's eyes lit up. 'I'll fetch the cups.'

John stirred. 'What's that? Davie, is that you, son?'

'I've brought you some baccy,' Davie grinned at his father-in-law, 'and a drop of the hard stuff.'

'Good on you, lad!' John's gaunt face smiled. He flapped a hand impatiently at Kate. 'Get them poured, woman.'

Kate ignored him as she pulled out a chair for Davie and took his coat from him.

'Sit yourself down. How was your trip? When did you get in? You should've sent word and we could've come to meet you. Couldn't we, Kitty? You're looking as thin as a poker. Have you been ill?'

Davie laughed, his eyes shining with affection. 'I'm grand. Come and sit beside me, Kate.'

'No, I can see you need feeding up,' she insisted. 'I'll fetch that pie – and I can fry up some tatties in half a minute.'

Davie caught her arm and swung her on to his knee. 'Stop fussing.' He kissed her cheek and poured out whisky into the cups. 'Pass this one to your grandda, Kitty.'

Catherine eyed him. She was not his skivvy.

'Gan on,' John said, prodding her with his foot, 'do as your da says.'

She got up, biting back a retort and passed over the cup Davie held out. The evening was ruined. They would finish the bottle, then she would be sent out to fetch more. Well, she wouldn't do it. Kate hadn't even bothered to wipe the flour off the table before starting to drink. Catherine's heart sank to think she would have to wait up until all the drinking and talking was over before she could make her bed on the hard settle. Sometimes, as a child, she had curled up and gone to sleep there while the noise and drinking went on around her. But she was too old for that now. It rankled that Kate wanted her warming the bed when Davie was away, but as soon as he was back she was turfed out.

'How long you back for?' Catherine asked.

'Till after Christmas.'

'That's grand,' Kate said in delight. 'We'll have the best time ever.'

'I've a present for you, Kitty,' Davie smiled. He rummaged in his bag and pulled out a wodge of newspaper, holding it out to her.

'Can't I keep it for Christmas?' Catherine said, keeping her arms folded.

'I'll buy you something else for that.'

Kate said, 'Gan on, Kitty, don't be so ungrateful. I want to see what it is.'

She took the parcel and unwrapped the foreign newspaper. Inside was a gaudy, painted doll. She felt like telling him she was too old for dolls.

'It's Russian. Open it up,' Davie urged. 'It pulls apart in the middle.'

Catherine twisted the doll in half, intrigued in spite of herself. Inside was another doll, smaller and painted with different patterns.

'Do it again,' Davie chuckled.

Catherine pulled off the top of the second doll, revealing a third one. She carried on until there were six dolls, the final one a tiny replica of the first with nothing left inside, just a hollow sound when she tapped it. Catherine was fascinated and appalled by the expressionless figures. They were just like her, a façade hiding an inner person that she did not dare show the world. If she stripped away all her faces, would she find a frightened hollow person at her core? The thought terrified her. So did the dolls.

Quickly she stuffed them back into each other.

'Aren't they bonny?' Kate demanded.

'Aye,' Catherine gulped, 'but I'm too old for dolls. Maybes cousin Ida would like them. I'll give them to her the next time Aunt Sarah's over visitin'. She'd love to play with them.'

Davie gave her a strange look. She had hurt him with her rejection. Or maybe it was his way of saying he could see right through her.

'There's no pleasing our Kitty,' Kate said in annoyance. 'Don't mind her. What you got for me, Davie man?'

20

Davie fumbled in his bag again and pulled out a piece of cloth wrapped in a jumper.

'You've brought me back a duster?' Kate teased.

'Look inside.'

She unfolded the cloth with the excitement of a child. Inside was a metal brooch. Kate held it up to the light: an exotic bird painted in china blue.

'Match your eyes,' Davie said bashfully.

Suddenly, Kate was crying.

Davie said in alarm, 'I thought you'd like it—'

'I do,' Kate sobbed. 'It's beautiful! No one's given me anything this grand in years.'

'Don't be so soft!' John snorted. 'What you want with jewellery, any road? Gan to wear it on your pinny?'

She glared at him. 'I'll find some'at to wear it on.' She wiped her eyes on her sleeve. 'Ta, Davie.' He poured her another shot of whisky.

Catherine watched them from her perch on the fender, wondering if her real father had ever given Kate such a brooch. Alexander would have given her something much grander, she was sure. But if he had, it was sold or pawned long ago, for Kate possessed no jewellery, save Davie's cheap wedding ring. How she wished there was something from her father that Kate could have passed on to her to keep – some hint of his tastes – tangible proof of his existence. But Kate would have sold it for drink long ago. Anger curdled inside her. She stood up.

'I want to gan to bed. Some of us have to work the morra.'

'Sit doon.' Kate waved at her to be seated. 'It's early yet.'

'You sleep in here then and I'll gan in the bed,' Catherine challenged, remaining on her feet.

'Just a bit longer, hinny.'

'You'll not notice the difference after that whisky,' Catherine muttered.

'Don't give me your lip,' Kate snapped, instantly riled. She was out of her seat and swaying towards her daughter. 'Don't look at me with his eyes!' she hissed. 'You've no right to speak to me like that. I've worked me fingers to the bone for you, you selfish lass. I'm entitled to a bit fun when me man comes home from sea. And you'll not tell me what I'm to do and not to do in me own home, do you hear?'

'It's my home an' all,' Catherine flashed back, 'not that you'd think it. Why should I have to gan on the settle like a lodger? I'm bringing in more wages than you – don't I deserve a bed?'

21

'Then gan in with your grandda.' Kate was dismissive.

Catherine glared at her mother. How could she suggest such a thing, knowing what a lecherous old man he was? She remembered times when old John had come staggering into their bedroom and fumbled drunkenly with Kate while she fought him off, with Grandma Rose lying helpless and bed-bound in the next room.

'I'll leave home,' Catherine threatened wildly, 'and I'll not come back!'

'Don't talk daft.'

'I mean it. I'll sign up with an agency and gan into place.'

'You wouldn't.'

'I would!'

John scoffed. 'You'd not last two minutes skivvying for posh folk. You've too many airs and graces.'

Catherine was riled. 'I can work as hard as any lass round here.'

'It's what's in your head's different,' John said. 'You take after me – won't be put upon by the bosses. They're no better than us, Kitty. Still have to wipe their backsides, whoever they are. You don't want to work for the nobs – that's for common lasses like Kate.'

'Don't call me common!' Kate blazed. 'That's the pot calling the kettle black!'

In an instant, John had seized the poker and was brandishing it at Kate. But he was slower on his feet than in times past, and she easily stepped out of his way. He cursed her and lunged again.

'I'll tak the frying pan to you again,' she threatened. 'You'll not get the better of me, you old fool.'

Catherine jumped aside as John kicked a chair out of his way. Davie got up and barged between them.

'Haway, there's no need for this.'

'Out me way,' John shouted. 'If you won't keep her in order, I will.'

'Put the poker down, man,' Davie said.

'This is my house,' John ranted, waving the poker at Davie. 'You'll not tell me what to do.'

Davie grabbed it and wrestled it out of his grip. It clanged on the table, smashing one of the cups. Whisky splashed across the floury surface. Davie pushed John back into his seat. Kate looked triumphant. Not since old Rose had died had she had an ally against the bullying John. Catherine knew from that look that her mother would not be encouraging Davie back to sea in a hurry.

Her protest had backfired. Now Davie would be ensconced at

Number Ten for weeks to come. It had been stupid to make threats about leaving, for she had nowhere to go. The walls of the hot cramped kitchen pressed in around her. She was trapped.

Chapter 5

Unofficial war was declared: Kate and Davie against Catherine. At least that was how Catherine saw it. Kate left her to run the house while she was out at work and expected tea on the table when she got in. But Catherine had the men demanding food and drink all day long, as well as trying to complete her Christmas orders. Davie would help with bringing in the coal and go out for the odd errand while buying his newspaper, but John did nothing.

When Kate got home, Davie's co-operation ceased. He sided with Kate over everything.

'Do as your mam says,' he constantly repeated. Or, 'Can't you see Kate's had a hard day? Just do as she asks, lass.'

Catherine seethed with resentment. Every day was a hard day for her. At the end of it she had to carry on working in the dim light with her paints while they sat around chatting and drinking. Kate never helped her with her Christmas orders like she had promised.

'Lend us sixpence for a jug of beer, hinny,' Kate whispered in the scullery. 'You're making good money.'

'Why can't *he*?' Catherine protested.

'Davie's money is his own – and he's generous with it. I don't like to ask.'

Catherine's look was contemptuous. Why should the men spend their money how they liked, while the women were expected to use theirs on the household? It would be different when she was married. Grudgingly, she gave her mother the sixpence. But she determined Kate would never get to know of the money she saved and hid in the rafters of the outside privy. Years of living in fear at her family's spendthrift ways had made her cautious. That was hers alone, gathered from hard work and saving. She would not let her mother drink it all away.

Apart from going to confession and Mass, Catherine hardly left the house all through December. She missed the youth club party.

'I can't, Lily man,' she said distractedly when her friend called, 'I've too much to finish.'

'You can do it later,' her friend said impatiently.

'Folk are relying on these as presents. I can't let them down. You'll have to gan with Amelia or one of the other lasses.'

Lily left in a huff and Catherine did not see her again until after Christmas. Catherine sat up late on Christmas Eve finishing her orders. Even Kate belatedly helped finish off some of the sewing, though her work was hurried. At midnight, Catherine tramped round Jarrow, making her final deliveries around the more well-to-do houses. By Christmas Day, Catherine was so exhausted she fell asleep during Mass and yawned all through the dinner she helped Kate prepare.

Work did not let up in January. Although there were layoffs at the yards, there seemed to be plenty of custom for her covers. Birthdays, weddings, christenings and the approaching Mothering Sunday gave her more work than she could cope with.

She grew tired and irritable, but would not turn work away. She had to save, so there was money put by. Davie's wages had run out, but bad weather and slackening trade had delayed his return to sea. At meal-times, Catherine served the smallest portions to herself until her appetite dwindled and she lost interest in food. No one seemed to notice, yet tempers grew fractious when there wasn't enough left of Kate's wages for drink. John hobbled down the hill to Tyne Dock to spend his pension round the pubs, but would give Kate nothing towards housekeeping.

'It's my money – I've slaved for it and I'll spend it how I like,' John declared when Kate complained.

'It's a war pension for our Jack being killed,' Kate rounded on him. 'It's as much mine as yours!'

'He was my son – my flesh and blood,' John snarled. 'You were just his half-sister.'

'I meant more to him than you ever did,' Kate said tearfully. 'He thought the world of me.'

'He thought you were a slut,' John spat into the fire. 'And I'll tak the belt to ye if you touch a penny of me money.'

Catherine tried to ignore their wrangling, but it left her insides knotted. She never knew when their bickering would erupt into violence. All she could do was work, save the pennies and pray for better times. She found solace in going to church, her one release of the week.

25

Catherine prayed for her mother and grandfather, terrified that they might die with their sins still unwashed. Kate would only go to confession once in a blue moon – 'for a good rake out' as she called it – but John never went at all. It was up to her, Catherine, to save them. Kneeling in the cavernous church, Catherine poured out her troubles to Our Lady. While confessing to the stern priest compounded her feelings of guilt, praying to the Virgin Mary gave her comfort and strength.

During one service, Catherine became aware of a strong, melodious voice. As she listened, a deep feeling of calm spread inside. The singing was both manly and beautiful. For a moment she imagined what the singer would look like and the picture of her father as a young man, described by Aunt Mary, came into her head. He would be tall, well-dressed, strong-featured, with a bold gaze and a ready smile.

Catherine's heart began to pound with a longing that was not wholly spiritual. She was almost reluctant to turn around in case the singer was a disappointment. But her curiosity was too great and she glanced over her shoulder. She gasped in shock. It was as if she had conjured the man out of her daydreams. He was not quite as tall as she had imagined, but his coat was well cut and his dark eyes shone with vitality as he sang.

Catherine had never seen him before. When the service was over, she watched him leave alone and hurried out to see which way he went. He strode off in the direction of Shields and too soon was out of sight. How old was he – thirty-two, thirty-three? Was he married? Had he settled in the town or was he just visiting?

As she made her way home, Catherine's mind spun with unanswered questions. By the time she reached East Jarrow, she had talked herself out of any illusions that such a man would look twice at a lass like her. But he had stirred a deep inner longing. This was the kind of man that she wanted, craved. She knew it was sinful to think about men in such a way, but she could not rid her mind of him.

Once home, the feeling of being hemmed in engulfed her more strongly than ever. Tired as she was, Catherine determined she must get out more, see her friends again. She had neglected them for too long. What was a girl of seventeen doing slaving away day and night like a worker in a sweatshop? No one thanked her for it.

That Saturday, she carried the tin bath into the bedroom, barred the door and gave herself a good wash and scrub. It surprised her to see how thin were her arms and legs. As she ran the soap over her body, she could feel her ribs jutting out. Her breasts felt smaller, her hair limp

26

and brittle. Catherine sank back in the cramped bath, suddenly too tired to bother going out.

She must have dozed off, for she was startled out of her torpor by Kate hammering on the door.

'Kitty, you still in there? You'll grow fins. Haway and shift yoursel' – or you'll miss the dance.'

'Don't think I'll gan.'

'Don't be daft,' Kate shouted, 'course you will. I'll not have your long face tripping us up all evening.'

Catherine roused herself at her mother's chivvying. Half an hour later, she was dressed in her favourite blue dress and matching shoes she had bought with her Christmas earnings, and hurrying towards the church hall.

She spotted Lily sitting on the girls' side of the hall next to Amelia. Lily waved, her face breaking into a surprised smile at the sight of her. Catherine grinned back, thankful she had come.

'Dragged yourself away from your business interests at last?' Lily teased.

'Aye, just for the night,' Catherine said.

Amelia shuffled up. 'Thought you'd become a nun – only time we see you is on your knees in church.'

'Well I'm here now,' Catherine laughed, plonking herself down, 'and ready to dance.'

She glanced across the room and saw Tommy and Peter staring over. They grinned and Catherine smiled back, her spirits lifting further. She was going to have fun tonight and banish all her home troubles.

'You missed a grand trip to Durham last Saturday,' Lily said.

'Aye,' Amelia nudged Lily, 'not that you saw much of it.'

Lily giggled.

'What d'you mean?' Catherine asked.

'Well, Lily saw more of the riverbanks than the cathedral,' Amelia sniggered.

'We never!' Lily blushed.

Catherine studied her friend. 'We?'

The other two dissolved into laughter. Before they could explain, Miss McGrath announced the first dance and struck up on the piano. Catherine saw Tommy and Peter detach themselves from the group of lads on the other side of the hall. She rose to greet them.

'Hello, Kitty,' Tommy smiled. 'Good to see you've broken your vow of silence.'

'It hasn't been that long,' Catherine protested.

'Seems like it.'

'Well, I'm glad you've noticed,' she laughed.

Then he reached past her and pulled Lily to her feet. 'Haway, bonny lass.'

Lily took his arm and they swept on to the dance floor. Catherine turned to Amelia with a questioning look.

'Aye, they're courtin',' she answered.

'Since when?'

'The Christmas party.' Amelia stood up and linked arms with the bashful Peter.

Catherine gaped at them as they followed the other couple. She sat down quickly, her legs feeling wobbly. Why had Lily never said anything at church? Two months of courting Tommy Gallon and she never knew.

Catherine felt sick and dizzy as shock gave way to sharp jealousy. She should've been told. Tommy had all but been going out with her! Even the quiet Peter had chosen Amelia rather than her. She felt suddenly alone and humiliated. She sat, gripping her hands in her lap, trying not to cry, swallowing tears.

When the dance finished and the girls came back, Catherine forced herself to make light of it.

'You're a dark horse, not telling me about Tommy,' she laughed.

'He walked me home after the Christmas party,' Lily smiled breathlessly. 'He's really canny.'

'You're not serious about him, though?' Catherine couldn't help asking.

Lily gave her a look. 'Course I am. He's good company,' she dropped her voice, 'and a good kisser!'

Her friends smothered their laughter. Catherine felt faint. Heat prickled her skin.

'But – but he's just a pitman,' she burst out.

Lily and Amelia stopped and stared at her. She had no idea why she'd said such a thing, but instead of retracting it, Catherine blustered on.

'Well, what's the future ganin' to be like as a pitman's wife? A life of drudgery, that's what. All that washing and getting up all hours of the night to see them fed and off to work. I know what I'm talking about – me Aunt Sarah's married to one and she's four sons down the pit an' all. It's never-ending – she's old before her time.'

Lily's expression turned from surprise to anger.

28

'Don't you preach at me, Kitty. What gives you the right to look down your nose at me and Tommy? He's a grand lad and it doesn't bother me two pins that he works down the pit. It's hard, honest graft. He's not sitting at home with his feet up, painting little bits of cushion covers – he's doing some'at useful. Maybe it's dirty and dangerous, but I love him all the more for doing it.'

'Well, more fool you,' Catherine said, wounded by Lily's words. 'You'll not catch me weddin' a pit lad.'

'Then you'll die an old maid, Kitty,' Lily said in scorn. 'The sort of lad you're lookin' for doesn't exist for lasses like us.'

'He does for me,' Catherine declared.

Amelia came to Lily's defence. 'Don't speak to Lily like that. Your nose is stuck that high in the air it's got ice on it!'

By now, the other girls were aware of the growing argument. Silence was falling around them. Lily turned her back on Catherine, her cheeks puce with indignation, eyes watery with tears. The others looked on, wondering what had been said. Catherine could not bear their accusing stares. She got to her feet, shaking uncontrollably. It was like being a child again. Her against the rest, excluded from the party.

Without another word, she grabbed her jacket and fled from the room. Falling into the street, she made her way blindly through the dark lanes of Tyne Dock. Hot tears streamed down her face. Why had she turned on Lily and said such hurtful things? She had only meant to warn her about life as a pitman's wife, not to bad-mouth Tommy. Or had she? Wasn't she so consumed with jealousy at Tommy choosing Lily instead of waiting for her that she'd lashed out at her closest friend? She had wanted to hurt her. She was despicable. No wonder no one wanted her for a friend. And that's all she ever really wanted – to have friends, to belong. Why did she have to be different?

Because you're a bastard on the inside and the out. The hateful words, spoken long ago by an angry neighbour, rang in her head. She was cursed from birth never to be one of the crowd. She would always be different, always set apart.

In her mind, she was a small girl again, climbing the back stairs to Bella's house, dressed in a clean pinny and her hair in ribbons. She could hear the shrieks of the other children in the middle of a party game. Her friends had forgotten to call for her, but she wasn't too late, whatever Kate said.

Catherine knocked on the door, hopping with excitement. No one came. She knocked louder. Finally the door opened. Bella stood

29

there smiling, the others crowding behind, breathless from blindman's buff.

'Sorry I'm late—'

'You can't come in,' Bella cut her off. 'You're not invited.'

'But—'

'Mam says you've got no da.'

The door slammed shut. She could hear the laughter behind it. Pain ripped through her like a sharp blade . . .

Catherine, sobbing at the memory, stumbled down the hill, away from the youth club, oblivious to the cries of a tram driver and the clanging bell as it narrowly missed her. Suddenly she found herself in complete darkness. She groped around and felt a cold, damp, slimy wall. Where was she? Where had the streetlights gone? Panic choked her. Spinning around her, the blackness seemed complete. She was entombed somewhere that stank of urine and mould. Above her was a strange rumble as if the earth was shaking. This was Hell. No warm fires and flames of light for her, just cold, stinking nothingness.

Catherine flattened herself against the wall to stop herself falling. She couldn't breathe. Out of the dark, shadows loomed and tried to sweep her away. Her head swam and her temples throbbed with pressure as if her brain was trying to burst its cage. All at once, she felt a gushing from her nose. She tasted blood in her mouth. Putting up her hands to stop the flood, she felt blood pouring through her fingers.

She cried out in horror. There was a sudden flash of light as a tram roared towards her. It lit the cavernous tunnel. Catherine saw she was under the railway arches of Tyne Dock. She half registered the thought, then the light went and the world closed in on her again as she lost consciousness and slipped down the slimy wall into oblivion.

Chapter 6

Catherine could hear hushed voices beyond the bedroom door.

'. . . but so much – she's never bled like that before, Dr Dyer.'

'She's very weak. Has she been eating properly, Kate?'

A pause, then, 'She's got the appetite of a flea. Lasses these days just want to look slim in their short dresses.'

'This has happened before, hasn't it?' Dr Dyer asked.

'No!'

'Not the bleeding, but collapse. At the end of the war, remember? She'd be about thirteen. Couldn't walk for weeks, yet I could find nothing wrong with her legs. Total exhaustion.'

'Not wanting to gan back to school, more like,' Kate snorted. 'Lay like a princess while I fed her fancy food to try and get her spark back.'

The doctor said kindly, 'That's what you'll have to do now, Kate. She's very run-down – and the nosebleed is worrying. You must give her plenty of liver to stop her becoming anaemic. Good food and rest for the girl.'

Kate sighed. 'It must be some'at that made her ill. She's a strong lass; it's not natural.'

'She'll have to stop her work for a while.'

'Aye, maybes it was the paints.' Kate seized on the idea. 'I heard that lead in paint can be harmful – poison you. Me mother used to work in the puddling mills and lasses died of lead poisoning in there.'

'Perhaps,' Dr Dyer mused, 'though I see no signs of poisoning – no vomiting. But just to be sure, keep them packed away until she's recovered.' The outside door opened. 'I'll be back tomorrow.'

'Thank you, Doctor,' Kate said. 'You've been that good to us. I daren't think what would've happened if you hadn't found her . . .' Kate's voice faltered.

'I'm glad I did too. Don't upset yourself. As you say, she's a strong girl. Good day, Kate.'

Catherine closed her eyes, the words washing over her. She felt detached, floating, as if in a dream. Yet her body felt as heavy as iron, pinning her to the bed. She was as weak as a kitten, too tired to move an inch. It was wonderful just lying in the feather bed, not having to do anything, not having to think. She was in a world of warm, scratchy blankets, the smell of camphor, the sound of Kate stoking up the kitchen fire. The distant cry of the rag-and-bone man down the lane was the last sound she remembered before surrendering to sleep.

In the days that followed, memory of that terrible evening washed back into Catherine's mind. Dr Dyer had been passing in his car and spotted her slumped on the pavement. The time between being picked off the street and put to bed was a blank, but there had been shouting and hot tea, crying and stanching of blood. She was back in Kate's bed, and Davie was sharing the parlour with a filthy-tempered John.

Time had stopped. Days were no different to nights, as she slept and woke and slept again. Kate would spoon soup and tea into her like a baby, cool her face with a damp cloth and croon quietly. Catherine lapped it up gratefully, knowing the tenderness and the sanctuary of the big bed would not last.

After a week, the bickering beyond the bedroom door grew.

'It's time you got your lazy backside off to sea,' John ranted at Davie. 'And when's me tea? The lazy bitch in there isn't the only one needs feedin'.'

'I can't be everywhere at once,' Kate snapped. 'You'll not die of starvation in the next five minutes.'

'She's puttin' it on,' John blustered. 'One nosebleed and she's in bed a week. You're too soft by half.'

'Aye,' Davie agreed, 'she's running you ragged.'

'You all are!' Kate cried. 'It wouldn't harm the pair of you to lift a finger for once and serve out the tea.'

'And it wouldn't harm the lass to get out of bed and come to the table,' Davie muttered.

'Since when have you been a doctor?' Kate demanded.

'Doctors!' John was contemptuous. 'Kill more than they cure. That Scotch doctor'll have us penniless and in the workhouse with the cost of all this fancy food for Kitty.'

'How would you know? You don't pay a ha'penny towards it – neither of you do!'

'I will as soon as trade picks up,' Davie said defensively.

'Then get yoursel' down the docks – you'll not find a ship, sitting with your feet up here all day long.'

'If that's what you want—'

'Aye, that's what I want!'

'Well, I'd rather be at sea than stop around here – put out me wife's bed and having to listen to him rant on all day long. A hurricane would be better!'

Catherine heard the slamming of the back door and Kate crashing about in the kitchen, banging things down on the table.

'Happy now?' she accused John.

He snorted, 'It's you and the lass are driving him out, not me. I'd tak the belt to you if you were my missus.'

'Aye, that's always your answer, isn't it?' Kate said bitterly. 'Why do you think I married Davie?'

' 'Cos he's too weak to stand up to ye.'

'No, 'cos he's man enough to keep his belt where it belongs – in his breeks.'

Catherine waited for the sound of the poker banging on the fender or crockery flying. But her grandfather's swearing petered out and the silence that followed was ominous. With a feeling of dread, she was sure that the anger and bitterness would turn its attention on her next.

A week later, Davie was bound for the Cape and Kate's patience had run out. She turfed Catherine out of bed and spring-cleaned the bedroom. Kate's way of coping with unhappiness was to work twice as hard, pushing herself physically so she had no time to dwell.

'Work it out, lass,' she ordered, when Catherine sat listlessly watching her. 'No point sitting around feeling sorry for yoursel'. You can start by helping me beat the mattress.'

'I'm too tired,' Catherine complained.

'You need a bit fresh air in your lungs, that's all. We'll get the mattress out in the yard.'

Catherine struggled to help her mother, while John sat by the fire ignoring the activity. She coughed as dust and feathers flew up around them, wary of Kate's grim look.

The next day, Kate roused her from sleep. 'I've got work decoratin' down Jarrow. You'll have to get your grandda's breakfast. There's washing to fetch from Simpsons' in Oswald Street and a parcel to tak down to Gompertz's – Davie's suit. Make sure you get a good price for it.'

'Not the in-and-out!' Catherine protested. She had never overcome the humiliation of being sent to the pawnshop, with the neighbours watching from their doorsteps.

'How else are we ganin' to eat this week?' Kate was sharp. 'I'll be back at dinner time.' Then she was gone.

Catherine sat for a long time feeling numb and alone. Was this to be her life, domestic drudgery and trips to the pawnshop? But what else was she fit for? She had turned her back on school at thirteen, with no pieces of paper to prove she knew anything. Her head might be full of dreams and stories, but she didn't have the education to make sense of them on paper. Since a child, she had tried to write down snatches of stories that flashed through her mind, but they never came out right. She blushed to think of the long story she had once sent into the local newspaper that had been returned the very next day, rejected and obviously unread. How that had rankled – still did.

She could start her painting again. But maybe it *was* ruining her health. It might sound tragically romantic to be an artist dying young, but she wanted to live. Catherine was filled with a sudden yearning for life, to experience a world beyond the New Buildings, even beyond Jarrow and Shields. Wasn't she the daughter of a gentleman?

Catherine forced herself to get up and dressed in her best. She would show them all. Today, she would go and find herself a job away from William Black Street. Simpsons' washing would have to wait, and as for the pawnshop – Davie's suit was Kate's affair; she could take it herself.

When Catherine reappeared that evening, Kate's worry turned quickly to fury.

'I've been looking all over for you – you never went to Simpsons' – and Davie's suit's still on the table. Where the devil have you been?'

'Signed up with Mrs Bridge's.' Catherine faced her triumphantly.

'What you mean, Mrs Bridge's?'

'The wife that runs that agency,' Catherine said proudly.

'For domestics?'

'Not just them – all kinds of work. She thinks I'd make a good lady's companion.'

John bellowed with laughter. 'Hark at her!'

Kate just gawped at her, speechless.

'It's true,' Catherine insisted. 'There's a lady up Cleadon village wants one. Mrs Bridge thinks I'm just right for the job. I'm to gan up there tomorra and be interviewed.'

'Interviewed!' crowed John. 'Our Kitty, a lady's companion? You bugger!'

Kate found her voice. 'Don't talk daft. You'll be a maid of all work – a skivvy. I can't believe you'd fall for that. You're not ganin'.'

'I am.'

'You're not fit enough. It'll finish you.'

'Oh, but I'm fit enough to skivvy for you and run up and down to the pawnshop?'

'Don't give me your lip—'

'Don't worry, you'll get no more of me lip. I'm not stoppin' round here any longer. If the wife up Cleadon'll have us, I'm off to live up there. Thought you'd be pleased for me.'

'Pleased that you're ganin' into place?' Kate was scornful.

'Well, what else can I do?' Catherine protested.

'Some'at you're more suited to, like shop work. You've a head for figures and business.'

'You just want me around here to do your chores for you.'

'And what about me?' John joined in. 'Who's ganin' to look after me while Kate's out workin'?'

'You'll manage.' Catherine eyed him boldly.

'Don't go.' Kate was suddenly pleading. 'Don't leave me with . . .'

Catherine knew from her look that her mother dreaded being left alone with John. But why should she pass up this opportunity of a better life? The fear of being stuck there for ever was stronger than her guilt at leaving Kate to put up with John alone. And some day soon, Davie would be back.

'There's Davie, remember. He'll be pleased to find me gone.'

'I don't know why you've taken against him so,' Kate snapped. 'He's done nothing to deserve it.'

Catherine knew she could never get her mother to understand that it wasn't so much dislike of Davie, as a deep longing for her real father, that made her act as she did.

'Me mind's made up.' Catherine stood her ground. 'I'm ganin' up Cleadon the morra.'

Kate hung her head in defeat, while John spat into the fire and cursed all women.

A week later, Catherine had secured the position at Oakside Manor, bought her uniform with a loan from the Church, and packed a small bag of possessions. Her mother walked her down to the tram stand.

'I still don't see what you need a uniform for if you're a lady's companion.'

'Oh, it's just for neatness,' Catherine said excitedly. 'You should see the size of the house – five bedrooms and a bathroom as big as our kitchen and two inside privies! And the gardens – you can't see the road for the trees, like a secret world. And greenhouses. Mrs Halliday says they grow peaches. Just think of it, I'll be eatin' fresh peaches this summer.'

Kate gasped and stopped. Catherine saw her hands fly to her mouth.

'What's wrong?' she asked in concern. Tears welled up in her mother's eyes. 'Do you have a stitch? Do you want to sit down?'

Kate shook her head but could not speak.

'I can walk the rest on me own,' Catherine assured her.

'N-no,' Kate gulped. 'It was just the talk of peaches.' She wiped her eyes fiercely with her sleeve.

'I'm sorry,' Catherine said in confusion. 'I didn't mean to gan on about them. I'll bring you some back if I can.'

Kate gave a sad smile. 'It's not that, hinny. You just reminded me of some'at.'

'What?'

'I used to work in a big house once, with great big greenhouses. The smell of the peaches . . .'

Catherine held her breath. 'You mean Ravensworth?'

Kate gave her a sharp look. 'Who told you that?'

Catherine shrugged. 'Maybes it was Grandma.'

Kate nodded. 'Aye, I lived with your Great-Aunt Lizzie at Ravensworth when I was about your age – helped her out when she broke her leg. Her husband, Peter, was one of the gardeners – canny couple. I got a job at the castle for a bit as a kitchen maid.'

Catherine marvelled to think her mother had worked in such a place. Aunt Mary had mentioned the coaching inn, but not the castle. Perhaps she had been jealous of Kate's job there. What stories her mother could tell about the gentry and their ways, if only she could get Kate to talk about it.

'What was it like,' Catherine asked breathlessly, 'working for the Liddells?'

Kate's look was instantly guarded. 'What do you know about the Liddells? Has our Mary been letting her mouth go?'

Catherine did not answer. Kate abruptly picked up the bag that Catherine had set down on the pavement and began to march down the bank. Catherine sighed in frustration. Her mother would never talk to her about her past, let alone about Alexander Pringle-Davies. All Catherine knew was that fresh peaches reminded Kate of a past she was too ashamed or frightened to remember.

As the tram for Cleadon approached, Kate touched her daughter's cheek with a roughened hand.

'Take care of yourself, lass.'

'I'll be back before you know it.' Catherine tried to make light of their parting. 'I get every Saturday afternoon off when Mrs Halliday gans over Sunderland way to visit her sister.'

'That's grand,' Kate smiled.

For a moment, Catherine saw a flash of beauty in her mother's face. She leant forward and gave Kate a peck on the cheek. The next moment Kate was pushing her on to the tram with her bag and waving her away. By the time she'd found a seat and looked back, her mother was gone.

Catherine felt a momentary pang of loss. But the thought of the grand house that was soon to be her home rekindled her excitement. This was the start to a new life away from the shame and poverty that dogged her in East Jarrow, and she could not wait to get on with it.

Chapter 7

'And the Blakes are coming for afternoon tea,' Mrs Halliday called at Catherine's retreating back. 'They like egg and cress sandwiches and lemon sponge cake – but not too much lemon – you can be a bit heavy-handed at times, Louisa.'

Catherine gripped the door handle, swallowing a retort.

'And you can serve it in the summerhouse. Unless it clouds over, then we'll have it in the dining room – with the French windows open to the garden. Unless it's too breezy, then you can shut them. Or maybe we should just take tea in here? What do you think, Louisa?'

That you're a fussy, ridiculous old wife, who should get off your backside and do something useful for once! Catherine itched to say it out loud to her fidgeting, querulous employer, sitting next to the fire, fanning herself in the stifling room. Only Mrs Halliday could insist on a fire in the middle of June, unable to make up her mind if it was going to stay fine or start to rain.

Catherine turned to face her. 'I'll serve tea in the dining room with the doors half open. Is that all, ma'am?'

'Yes, yes, I think so, for the moment,' Mrs Halliday panted. 'And I hope you're not going to be sharp with my visitors, Louisa. You're becoming more brazen by the day.'

Catherine left the room, clenching her fists to stop herself screaming. She stomped into the kitchen where old Sam, the gardener, was slurping tea.

'I'll give her brazen! Some of us have been up since five this morning laying fires and heating water – though we're in the middle of a hot spell. And now she's got company for tea and expects me to go tappy-lappying all over the garden and house with tea trays, when I've got all the polishing to do and the beds to make up for her snobby sister and brother-in-law coming tomorra.'

'Aye, well,' Sam ruminated, 'that's what you're paid for, Louisa.'

'Not nearly enough,' Catherine railed. 'And don't you gan calling me Louisa, do you hear? I'm Kitty, except to that daft Mrs Halliday and her friends.' Catherine imitated her employer's breathless voice. 'Oh, no, no, no! We can't have a lady's maid called Kitty, it's too common, don't you think? You shall be called Janet – no, Rachel. Or maybe Sarah. Something plain but dignified. Louisa. That's it, Louisa.'

Sam chuckled at the mimicry. 'You should be on the stage, lass.'

'I should be anywhere but here,' Catherine sighed. 'Lady's companion, my foot. I've never worked so hard in me life. Me mam was right, I'm just a skivvy with a posh name. And the way they look at me, the missus and her snooty friends, as if they're doing me a big favour letting me stand around serving them. I can't believe I've stuck it for a whole year.'

'Worse things happen at sea,' Sam said amiably.

A bell jangled on the wall above them. Catherine gritted her teeth.

'She'll have changed her mind again. It'll be cucumber sandwiches and currant loaf, served on the lawn and me dancing the tango with a rose between me teeth.'

Sam got up chuckling, while Catherine braced herself to return to the drawing room and the vacillating Mrs Halliday.

Later, as she sweated in the hot kitchen over a rhubarb tart, she wondered for the umpteenth time why she stayed. The dream of being a lady's companion and a life of gentility in the countryside had evaporated after a few weeks. The day she was rechristened Louisa, Catherine knew her mother had been right and that she was to be a maid of all work in all but name. She had been tricked. Apart from Sam's wife, who came in to help with the laundry, there was no domestic help at Oakside Manor but her.

'But you're so capable,' Mrs Halliday had cried in astonishment when Catherine had suggested another pair of hands in the kitchen. 'I wouldn't want anyone else. Besides, there's only me to look after. It's not very hard work for a young girl like you.'

Catherine had to admit that the reason she had stayed was stubbornness and not wanting to admit to Kate that she had been right all along. She put up with her employer's carping and indecision, only standing up to her about her days off. Mrs Halliday tried to wheedle out of the Saturday afternoon arrangement whenever she wasn't visiting her sister, but Catherine had been quietly stubborn and made a point of leaving Cleadon every Saturday afternoon so that she could not be at the woman's constant beck and call.

Her free hours slipped by too quickly, and there was time for little else than a couple of hours at home and attending benediction before returning to Oakside Manor. The one source of joy in her week was hearing the deep bass voice of the mysterious man who sat behind her in church. When he was there her spirits were lifted, when he was not, Catherine was gripped with disappointment. She had heard the priest call him Mr Rolland, but she could discover nothing more about him.

If Davie was at home, Catherine would brace herself to find her family already drinking from the 'grey hen' in the middle of the afternoon, the kitchen door thrown open to catch the river breeze. After handing over most of her wages to Kate, she would retreat up the street to Aunt Mary's orderly house.

'Why don't you call on Lily?' Kate had suggested recently. 'All you get from our Mary is her complaining. You need a bit of fun on your day off – a bit company your own age.'

'Lily's courtin',' Catherine sighed.

'Well, what about Amelia?' Kate persisted.

Catherine shrugged. She had not dared go back to the youth club in over a year, afraid of being cold-shouldered by her former friends. She had lost touch with them all.

Thinking about it now, as she shoved the rhubarb tart into the scorching oven, she was overwhelmed by loneliness. She was nearly nineteen, but her life was one of drudgery and isolation. She suddenly longed for the quick laughter and chatter of Lily, Tommy and the others.

The next Saturday, she plucked up the courage to seek out her old friend. Mrs Hearn answered her knocking.

'No, pet, our Lily's gone on the outing to Hexham – with the youth club. Did you not hear about it?'

Catherine swallowed. 'I've been that busy with work.'

Lily's mother nodded. 'Eeh, it's grand to see you. I've missed you comin' round, Kitty. Hearing you lasses chattering and carrying on together.'

Suddenly Catherine's eyes flooded with tears. 'I miss it an' all.'

A moment later she was openly crying on the Hearns' doorstep. Quickly, Mrs Hearn had an arm about her and was bustling her into the kitchen. She produced a clean starched handkerchief, a cup of tea and a large wedge of currant loaf still warm from the oven. By the time Catherine had finished it, she felt ten times better.

'If you're that unhappy up Cleadon way,' said Lily's mother, 'why don't you come back home, find some'at round here?'

'I don't want to gan back to me family,' Catherine confessed. 'I don't get on with them.'

Mrs Hearn sat and pondered this. Her face suddenly brightened. 'Our Lily says they're needin' lasses at the laundry.'

Catherine tried to hide her lack of enthusiasm. Harton workhouse still invoked terror. It was never to be mentioned at home for fear of inciting her grandda's temper. It conjured up a terrible time in Kate's childhood when she had been sent out to beg round the streets and John had been reduced to hard labour at Harton in order to eat.

'You could live in,' Mrs Hearn suggested. 'Why don't you ask Father O'Neill to put in a word for you? A little word from the priest dropped in the right ear works wonders. And you and our Lily could be together again. She'd be that pleased.'

Catherine looked up in surprise. 'Would she?'

'Why, of course,' Mrs Hearn smiled. 'Whatever it was you two fell out about, wasn't worth the bother. I know Lily misses you – she's said as much.'

Catherine was not sure if the woman was just being kind, but the words gave her courage. She left the Hearns' feeling a new surge of optimism. Even a job at the workhouse laundry would be better than her present situation – if Lily would be her friend again.

She plucked up courage to speak to Father O'Neill after the Saturday evening service. He glowered at her from under wiry grey eyebrows as she asked for his help, and she felt her familiar fear of him. How many times as a child had she woken screaming from a nightmare in which a black-robed priest loomed out of the dark of the confessional box from which she could never escape? In her childish mind she had always linked the nightmare with the censorious Father O'Neill.

Catherine braced herself for rejection, but he finally nodded.

'I know the matron; I'll go and speak to her.'

'Thank you, Father,' Catherine said quickly, and escaped.

The following week, there was a letter waiting for her at home.

'Open it then,' Kate said excitedly. 'What does it say?'

Catherine glanced at old John, snoozing in his chair.

'I've got an interview,' Catherine whispered, 'up at Harton.'

Kate gasped. 'Not the workhouse?'

'Aye, in the laundry,' Catherine said defiantly.

41

Kate snorted in disbelief. 'You'd not last five minutes in a laundry. Got to be strong as an ox – I should know, I've done it.'

'Done what?' John asked, rousing from sleep.

'Nowt,' Kate said nervously.

Catherine faced him boldly. 'I've got an interview up at Harton laundry.'

John's craggy face went puce. 'Harton? You're not ganin' to work there!'

'Why not?'

' 'Cos I say so, you cheeky bitch!'

'The pay's better than what I get from Mrs High-and-Mighty-Halliday – I know that from what Lily's said.'

'And she'll be able to come home more often,' Kate tried to placate him. 'You miss her being so far away, don't you?'

'I didn't ask for your opinion.' John kicked the fender in a temper. He rose and glared at Catherine. 'Me and your grandmother saved you from that hellhole, you ungrateful lass. It killed your grandma having to bring you up – but we did it, to save your slut of a mother and you from the workhouse. And now you say you're ganin' to work there! It's a disgrace on the name of McMullen to have one of mine gan in such a place!'

'It's honest graft, Grandda,' Catherine stood her ground, 'and I'll be gettin' paid, not ganin' cap in hand for relief work—'

Kate gasped and Catherine realised too late what she had said. In an instant, John had seized the steel poker and was brandishing it at her.

'You dare say that to me face,' he roared. 'I only went there so as I could feed your grandma and her brats. McMullens don't gan cap in hand to anyone!'

As he raised the poker, Kate barged between them and pushed Catherine towards the door.

'Go, Kitty!' she ordered, shoving her stubborn daughter out of the room.

'I'll kill her!' John bawled as Catherine escaped into the street. But Kate barred the doorway with her bulk.

'See what you've done with your big mouth?' she barked. 'Make yoursel' scarce and don't come back in a hurry!'

Catherine wandered the streets of South Shields until the pounding in her heart eased. She was shaken by John's outburst, but all the more determined to win the job. His opposition was based on prejudice and

42

fear. Kate's derision that she was not strong enough for such work rankled too.

Yet, when the time came, Catherine had to screw up all her courage to walk through the forbidding gates of the soot-blackened brick fortress. This was the paupers' prison, the place of no hope for the destitute and outcast. The long corridors were stark and echoing, the windows too high to afford a view. In the distance, she heard doors clang and the occasional shout.

Matron Hatch walked her through the large, noisy laundry. It clanked and hissed with huge rollers and presses, the air suffocatingly hot and dusty. Rows of young women, the paid laundry workers in pale blue overalls and the inmates in brown, stood sweating over the machinery. Catherine's heart sank. She looked about nervously for Lily but could not see her.

'Father O'Neill thinks you are a bright girl and a good worker,' Matron Hatch said, as they reached her office. Her features were sharp, her brow furrowed under a starched white cap, her uniform immaculate.

Catherine nodded, hiding her surprise.

'Can you add up?'

'Aye, ma'am, I can.'

'Do you have a school certificate?'

Catherine flushed. 'No, but I've run me own business.'

'Is your writing neat? Write something here for me. Then add up these figures.'

Catherine did so, puzzled as to why pressing sheets all day would require such skills.

Matron Hatch scrutinised her work, sucked in thin lips and announced, 'Good enough, I suppose. I'm going to try you out as a checker, but only because Father O'Neill says you're up to it. So don't let the pair of us down, do you hear?'

'I'll do me very best, ma'am,' Catherine promised, wondering what a checker did.

'Call me Matron from now on. Come and I'll show you where you'll work.'

She followed her back into the steamy laundry and was shown a cubicle in the corner.

'It's your job to count all the laundry,' she shouted over the din, 'and keep an eye on the inmates.' She nodded towards the girls in brown.

Catherine's heart gave a jolt to see these workhouse women. They were the incarcerated, women less fortunate than Kate, doing the most menial tasks.

Matron continued, 'You'll live in, with a full day off a fortnight. Every other weekend you have to help out on the vagrants' ward. Is that agreed?'

Catherine gulped and nodded.

'As you are one of the officers, you must live in. Will that be a problem with your father or mother?'

Catherine looked alarmed. 'N-no,' she said quickly. 'I'm living away from home at the minute.'

'Good. So how soon can you start?' Matron asked.

'I have to give a week's notice.' As she said the words, she felt a soaring of her spirits. No more tugging her forelock to Mrs Halliday and her like. She was going to be a clerk with responsibility over others.

Catherine wasted no time in telling her employer.

'A laundry?' Mrs Halliday cried in a fluster. 'What do you want to work in a laundry for? Heavens above! You'll be wasted in such a place.'

Catherine went calmly about her work, while Mrs Halliday blustered on. 'No, no, Louisa. If it's the half-days you're worried about, I'll make sure you have your Saturday afternoons off.'

'Me mam wants me back in Shields,' Catherine said, which was not a lie but not the whole truth.

'But you have a future here! In time, you could become an excellent lady's maid.'

Catherine bit back the retort that she would never be anyone's servant ever again. She was the daughter of a gentleman. Nothing Mrs Halliday said could dissuade her. When she packed her small bag and left by the servants' entrance, she glanced back at the solid stone mansion surrounded by the fresh green of early summer.

'I'm ganin' to live in a house like this one day,' she suddenly determined. 'And I'll not gan sneakin' in the back way. I'll walk right up the front steps, 'cos it'll be mine!'

'Who you talkin' to, Kitty?' Sam asked, looking up from his hoeing.

She swung round, startled to think she had been overheard.

'Just mesel',' she laughed, self-consciously.

He shook his head as if she were mad. Perhaps she was, for daring to think so far above her station. But she hungered for it. Deep down, the ambition to live this other life she knew she was born to smouldered like a new fire.

'Take care of yoursel', lass.' Sam waved her away.

She shouted farewell, then left through the gates without a backward glance.

Chapter 8

For the first few weeks, Catherine doubted whether she should have taken the job at the workhouse. It was hot and noisy in the laundry during the summer months, and after nine hours her head pounded and eyes ached. The laundry workers were either shy or sullen while her fellow officers viewed her with suspicion.

'How come a lass like her gets the checking to do?' Hettie, a bullish woman in her thirties, asked loudly in the officers' mess where they ate. 'She's just turned nineteen. I've been working here sixteen years and I'm still a warder. And it's not as if she's got any education.'

Catherine carried on eating, forcing herself to swallow each mouthful. She and Hettie were sharing a small room together, and the waspish woman had made it plain she resented the arrangement.

'Mind you, it's like living with Saint Catherine – crucifix and holy pictures all over the walls,' Hettie continued, making the others laugh. 'Wearing out the lino with all that kneeling.'

Catherine smiled, as if she found it amusing too. 'Just thanking Our Lady for giving me such a canny room-mate.'

This caused a few sniggers and Hettie to frown. Catherine knew by the hateful look she gave her that she was foolish to spark back, but she could not help it. She had done nothing to offend the woman and she would not be blamed for her youthfulness or willingness to work hard.

She wished she could discuss it with Lily, but she hardly got a chance to talk with her old friend. They had smiled at each other on the first day and Lily had generously whispered good luck, showing no envy at Catherine's superior position. Catherine had felt a flood of relief, soon followed by frustration at their lack of contact. She was staff, while Lily was rank and file. Lily was on ironing duties – a step above the inmates in the washhouse – and spent all her time behind the hot pipes and whirring leather belts of the ironing benches. At midday, Lily ate with the other paid workers and at five o'clock she went home.

46

She and Catherine had only snatched conversations when handing over piles of sheets ready to return to the hospital.

'Hettie Brown's jealous of her own shadow,' Lily told her. 'Steer clear.'

'How can I when we share a titchy room together?'

'Well, don't cross her,' Lily warned. 'Once she gets her claws into you, she'll make your life a misery. I've seen her make the inmates cry often enough – she used to be on ironing till Matron moved her to the hospital. Talk of the devil.'

Matron Hatch appeared at the door and Lily hurried away, leaving Catherine to check the stock of fresh ironing.

Awkward with the older women who made up the majority of the workhouse staff, Catherine threw herself all the more determinedly into her new job. After a full day's work in the laundry, she often spent half the evening on the infirm wards with the elderly. It reminded her of attending to her bed-bound Grandma Rose as a child, and it did not frighten her when the old people babbled in confusion or wandered about looking for their front doors and people long dead.

One Saturday, Matron told her, 'We need someone to accompany the women to the cottages this afternoon, Miss McMullen. I'd like you to go.'

Catherine nodded in agreement, wondering what cottages.

'You must supervise them and make sure there is no unseemly behaviour. They assemble at the main gate at two o'clock. Miss Brown will be on duty with you.'

Catherine's heart sank. The unexpected outing would no doubt be ruined in Hettie's company. Still, she was intrigued to discover where they were going, and perhaps, away from the workhouse, she could win Hettie's friendship.

The women who gathered in the sunshine, in their drab brown uniforms and woollen stockings, looked young. Some were smiling and joking, an air of expectancy about them.

'Keep quiet, or you'll be left behind,' Hettie commanded, and silence quickly followed.

She looked at Catherine in satisfaction and winked. Encouraged by her sudden friendliness, Catherine smiled back. An old army ambulance chugged up to the gates and Hettie shooed the women on to the makeshift bus.

'We'll sit at the front,' she told Catherine and arranged herself neatly into the seat close to the driver.

'How far is it?' Catherine asked.

'Half an hour or so,' Hettie said, then turned away and spent most of the journey chatting to the driver. The sixteen women behind spoke in whispers only occasionally, drawing the censure of Warder Brown. By now, Catherine did not dare ask Hettie what the trip was for, in case she ridiculed her in front of the others.

The bus took them out of the town and followed the coast south. Catherine was so mesmerised by the swaying cornfields and the distant hazy cliffs that it came as a surprise when the bus swung up a rough road and drew to a halt. About them were long, one-storey huts arranged around a bare courtyard, where hens pecked in the dust. Beyond, she glimpsed a vegetable patch.

'You've one hour,' Hettie called out. 'Anyone acting daft gans straight back on the bus.' The women got up quickly, their excitement palpable. 'I'll lead them in,' Hettie said to Catherine, 'you follow at the back and make sure no one scarpers.'

One woman, whom Catherine recognised from the laundry, raised her thick eyebrows in the only hint of defiance. 'Scarper where?' she muttered.

The driver settled to read his newspaper while Hettie marched her wards into a long, low hall. At the door, Catherine noticed a group of girls standing around with a skipping rope, staring at the visitors in curiosity. The laundry worker smiled at them, but got no response.

'Poor bairns,' she murmured to Catherine, 'they've got no mams.'

'How do you know?' Catherine asked in surprise.

The woman gave her a strange look. 'They'd be waiting inside if they had, wouldn't they?' She stepped closer. 'Miss, do you have any sweets on you?'

Catherine felt in her pocket and pulled out a humbug. 'That's all I've got.'

'Ta, miss.' The woman beamed as if she had given her something precious.

As they stepped through the door, Catherine caught sight of two rows of children, one line of girls in starched white pinafores, one of boys in grey shorts and jumpers. They stood waiting, craning to see who came through the door, their faces brightening as they saw someone they knew. At the far end, a nurse clutched a pair of babies.

Realisation hit Catherine like a hammer. This was the workhouse orphanage. These children must belong to the women. This was a visit; an afternoon in which to pretend to be a mother, to not be an orphan, to

48

say all that had to be said. She stopped in shock. How often did they get to see their children? Once a fortnight, once a month? Not long enough to do anything. But then, no doubt, that was the point, as far as those in authority were concerned. Not long enough to be of influence, to taint their offspring with their wickedness.

The women lined up opposite, waiting for Hettie to stop talking to the children's matron and give them permission to start their visit. The hall clock struck a quarter to three.

'Right then, one hour.'

The tense silence broke as the mothers rushed forward and hugged their children and the hubbub of chatter began. The smaller girls and boys climbed on to their mothers' knees and let themselves be cuddled. The older ones were more awkward, shifting legs, twiddling hair, biting nails.

Some mothers handed over small treats they had managed to save from their rations, or twists of sweets they had bribed staff to buy with their meagre pocket money. The young women who fiercely cradled their babies seemed the happiest, their crooning almost frantic.

Catherine looked on appalled. She felt wretched, nauseous. This could so easily have been her and Kate. Would she have rushed to embrace her mother, or shrunk from her in shame? She could tell by the resentful looks of some of the older children that the moralising of their guardians had poisoned any love. Their unmarried mothers were sinful, beyond saving. They must grow up away from them or risk going the same way.

The laundry woman was trying to engage her sullen son. He scowled at her from under dark eyebrows just like hers.

'Feeding you well, are they? Are you workin' in the gardens still? Must be canny to work outside this time o' year. Hot as hell in the laundry—'

He gave her a look of alarm and she glanced round quickly to see if anyone had heard. Catherine pretended she had not. The woman ploughed on with the one-sided conversation, the boy giving occasional grunts. Eventually, she produced Catherine's boiled sweet like a trump card and handed it over. She lapsed into silence, watching him suck.

The hour dragged on and one of the babies grew fractious. Glancing at the clock, the mother bounced her desperately, but she began to howl louder.

'Hand her back,' the nurse ordered, 'it's nearly time for her feed.'

'Just a minute more,' the mother pleaded, not letting go.

Hettie intervened. 'Give her over.'

'But I haven't had me hour,' the woman wailed, bursting into tears.

Hettie wrestled the baby from her and pushed her away. 'Get back on the bus, or I'll make sure you don't come next time.'

The young woman pressed her hands against her face, sobbing as her baby was taken away.

'Witch,' the laundry worker muttered. Suddenly she stood up. 'Haway, give the lass back her bairn. She's not had her time.'

There was a stunned silence in the hall, apart from the weeping mother. Then Hettie was marching down the hall, barking orders.

'You can get out now, Jenny McManners! Time's up for all of you. Line up by the door!'

Murmurs of disbelief rippled down the hall.

'Do as I say, or you'll not be here next month,' Hettie threatened.

The matron clapped her hands. 'Come, children, say goodbye to your mothers.'

The smaller ones started to cry and cling on. Some of the women burst into tears too. Briefly, Jenny seized her son and hugged him. Catherine saw how the boy gripped his mother in return, just for an instant.

Suddenly, Catherine's throat flooded with tears. It was too cruel on the children. Whatever their mothers had done, none of them deserved to be treated like this. She glared at Hettie, as she bowled up the hall, shoving the women towards the door and pushing the children away. Catherine was so angry and upset she could not speak. She stood, clenching and unclenching her fists.

The mother of the baby came past crying, and she put out a comforting arm, steering her out of the hall.

'You'll see her again soon,' Catherine encouraged.

As the bus trundled back to town, Hettie reprimanded her. 'You don't touch the inmates like that.'

'But it's all right to hit them and shove them around?' Catherine snapped.

Hettie stared at her. 'What you getting all upset about? They're just a pack of loose women and their brats – scum of the earth.'

'They're just bairns,' Catherine said, choking back tears. 'It's not their fault.'

'I can't believe you're crying over the little bastards.'

That word was like a kick to the stomach. Catherine felt her insides heave.

'Stop the bus,' she gasped, jumping from her seat.

The driver lurched the bus to a halt. Catherine jumped out, bent over the verge and vomited into the ditch. The memory of that terrible hour in the comfortless hall made her retch until her stomach was empty and aching.

She turned in humiliation to see the women peering at her from the open door. Catherine scrabbled for a handkerchief and wiped her mouth.

Climbing back on, she muttered, 'It's the travel – always makes me sick.'

Hettie eyed her. 'Well, well, what a fuss.'

Catherine felt an anxious flutter at her curious look. If the woman ever discovered Catherine's own shameful origins, she knew her life would not be worth living.

Chapter 9

After her defiance, Jenny McManners was transferred from the laundry and put to work with the vagrants and tramps. Occasionally, Catherine saw her scrubbing floors when she did Saturday duties on the vagrants' ward. But the worst punishment was being forbidden the monthly trips to the cottages.

At harvest time, when a special service and tea was laid on at the orphanage, Catherine spoke to Hettie.

'Couldn't McManners be allowed to go? She's done her punishment.'

'She broke the rules – nearly caused a riot,' Hettie said severely.

'She'll not do it again, I'm sure.'

Hettie's look was sharp. 'It's no concern of yours.'

Catherine said no more, fearful that the vindictive woman might start poking into her own background. All she could do was slip sweets to Jenny's boy and say they were from his mother. He never said a word, just looked at her with sad, angry eyes. How she recognised that look: the same confused feelings of resentment and shame about being born with no da.

Catherine came to realise the best way to cover up her own past was self-improvement. She had left school without qualifications, but she would teach herself.

One free Saturday, she plucked up the courage to enter the public library. Heart hammering, she pushed open the heavy doors and went in. Never had she imagined that a place could hold so many books. As a child, she had sometimes sneaked a look at novels belonging to their lodgers, or those at her Great-Aunt Maggie's, further up the street, but Kate had always scolded her for touching what did not belong to her. The McMullens possessed no books, apart from Uncle Jack's well-thumbed history of the Boer War, and a copy of *A Christmas Carol* given by their upstairs neighbour. Catherine had often saved up her tram fare to school to buy comics and had once borrowed an annual from a girl at school and never returned it. She had read it until it fell to bits and was too ashamed to hand it back. The memory made her hot with guilt.

As Catherine stood gazing around her, wondering where to start, a librarian came to her rescue.

'What are you looking for?' she whispered.

Knowledge, learning, a new life.

'Er – Shakespeare – and, em, poetry,' Catherine floundered.

Instead of ridiculing her as she feared, the woman nodded and led her over to a vast bookcase and indicated the works of Shakespeare.

'Poetry is over there. When you've chosen what you want, come to the desk and be registered.'

Catherine, almost losing her nerve in the vast hushed library, grabbed a book randomly and hurried to the desk. Outside, she hid the book in her jacket and rushed back to her quarters. With Hettie out, she spent the afternoon immersed in *Romeo and Juliet*. Even though there were words she did not understand, she revelled in the sound of the language, speaking out loud to the empty room.

The next week she went back and borrowed more. That winter, she worked her way through two more plays, three novels by Dickens, poetry by Wordsworth and Matthew Arnold, *The Mill on the Floss* by George Eliot, and *Tess of the D'Urbervilles* by Thomas Hardy. She especially identified with the tragic Tess, noble-blooded but born into poverty.

Catherine bought an exercise book and began scribbling her own short stories about luckless heroines and grand houses, trying to imitate what she had read. Her Uncle Jack had once given her a jotter and she had written a rambling tale of an Irish girl. But Kate must have used it on the fire or thrown it out during a spring-clean, because she had not seen it for years. And she still blushed to think how the local newspaper had returned her one attempt at publishing a story, after she had paid precious pennies to Amelia to type it up. No one would see these stories, especially not Hettie, so she hid them under her mattress. They were just for her – a way of losing herself in another world where she could make anything happen – for a few snatched, magical minutes.

But one book more than any other spurred on Catherine's ambition to better herself in the eyes of the world. Someone in the queue at the desk was returning Lord Chesterfield's *Letters to His Son*. Something about the title, or perhaps the author's aristocratic name, excited her interest and she asked to borrow it next.

That evening, by lamplight in her room while Hettie played cards in the staffroom, Catherine discovered the key to her ambition. The letters were addressed to Chesterfield's illegitimate son and laid down how he should behave in order to get on in the world. Manners and appearance were everything. She lay awake long into the night, pondering the advice, and all that following week spent every free moment reading more. When she got to the end, she started again, underlining and making notes in the margin in faint pencil as if it were a textbook. Month after month, she renewed the library book, until the pages became loosened from their binding.

With it, she strove to transform herself into someone new, refining her speech and table manners and saving up part of her wages to spend on better clothes. She was very cautious with money, putting aside some of the two pounds and ten shillings a month into insurance for Kate's life and her grandda's funeral. She feared either of them dying penniless and suffering a pauper's funeral. So while she prayed every week for their sins to be forgiven and Hell be avoided, she also insured against a shameful death.

Catherine took up French and drawing lessons as accomplishments fit for a lady. She put up with Hettie's ridicule by ignoring her, which only goaded the woman further.

'Look, here comes bloody Saint Catherine,' she jibed in the staff hall.

'You shouldn't swear, Hettie,' Catherine said, offended.

'Ooh, hark at her! Thinks she's better than us, doesn't she? But we all know she's just a common lass from East Jarrow with a mam who drinks in public houses, don't we?'

Catherine went puce. Who had been spreading tales about her? Not Lily, surely? But she knew how easily scandal travelled in a close-knit town. If Hettie had determined to make Catherine's family her business, there were plenty of gossips around the New Buildings happy to talk. The thought made her panic.

'I don't know what you mean,' Catherine retaliated. 'I come from a good Catholic family. We McMullens work hard and keep our noses clean.'

Hettie guffawed. 'Keep your noses six feet in the air, more like.'

Hettie's friend, Gert, gave her a sly look. 'You're related to old John McMullen, aren't you?'

Catherine nodded cautiously.

The woman grunted. 'Used to fight his way round the town, me mam said. McMullens lived near us when I was a bairn – Leam Lane.

54

I remember him chasing us lasses with a fire poker, just for lookin' his way.'

At the mention of Leam Lane, Catherine's heart began to pound. That was where she was born and had lived for six years, until neighbours had grown suspicious of Grandma Rose's attempts to pass Catherine off as her own child. Kate had once drunkenly told her they had moved to the New Buildings to try to escape the rumours.

'Me life's a misery 'cos of you,' Kate had accused. 'Worked me socks off to keep you, then you all did a flit to the New Buildings without even tellin' me! But nobody believed that rubbish about you being Mam's bairn – I knew they wouldn't. You're the millstone round me bloody neck!'

'Must be a different McMullen,' Catherine said, sweating at the memory of Kate's bitter drunken words. 'Jarrow and Shields are full of them.'

'Well, this John was a fightin' sort – and a foul-mouthed drinker,' Gert continued.

Hettie laughed. 'I bet our holy Kitty here doesn't stand for that.'

'Aye,' Gert joined in, 'and his daughter Kate's just as bad, so I've heard.'

'Kate?' Hettie needled. 'Isn't that your mam's name, Kitty?'

Catherine stood up, her meal half-untouched. She walked from the hall with as much dignity as her shaking legs could muster. She thought of rushing to her room to cry, but Hettie might pursue her there with her hateful insinuations. How much did she already know about her past? She doubted if Gert had ever lived in Leam Lane for she did not remember her. She was probably just repeating tittle-tattle. Catherine could not bear to stay a moment longer.

Fighting back tears, she stumbled into the spring evening chill and found herself making towards the sanctuary of Lily's. How often had she gone to the Hearns' house for comfort and found refuge in its ordered neatness and warmth?

'Kitty!' Lily exclaimed. They stood awkwardly for a moment, then her friend pulled her in. 'Thought you'd grown too grand to visit us,' she teased.

Catherine tried to smile, then burst into tears.

'I didn't mean it,' Lily said in consternation, putting an arm around her. Catherine sobbed into her shoulder, unable to speak. 'Is it that bitch Hettie Brown again?'

'Y-yes.'

'Told you she was trouble. Haway in me bedroom and spit it out.'

They sat on Lily's bed in the dying light while Catherine poured out her troubles.

'She makes me life a misery – puts things under me pillow to make me scream. She and Gert made the sheets so I couldn't get into bed – and I know she messes it up for inspection to get me in trouble with Matron. Last week she stuck these pictures up on me wall of these muscle men – and I only got them down in the nick of time before Matron came round.'

'Ooh, have you kept them?' Lily joked.

'Lily man, I'm serious. She's trying to get me the sack, I know she is. Why does she hate me so much?'

Lily gave her a hug. ' 'Cos you're young – and you're trying to make some'at of yoursel'. Folk like Hettie cannot stand that. Listen, why don't you ask to move rooms?'

'But what would I say? Matron will want to have a good reason.'

'Say you need your own room to pray in.'

Catherine winced. 'Don't you start.'

Lily laughed. 'Well, you must admit, you can be a holy Mary at times.'

How could she explain that telling her worries to Our Lady gave her comfort? She could not expect Lily to understand that she had to keep praying for her family, else all the guilt and fear that had lurked inside her since she was a child would rise up and swamp her. She was born in sin and would be thrown into the flames of Hell if she stopped praying or asking forgiveness for one minute – the priest had said as much. Her grandda and Kate would end up there too, with all their drinking and cursing, so it was up to her to save them as well.

When she said nothing, Lily tried to cajole her. 'Show them your funny side, Kitty. You're good company when you let your hair down. And you should get out more. Why don't you come on the Easter outing to Morpeth?'

Catherine brightened. 'I'd like that. Can I go with you – or – are you – will you be sitting with Tommy?'

Lily gave a dismissive laugh. 'Tommy? I'm not courtin' him no more.'

'Oh, I didn't know, I'm sorry.'

'Don't be. He got drunk at Christmas and gambled away his wages – couldn't afford to buy me a present. Don't want to end up with a lad like that, do I?'

56

'No,' Catherine said ruefully.

'We'll gan on the outing and forget about lads,' Lily declared, jumping up. 'Do you fancy a bit of Mam's currant loaf?'

'Please,' Catherine smiled gratefully.

By the time she left to go back to Harton, she was filled with a new determination not to let Hettie and the gossips hound her out of her job. She would take Lily's advice and win them over by playing the clown and laughing at herself, however hurt she felt inside. She would show them Kitty McMullen the performer, just as she had as a girl. By playing the fool, she had made friends again with those children who had turned on her for having no da. Make them laugh, Catherine determined. People forgot to be cruel if you made them laugh.

Catherine went on the trip to Morpeth with Lily and enjoyed picnicking in the park and taking a boat on the river. Over the summer they became firm friends again, cycling the countryside on days off, visiting the picture houses and local fairs. Catherine worked hard at pleasing the staff at the workhouse and wrote a play for them to perform at the summer fête, giving Hettie the leading role.

The woman preened with self-importance and, although she forgot half her words, believed it a great success. Hettie was so pleased, she agreed to Catherine's request to allow Jenny McManners to visit her son again. Catherine had seen Jenny's anger fizzle into moroseness as she accepted defeat. The unhappy mother had only been allowed on the trip to the orphanage at Christmas time because Matron was in charge and Hettie did not dare prevent Jenny.

Catherine was secretly triumphant at Hettie's change of heart.

Shortly afterwards, Matron summoned her into her office.

'You've worked hard, Miss McMullen,' Mrs Hatch acknowledged. 'And I'm glad to see you're getting on better with Miss Brown and the others. I did fear that your opinion of yourself was a little high when you first came.'

Catherine bit back a retort that high opinions were Hettie's problem, not hers. She simply nodded.

'So I'm going to promote you to assistant head laundress.'

Catherine gaped at her.

'Do you not want the promotion?' Matron asked sharply.

'Y-yes, of course I do,' Catherine said quickly. 'Thank you, Matron.'

'It means you can have a room of your own.'

Catherine broke into a grin of relief. 'Thank you.'

The news was greeted with grumbles by some of the staff, who thought twenty was far too young for such a position.

'You should have got it, Gert,' Hettie said loudly to her friend.

Catherine's insides churned at the jealous look on Hettie's face. Shortly after she moved into her own room, the rumours about her started with renewed venom.

Chapter 10

Autumn 1926

'Where do you think she gets her fancy clothes from?' Hettie said in the hushed tone of the gossip. 'I mean that winter coat with the fur collar – she couldn't afford that on her wages.'

'Aye, that's true,' another warder agreed.

'She's got a fancy man, that's what,' Hettie declared. 'And we all know what men like that expect in return.'

Catherine froze in the doorway of the staffroom, hidden behind the half-closed door.

Gert joined in. 'She got that bunch of flowers last week, an' all. Delivered to the door, brazen as can be.'

Catherine flushed to think of Tommy Gallon's impulsive gesture. He had won a game of pitch-and-toss, and had come round with an armful of chrysanthemums. He had meant nothing by it. They were just youth club friends and Tommy had given up trying to court her or Lily a long time ago.

'No, that was from a pitman friend, she said so.'

'And them on strike and supposed to be hard up? Shows they've more money than sense.'

'Who is it then, this fancy man?' another woman asked.

'I don't know,' Hettie snorted. 'She's too high-and-mighty to speak to the likes of us any more. But there must be someone.'

'Bet it's a man she's met at those Catholic dances she goes to,' Gert speculated.

'Aye,' Hettie agreed. 'She puts on this act of being all holy – but underneath she's free and easy with her favours.'

They all began to join in.

'And tries to sound all posh—'

'As if she's better than us.'

'But she's not – she's common as they come.'

'East Jarrow.'

'With a drunk for a grandfather—'

'And a *mam* who drinks.'

'That's terrible!'

'Well, the da's away at sea most of the time, isn't he, Gert?'

'I've heard that's just her stepda.'

'What do you mean?'

'Well,' Hettie said breathlessly, 'I don't rightly know, but remember how upset she got over Jenny McManners and her bastard son? Takes one to know one, I say.'

There were gasps of shock.

'Never!'

Catherine clutched the doorframe for support, fighting waves of nausea. She wanted to run away. They were hateful! But she had to go in, show them that she did not care. It was gossip and nothing more – they had no proof, just Hettie's vile thoughts. She had done nothing wrong and there was no fancy man.

With heart pounding, she forced herself to walk in the room. The talking stopped at once. Two women returned to their knitting, the others stared at the jigsaw on the table.

'I've brought some rock cakes from me Aunt Mary,' Catherine said brightly. 'Thought you all might like to share them.'

She smiled at each of them in turn, relishing the guilty looks on some of their faces.

'That's canny,' mumbled one of the knitters.

'No, thank you, they give me indigestion,' Hettie said dismissively and stood up. 'You coming, Gert?' Her friend hesitated, then followed.

Catherine felt her mouth drying. If they all walked out, she would crumble like dead leaves.

'Don't worry,' Catherine said with forced joviality, 'if they're too hard we'll donate them to the stone-breakers' yard.'

One of the women laughed. 'Haway, I'll try one. Like anything with raisins in.'

It broke the awkwardness and Catherine rushed to the table in relief, tearing open the greaseproof paper. She made a pot of tea and soon the talk was of the shortening days, the collapse of the miners' lockout and whether Matron could afford to lay on mince pies at the Christmas dance.

That night, as Catherine lay in bed, it was not for herself that she worried, but Tommy. It was so easy in the enclosed world of the workhouse to forget what was happening outside. But the casual talk of the lockout by the miners' bosses made her ashamed she had not thought of it more.

Tommy had been on strike for six months and she could imagine only too well how they were getting by on no money. His mother taking in washing or lodgers, trips to the pawnshop until their house was bare, scratching along the wagon ways for fallen bits of coal, risking arrest stealing timber. Children going to bed with stomachs aching, men tightening their belts, the women huddling over cups of hot water because the stores would no longer give them credit for tea. She had known times of hardship as a child, when there had been little work at the yards and what money came into the house was never enough to clear their debts.

Her eyes stung with angry tears. Why should working people be treated in such a way, when the bosses lived in huge mansions and never had a day's worry over money? The world was topsy-turvy. There were people who slaved hard all their lives and never earned enough to live on – like some of the wretches who ended up in the workhouse. And there were those who never did a day's work and had more money than they knew what to do with – like Mrs Halliday at Oakside Manor. Even in her short life Catherine knew of injustice, and it rankled.

And there was big-hearted, foolish Tommy throwing away precious pennies on a bunch of flowers because he knew how much pleasure it would bring. He was worth ten Mrs Hallidays.

Unable to sleep, Catherine sat up and pulled on her new winter coat that had caused such a stir. It was paid for with her own hard-earned money and she would wear it with pride. Pulling out a half-filled exercise book, she began to jot down characters for a story, pithy little thumb-sketches based on people she knew – members of staff, long-ago lodgers of Kate's, characters around the docks, spiteful children. Maybe the story would never be written, but it helped calm her anger at the unfairness of life, and finally it helped her sleep.

The next time she saw Tommy, she slipped him half a crown that she had saved especially. He tried not to take it.

'So you can buy your mam something for Christmas – and your little sisters,' Catherine encouraged. She did not add that it was the worst feeling in the world to have nothing in your Christmas stocking. One year, Kate had filled hers with wrapped vegetables because she had nothing else to give, and Catherine had wept with fury and disappointment. It seemed even crueller than an empty stocking, to have a bulging one that turned out to be full of potatoes and carrots. She would not wish that on any child.

Tommy gave her a kiss on the cheek, but Catherine pushed him away with a quick laugh. They were standing outside church after Mass and she wanted no one to get the wrong idea about them.

As she turned, she almost collided with a tall man behind. He raised his bowler hat and smiled.

'Excuse me.'

'No – it was my fault,' Catherine stuttered, as she stared into his face. Her heart thumped. It was Gerald Rolland, the man with the deep, sensual voice who sang at the back of the church. The man she had watched for the past two years, who had not so much as returned a look. Here he was smiling at her and raising his hat as if she was a lady.

'Lovely music today, wasn't it?' she said on impulse.

'Indeed it was,' he agreed. 'This is my favourite time of year – all those carols, all those great tunes.'

'Me too,' Catherine enthused, aware how much she was blushing. 'And you've such a beautiful singing voice.'

He shot her a look of surprise. She felt weak at the knees under his dark-eyed, scrutinising gaze. 'How kind of you,' he smiled again. He had a broad sensual mouth. Adjusting his hat, he added, 'No doubt I'll see you at church again. Good day.'

Catherine nodded and smiled and watched him stride away in his well-cut black coat. Her heart was jerking like a yo-yo. Tommy coughed and she turned to see him grinning with amusement.

' "You've got such a beautiful singing voice",' he mimicked.

She gave him a shove. 'Well, he has.'

'Kitty, your cheeks are on fire. Could this be love?'

She covered her face and told him to shush. 'I was just being polite.'

'You've never told me I'm a beautiful singer,' he teased.

'That's 'cos you sing flat as a pancake,' she laughed.

'I can tell when I'm well beaten,' Tommy said ruefully. 'Maybe all those French lessons and talking posh will pay off.'

'What do you mean by that?' Catherine bristled.

Tommy grinned, 'Well, you didn't do all that to impress the likes of me, now did you, Kitty?'

Catherine said nothing, because she knew he was right.

The following Saturday, Gerald approached her after benediction and gave her a diffident smile.

'Which way are you walking?'

She stared at him, speechless, heart knocking against her chest.

'Sorry, I just thought . . .' He gave an embarrassed cough. 'But maybe you're waiting for your young man?'

'Young man?' Catherine stammered. 'Oh, you mean Tommy? Goodness, no, he's not me man! I don't have one. And yes, I'd like to walk with you.' She blushed crimson.

They stood for a moment, smiling awkwardly.

'Well?' He looked at her quizzically.

'Yes?'

'Which way do you live?' he prompted.

'Oh!' Catherine exclaimed. Panic seized her at the thought of him walking her back to William Black Street where she was due to spend the night. Davie was home and he and Kate would be drunk by now. Her mother would give Gerald the eye and pull him into their fusty kitchen, for raucous singing and whisky drinking. Gerald did not look like the type who drank liquor. But neither did she want him walking her to the gates of the workhouse, where they might be spotted by the malicious Hettie or one of her spies.

'I-I'm not going straight home,' Catherine improvised desperately. 'I thought of going to the pictures.'

'Oh, I see,' Gerald said in surprise. 'Is there something good on?'

'Yes – well – I don't know – I was going to find out. Do – do you like the cinema?' She felt herself sweating as she asked him. What had possessed her to be so forward?

He looked taken aback, then nodded. 'Yes, I do. Are you meeting someone, or were you going on your own?'

Catherine felt herself squirm. He might think her odd for going to the pictures alone, but she had done so since she was a small girl. Her greatest pleasure in childhood was to be slipped a penny by her Uncle Jack and dash off to the noisy fleapit to gaze at the moving pictures, while organ music burst over her and swept her into a magical world.

'I was going alone,' she said, meeting his look with a touch of defiance.

Suddenly he smiled. 'May I join you? I have no other plans this evening.'

Catherine was elated. 'Of course, I'd like that very much.'

He nodded, and together they set off towards the centre of town. By the time they had found a film to go to, she had told him her name, that she lived in Jarrow and worked as an officer at Harton, that she loved reading and painting and cycling in the countryside. He listened attentively to her chatter and laughed at her descriptions of her fellow staff, and Catherine could not help exaggerating their foibles to amuse him.

Gerald insisted on paying for good seats in the stalls to see a Rudolph Valentino film, and buying chocolates for the interval. Catherine thought she must be dreaming; never could she have imagined such luck. If Hettie Brown could see her now, sitting in the dark next to the handsome, well-to-do Gerald Rolland – insurance agent, bass singer – the woman would have a pink fit. Catherine felt a delicious thrill at the thought of introducing such a man to her family and friends.

Afterwards, she had a strong desire to slip her arm through his and stroll through the streets of South Shields. But he made no move towards her.

'Can I see you to your tram?' he asked politely. 'I go in the opposite direction.'

She felt a stab of disappointment as she nodded.

'Thank you very much for treating me to the film,' she said, as the tram rattled to a stop in front of them.

Gerald tipped his hat. 'Perhaps we can do it again some time?'

Catherine smiled eagerly. 'I'd like that very much.'

He waved her away and she craned for a view of him out of the dirty window as the tram laboured up the bank towards East Jarrow. She could not wait to see Kate's expression when she told her about the grand man who had bought her chocolates. It was something they could share over a cup of warming tea, something to make Kate's eyes widen in admiration.

'Where've you been?' Kate demanded angrily, when she reached home. 'You never said you'd be this late.'

'To church, then the pictures,' Catherine said, unable to hide her smile of satisfaction.

Kate's eyes narrowed in suspicion. 'Your tea's ruined – burnt to a cinder. You never said owt about the pictures. Who you been with?'

Catherine's heart sank. She could tell by her mother's look and the smell on her breath that she was in a belligerent mood. There was no sign of Davie or John. Perhaps they had gone to the pub and left her, or maybe there had been a row. Kate grabbed her by the arm.

'Don't turn your back on me. I asked you a question. Who you been with? Look like the cat that got the cream.'

'A friend took me to see Rudolph Valentino,' Catherine admitted.

'A lad?'

'Not a lad – a man – a nice gentleman.'

'What man? You've never said owt about a man friend. Your grandda'll go light if he hears about this.'

'I've done nothing wrong,' Catherine said, resentful of her mother's tone. 'I'm a grown woman, I can see who I like.'

'Not while you're still under my roof,' Kate snapped.

'I'm not under your roof,' Catherine challenged. 'I pay me own way in the world now. I only come back on me day off to keep you happy and see Grandda.'

This seemed to madden Kate further. She shook her daughter.

'Don't you give me your lip. You're still just a lass, for all your airs and graces. And you're too young for men friends. Have you been doing owt you shouldn't have?'

Catherine shook off Kate's hold. 'You mean like you did?' she accused. 'I'm not that daft.'

In fury, Kate slapped her across the cheek. Catherine gasped and clutched her face. In an instant Kate was remorseful.

'I'm sorry, hinny,' she said tearfully, trying to hug her, 'I didn't mean to hit you. I'm just that scared of some man taking advantage of you. Let me look at you. I'll get a wet cloth. Sit here, hinny. Don't cry, please don't cry.'

But it was Kate who was soon in floods of tears, berating herself and false men and the world in general for all her troubles. She sat looking old and worn out, wiping her eyes with a grubby apron, while Catherine made her sip water. How quickly Kate could ruin a good day or a special feeling with her drunken suspicions and her grasping neediness. Catherine fought down resentment at her volatile mother. Why did she bother trying to please her? She should have kept quiet about Gerald and the cinema, pretended she'd been with Lily. But she could never lie to her mother.

'Tell me about your man,' Kate sniffed, trying to smile.

Catherine felt tired and deflated. She no longer wanted to talk about Gerald. She wanted to keep the young shoots of their courtship to herself, where her mother could not spoil them. Kate would be especially suspicious of an older, well-to-do man who might remind her too painfully of her failure with Alexander Pringle-Davies.

'There's nothing to tell,' Catherine said wearily. 'He's just a friend from church, that's all. I'm sorry about the tea.'

'I'll make you some'at now,' Kate said, brightening, the storm suddenly over. 'Egg and fried bread, eh?'

The sweet taste of chocolate was still on Catherine's lips. 'No, ta. I'll just have a cup of tea.'

'Nonsense,' Kate said, rising, 'you need fattening up – just skin and bone. Can't trust you to eat proper at Harton, but I can make sure you do in my house. And the men'll want some'at when they roll home.'

Kate was in command again. Knowing it was easier not to argue, Catherine set about helping make the eggs, hugging to herself the thought that she would see Gerald tomorrow at Mass. She could hardly wait.

Chapter 11

Catherine tried to hide her disappointment when Gerald did not seek her out the following day. It was crowded outside St Peter and St Paul's, and he was gone before she could speak to him. All that week she thought of him and wondered if she had imagined their magical evening together. But she still had the remains of the box of chocolates, which she kept in her cupboard and did not want to finish because they were a sweet reminder of the best evening of her life.

What did she know about him, apart from his respectable job with an insurance company? He had hardly spoken about himself, parrying her questions with the briefest of answers. Gerald had a mother still alive somewhere in Newcastle. He loved music, especially Bach and Haydn. He lodged in a large house that overlooked the park and the seafront. That was all she knew about him. Perhaps he was a widower, or jilted in love and wary of young women. Maybe he was not interested in her and had simply been at a loose end the previous Saturday.

Still, she attended benediction this Saturday as usual, as much in hope of seeing him, as a sense of duty.

Ignoring her during the service, he caught her up outside in the dark. 'Kitty!'

She stopped and swung round. 'Mr Rolland.'

'Gerald, please,' he chided her. 'Are you walking into town?'

'I was going to call on my friend Lily.'

'Let me accompany you.'

Catherine nodded, trying to appear calm. They set off through the frosty streets, their footsteps ringing on the cobbles. He chatted to her as if they were old friends, asking her about the past week. Halfway to Lily's house, he suddenly asked, 'Is your friend expecting you?'

Catherine blushed. 'Not really, but she doesn't mind me just calling.'

'Then she won't be offended if you don't call at all?' he pressed. 'I was thinking how nice it would be if we went to the pictures together again, tonight.'

Catherine's heart leapt. 'Yes, it would. Carole Lombard's on at the Palladium.'

'Then let's go,' Gerald urged.

Catherine grinned back. 'If you let me buy the chocolates this time.'

They sat in the packed cinema, squashed close together, eating chocolates. At one point his hand touched hers and he left it resting there for several minutes. Catherine thrilled at its warm heaviness, at skin touching skin.

Afterwards, he took her arm and linked it through his own as he walked her to the tram.

'Next Friday, they're doing Handel's *Messiah* at St Benedict's,' Gerald said. 'Would you like to go?'

'That would be grand,' Catherine beamed.

'Good, I'll get us tickets. Meet you there, outside the hall, half-past seven.'

Catherine went home, wrapped in happy thoughts of the following Friday. It was only later that she thought it odd that they had not mentioned seeing each other at Mass the following day. Sure enough, when Sunday came, Gerald slipped away from church without speaking to her and she was left puzzling over his erratic behaviour. When they were on their own, he was sweetly attentive and full of interesting conversation. But on a crowded Sunday at church, he did not even glance in her direction.

Despite this, Catherine was happy to be with him when she could. He was, she thought, a shy man and given time would become outwardly more demonstrative towards her.

They had a happy evening at the *Messiah*, and at the end Catherine dared to suggest, 'It's the staff Christmas dance next Saturday – would you like to come?'

He looked startled, then glanced away. 'I don't – can't dance.'

'You don't have to,' Catherine laughed. 'We can just sit and eat mince pies and watch the others.'

'No, sorry. I promised to visit my mother. I won't be in South Shields that night.'

Catherine hid her disappointment. He was making excuses, she knew it. But perhaps he hated dancing and did not want to be shown up. She would do nothing to make him embarrassed, so dropped the idea.

'So I won't see you for a fortnight?' she said glumly.

He reached for her hand. 'I'll take you into Newcastle for a Christmas concert,' he suddenly suggested. 'The Saturday before Christmas. What do you say?'

'Yes, of course!' Catherine cheered up at once. 'I've never been to Newcastle. Will we go on the train?'

'Train and a concert – and tea at Fenwick's,' he promised, with his sensuous smile. Then he raised her hand to his lips and brushed it with a kiss.

Catherine was shaking with excitement as she mounted the tram, quite forgetting that moments before he had spurned the idea of going with her to the workhouse dance. She attended it with Lily instead, but could not help telling her friend about her secret courtship.

'Not Mr Rolland from church?' Lily gasped.

Catherine grinned. 'Aye, and next Saturday we're going to Newcastle for a concert and tea. He's such a gentleman – and that interesting about music. Did you know he used to play the organ in a cinema in Newcastle?' Catherine hesitated. 'What's wrong?'

Lily shook her head. 'Nowt. It's just – well, I thought I'd heard he was married.'

Catherine stared at her, stunned. 'No he isn't! He can't be. Gerald isn't the type to lead a lass on.'

'Must have got it wrong,' Lily said hastily. They looked at each other warily. Maybe Lily was a touch jealous of her being courted by such a man. After that, they did not speak again of Gerald Rolland, except at the end of the evening when Lily said, 'Take care, Kitty. Don't do anything daft in Newcastle.'

Catherine was hurt that her friend should doubt her, knowing how cautious she was with lads. She had never let Tommy Gallon kiss her full on the lips like Lily had, so she was one to talk! But as the trip to Newcastle approached, she grew nervous and began to feel unwell. On the Friday evening, to her consternation, she began a heavy nosebleed. Gert called Matron Hatch and Catherine was confined to bed.

'Has this ever happened before?' Matron asked.

'Yes,' Catherine admitted, 'but it'll pass.'

'You'll want to rest at home over the weekend. We'll call for your mother.'

'No,' Catherine said in alarm. She did not want Kate coming anywhere near the workhouse or showing her up in front of Matron and her colleagues. 'I'll be right as rain by tomorrow.'

But on Saturday morning, she could hardly climb out of bed with weakness. Catherine asked if Lily could visit her to take a message to her family. To her dismay, Hettie stood guard at the door, listening to their conversation.

Catherine added desperately, 'You will tell the choir master, Mr Rolland, that I cannot come to practice.'

Lily nodded. 'Where will I find him?' she whispered.

'Tyne Dock, quarter past one,' Catherine mouthed, fighting back tears of frustration.

It was three days before she was back on her feet and in the laundry. Lily could tell her little.

'Aye, he was there,' she told her hurriedly in the drying room. 'Didn't seem best pleased when I told him you were ill. Hardly said a word – didn't even thank me for me trouble,' she added indignantly.

Dismayed, Catherine put a hand on her arm. 'Ta for going. You're a good friend, Lily.'

Christmas Day came and Catherine saw Gerald at Mass. He gave her a searching look as he passed on the church steps and tipped his hat, but said nothing. Kate was standing beside her and did not miss the look or her daughter's blushing.

'That's him, isn't it?' she said, staring at Gerald's retreating back as if she had seen a ghost. 'The man who took you to the pictures.'

Catherine shushed her and began walking away. Kate limped after her.

'I know his type,' she said with a bitter little laugh. 'All posh clothes and syrupy words, but a heart of bell metal.'

Catherine was furious. 'You don't know anything about him,' she hissed.

'So why's he ignoring you?'

'He's a shy and private man,' Catherine defended.

Kate snorted. 'Don't fall for any lad who thinks he's better than you. Doesn't matter what they say – you can see it in their eyes. Look into their eyes, Kitty.'

They walked home in tense silence. What did Kate know? She was too embittered by her own mistakes with men to see good in any of them. Even Davie, who adored her, got the sharp end of her tongue when black moods took a-hold.

Catherine tried to shake off her anger at her mother and the disappointment that Gerald had not spoken to her on Christmas Day. While Kate took nips of whisky in the scullery, Catherine busied herself with preparing the lunch of pork, stuffing and vegetables. She was gladdened by John's glee at the new pipe she had bought him, and even Davie seemed pleased with the tobacco pouch and lighter she gave him. But the mood changed abruptly with the opening of Kate's present. Her mother burst into tears at the sight of the pearl hatpin and navy gloves.

'You shouldn't gan spending good money on me,' she blubbered. 'I don't deserve it. I haven't had gloves like this since . . . such a long time.'

'Something smart for church,' Catherine said awkwardly.

Kate shot her a look. 'What d'you mean? You saying I don't gan enough?'

'No—'

All at once, she was belligerent. 'When do I get the chance? I've a house full of lazy men demanding this and that.'

Davie said good-naturedly, 'The lass didn't mean anything by it.'

'What would you know?' Kate snapped. Catherine felt a familiar dread at the angry gleam in her mother's eyes. She was itching for a fight.

'It wasn't always like this, you know. I remember when I was a lass, we'd go every Sunday to Saint Bede's in Jarrow.'

'Shurr-up and get the dinner served,' John ordered.

'What a grand place – built by the men themselves.' Kate gave John a defiant look and Catherine tensed. She knew where this was leading. 'Aye, me own da was one of them. William Fawcett.'

'That's enough,' John growled, picking up the poker and clanging it on the fender. 'Don't you mention that name in my house!'

'The Fawcetts were well respected round Jarrow,' Kate goaded. 'Good Catholic family – regular churchgoers – and we lived in a respectable part of town.'

'Kate . . .' Davie warned.

'Not like the McMullens. They lived in the cottages – like middens they were – not fit for pigs.'

John let out a roar. 'Just let me at you!'

But Kate knew John was too unsteady on his legs these days to catch her. 'Mam cursed the day she ever set eyes on you,' she said savagely. 'It was me real da she loved with all her heart, not you.'

'No!' John cried. 'It was me saved her from the puddling mills, not bloody Fawcett.'

'You killed her,' Kate said, trembling, 'with your drinkin' and fightin'. You put us on the street, turned us into beggars.'

71

John hurled the poker at his stepdaughter. It gave Kate a glancing blow on her shoulder and smashed on to the table, toppling the jug of gravy. Kate grabbed at the poker, revenge in her look.

'No, Kate!' Davie pleaded.

Catherine barged at her mother, wresting the poker from her grip and shoving her towards the door. Davie pushed the struggling, cursing John back into his seat. Out in the yard, Catherine stood blocking the back door until her mother calmed down, praying none of the neighbours had heard the commotion. The back lane was deserted.

Kate stood panting with rage for several minutes. Abruptly, her shoulders crumpled and she began to sob hysterically. Catherine felt a strong mix of anger and pity and shame for the woman. What had possessed her to rake up the past like that and cause such a scene? There was nothing to be gained by riling old John.

'Ta for ruining Christmas,' Catherine muttered, upset by her mother's excessive tears. This was what whisky did to her, turned her into a howling, unpredictable monster. It reminded her of how Kate had wailed over Grandma Rose's grave, sodden with drink, shaming them all, while she had clutched at her grandda's hand for comfort. He had been stoical and dignified, while Kate's wild grief had been terrifying.

'I-I'm s-sorry,' Kate wept.

Catherine turned away, peering into the kitchen where the shouting had subsided. Gravy dripped from the tablecloth and she wondered if the meal could be salvaged.

'Don't go,' Kate sobbed, 'please don't go. I need you, Kitty.'

'No you don't,' Catherine said in irritation. 'You just want someone to clear up the mess you make.'

'Don't speak to your mam like that.' Kate looked wounded. 'I don't know what came over me. It was just seeing him – today at church.'

'Seeing who?'

'Your man. He just reminded me of . . .' She hung her head.

Catherine's heart squeezed. 'Of who?' she whispered. 'Me da?'

'Aye,' Kate said hoarsely. She looked up with bleary, desolate eyes. 'It made me think how different things would've been if I'd still been a Fawcett and not a McMullen.'

Catherine held her breath, not wanting to stop her mother's confiding.

'How would it have been different?' she asked softly.

Kate's voice shook. 'He loved me as Kate Fawcett – the daughter of William Fawcett, a friend of the Liddells. He knew me da – knew him for a gentleman.' Kate's tone hardened. 'But when he discovered I was a common McMullen, he couldn't get away quick enough.'

Catherine's mind spun. Alexander had known her grandfather, William Fawcett. William was a friend of the Liddells! Did she mean the Liddells of Ravensworth, and was Alexander one of them? If so, Aunt Mary's story of her aristocratic father could really be true. The blood hammered in her head.

Kate took a step forward, swayed and steadied herself against the brick wall. She looked worried, as if she had said too much.

'Don't make the same mistake I did, Kitty,' she urged. 'Don't pretend you're someone you're not. 'Cos sooner or later you'll be found out.'

Chapter 12

The raw January winds came along with growing stagnation at the yards. The nearby pits were working on short time and the steel mills were mothballed. Davie had managed to get a job on a coal boat between Newcastle and Gothenburg, and Kate was morose without him. But Catherine's biggest upset was that Gerald had disappeared without trace.

She threw herself into her work and her reading, redoubling her efforts to improve herself. Her mother was wrong: it was possible to change and become someone else. Her words of warning on Christmas Day had only served to make Catherine the more determined to break free of her shameful past. Perhaps Gerald had somehow learnt of it. Or maybe he thought her too ill-educated and ignorant to be his life-long companion. An assistant head laundress might be a huge step up for Kitty McMullen of the New Buildings, but it was only the first rung on the ladder that would take her up and out of the unskilled classes.

She would become a nurse. Nursing was a respectable profession that recruited from the middle classes too. Catherine scoured the public library for books on anatomy and studied late into the night.

One evening Matron surprised her with a visit. Catherine leapt up and closed her books.

'Sit down Miss McMullen. Your light's on very late,' Matron observed.

'I'm studying,' Catherine said proudly.

'Can I see?'

Catherine handed over a textbook. Matron flicked through it and looked up in surprise. 'Why such an interest in the human body?'

Catherine flushed. 'I-I want to become a nurse,' she stammered.

Matron raised an eyebrow. 'You've never mentioned this before.'

'No.'

'Do you have a young man?' Matron's look was sharp.

Catherine blushed deeper in confusion. 'No, Matron.'

'That's not what I've heard.' Mrs Hatch closed the book and handed it back. 'And there has been concern that your interest in such matters is – a little – unhealthy. I wouldn't want you to do anything to sully the reputation of the workhouse staff. So perhaps you should limit the number of books of this type you leave lying about the staffroom.'

She went, leaving Catherine gawping in stupefaction. She didn't leave them lying around; someone had been poking about in her room. Hettie and Gert, more than likely, trying to get her into trouble! What else had they been telling Matron? How dare they spread lies about her. Was she never to escape their poisonous whisperings? How could Matron Hatch have believed them? Catherine flung herself on the bed and wept in fury.

That Saturday evening, she went to church to find comfort among the flickering shadows and the calm patient face of the Madonna. Halfway through benediction, she was struck by a familiar deep voice. Glancing round, she caught sight of Gerald and could not help a broad smile of joy. Briefly he returned it.

Afterwards, they walked into Shields as if there had been no hiatus in their courtship.

'I've been working in Newcastle – my mother hasn't been well,' he explained.

'Oh, I am sorry,' Catherine said in concern. 'Is she better now?'

'Yes, thank you.' The wind buffeted them. 'Let's go to a café for a hot drink,' he suggested.

Warming themselves over cups of hot chocolate, Catherine blurted out, 'I was so worried that you'd gone for good.'

He eyed her. 'I thought you'd made excuses not to come with me to Newcastle. I was annoyed that you'd sent your friend, as if you couldn't face me.'

Catherine reached out and seized his hand. 'No, I was ill – I had a terrible nosebleed and could hardly lift my head off the pillow. I so wanted to go with you to the concert. And then when you ignored me outside church at Mass – I was that miserable.'

Gerald gave his quizzical smile that made her insides twist with longing.

'So you've really missed me, Kitty?' he asked.

'Yes,' she blushed. 'Not a day goes by when I don't think of you.'

He squeezed her hand. 'I've missed you too. But I'm back now and we can carry on seeing each other again – on Saturdays – maybe other times when you're not working.'

Catherine thrilled at his words. 'That's grand!'

'But one thing, Kitty,' he cautioned, 'I don't want you telling everything to that friend of yours – or gossiping about us to anyone else. This is private between us.'

Catherine had a moment of doubt. Lily's words about him being married suddenly came back to her.

'What's wrong, Kitty?'

She had to ask him. 'You're not married, are you?'

He recoiled as if she had slapped him. 'What sort of man do you think I am?' he asked in offence.

'I mean, you've never been married in the past, have you?' Catherine said wildly. 'I wouldn't mind if you were a widower or anything. I just wondered . . .'

The look he gave her made her hot with shame. How could she have suspected such a thing?

'I'm sorry,' she mumbled.

He surveyed her with sorrowful dark eyes. 'I forgive you, Kitty. I don't blame you for thinking it possible that a man of my age might have already been married.' He took hold of her hand again. 'But I can assure you I never have been. I've never found the right woman.'

The way he looked at her and the touch of his hand made Catherine's heart race with excitement and hope.

They began to see each other regularly on Saturday evenings and as spring arrived and the days grew longer, Gerald would suggest evening walks in the countryside around South Shields, away from the busy streets. She delighted in his company, eager to learn from him about everything from music to insurance. He took her to concerts and encouraged her to take up the piano again. Kate had tried to make her learn as a child, but Catherine had been paralysed by the fear of how much debt was being amassed in unpaid lessons and a beautiful piano bought on tick. She had rebelled by being determined to fail and refusing to learn.

But Gerald rekindled a love of the piano and a thirst for classical music. She had grown up with traditional singsongs and Irish tunes passed down from John. Kate could sing like a bird and once had brought tears to Catherine's eyes with a bitter-sweet rendering of

'Thora', about a wintry landscape and a child lost. But too often Kate's singing degenerated into raucousness and ribald songs that made Catherine blush.

Gerald's love of music was noble and pure, and she begged him to teach her all he knew. He was patient and considerate. Most of all, he did not scoff at her attempts at self-improvement as her workmates did.

'Don't listen to them, Kitty,' he said dismissively, 'they're only jealous. You have a sweetness and refinement that they will never have – and an eagerness to learn. You must carry on with your studies. You're too good for a workhouse laundry – a nurse's training would be just the thing.'

As summer came, Catherine's dissatisfaction with her job grew. After Matron's warning, she felt wary of confiding in her employer, so plucked up courage to approach Father O'Neill for help.

'Nursing?' he barked at her in astonishment.

'Yes, Father, it's what I've set me heart on.'

The priest shook his head. 'They'd never take you on,' he said bluntly. 'You've not got the education. It's a hard training, Kitty; you wouldn't cope. Be thankful for what you've got. You're getting on well at the laundry – it's a great achievement for a girl with no learning.'

Catherine wanted to run out of the church hall screaming. She was deeply hurt by his dismissal of her ambition. *A girl with no learning.* She hated him for belittling her. She would show them all! Stubbornly, Catherine continued to borrow heavy medical books and ploughed through them, making notes in her rough scrawl.

In moments of self-doubt, she surveyed her notes and thought Father O'Neill was right. She could draw competently, but knew her writing was jumbled and the words misspelt. She did not have the learning to write long essays or put her thoughts into grammatical English. Her mind was a wilderness, untended, and she was bowed down with the effort of improving it.

Only being with Gerald made her feel better. With him, she could practise speaking in a genteel way and talk of art and music without feeling self-conscious. Sometimes she wished he would be more demonstrative, do more than walk arm in arm along quiet lanes or kiss her hand at the end of the evening. She dreamt of him holding her tight and kissing her lips like they did in films, but there was always a reserve about him that she could not breach.

But soon Catherine would be twenty-one and an adult. No longer would she be bound by Kate's rule. She would be a fully-grown woman, free to marry. Perhaps this was the moment Gerald was waiting for too.

It was Kate's suggestion to throw a party.

'You must do some'at to mark your comin' of age,' she declared. 'Me and Mary'll put on a grand tea – have our Sarah and your cousins over from Birtley. And you can have your friends round, eh? We'll have a right good party – Uncle Alec on the fiddle – push back the furniture and have a bit dance.'

Catherine eyed her mother with caution. The last thing she wanted was Kate making a spectacle of herself in front of all her friends. And which friends would she invite? Lily and Amelia, of course, and Tommy and Peter and cousin Ida. But what about Gerald? This would be a golden opportunity to introduce him to the family – as long as Kate did not get drunk.

'Gan on, Kitty,' Kate urged, 'you like a party as much as I do. And don't give me that look. I'll not show you up. Promise I'll not touch a drop.'

Catherine smiled in relief and nodded. 'I'd like a party.'

'If it's canny weather we can tak the tables outside and have a street party – like after the war,' Kate enthused. 'All the more room for dancin'. And some of the neighbours can join in – like Bella and her mam.'

Catherine's insides clenched. She might have been only eight when Bella and the other girls had shut her out of their birthday party, but the shock and humiliation would stay with her for ever. She felt the hurt like a raw wound as if it had happened yesterday.

Kate saw her look. 'Maybes not Bella. But the McGraths – they've got a piano – we could pull it outside.'

Catherine felt dizzy at her mother's plans; the whole of Jarrow would be turning up for her birthday at this rate.

'Could we have it round at Aunt Mary's?' Catherine asked. 'She's got more room.'

Kate looked wounded. 'You mean she's more posh. I'll not have her lording it over us on such a day. You're my bairn and we're having the party here.'

Catherine felt a guilty twinge, for she had been thinking of Gerald's reaction.

'Well, let's just keep it to family and close friends,' Catherine said firmly.

Kate scrutinised her. 'Close friends? So are we ganin' to meet your mystery man, Mr Rolland?'

78

Catherine reddened quickly. 'He's not a mystery man, he's just shy of company.'

Kate snorted. 'Keeping him hid 'cos you're ashamed of your family, more like.'

'No, I'm not!'

'Then bring him to your party,' Kate challenged.

'I will,' Catherine glared.

The next time Gerald took her walking she told him.

'Me birthday's on the Monday, but we're having the party on the following Saturday afternoon when I'm off work. You will come, won't you? Me family want to meet you – they tease me that you don't exist.' She laughed, trying to make light of it, but her stomach knotted at the alarm on his face.

'I'm not sure,' he said gravely. 'I may have to visit Mother.'

Catherine withdrew her arm. 'You can see your mother on the Sunday. This is me twenty-first! Tell her – she'll understand. Unless you've never told her about me?'

He glanced away.

'You haven't, have you?' Catherine looked at him dismayed. She clenched her fists. 'It's plain as glass I don't mean owt to you! If I did, you'd want to come and meet me family and share in me special day.'

She turned and stalked away down the cinder track by the railway line. Butterflies flew up as she pulled savagely at the long grass. Gerald did not love her. He was too grand to deign to come to a party in East Jarrow. She had seen the look of distaste on his handsome face and known the void between them.

'Kitty, wait! Stop,' he shouted, running to catch up. He swung her round. 'Of course I'll come. I didn't know it meant that much to you.'

She swallowed angry tears. 'Course it does. How could you not know?'

He smiled down at her. 'I'm glad you value our friendship so much. These times together mean a lot to me too.'

She smiled back, encouraged. 'They mean the world to me, Gerald.'

He bent and kissed her forehead. It was a fatherly kiss, like a blessing. She stood with face upturned, hoping he would kiss her on the lips too. But he stood back and held out his arm for her to hold. Catherine smothered her disappointment and took it, reminding herself that she had won him round. Gerald would be the guest of honour at her coming of age.

Chapter 13

June came, hot and blustery. On the Saturday of the party, Catherine hurried round to William Black Street to help with the preparations.

'It's too windy to have it outside,' Mary decreed. 'Me tablecloths'll fly off to China.' She had brought beautifully embroidered covers, and Alec had staggered round with their china plates and tea cups.

Kate looked disappointed, then nodded. 'I'll swill the yard out and we can dance out there.'

Mary muttered loudly to Catherine, 'You'll not catch me dancing in her yard if the Pope himself were to come.'

Kate winked. 'There's a far more important guest comin' than the Pope. Isn't that right, Kitty?'

Mary smiled, 'Aye, of course. Will we have to curtsy when he comes in?'

'Stop it, the pair of you,' Catherine laughed in embarrassment. 'Just act normal. But don't ask him lots of questions or make a fuss or tell him things about me as a bairn. And don't say he's the first lad I've brought home.'

'But he is,' Kate pointed out.

'Well, just don't say anything.'

Her mother and aunt exchanged looks. 'McMullens not say owt? That'll be the day,' Mary said.

'Aye,' Kate chuckled, 'Hell will freeze over first.'

Catherine gasped. 'And don't say things like that.'

The women burst out laughing at her consternation.

'By, he must be special,' Davie joined in, clomping in from the street where he was hanging bunting over the front door.

Aunt Sarah and four of the cousins arrived off the train from Birtley. The noise of chatter, clattering crockery and banging oven doors rose as everyone helped or got in the way. A chair was put outside for old

John while Davie and two cousins went off to fetch some beer to quench their thirst. Not for the first time did Catherine wish her stepfather was far at sea. If he enticed Kate to get drunk and loud-mouthed, she would never forgive him.

By quarter to four, the parlour was dusted and table beautifully laid with an assortment of sandwiches, scones and cake. The kitchen floor was scrubbed, the fender and fire irons gleaming, and more baking sat cooling by the open window, ready to replenish the plates. All traces of washing and ironing had been banished to the wash house, and flowers decorated the mantelpiece and windowsills.

Catherine wore a new pale blue dress, with clip-on earrings that Aunt Mary had given her. Kate had given her a garish scarf that she had tried to look pleased about, but would probably never wear.

She looked at her mother, still flushed from her marathon of baking, the sweat stains darkening her dress, her apron floury.

'Haway, and get your pinny off,' Catherine fussed, trying to calm her nerves. 'I'll help you pin up your hair again. You are going to change your dress, aren't you?'

Kate blew out her cheeks. 'You would think the King was inspectin' the troops,' she teased. But she allowed Catherine to bundle her into the bedroom and look out a clean blouse and skirt.

As she combed Kate's thick brown hair, Catherine mused, 'You haven't a single grey hair. Lily's mam has lots.'

'It's a miracle,' Kate grunted. 'Your grandda's given me enough trouble to turn me white five times over. Not to mention the rest of you.'

She turned and put a rough hand to her daughter's face. 'By, but you're bonny in your new frock.'

Catherine's eyes pricked at her mother's soft tone. How rarely she heard it, yet how much she had craved it in childhood. Now her girlhood was officially over and she could look this woman in the eye as an equal. Except she didn't feel equal; inside she was still a child seeking Kate's approval.

'I hope you like him,' Catherine said, suddenly seized with doubt.

'Your mystery man?' Kate's look was reflective, wistful. 'You're a better judge of character than me. I'm sure he's a real gentleman. As long as he does right by you, I'll welcome him into this home like family.'

Catherine felt a surge of gratitude. She quickly hugged her mother. 'Ta, our Kate. Ta for doing all this.'

Kate's lip trembled. Catherine, thinking she was going to cry, pulled away. It would not do for either of them to be red-eyed for their guests.

Kate turned away. 'Haway, let's start the party,' she said briskly.

Back in the kitchen, Lily and Amelia had arrived with presents of lavender water and handkerchiefs. Tommy and Peter brought flowers and a canary.

'What in the wide world am I supposed to do with that?' Catherine laughed.

'Have it as a pet,' Tommy said cheerfully.

'Matron doesn't allow pets.'

'I'll keep it for you,' Kate said. 'Bet it speaks more sense than old John.'

The laughter and noise in the kitchen grew. Kate shooed them into the parlour and told them to help themselves to the food.

'Can't we wait a few minutes?' Catherine said, her insides taut. She kept glancing at the door, looking for Gerald's arrival.

'What time did you tell him?' Mary asked.

'Four o'clock – four-ish,' Catherine stammered, 'I think.' Her mouth and throat were dry with nervousness.

She glanced at the clock for the umpteenth time. Twenty past four.

'We'll not cut the cake till he comes,' Kate promised. 'Haway, Sarah and get the tea poured. Everyone's parched.'

Catherine busied herself in the parlour, handing out sandwiches and chatting to the guests.

'I'll just take these round,' she said, slipping out of the room. Lily followed with a plate of scones.

At the open front door they peered into the street. John was turning red in the June sun, mug of beer in hand.

'I'm still on sentry duty,' he said. 'No sign of the enemy yet.'

'Grandda!' Catherine chided. Her heart sank. Two neighbours across the street stood cross-armed at their doors, watching. Catherine nodded and they waved back. How many of them were looking out to see whom Kitty McMullen was courting?

Catherine retreated inside again. Quarter to five. Panic began to seize her. Something had happened to him. He had promised to come; he wouldn't let her down deliberately.

'Maybes he's waiting for a tram,' Lily suggested.

Catherine nodded. But by five o'clock she knew that was unlikely. Gerald could have walked from his boarding house by the promenade

82

to Jarrow in an hour. While she smiled and joked with her cousins and friends, her stomach heaved like a rough sea.

Doubts crowded in. How did she know where he lived when she had never been there? She had never met any of his friends or family. His precious mother did not even know she existed. Why was he so secretive? Why did she only get to see him when he decreed it? He was living a double life. Lily was right, he must be married. She was as foolish as Kate to be taken in by his sophisticated clothes and his cultured ways. But that was ridiculous. Gerald was a devout churchgoer, a man of honour, and he had given his word he had never been married. How dare she doubt him?

Half-past five. Catherine's worry turned to anger. Gerald had discovered that her mother was a fallen woman and she was illegitimate. That was the truth of it. What other reason could there be for humiliating her in front of all her family? Kate's sinfulness with her father had blighted her life yet again. Why was her mother so weak? She wanted to run out of the house, escape from the pitying glances, the worried looks.

Finally the cake was cut and they all sang 'Happy Birthday'.

'Make a wish,' someone shouted.

Catherine closed her eyes, knowing that her greatest wish, for Gerald to walk through the door, was not going to happen now. So she wished with all her might for escape from Number Ten, William Black Street and the humiliation of being Kate's daughter.

For the rest of the party she looked on like a bystander observing strangers. Uncle Alec played his fiddle and Tam McGrath joined in on the tin whistle. The table was pushed back and dancing began in the parlour, the dancers knocking into John's iron bed. Tea drinking gave way to beer and whisky. Tommy and the Birtley cousins arm-wrestled on the kitchen table while Sarah and Kate grew louder with each drink.

Catherine was glad Gerald was not there to see her mother swaying on the hearth singing 'Cushie Butterfield' and bursting into tears when someone mentioned it was Jack's favourite. What did it matter if Kate got drunk and took over her party? The spark had gone out of it the moment she realised that Gerald was not coming.

It was late when the last of the revellers staggered off into the night. Sarah and Ida were staying at Mary's, while the boys piled into the parlour with the snoring John. Catherine lay down on the settle, drained of emotion.

'Sorry, hinny,' Kate said, lurching over her. Catherine felt queasy at the familiar reek of whisky.

'Doesn't matter,' she muttered, burying her face in her arm.

'You deserve better than him,' her mother slurred.

'I'll not find better round here.'

'Course you will, Kitty. Don't let one rotten apple spoil the what's-it.'

'Barrel.'

'Aye, the barrel.' Kate hiccuped.

'Come to bed, woman,' Davie called wearily from the back room.

Kate chuckled. 'See, I found one in the end.'

Catherine snorted. She would never settle for a man like Davie, or a life like Kate's.

Once Kate had gone, she got up and padded outside, a blanket thrown over her nightdress. The smell of the sea was strong on the night breeze, the clouds racing across the stars.

She felt bruised from Gerald's rejection. She ached for him, yet he was a huge disappointment. Longing weighed her down. But for what? Maybe not just for Gerald, but for something out there under the stars, out of her reach. For the first time, Catherine thought of escape, real escape, of leaving not just William Black Street, but Jarrow itself. The thought wriggled in her mind, frightening and unsettling. There was a world out there beyond Shields, far from Tyneside, which people like her father inhabited.

She shivered in her bare feet. One day, she was going to find it.

Chapter 14

The following Saturday evening, Gerald was waiting for her outside church. Catherine brushed past him and stalked off down the street. He chased after her and caught her by the arm.

'Kitty, wait. What's wrong?'

She shook him off. 'What's wrong? You made a laughing stock of me in front of all me family, that's what!'

'When?'

'On me twenty-first,' she glared.

'You mean your birthday party?' He sounded bemused.

'Aye, the one you promised to come to,' she accused. 'All me family were there and me friends – all waiting to meet you, and me looking at the clock every five minutes, fretting and thinking some'at terrible's happened to you. And them looking at me as if I've made the whole thing up – you and me.'

Suddenly, Catherine was seized by a huge convulsion. A sob rose up from the pit of her stomach.

He seized her hands in consternation. 'I'm sorry, truly sorry.' Quickly, Gerald pulled her round the corner. He stared down at her, his dark eyes contrite. 'I had no idea it meant that much to you. I was in Newcastle – Mother has been unwell again and I didn't like to leave her. I didn't know how to get a message to you. I knew you would understand once you heard my reason. And with all your other friends there – well, I didn't think you'd miss me.'

She stared at him in disbelief, shaking and crying. How could he not know how much she loved him?

'Please forgive me, Kitty,' he begged, squeezing her hands in his.

She wanted to, but the humiliation of her terrible birthday was still too raw.

'Y-you d-didn't even send me a card,' she said miserably. 'Nothing to show you cared even a little.'

'But I do,' he insisted, producing a handkerchief and dabbing at her tears. 'I have a present for you, but it's not one I could send in the post.'

'What is it?' Catherine sniffed.

'Dear, sweet girl, please don't cry any more. Come, let's walk up Simonside – you'll feel better for the fresh air – and I can explain.'

Her curiosity raised, Catherine allowed him to link her arm through his and march her briskly away from the town. Along the railway embankment, the smell of newly cut grass mingled with cinders from the track. The evening call of birds grew as the clank and din of the yards receded. Above the embankment, hidden by briars and hawthorns, Gerald sat her down on a rough bench made from an old railway sleeper. It was their favourite sitting place, sheltered and secluded, and Catherine was suddenly desperate that he would put everything right again.

He took her hand and began to stroke it. 'I have a confession,' he said in his deep voice. 'My mother was ill, but I knew I should have made every attempt to come to your party. I hate myself for letting you down.'

'I don't blame you for your mam being ill,' Catherine said generously.

'It wasn't just that,' Gerald said, gazing at her intently. 'I was afraid to come.'

'Afraid? What do you mean?'

'Your family . . .'

'I knew it,' Catherine trembled, withdrawing her hand. 'You're ashamed of us 'cos we're from the New Buildings and me grandda has no trade, and me stepda's a common seaman. And you've been listening to gossip about me mother, no doubt.'

'No,' Gerald said, surprised by her outburst. 'I don't know much about your folk. But I'd heard the McMullens were a large family, a close family that looks after its own – doesn't take to strangers easily. Quite frankly, I was worried your folks might get the wrong impression about us.'

'What impression?' Catherine asked in confusion.

'That we might be courting.'

She felt suddenly leaden. 'But I thought we were.'

He gently tilted her chin so she had to look into his dark brown eyes.

'We don't know each other very well,' Gerald murmured. 'We need to have time together – alone together – to find out if we are suited.'

Catherine's heart began to hammer. 'What do you mean?'

He smiled. 'That's my present to you, Kitty. We'll go away on a holiday together, just you and me. No Mother, no McMullens, no nosy neighbours. I'll pay for everything, of course.'

Catherine could feel an excited flush spreading up from her neck into her fair face.

'Go away where?' she whispered.

'The Co-operative Hotel at Gilsland. It's in Cumbria – beautiful countryside. We can go on long walks and the food's very good. I've been before.'

Catherine eyed him cautiously. 'Who with?'

'On my own,' he said. 'The hotel caters for single working people.'

Catherine smiled in relief. 'So we don't have to pretend that we're—' She broke off, flushing deeper with embarrassment.

Gerald laughed. 'Kitty McMullen, did you for a moment think I'd be proposing something improper?'

'No!'

'Well, I'm not. I'd never do anything to take advantage of your sweet, trusting nature. It's what's so appealing about you, Kitty. Your youthful innocence.'

He made her sound childish. 'I'm a grown woman now,' Catherine reminded him.

He leant forward and kissed her forehead. 'Of course you are. You're entitled to go to Gilsland of your own accord, as a working girl on a good wage. That's what you must do. We'll both go separately, so as not to cause tongues to wag, but once we're there we'll have as much time together as we want.'

Catherine felt a slight niggle. 'Why should they wag when it's all above board?'

'You know what folk are like. We don't want any tittle-tattle to the priest or your employers, do we? You can book in a couple of days before me and then I'll join you. What do you say?'

Catherine yearned to go, yet the idea made her nervous. 'When will we go?'

'August would be best for me. Mother goes to stay with her half-cousin at the coast and I usually take my holiday week then.' He leant close. 'Say yes, Kitty.'

She had a strong urge to throw her arms about his neck and kiss him on his sensual lips. She would put up with the charade of not courting publicly so as to be with him at Gilsland. And perhaps after the holiday, he would officially be her intended. She felt a sudden surge of hope.

'Aye, I'd like to go,' she smiled.

Unexpectedly, Gerald leant over and brushed her lips with a brief kiss that left her full of longing.

The summer dragged on as Catherine waited impatiently for Gilsland. She had never been away from Jarrow for a whole week on holiday, let alone with a man. The thought made her insides churn with fear and excitement. She told no one but Lily that Gerald would be at the hotel too. Kate was surprised but pleased at her holiday plans.

'I think it's grand, you letting your hair down for once. But don't you want to gan with Lily or Amelia?'

'They can't afford it,' Catherine said with a shrug. 'Anyway, I'll meet other lasses there.'

Kate eyed her. 'And lads. Find someone more your own age, eh? Not like that Mr Rolland.'

Catherine quickly turned away to hide her blushing. She had never told her mother about making up with Gerald.

'Aye, find a lad that trets you right,' Kate continued as she pounded bread dough. 'Plenty more fish in the sea.'

Catherine managed to meet Gerald briefly on Saturday evenings for walks if the weather was fine, or to go to the cinema if it rained. She could hardly contain her excitement about the approaching trip but he would merely smile and pat her hand as if indulging a child.

Two weeks before they were due to go, Matron summoned Catherine into her office. Catherine was terrified word had somehow got out that she was holidaying with a man. Had Lily let slip her secret? She sat opposite Matron Hatch, clutching her hands to stop them shaking.

'Miss McMullen, I'll come straight to the point. Do you still have ambitions to become a nurse?'

Catherine gawped at her. 'A nurse? I-I don't know. I suppose so. Well, yes.' Her heart was hammering with relief that this was nothing to do with Gerald.

Matron nodded and picked up a piece of paper. 'There is one way into nursing for girls like you who don't have the qualifications or background,' she said bluntly. 'You can train to be a midwife.'

'A midwife?' Catherine said in astonishment.

'I have details here about such a course. If you are interested I could put a word in for you. You're a quick learner and a hard worker. I don't see why in time you couldn't go on to becoming a fully trained nurse.'

Catherine sat speechless. Here was the opportunity she had dreamt of, to become a skilled nurse, a woman with a profession. She saw herself in a smart matron's uniform with a starched headdress. Gerald would admire her, maybe enough to marry her.

'Of course, it's not just a matter of training,' Matron continued. 'You will need to support yourself away from home. Some funding will need to be found.'

'Away from home?' Catherine queried.

'Yes, the training is in London. It would be an excellent grounding for you – and I wouldn't be suggesting it if I didn't think you were up to it.'

'London!' Catherine exclaimed. 'Oh, I couldn't gan there. It's too far away . . .' She could not go that far from Gerald, not now that there was an understanding between them.

Matron gave a sharp look. 'If you're serious about getting on, Miss McMullen, you'll have to be prepared to move away.'

Catherine felt a rush of disappointment. A few weeks ago, after her birthday, she might have snatched at the chance to leave Tyneside. But now she was deeper in love than ever. Gerald was her future more than midwifery. The midwives she knew were common, illiterate women, helping out their neighbours for a few pennies. Besides, the idea of childbirth appalled her. It was the messy, mysterious side of nursing about which she had no wish to be enlightened. Kate had once said that giving birth was worse than torture and Catherine feared it. When she daydreamed of sweeping about in a matron's uniform, it had nothing to do with the blood and sweat of a midwife's lot.

'If it's the money you're worried about, I'm sure we could ask Father O'Neill for help with a loan for the train fare and books.'

'I'm sorry, Matron, but I don't want to be a midwife,' Catherine replied.

Matron frowned. 'Go away and think about it. If you change your mind, come back and tell me before the end of the month. The training starts in September.'

Catherine nodded and rose quickly. As she opened the door, Matron added, 'Lots of girls would jump at such a chance. This isn't backstreet midwifery; it's a proper training. So don't go thinking you're too grand for it, Miss McMullen.'

Catherine hurried from the office, feeling rebuked. She had disappointed her employer, but she could not tell her the real reason for her reluctance. Perhaps, when Gerald proposed to her, Matron Hatch would understand.

Yet part of her agonised that she was making a mistake. She could just imagine Kate saying, 'Tak the bull by the horns, Kitty, and get yoursel' doon to London. You can come back to Jarrow, hinny, once you've got your trainin'.'

She confided in Lily. 'Do you think I've done the right thing?'

Lily shrugged. 'It's a grand opportunity, Kitty. I'd gan if I was given half a chance.'

'Would you?' Catherine asked in surprise. Lily had always seemed such a home-bird.

'Aye,' Lily nodded, carried away by her own brave words. 'Just think of being in London. Seeing the King and Queen and all them big shops.'

'Would you come with us?' Catherine asked, curious.

'Course I would,' Lily declared.

They stared at each other and burst out laughing at their daring.

Then Lily said, 'They'd not have me on the trainin' and old Hatchet wouldn't put a word in for a laundry maid like me.'

Catherine sighed. 'Maybes not. But wouldn't it be a laugh to gan away together?'

Lily studied her. 'Have you told Gerald about this?'

Catherine looked away. 'No.'

'Why not?'

Catherine could not answer. Deep down she feared he might encourage her to go.

Chapter 15

From the train window, Catherine could see the moors covered in purple heather, and when she stepped out on to the quiet platform a blast of scented air nearly knocked her over. A charabanc from the hotel was there to meet the new arrivals and she found herself sitting next to a talkative girl from Edinburgh. By the time they reached Gilsland, nestling in a dip below the blustery fell, she knew that her companion was called Helen, had three brothers, worked in a telephone exchange, played tennis and was in love with Douglas Fairbanks.

Catherine's fear of being on her own for two days before Gerald arrived evaporated in minutes. By tea time, she and Helen had become firm friends and by bedtime had made arrangements to play tennis with two bank clerks from Preston.

'But I've never played before,' Catherine exclaimed.

'Doesn't matter,' said Terence, a tall, loping man with ears that stuck out, 'neither has Billy.'

'Yes I have,' Billy protested.

'Not that you'd notice,' Terence grinned.

That night, Catherine knelt by her bed and gave thanks for the spotlessly clean hotel, the heady view of vast open sky above mossy lawns and her new cheerful companions. Unable to sleep, thinking of Gerald's arrival, she threw wide her window and leant out.

In the dusk she could hear the distant bleat of a sheep and then silence. The air smelt of honey and grass. She breathed in huge gulps, marvelling at its purity. There was not a trace of coaldust or pitch or the raw effluent of the tide. Something else puzzled her about the night sky, deepening by the minute. At home, it was a yellow haze of smoke and lamplight like a blanket thrown over the town. Here the sky seemed to go on for ever, glinting with thousands of stars. She had no idea so many existed. She could hardly wait to share such a romantic sky with Gerald.

Catherine stayed by the window until she was chilled through, thinking fantastical thoughts. Was her father leaning on another windowsill in some other country house, gazing out at the starry sky at that very moment? Had Kate ever leant out of Ravensworth Castle and longed for her lover as she now did? Catherine shivered and pushed away such disturbing thoughts. She climbed into bed, leaving the window open, and was asleep in minutes.

The two days of waiting passed swiftly in the company of Helen and the bank clerks. They played tennis in the morning, took a packed lunch and went for a walk in the afternoon. After tea, Terence organised a mixed game of cricket on the lawn and in the evening they gathered round the piano and sang while a store manager from Newcastle rattled through his repertoire of music-hall tunes.

'Go on, Kitty,' Helen pushed her forward, 'give us some Geordie songs.'

Catherine needed little encouragement. All those times she had stood on the fender performing for her Grandda John and Grandma Rose came flooding back, and she sang the traditional songs with relish.

Her friends clapped and Terence swung an arm round her and declared, 'I'd pay to sit in the grand circle to hear you any day, Kitty McMullen.'

Gerald's arrival in the middle of a tennis game the next morning took Catherine by surprise. She had imagined he would come on the afternoon train as she had, but he had taken an early bus.

She was laughing from having delivered a fluke service that Billy had not seen coming.

'Well done!' Terence cried, patting her shoulder.

'Someone's staring at you,' Helen remarked, pointing beyond the fence. 'Has your dad come to check up on you?' she laughed.

Catherine swung round in alarm and squinted into the sun. 'Gerald!' she gasped and waved him over.

He nodded at her, then turned and walked away, hands clutched behind his back. She turned back in embarrassment. 'He's a friend.'

Helen raised her eyebrows. 'I think he's a wee bit jealous,' she teased.

'Don't be daft.'

'Do you want to finish the game?' Terence asked, unsure.

'Course I do. Gerald won't mind.'

But it seemed Gerald did. Catherine rushed to find him after their match and found him sulking in the lounge behind a newspaper.

'Don't let me drag you away from the fun,' he said. 'I see you've wasted no time making new friends.'

'Well, what was I supposed to do?' Catherine retorted. 'Sit in my room and mope? Come on, I'll introduce you. Helen's from Scotland – she's really canny – and the Preston lads are a laugh.'

'I came here to be with you, not a bunch of boys from the cotton mills.'

Catherine flushed. 'They're bank clerks – and it was you suggested we come here.'

A middle-aged couple walked into the room and glanced at them. Catherine prised the newspaper from Gerald's hands and pleaded, 'Let's go outside. I've been counting the minutes. Don't let's fall out over a daft game of tennis.'

Mollified, Gerald led the way into the garden. They found a quiet spot beyond the kitchen garden and she slipped an arm through his.

'I'm glad you suggested we come here – it's a grand place. I couldn't wait for you to get here – all the tennis and that was just to fill in time. Those lads don't mean anything to me.'

'That tall one has his eye on you,' Gerald said suspiciously.

'Terence?' Catherine laughed. 'Well, he's wasting his time. It's you I want to be with, Gerald, no one else.'

For the first time he smiled at her, his handsome face lightening. 'Come on, we'll take a walk up the hill. There's a stretch of the old Roman Road further on, don't you know?'

Catherine did, but she kept quiet about having walked there with the others the day before.

'Show me,' she smiled back.

The rest of the week passed too quickly and they spent every waking hour in each other's company. Gerald had never been so possessive over her, steering her away from the others and declining invitations to tennis or cricket or board games in the evening. The weather held and they went back out for evening walks along the river. Catherine had only momentary twinges of disappointment that she could not join in the occasional game with Helen and the younger ones. But walking alone in the twilight with Gerald was better than anything else. He was so much more affectionate and relaxed when they were on their own that she had a glimpse of what life could be like for them together.

On the last evening, she tried to steer the conversation towards the future.

'I love it here – the moors and the smell of the place. I don't want to gan back.'

'It is beautiful,' Gerald agreed. 'Didn't I tell you you'd love it?'

'Wish we could stay here together for ever,' she said, squeezing his hand.

He laughed. 'Well, we can't – we both have work awaiting us – and we should be thankful we have in this day and age.'

'Aye, I know that, but it doesn't do any harm to have dreams. What do you wish for, Gerald?'

He stopped, his face wistful in the glow of the setting sun. 'To lead a good life, I suppose, and be happy. To find the right companion and make her happy too.'

Catherine's heart missed a beat. Did he mean her? Tentatively, she put a hand up to his face and felt the roughness of his chin. He kissed the palm of her hand.

'Gerald . . .' she whispered.

In a swift movement, his arms came about her and he pulled her close. He leant down and put his mouth over hers. His lips were surprisingly soft and moist as they pressed on hers. It was their first real kiss, the one she had longed for all summer, but now it was happening, she was seized with panic. While his mouth sucked at hers, his strong tongue was probing, trying to force her lips apart. Catherine clamped them tight. She had a vague idea that to allow him into her mouth would lead to pregnancy. Why was she so ignorant about these things? Why had she not asked Lily for more details about how far it was safe to allow a man to go? Lily had kissed Tommy and she would know.

Instead of feeling exultant that Gerald was finally kissing her as a man kisses a grown woman, she was gripped with panic and anxiety that she was doing something wrong. She stood as rigid as a statue, eyes squeezed tight shut, until he stopped.

When Gerald pulled away, she could feel the coldness of the evening breeze on her wet lips.

'Kitty, what's wrong?'

'Nothing.'

'I'm sorry, I thought . . . I was overcome by the perfect evening. I shouldn't have.' He sounded offended.

Catherine said quickly, 'Oh, but I wanted you to.'

'No, it was wrong of me. You are so young.' Gerald turned away. 'We should be getting back.'

Catherine's eyes flooded with tears. She had spoilt everything with her stupid fears. She swallowed hard. 'I love you. Please don't go.' She grabbed at his arm. 'I have to tell you something. I turned down the chance to go to London – couldn't stand the thought of ganin' so far away from you.'

He stopped and stared at her. 'What chance?'

'Matron wanted me to gan to London to train as a midwife. I said no.' Catherine searched his face for approval.

'You didn't say it was because of me?' he said, startled.

She shook her head, feeling dashed. 'I said it was too far from home. Anyways, I couldn't afford it – haven't got enough saved up.'

'But isn't that what you wanted to do, nursing?'

Catherine looked him in the eye. 'I don't want to be in London – I want to be with you.'

They stared at each other. Gerald reached out and touched her hair. 'You turned all that down just for me?'

She nodded. He let out a long sigh and pulled her gently into his arms.

'Oh, dear Kitty. I don't deserve it.'

'You do to me, and I don't regret it,' she assured him, pressing her cheek to his chest and returning his hug.

They stood in the dying light, holding on to each other wordlessly. Catherine wished she could stay like that for ever, listening to the quiet beat of his heart and feeling the warmth of his breath on her hair. But as the night breeze strengthened, he broke away.

'Come on, we should go back before they lock the doors.'

Catherine tried to delay the moment. She felt there was so much unresolved between them, about what happened once they left the haven of Gilsland.

'When we get back home,' she said, 'will we be courtin' proper? I mean, we've got on like a house on fire this week, haven't we? And you said we had to find out if we were suited. Well, we are, aren't we?'

She could not see his expression in the half-dark, but his voice was full of warmth.

'It's been a grand week, Kitty, one of the best I've ever had. And if it means so much to you, we can say that we're courting.'

Catherine felt a surge of relief.

'That's champion!' she cried. She heard him laugh softly. 'Gerald,' she said impulsively, 'kiss me again, please.'

He hesitated a fraction, then stepped close and kissed her gently on the lips. It was a chaste kiss, empty of passion, but tender. Catherine's heart swelled at the thought that she could finally parade Gerald as her intended. No more skirting around town avoiding busy places. She would have him home for tea – or at least to Aunt Mary's. They would go to the Harvest Festival dance together.

As she pressed her lips against his, a delicious thrill went through her at the thought of showing him off to Kate. She had found a gentleman who would give her the respectability she craved. Kate would be pleased and proud, and fuss around Gerald. She would have her mother's approval – and a little touch of envy.

Chapter 16

On the evening she arrived back in Jarrow, Catherine could not resist rushing round to William Black Street to tell her news. The hot weather was ending abruptly in a thunderstorm and Catherine arrived soaked. Davie was back at sea, so a subdued Kate brightened at once on seeing her. Her jaw dropped when she heard Gerald Rolland had been on the holiday too.

'Did you know he would be there?' she asked in amazement, helping her daughter out of her dripping coat.

'Well, I had an idea,' Catherine admitted.

'You're blushin',' Kate declared. 'Look at that! He must've found out you were ganin'. I hope you gave him an earful for missin' your party.'

'That's all in the past,' she said hastily. 'We have an understanding now.'

'Meaning?'

'Me and Gerald Rolland are courtin',' Catherine said with glee.

'By the saints!' Kate gasped. 'Are you havin' me on?'

'No!'

John woke up by the spitting fire. 'What you wake me up for?' he grumbled. 'Kitty, is that you? Have you brought me any baccy?'

'Aye, Grandda, and a pot of honey from Gilsland.'

'Our Kitty's courtin',' Kate said in a fluster. 'You'll bring him round for tea on your next day off, won't you?'

'I'll believe it when I see it,' John snorted.

'It's true,' Catherine insisted.

'Don't listen to him,' Kate sniffed. 'We'd all die old maids if he had his way.'

'What you sayin', you old bitch?' he snarled. 'Get me a bit bread and put some o' Kitty's honey on it.'

Kate ignored him. 'Tell me what you did all week. Was the hotel very grand?'

Catherine revelled in telling her mother all about it, while she fetched bread and spread on honey, to keep the peace between John and Kate. Her mother laughed and made little comments at her pithy descriptions of the other guests.

It was late by the time Catherine got up to go. Kate pressed her to stay.

'It's raining cats and dogs still. Why don't you stop the night, hinny?'

'No, I'm on duty first thing in the morning.' She pulled on her coat and hat, which had been steaming by the hearth.

Kate saw her to the door. 'This man,' she said with a serious look, 'he's not leadin' you on?'

Catherine bristled. 'Course not. He cares for me. That business with me party – his mam was ill – and he'd heard about the McMullens being clannish – was afraid we wouldn't take to him.'

Kate grunted, 'Well, there's nowt we can do about that. He'll have to tak us as he finds us.' She scrutinised her daughter, her blue eyes still vivid despite the shadows and lines. 'I just hope he's not ganin' to lead you a dance.'

They both knew she was thinking of Catherine's father. His unspoken presence hung between them like a question unanswered.

'He's not like that,' Catherine said, shrugging into her wet coat.

'I hope not,' Kate replied, her voice heavy with regret.

All the way back to Harton, in the teeming rain, Catherine could not rid her mind of her mother's dispiriting words. That night the temperature dropped and she could not get warm, yet the narrow room with its view on to another brick wall seemed airless and oppressive. By morning she was sneezing violently and her head throbbed; by evening a nosebleed had started and she took to bed.

Matron came to visit her and asked her strange questions about her holiday.

'Perhaps you've picked up an infection,' she said.

Catherine's head swam. She felt too ill and tired to answer.

'Sorry, Matron,' was all she could mumble.

Lily slipped in to see her the next day. 'Not supposed to be here, but I've brought you some of me mam's ointment to rub on. Cures everything from colds to lumbago. Did you have a canny time? Was Gerald good to you?'

Catherine managed a weak smile and nodded. 'Best time ever. We're courtin'.'

Lily gasped. 'That's grand. Shall I get word to him you're poorly?'

But before Catherine could answer, Hettie barged into the room.

'You, out!' she ordered. 'If I catch you up here again, you'll be straight to Matron.'

Lily hurried off. Hettie hovered over the bed.

'Was there some'at you wanted Lily to do?' she asked.

Catherine shook her head, worried at what she might have overheard.

'Had a good time then? Must have spoilt it, being ill. I wouldn't have done it meself – ganin' off on me own like that – doesn't seem proper. But you young'uns . . .'

Catherine turned her face away and clutched a wodge of torn sheet to her nose. She could not be bothered arguing back at Hettie's snide remarks.

The following day, as she struggled to dress for work, she noticed in alarm she had come out in a rash. It made her itch and she could not stop scratching. Her colleagues were quick to notice.

'You got that all over?' Gert asked with disgust.

'It's from Lily's ointment, that's all,' Catherine said, unnerved by all the staring.

That evening, Hettie and Gert came to tell her she was being moved to the sick bay.

'But I'm not infectious,' she protested weakly.

'Matron's orders. We've got to help you move,' Hettie said with satisfaction.

Catherine was taken to a windowless room in the sanatorium away from the others. She could hear the hacking cough of a consumptive somewhere else on the wing. Lying back, she felt dizzy and frightened. What did they think was wrong with her?

She seemed to lie there for an eternity, until Matron appeared suddenly with a doctor.

'Dr Lovell is going to examine you,' Matron Hatch said brusquely. Then she was gone, closing the door behind her. Catherine sat up in alarm. She did not want to be left alone with this man. She had heard him talking sharply to the inmates. He eyed her fiercely under bushy grey eyebrows.

Without a word of greeting, he began poking around her ears and mouth and shone a small torch into her eyes. She flinched as he touched her with cold fingers and examined her hands and arms. Thinking of the kind Dr Dyer, Catherine wished she could be lying at home being fussed over by their local Scots doctor.

'Lie down and pull up your nightgown,' Dr Lovell ordered.

Catherine stared at him in horror. 'Why?'

'Don't ask questions, just do as you're told,' he snapped.

She lay back, feeling sick, and closed her eyes tight as his hands prodded every inch of her. He pulled her legs apart and examined her with a cold instrument. Catherine began to whimper with the discomfort and shame.

'With whom have you been in contact recently?' he demanded.

She opened her eyes and asked in bewilderment, 'What do you mean?'

'You've been away on holiday, Matron told me. Have you been in close physical contact with a man?'

Catherine stared in confusion.

He added impatiently, 'You have a suspicious rash. We need to know if you might have caught it from being intimate with a man. You are known among the staff as being familiar with men.'

Catherine went puce. They thought she had been with a man! She, who was so terrified of intimacy that she kissed as if her lips were sewn together, was being accused of loose behaviour. Worse still, they thought she was diseased because of it. How dare they accuse her so? She was more devout and upstanding than the rest of the staff put together.

Catherine went hot and cold with shock. She could not speak. Not only had this hateful man touched her all over, but Matron had ordered it. Mrs Hatch thought the worst of her too. But what could she say? She had been on holiday with Gerald and allowed him to kiss her alone. Did that count as intimate contact? Surely she could not have caught this rash from one long kiss?

She swallowed hard and forced herself to say, 'I got the rash from some ointment. Lily thought it would help me cold. I never came back from holiday with any rash,' she said defiantly, 'and I've never been intimate with a lad.'

Even as she denied the words, her face burnt with the shame of it all. They had ruined her romantic thoughts of Gerald, sullied the innocent memories of their holiday together. Now she could never share them with the others. Hettie must have overheard her talking to Lily about Gerald and used the information against her.

Dr Lovell wiped his hands on a cloth and shut his bag.

'I don't think there's any cause for concern,' he said brusquely, 'but I'll recommend that you stay in isolation until the rash goes, just to be sure.'

He left. Catherine sat on the bed clutching her knees and shaking. She was furious and miserable. Part of her wished to storm out of the workhouse and tell them all to go to the devil. She had never felt so ashamed in all her life. But to do so would be to admit defeat. It would make her look guilty and the bigots like Hettie and Gert would have triumphed.

Through the long sleepless night, Catherine tossed on the bed, besieged by black thoughts. She must have done something wrong to be in such a position. She was sinful to have gone on the holiday in the first place. In the depths of her mind, were her thoughts about Gerald just as carnal as Kate's had been for her father? Maybe the rash was a punishment. She was tainted with the same weakness as Kate.

People must be right when they said that the sins of mothers infected their daughters and that's why they had to be brought up apart, so they would not go the same way. That's why Rose and John had sent Kate away and brought her up as their own. They had wanted to keep her from Kate's corrupting weakness. She should never have been allowed to return and look after her. From the moment Kate had begun to run their household things had started to go badly wrong – the drinking, the debts, the fighting and violence, the rough men who had come into the midst of their home as lodgers . . .

Catherine had a brief flash of memory, as vivid as a moving picture, of a lean-faced man with cropped dark hair and jade-green eyes smiling at her.

Come here, pretty Kitty, and I'll tell you the story of Osian and the magic horse.

He had swung her on to his knee and she had felt the coarseness of his serge trousers on her bare legs, the warmth of his hands. As he told the tale, his breath was hot on her neck and he bounced her up and down as if he were the galloping horse. She wanted to climb down, but the horse was galloping too fast and she clung on in fear.

The memory faded before she could remember his name or who he was, but it left her feeling queasy and desolate.

Her fear subsided with the new day. By then Catherine had decided that she would stay on and redouble her efforts to appear respectable in the eyes of the other officers. She would give them no excuse to besmirch her character or carry tales to Matron. She would not let Gerald kiss her again until they were engaged.

Two days later, she was back working at the laundry and in the evening went straight to confession. She poured out her guilty thoughts about kissing Gerald and dwelling on the carnal, and recognised Father O'Neill's stern voice rebuking her behind the confessional. Catherine came away feeling frightened of the flames of Hell, of kissing Gerald and going the way of her mother.

Yet she longed to see him again. With being ill, she had missed him on Sunday and went eagerly to church the following one. There was no sign of him and no sound of his deep, melodious voice. When she went home, Kate was full of questions, impatient to meet him.

'He's working away,' Catherine said evasively.

'Have you seen him since the holiday?'

'No.'

Kate tutted. 'That's a bad sign.' She gave a piercing look. 'You haven't – you didn't . . .?'

Catherine rounded on her. 'Did what? Let him have his evil way?'

Kate flinched. 'I just don't want to see you taken in . . .'

'Like you were, you mean?' Catherine said bluntly, hurt that her mother should think as little of her as the women she worked with. She stormed out and did not visit again for two weeks.

Chapter 17

The following weekend, Gerald reappeared. Catherine, sick with relief, hung back waiting for him after benediction.

'You've been away? It seems ages. Is your mother all right? I've missed you that much,' she gabbled as they walked down a side street.

He nodded at her questions without looking at her, his mind somewhere else. 'Yes, it does seem an age,' he said distractedly.

'Shall we go up to the railway cutting?' she asked eagerly. 'I want to hear all about where you've been.'

'You weren't there the Sunday after we got back,' he said accusingly.

Catherine coloured. 'No, I was ill in bed for a few days – a bad cold.'

'Oh, I'm sorry. I thought perhaps . . .' His voice trailed off.

She looked at him in concern. 'Is something wrong?'

He shook his head as if ridding it of difficult thoughts. They walked up to Simonside in near silence, Catherine anxious not to upset him with too many questions. They sat on their bench, though the September wind gusted around them and spattered them with drops of rain.

'Me family would like to have you round for tea,' she broke the silence, 'nothing fancy. Maybes next Saturday?'

He frowned at her as if he were finding it hard to focus on what she was saying.

'Saturday? Oh, yes, very well.'

'Gerald,' she said, puzzled, 'tell me what's on your mind. You seem a million miles away.'

'I was thinking about Gilsland,' he murmured.

Her heart began to race. 'I think of it all the time. Wasn't it just grand? The best time in me life.'

'Have you thought any more about it?' he asked.

Her stomach jerked. 'About us, you mean?'

He gave her a strange look. 'No, about the midwifery course.'

Catherine stared at him, baffled.

'I was thinking what a great opportunity it is for you,' Gerald continued. 'And I would like to help you out – lend you the money so that you can go.'

Tears stung her eyes. She blinked quickly, forcing them back.

'It's too late. I had to tell Matron by the end of August,' she said.

He pursed his lips. 'I'm sorry, I would like to have helped. You deserve to get on.'

Catherine blurted out, 'I don't care about being a midwife – I never wanted to be one. I want to stay here and be with you.'

He shifted uneasily. 'You're very sweet.' But he did not lean close and try to kiss her or talk about their future together. Instead he rambled on about a concert he had been to in Newcastle and his mother's visit to the coast.

As spots of rain turned heavier, they hurried back to town. At the foot of the bank they parted. Catherine clenched her fists in frustration.

'You'll come next Saturday then?'

'Next Saturday?' he queried.

'To tea at my house,' she prompted.

'Oh, tea, yes, of course.'

'It's Number Ten, William Black Street, remember. Four o'clock be all right?'

He nodded, tipped his hat and walked away. Catherine swallowed the panic she felt rising inside. Gerald had given her no reason to be optimistic that he would come this time. She plodded up towards East Jarrow in the fading light, oblivious of the rain. She would need to tell Kate just in case he did turn up. By the time she reached the New Buildings, she had convinced herself that Gerald would keep his promise. The talk of the midwifery course had meant nothing ominous, it had just been a sign of his generous nature, wanting to provide for her, thinking of her future and wellbeing.

All that week, Catherine went around with a feeling of dread in the pit of her stomach. She would get home early to make sure Kate had the house clean and looking respectable and make sure John was either sober or put to bed.

On the way up to East Jarrow, she bought a large sponge cake with a cream filling that she knew Gerald would like. Arriving at the house, she was dismayed to see wet washing strewn around the hearth. The table was unlaid and cluttered with ironing.

Catherine dashed about, seizing wet sheets. 'Kate! He'll be here in an hour. What you doing washing on a Saturday?'

Her mother appeared from the scullery, her hair dishevelled, sleeves rolled up.

'Your grandda wet his bed,' she said shortly. She gave Catherine a wary look.

'What is it?'

'You better read this – it came this morning,' Kate said dully, pulling out an envelope from her apron pocket.

It had already been opened. Catherine shot her mother an angry look.

'You've read it.'

'It's from him. I'm sorry, hinny.'

She could not bear the look of pity on Kate's face. Turning away, she unfolded the letter with trembling hands.

Dearest Kitty,

I cannot come for tea on Saturday, or any other day in the future. I am truly sorry for causing you such pain. I never meant for you to become so attached to me. My regard for you is too high to allow the situation to continue.

You see, my dear, I have been grieving these past two years for another. I was engaged to be married to the daughter of a clerk in a law firm, here in South Shields, but being unsure of my feelings and hers, broke off the engagement just before our marriage. You, sweet Kitty, have been a solace to me in these trying times and given me back my will to love again. But I see clearly now that it is this other woman whom I truly love and that I could marry no other.

You have been the rock to which I have clung in my despair. Please forgive me for leaning on you thus. I hope you will find a man worthy of your love in the years to come.

With kind regards,

adieu,

Gerald Rolland

Catherine wanted to scream as she crumpled the letter in her fist and threw it on the fire. How could he do this to her? He had been promised to another all along. What a coward he was! Hot tears welled in her eyes.

'You're better off without him,' Kate declared. 'His type never make a lass happy. They're all sweet words and false promises. Here one day, gone—'

'Shut up!' Catherine rounded on her. 'You don't know what you're talking about. You never knew him, so don't you go judging him. And you should never have opened me letter!'

'Well, it makes no difference.' Kate was defensive. 'He's done the dirty on you anyroad. I've never trusted him since he spoilt your party – and all that sneaking about the place not wantin' to be seen with you – well, we know why now. He had another lass all along.'

'Aye, he did,' Catherine said tearfully. 'Happy now? Bet you're pleased I'm just as daft as you – being taken in by posh clothes and a la-di-da voice.'

'I never said—'

'But at least I never got mesel' into trouble,' Catherine blazed.

'Don't you speak to me like that,' Kate snapped.

'I don't believe he had another lass,' Catherine cried, unable to stop. 'He just thought I wasn't good enough for him. I bet some snotty gossip from round here told him about me and you. You're not the only one never gan to be rid of the shame – 'cos I'm stuck with it an' all. Do you ever think about that?'

Kate gave her such a look of angry despair that Catherine turned away.

Kate came after her. 'I'll not be spoken to like that by me own flesh and blood as if I'm worth nowt.' She grabbed her arm. 'I've brought you up as best I can, but do I get any thanks for it? Not a word!' She shook her. 'So don't blame me for your troubles with this man – they're all of your own making. I warned you about him, but you always know best.'

Catherine threw off her mother's hold. 'Leave me alone!'

'Gladly.' Kate trembled with fury. 'Gan stew in your own misery. Get out!'

Catherine fled into the muddy lane, not caring if the neighbours stared from their rain-splashed doorsteps. No one would be surprised at shouting coming from the McMullens' house.

She slipped and slid down the bank, shaking and sobbing with shock. Gerald had deserted her, Kate thrown her out and the women at Harton despised her. Where could she go to escape? Catherine stumbled aimlessly through the town, distressed and fearful. But she knew she had to keep moving, for if she stopped for one moment, the demons that chased her would catch her up.

Chapter 18

Catherine found herself at Tyne Dock station. It was just after three in the afternoon. Not knowing quite why, she bought a ticket to Lamesley. As she sat on the train and watched the dockyards and terraced housing of Jarrow and Hebburn slip by, she felt her panic and misery begin to ease.

It was obvious she did not belong here. She would never be accepted by its people as long as the disgrace of illegitimacy was known. It bound her up like a shroud, defined who she was in the eyes of neighbours and workmates. To them she was common Kitty McMullen, daughter of a fallen woman, tainted with sin. No matter how hard she tried to improve herself, how devout she was, she would never achieve respectability round the streets of Jarrow or Shields. She was saddled with Kate's mistake.

Kate! she thought resentfully. Her mother had blighted her life, not only with her weakness with men, but her drinking and volatile moods. She had seesawed between possessiveness and rejection, smothering love and sudden beatings. When she thought of her childhood, the humiliations outnumbered the kindnesses: the weekly trek to the pawnshop, queuing for whisky beside grown men, the savage name-calling of the neighbours' children.

Catherine squeezed her eyes shut to try to rid herself of the memories. She and Kate would never get on: they were chalk and cheese. But she was only half Kate's daughter – the lesser half – the argumentative, coarser half. Somewhere she had a father whom she took after, an impulsive romantic, a refined gentleman. It was from him she must have inherited her taste for fine things, the drive to better herself.

The desire to discover who he was burnt within her more than ever. She felt reckless in her search for him, no longer caring what people would think of her questions. If she could only find him, she felt sure he would rescue her. She had been living the wrong life in the wrong place, whereas she was more suited to this other life of beauty and learning that had eluded her.

Catherine stood on the platform at Lamesley, gazing at the cornfields. In the near distance, the woods of the Ravensworth estate were tinged with russet and gold, while beyond, a pit village puffed smoke like a train pulling up the far hills.

Now she was here, she had no idea where to go first. But the air was clear and sweet after recent rain, and she was content to walk along the lane, breathing in its freshness. She stopped by the squat, grey church and put her hand to the cold stone wall. Was this where Grandma Rose had sat and watched a Ravensworth bride as a very small girl? She had loved to hear her grandmother's stories of visits to the countryside and its tales passed down by Rose's own grandmother. Stories from a woman who had been alive a hundred years ago, of the gentry riding by flaming torchlight and women in crinolines. She shivered to think she might be standing on the same spot as someone who had seen the Duke of Wellington.

Suddenly, Catherine thought of Great-Aunt Lizzie. The last they had heard was that she was widowed but still living somewhere on the estate with her son, George. They had not set eyes on each other for years. Perhaps her great-aunt had known who her father was.

It took half an hour of asking around the village before she was directed up the hill to a row of cottages in the woods. She passed under an old gateway with a deserted and boarded-up lodge. The tunnel of trees rustled above, showering her with the first autumn leaves. The driveway was mossy and overgrown, and Catherine felt the ghosts of the past watching her as she walked.

Catherine did not recognise the stooped, grey-haired woman who hobbled to the door after much knocking. She squinted at her with a wrinkled, weather-beaten face.

'It's Kitty, your grand-niece,' Catherine repeated more loudly, 'from Jarrow.'

Lizzie's face broke into a grin of recognition. 'Little Kitty? Well, I never! Haway in, it's grand to see you. You don't mind cats? Sit yourself down. I've just made a pot of tea. What brings you here? Is your mam all right?' She swung round in concern.

'Yes,' Catherine said hastily, 'everyone's canny.'

'A grand lass, your mam,' Lizzie wheezed. 'Happy times we had when she lived here. Our George and Alfred thought the world of her. Good with bairns is Kate.'

Catherine felt uncomfortable. If only her aunt knew the half of it.

'Let me pour the tea,' she insisted, and jumped up to help. A ginger cat stalked up to her and rubbed against her legs.

They chatted for a few minutes, Catherine shouting loudly into Lizzie's ear trumpet, giving news of the family. But it was not difficult to steer her back to talk of the olden days when Kate had been at Ravensworth. The old woman's face lit up at mention of the past.

'Came to help out when I'd had a fall,' she explained. 'Bonny lass – such a clear skin for someone brought up in the town. She was a real favourite round here, always quick to lend a hand – and singing, always singing like a bird. Went to work at Farnacre for the old dowager.'

'Farnacre?'

'The old dower house yonder,' Lizzie said, with a jerk of her thumb. 'Then Lady Ravensworth noticed her and the next minute she's a maid at the castle. Such a willing worker, you see. And Lady Emma – well, she was a bright spark – liked to have lively young'uns around her all the time.'

Lizzie went off on a long ramble about the former Lady Ravensworth and a scandal concerning a footman, until Catherine steered her back.

'So why did me mam end up working at the inn?'

'For the reason I told you,' Lizzie said impatiently. 'The earl died and Lady Emma took Kate to Farnacre, then Lady Emma ran off with the footman and the next earl died an' all, so there was no job at the dower house, so she went to the inn.'

Catherine was still puzzled, but the real question still burnt on the tip of her tongue. She screwed up her courage.

'Aunt Lizzie, did she meet me father when she worked at the castle?'

The old woman was suddenly flustered. 'Your father? Well, I don't rightly know.'

'But it's possible?'

Lizzie sucked on her gums in thought. 'Kate would never talk about it. She never told me who he was. I always thought . . .'

'What?' Catherine pressed.

'A lad who worked in the gardens was sweet on her – Robert. Aye, he spent all his spare time down at the inn, according to my Peter. And he got wed soon after Kate left, so perhaps he never knew about her carrying his bairn.'

Catherine was disbelieving. Kate would not have risked disgrace for a mere gardener.

'Aunt Mary said me father was a real gentleman – had connections with the Liddells.'

Lizzie nodded. 'Well, Robert had the manners of a gentleman – and he worked for the Liddells until they left the castle. He went with them to their country estate in Northumberland.'

'Aunt Mary said he was called Alexander Pringle-Davies. Do you know that name?'

Lizzie stared at her, then abruptly laughed. 'Master Alexander? Don't be daft! Our Mary's full of tales and nonsense.'

'So you knew him?'

'Not exactly. He used to stay at the castle on business – handsome as they come. He was some sort of relation of the old earl – and a friend of Lady Emma's. Now there was gossip about him and Lady Ravensworth . . . but him and Kate? No, that's our Mary being fanciful.'

Catherine was hurt by her aunt's dismissal of such an idea, as if it was impossible she could have had such a father. But instead of discouraging her, it made her all the more convinced that this gentleman must have been Kate's lover. If it had been Robert the gardener, there could have been a hurried wedding. But Kate must have aimed too high in her expectations of love, and fallen for a man so beyond her social class that marriage would have been out of the question.

'So he was related to the earl, you say?' Catherine was desperate to glean anything about him.

Lizzie frowned. 'I think so – it's so long since I've thought about him. Used to see him out riding.' She sighed. 'No, I don't remember the story. My Peter could have told you – he knew Master Alexander when he was a lad. Bright as a button and a whole lot of mischief.'

Catherine's insides twisted in frustration. If only her great-uncle was still alive to unlock the secrets Kate refused to tell.

'Where is Mr Pringle-Davies now?'

Lizzie shook her head. 'I wouldn't know. There haven't been Liddells at Ravensworth since the end of the war. It's a girls' school now, did you know? My Peter's bonny lawns turned into hockey pitches. The gardens gone to rack and ruin – though my George tries his best – and they're building villas where the glasshouses used to be.' She tutted and sucked hard on her gums.

The light was fading from the low-ceilinged cottage and Catherine got up to leave. She would get no more from her aunt and her fading memory.

'Why don't you stop the night?' Lizzie suggested. 'It's getting late and you'll not be home before dark. George'll be in shortly – he could show you around the old gardens.'

Catherine brightened, having no desire to return to the town. 'I'd like that.'

She helped her aunt peel some potatoes and carrots for the pot, until her cousin appeared. George stooped to enter the kitchen, taking off his cap and scratching his thin reddish hair, awkward at finding a visitor.

But Catherine put him at ease by showing interest in the models he made out of corn stalks. After a tea of rabbit stew and baked apples, he was gruffly willing to show her around the estate before nightfall. George was employed by the private school as its gardener.

'Don't have time to keep it like it should be,' he said in apology, as they approached the shadowy castellated mansion and skirted the old stables. A clock above the archway chimed seven and someone practising piano scales could be heard from an open window. A strong, sickly smell of overblown roses wafted at them as they rounded the corner on to a terrace. The flagstones were uneven and cracked, the flowerbeds choked with wild grasses, but the lawns that swept away towards the woods were neatly trimmed. One was marked out as a tennis court.

Her cousin pointed out two newly built houses on the fringe of the woods. 'Used to grow peaches and melons over there. We still grow vegetables, but nothing fancy. The sheds are used for storing trunks. Used to grow the sweetest asparagus – and chicory – and the best runner beans.'

Behind, the castle stood dark and brooding in the twilight.

'Why are there so few lights on?' Catherine asked.

'They don't use that half,' George explained. 'It's not safe. Floors caving in. Old mine workings underneath.'

'Is that why the Liddells left?'

George nodded. 'Made their castle from coal – and lost it to coal. Makes you think, doesn't it?'

Catherine glanced at her cousin. There was more to him than his taciturn shyness.

'Do you remember a man called Pringle-Davies?' she asked as they walked on. 'Used to visit here years ago when you were a boy.'

George removed his cap, scratched his head and replaced the cap in a swift movement. He shook his head.

'Maybe you knew him as Master Alexander?' Catherine pressed.

He kept walking as if he had not heard. They rounded a corner of overgrown rhododendrons and were suddenly standing before a lake. It was half silted up with pale reeds that rustled and moaned in the evening breeze. The water glittered in the dying light and rippled where small fish nipped the surface.

'How beautiful!' Catherine gasped. At the far end, a boathouse stood abandoned, its roof half gone.

'The pupils aren't allowed down here, but I sometimes bring me rod and catch a fish or two,' George confessed.

Catherine stood entranced. Here, more than at the run-down castle, she could imagine the former glory of this mighty estate. She pictured the gentry being rowed on the lake, or picnicking in the shade of the overhanging trees. For all its forlorn, overgrown state, it was still a place of faded romance; a lake created for no other reason than aesthetic pleasure. She breathed in the pungent smells of ripe fruit and weed-choked water.

Suddenly George said, 'Aye, I do recall him. Master Alexander.'

Catherine stared at him, her heart tripping.

'He gave me a shillin' once.'

'Why?'

'For carrying a lantern – so he and Lady Ravensworth could see their way home. Came into the hothouse to try the peaches. We were closing them up for the night – Father and me.'

Catherine felt a wave of disappointment. So it was true that Pringle-Davies was more likely to have been Lady Ravensworth's lover than Kate's.

'Your mam was there an' all,' George said. 'She was carryin' Alfred, 'cos he was tired out.'

Catherine's stomach lurched. 'Are you sure? Kate met him too?'

Her cousin nodded. 'Now I come to think of it, they were on speaking terms.'

'What do you mean?'

'Well, once I was down by the lake fishing. Shouldn't have been there,' he said, blushing. 'Saw them across the other side.'

'Together?'

'Aye, walking and talking. Heard him laughing. Must've bumped into her. Kate often took that way back to the castle when she'd been to see us. He would talk to anyone, would Master Alex.'

Catherine trembled in the chilly breeze. She looked across the lake and could almost see Kate with Alexander. A young, pretty Kate with a slim face and lustrous brown hair, laughing with the tall, handsome cousin of the Liddells.

'When's the last time you saw him?' she asked in a hushed voice, as if any noise would shatter her vision.

'Years ago,' George said, leading them back along the path. 'Don't remember seeing him much after the old earl died. Was a lot of chopping and changing in them days – three men inheriting the estate in as many years. Maybe he fell out of favour. Was a canny man, though Father said he was a wild'un.'

Catherine felt her frustration mount. She had a strong sense of Alexander's presence, yet he eluded her.

'Who would know what had happened to him?'

George turned and gave her a wary look. 'Why do you want to know? What you asking about him for, anyroad?'

She shrugged and smiled. 'Just wanting to know more about what life was like – when me mam worked here – that's all.' She slipped her arm through his. 'Ta for showing us round. I've enjoyed it – and I won't tell on you for fishing where you shouldn't if you don't tell on me for being nosy.'

But all that night, as the wind picked up and whistled down the chimney, Catherine lay awake imagining Kate's secret assignations beside the secluded lake. How easy it would be to fall in love in such a place. For the first time she had a glimpse of Kate's point of view: a naïve, gregarious girl, flattered by the attentions of sweet-talking, reckless Alexander.

She tossed on the hard truckle bed, disturbing the ginger cat. Yet what had happened to Alexander? He had vanished without trace in the upheaval of dying earls and disruption of business. Since then the gentry had been decimated by the war in Europe, the castle was subsiding into old mineworkings and the Liddells were long gone.

In the morning, Catherine rose early and made porridge for her aunt and cousin. After breakfast she said her farewells.

'Think I'll take a walk around the village before I get the train,' she explained. 'Thank you, Aunt Lizzie, for everything.'

'Tell your mam and Mary that I'm asking after them.'

'And Grandda?' Catherine prompted.

Lizzie sucked her gums in disapproval. 'Aye, if you must.'

As they kissed goodbye, Lizzie's face suddenly lit with a memory.

'He was an artist,' she announced.

'Who was?' Catherine queried.

'Master Alex. I've been trying to remember since you were asking. Used to go about the place sketching folk in a little book. Did one of my Peter and the bairns. Kept it all these years in the back of the Bible.'

'Can I see it?' Catherine gasped.

She hobbled across to the fireside and pointed to two large books jammed in a nook beside the range. 'Lift them down, hinny. It's in the Old Testament.'

Catherine laid them carefully on the table. Lizzie pulled out a yellowed piece of paper with shaking hands.

'There. It's just the spit of my Peter,' she said fondly.

The charcoal drawing was smudged and faded, but the figures were neatly drawn: a man in a cap sitting up on a flat cart, two boys grinning over his shoulders. From her own drawing lessons Catherine knew how difficult it was to depict people.

'I can tell it's George,' she said in delight, tracing the sketch with her finger. In the corner were the initials, APD. She felt a thrill at this tangible evidence of his existence.

Lizzie nodded. 'Like I said, he was an artist.'

Catherine longed to take the picture with her, but knew how much it meant to her aunt and did not ask.

Walking back down the hill, with the bells of Lamesley church ringing across the fields, she wondered if Alexander had ever sketched her mother. She was convinced that this man was her father, felt it deep inside. All she needed to do was discover where he had gone.

Catherine circled the inn at Ravensworth for half an hour before plucking up the courage to approach. The front was locked up, so she went round to the back, past stables and outhouses where hens pecked in the dirt.

'What you want?' a large woman in a faded apron demanded, as she threw scraps to a dog at the door.

'Can I have a glass of water?' Catherine asked, feeling foolish.

The woman jerked her head. 'Come in.' Catherine followed her into the gloomy kitchen and watched her splash water into a cup. 'You're not from round here. Lost your way, eh?'

'Visiting an aunt,' Catherine explained, sipping quickly. 'Two of me family used to work here. Kate and Mary McMullen. Did you know them?'

The woman shook her head. 'Must have been a while back. We've had the inn for ten years. Took over from old Bram Taylor.'

'Is he still living round here?' Catherine was hopeful. He of all people would remember Kate and her father, for it was here that they courted, according to Aunt Mary.

The woman shook her head again. 'Died in the war, heart gave out.'

Catherine tried one last time. 'Did you know a man called Pringle-Davies? Used to come to the castle on business.'

The landlady frowned and repeated the name. 'Sounds familiar.' Then realisation broke across her face. 'Aye, there was a man called Davies used to come now and again. We'd water and feed his horses while he went up to the castle.'

Catherine's heart leapt. 'Well-dressed gentleman?'

The woman nodded.

'Do – do you know where he lives?' She held her breath.

'Oh no, lass, he's dead. About the time the Liddells left Ravensworth, if I remember rightly.'

Catherine felt punched. 'Dead . . . are you sure?'

'Aye. I remember types like that with money to spend on the best rooms.'

'What did he die of?' she forced herself to ask.

The woman looked surprised. 'Old age, I wouldn't doubt.'

'Old age? But wasn't he quite young?'

The landlady snorted. 'He was eighty if he was a day. Anyway, what you so interested in him for?'

Catherine felt light-headed. She must be talking about the wrong Davies. But at least that did not mean that Alexander was dead. She thanked the woman and departed swiftly, mumbling about a train to catch. The landlady stood at the door watching her go.

She trailed back to the station, frustrated at the fruitless search. It had all happened over twenty years ago. Who was going to remember a maid from the town who left in a hurry or a casual guest at the inn with a well-cut coat and a silver-topped walking stick?

Still wrapped in her thoughts on arriving back at the workhouse, Catherine was shocked by what awaited her. The women in the staff room turned to gawp as she sauntered in.

'Where you been?' Hettie demanded, breaking the stunned silence. 'Matron wants to know.'

'It's me day off.' Catherine was indignant. 'I can do as I like.'

'That's what you think,' Hettie said, with a gleam in her eye that was unnerving.

115

'Been searching the town for you,' Gert said excitedly. 'Last night your mam came looking for you – said there'd been a row and she was worried you'd do something daft.'

'She was very upset,' Hettie declared, 'so Matron said we had to help look for you. Went to that Catholic club of yours – even asked the priest but you hadn't been at church.'

'And Lily's,' Gert said, 'but we couldn't find you anywhere.'

'Then your mam started crying and said you might have gone to have it out with a man called Gerald Rolland,' Hettie said, revelling in the telling.

Catherine looked at her stunned. 'You never . . .?'

'But your mam doesn't know where he lives, so Matron called out the police,' said Gert.

'The police!' Catherine's hands flew to her face. She felt faint.

'Had to,' Hettie said. 'Thought you might be in real bother. It all came out about you being on holiday with this man. But you weren't there and he swore blind he'd never seen you in a week.'

Catherine's knees buckled. She grabbed the back of a chair. What had Kate done now? Fear made her sick.

'So where were you?' Hettie demanded. 'If you weren't with that man Rolland, then where?'

'Visiting me Great-Aunt Lizzie,' Catherine croaked, gulping back tears. 'You had no right to gan looking for me, you had no right.'

Hettie snorted. 'That's not the way Matron sees it. What a carry-on. You're for the high jump, that's for sure.'

One of the older women said anxiously, 'Better get along to Matron, Kitty, and sort it out. Sooner the better.'

116

Chapter 19

Matron was livid. 'You are a very selfish young woman,' she scolded, 'taking off like that without letting anyone know. Your mother was worried sick. And as for all that business with this man Rolland – I was obviously right to have my doubts about you when you picked up that strange rash.'

Catherine was puce and sweating. 'I've never done anything improper,' she stuttered.

'Well, it doesn't look good,' Mrs Hatch snapped. 'Gallivanting off on holiday without anyone to chaperone you – and with what sort of man? The type who has no intention of marrying you. You've brought disgrace to this institution. And you such a devout churchgoer. You've been very foolish, very foolish indeed.'

Catherine swallowed her panic. Was she going to be sacked?

'I'm sorry for causing all the bother. But it was me day off and I just decided at the last minute to gan and see me Great-Aunt Lizzie.' She held her look. 'I'm a grown woman; I didn't think I needed anyone's permission to visit family.'

Matron regarded her coldly as if she did not believe her story. 'Just on a whim, was it?'

Catherine glanced down. She could hardly tell her she was searching for her father.

Matron continued. 'Your mother came here in a terrible state – we had to do something.'

Catherine felt queasy. Had Kate been the worse for drink? What else had she told them about their argument or let slip about their family?

'You will go at once to the police station to report that you are no longer missing and then you will go and make your peace with your mother.' Matron stood up. 'You will be back here by four o'clock and help out on the vagrants' ward. As punishment, you will not be allowed time off for a month.'

Catherine opened her mouth to protest.

'Think yourself lucky that I'm taking this no further,' Matron warned. 'The Board of Guardians might not be so sympathetic.'

Catherine swallowed, nodded and hurried from the room.

Suddenly she was angry. She had done nothing wrong. It was just the poisonous minds of the other staff who had got her into trouble. And her meddling mother. She seethed with anger against Kate. It was her garrulous tongue that had caused all this and exposed her affair with Gerald. Oh, Gerald! Catherine felt a wave of shame to think how he had been dragged into this too. How he would despise her now for bringing the police to his door.

With each grim step her fury grew. It was fuelled by the indulgent laughter and mild rebukes from the police, so that by the time she paced up the bank to East Jarrow, she was fit to burst with the unfairness of it all. All the tenderness she had experienced at Ravensworth for the young Kate was gone. That Kate no longer existed. She had turned into a drunken, manipulating, vengeful old woman.

Catherine burst into the kitchen, startling Kate out of her nap.

'You've done it now!' she blazed. 'What do you think you were doing, coming to the workhouse and causing trouble?'

'Kitty,' she gasped, clutching her chest, 'what a fright. Where've you been? I was that worried—'

'No you weren't. You'd just hoyed me out the house, remember? Must have put on a right act for Matron – pretending you cared – but it's all a load of rubbish. You just wanted to get your own back, didn't you? I never thought you'd sink so low – trying to get me the sack, were you?'

Kate looked stricken. She struggled to her feet. 'I wanted to say sorry, but you weren't there. I got all panicked you might've gone to Rolland, you were that upset.'

'Is that why you told them all about me and him on holiday?' Catherine trembled as she spoke. ' 'Cos they all think I'm worse than muck now. Think I'm a slut who runs around after men. Is that what you wanted them to think?'

'No, never!'

The bedroom door opened. 'What's all the noise?' Davie stood in trousers and vest, his face creased from sleep. He caught sight of his stepdaughter. 'Where've you been? Your mam was in a right state when I got in last night.'

Catherine clenched her fists. She was sick of people asking her that question and she was not going to be lectured to by Kate's husband.

'I was visiting family, if you must know,' Catherine challenged. 'I spent the night at Ravensworth.'

Kate gasped and sat back down. 'Ravensworth?' She looked bewildered.

'With Great-Aunt Lizzie.' Catherine watched her mother intently. 'We talked of the old days when you lived there – when you worked at the castle. Cousin George told me things too.'

'Things?' Kate said, flustered.

'Aye, we had a canny walk around the place – down to the lake.'

Kate looked grey with shock. 'Why?'

' 'Cos I wanted to find out about me father. Alexander Pringle-Davies. Isn't that who he is?'

Kate let out an agonised moan.

'That's enough,' Davie said, rushing to Kate's side and putting a protective arm about her.

'Who told you?' Kate whispered, her eyes flooding with tears.

'Aunt Mary,' Catherine said, suddenly hating her mother's distress. 'I wanted to know about him,' she tried to explain, 'wanted to find him. I asked at the inn, but they didn't know anything.'

At this, Kate burst into tears. Davie hugged his wife to him and rocked her in his arms. Catherine felt miserable. She could not begin to explain how she only felt half a person, not knowing about her father. Finding him would make her whole, fill up the strange emptiness that was always there inside.

'Can't you tell me about him?' Catherine pleaded. 'Help me find him.'

'Don't!' Kate sobbed. 'It's too late.'

'Not for me,' Catherine said, springing forward and seizing her mother's hand. 'Just tell me where he comes from—'

'Kitty,' Davie interrupted, 'you don't understand. Your father's dead.'

Catherine recoiled. 'How would you know?'

Davie gave her a pitying look. 'I've seen his gravestone – in Sweden. It's in a cemetery for foreigners.'

Catherine stared in bewilderment. 'Sweden?'

He shrugged broad shoulders. 'It was his, that's all I know. Died years ago.'

She looked at Kate for explanation, but her mother's look was hard and desolate.

'He's gone,' she said in an empty voice. 'Don't ever ask me about him again.'

Chapter 20

Nothing was the same for Catherine at the workhouse after the furore of her disappearance. Matron watched her hawkishly and the others made ribald remarks that once she might have laughed off, but now were too hurtful. She kept apart and buried herself in work. She volunteered for any extra shifts, driving herself to exhaustion, until she could collapse into bed and a dreamless sleep. Sometimes, she drove herself so hard it brought on bleeding from her nose and tongue, and she hid away in embarrassment.

In the privacy of her room, she read library books and wrote stories. She was gripped by a compulsion to write; it made her forget the dreary hours and where she was. Time and again, her tales of tragic love would be set in huge mansion houses, with terraces and lawns, and a mysterious lake surrounded by dense woods. Even a year after her visit to Ravensworth, the colours and smells of the countryside were still vivid. She poured out her loneliness in poetry and enrolled on a correspondence course to develop her literary style and technique.

One autumn day in 1928 Lily found her crying in her room.

'The course teachers – they think me writing's rubbish,' Catherine told her. 'Said me grammar and spelling's that bad I shouldn't ever think of writing as a career.'

Lily put an arm round her friend. 'Never mind what they think. You can do owt you put your mind to.'

'No I can't.' Catherine was forlorn. 'I'm ganin' to hoy it all away.'

Lily watched as she tore up the notebook she had been writing in for months.

'Kitty,' Lily said firmly, 'forget about writin'. You're not ganin' to sulk in here for the rest of your life. On Saturday we'll tak off on wor bicycles – gan to the coast or some'at. Tak a picnic – the weather's still warm enough. What do you say?'

Catherine suddenly yearned for sea air. She flung her arms around the kind girl. 'Thanks, Lily. Life wouldn't be worth living without you as me friend.'

That autumn, the two of them went on several bike rides into the countryside and Catherine returned feeling the pleasant tiredness of a day's vigorous exercise and fresh air. She learnt to laugh again at trivial things, to share jokes and forget about life at Harton.

Occasionally, when it was too wet to go out, she would visit Kate and old John, sit by the fire toasting stale bread on the fire iron. Davie was away most of that year at sea and Kate missed him. Catherine listened to her mother and grandfather snapping and snarling at each other and wondered how they had managed to live under the same roof for so long.

Conversation with her mother was still strained; neither able to forgive the other for the hurt inflicted the previous year. Catherine had not seen Gerald since. He had disappeared from the congregation, perhaps moved away; she was too embarrassed to ask.

Sometimes, a forgetful John would ask, 'Are you courtin', lass?'

'No, Grandda.'

'Brought me any baccy?'

'I gave it you when I came in,' Catherine said.

'You're smoking it, you daft old man,' Kate reminded him.

John scowled and pulled on his pipe for a few minutes, then asked again, 'Well, lass, are you courtin' yet?'

'No I'm not!' Catherine said impatiently.

' 'Cos if you are, I want to see the bugger.'

Catherine rolled her eyes. 'Grandda, I'm not courtin'. I can't be bothered with lads. So stop askin'.'

John grunted and sank into his own thoughts behind a veil of smoke.

'He's ganin' backwards in his mind,' Kate said as Catherine made to leave. 'Doesn't remember what day it is half the time. But he perks up when you come in the house, Kitty. He lives for you, hinny.'

Catherine sighed. She found these visits depressing, but the guilt she felt if she skipped them was the more overwhelming. It was this same sense of duty that drove her regularly to church and confession. At least there she was no longer troubled by Gerald's presence. She went to pray for Kate and John, an insurance against them being sent to Hell, and she prayed for herself and the soul of her father, finding comfort in the familiar words and the echoing building. But her heart was sore to think she would never meet her father, or be rescued and swept off to another life, assuming Davie's story had been true.

Perhaps life would never be any better than this, Catherine pondered on her knees, rosary in hand. And what did she have to complain about? She earned a fair wage and her family had a home, when increasingly trade in the town was grinding to a halt and the iron mills had ceased production. She knew by the way the wards were filling up at the workhouse that the numbers of destitute were on the increase.

Yet the docks still rang with ships unloading, and the town bustled with shoppers and Arab seamen just as before. She had a good friend in Lily, and could live without a man. Maybe she would dedicate her life to God, become a nun. At tranquil times of prayer, watching the sun stream through the stained-glass windows and throw coloured light on to the pews, she contemplated such a future.

Then Frank bowled into her life. It was springtime and the position of head laundress had just become vacant. Catherine had put in for it, hopeful that the scandal of eighteen months ago was now well behind her. She was feeling light-hearted and singing snatches of 'Red Sails in the Sunset', when a tenor voice in the storeroom startled her by joining in.

She stopped in astonishment as a young man with reddish hair and moustache appeared from behind a pile of boxes, grinning.

'Frank Pearson,' he said, holding out a hand. 'Got a supply of soap for you.' He patted the top box. 'Anyone told you what a bonny voice you've got, miss?'

'Are you from Proctor's?' Catherine asked, hesitating to shake his hand.

'Lumley's, miss. Best soap this side of the Atlantic. Powder for the heavy wash, bars for those collars and cuffs. Better smelling than that carbolic you're using. Just take a look.'

He had the top box open before she could answer. 'Can offer you cracking terms as well. Better than Proctor's. Why don't you just try it for a month?'

'It's not my decision,' Catherine said.

'But I can see you're an officer – and a young woman who knows her own mind,' he persisted, 'so maybe if you suggested it?' He had very blue eyes. 'Don't I know you from somewhere?' he asked.

Catherine felt a twist of anxiety. In childhood that question was usually followed by a derogatory snort: 'Aye, you're that Kitty McMullen from the New Buildings.'

'I've never seen you before,' Catherine blushed.

He clicked his fingers. 'I've got it – the Palace, last week. You're the double of Clara Bow.'

Catherine burst out laughing. 'By, you've swallowed a tin of treacle.'

He stepped forward and she caught a pleasant waft of cologne.

'Forget the soap. Can I take you to the pictures on Saturday? They're showing Rudolph Valentino at the Essoldo.'

Catherine liked him at once. How did he know that her earliest passion had been Saturday matinées at the flicks with a stick of liquorice and no errands for a whole afternoon?

'Yes, I'd like that,' she smiled. Holding out her hand, she added, 'I'm Kitty, by the way.'

He took it and held on to it longer than was necessary for a handshake.

Frank failed to get his soap order, though Catherine assured him he would if she became head laundress. But he got his afternoon with her, and several Saturdays after. She found his fresh looks and cheerful chatter just the tonic she needed after months without male company. She had forgotten the fun of flirtatious conversation and the feel of a man's hand holding hers in the dark of a picture house. Frank was uncomplicated and out to enjoy life. He worked hard and lived across the river in Percy Main.

Lily seemed a touch jealous of Catherine's new romance.

'You never have time for your friends any more,' she chided.

'I only see him Saturdays,' Catherine pointed out. 'He plays in the Sally Army band on Sundays, so you and me can do things together then.'

'Bet your grandda doesn't know he's in the Salvation Army.'

'No, and I'm not ganin' to tell him. We're just having a bit of a laugh, nothing serious.'

'It's all right for some,' Lily said. 'Can you find me one like that, an' all?'

Catherine's new-found happiness was blunted by a setback at Harton.

'They've passed me over!' she railed tearfully at Frank one week in late May. 'Matron's given the job to some lass from Gateshead. Can you believe it? And after all the hours of hard work I've put in over the years. That job should've been mine.'

'Course it should. They can't see quality when it stares them in the face. Something else will come along – don't you worry.'

Frank took her to the pictures. In the back stalls he soothed her with soft words, murmuring in her ear, 'I think the world of you, Kitty.' Slipping a hand around her waist, he pulled her close and kissed her full on the lips.

They did not see much of that day's film, as they cuddled and kissed and Catherine forgot her bruised pride for a while. Afterwards, they walked around the town, glancing into shop windows. She had a feeling Frank was trying to say something. He kept looking at her and smiling and shaking his head.

'You're a grand lass. I'm the luckiest man on the Tyne, eh?'

A few days later, Lily waylaid Catherine in the drying room.

'Kitty, don't go light with me, but I've heard some'at about Frank.' She looked nervous, twisting her hands in her apron pocket.

Catherine, still morose from her lack of promotion, felt a stirring of apprehension.

'What about him?'

'It's just gossip I've heard among the lasses – one of them comes from Percy Main.'

Catherine eyed her warily.

'They say he's got a lass – across the river.'

'Don't be daft, I know he hasn't,' Catherine dismissed the idea at once. 'You shouldn't listen to gossip – specially round here. You know they're always trying to bring me down.'

She walked away from Lily, offended that her friend should even think of trying to spoil things between her and Frank. Since losing out on advancement, being in love with him kept her going through the long hot days in the laundry.

But as Saturday approached, she felt a familiar sense of unease at seeing him. Surely he could not have deceived her as Gerald had?

The open smile on his face and the kiss with which he greeted her gave reassurance. The early summer day was too hot for the cinema and they caught a tram to the promenade. As they bought ice creams from a barrow and walked arm in arm, the desire to know the truth was overwhelming.

Catherine blurted out, 'The lasses at the laundry are saying things about you – bad things.'

Frank stopped and gave her a quizzical look.

'They say you've got another lass over the river.'

His fair face reddened. 'They say what? I hope you don't believe them.' His look was so wounded, she felt terrible for even mentioning it.

'No, course not, but . . .'

He threw down his ice cream and grabbed her so suddenly that she dropped hers. 'Kitty, I'm daft about you. There's no other lass for me. You must know that? Don't listen to what anyone says.'

'No, I won't.'

'Listen, Kitty, will you marry me?'

She blinked at him as if she had misheard. 'Marry?' She gave a nervous laugh.

But his look was urgent. 'I mean it, lass. Marry me now. We'll get a special licence. We could gan anywhere, you and me.'

Catherine's surprise gave way to alarm. 'It's too soon. We hardly know each other.'

'We know enough. You're the only lass I ever want to be with,' Frank insisted. 'I love you. Don't you love me, Kitty?'

'Y-yes—'

'Then show it. Say you'll marry me. Say it!'

Catherine was aware of passers-by staring at them. She pulled away from his grip.

'I can't. It's too quick.'

'It's not,' Frank said, with a pleading look. She had never seen him so agitated. 'We love each other and that's all that matters. It has to be now or never, Kitty.'

Catherine felt a ridiculous desire to laugh. He sounded like a hero from one of the new talkies. But she could see from his face that he was completely serious. It did not make sense. Why so sudden? Why was he so on edge after her questioning?

Catherine's insides clenched.

'There is another lass, isn't there?' she whispered.

Frank looked cross. 'I can't believe you're asking me again.' He turned away, plunging his hands in his pockets and began to walk off.

Catherine, embarrassed to be left standing alone, hurried after him. 'Frank, stop. I didn't mean it. I just don't see what all the hurry's about. Can't we just carry on seeing each other for a bit? I've been hurt before, you see . . .'

He stopped and faced her. After a long moment he smiled, though his blue eyes looked sad.

'Aye, course we can.'

With relief, she slipped her arm through his and they walked back into town. Although they spoke now and again, Catherine felt weighed down by the failure of the afternoon. She swallowed her disappointment when he left for the ferry without making a date for the following week.

When Saturday came, Catherine was not surprised when Frank did not. She knew something had gone badly wrong between them, though she was not clear quite what. Should she have said yes to marrying him? How different her life would be. No more laundry, no more snide remarks about her morals or her background. A clean start. Mrs Francis Pearson. A married woman's name to bear like a badge of honour. Catherine wandered around town aimlessly, heart lurching to see figures in the distance that looked like Frank but were not. All weekend she wished she had said yes, cursed herself for her caution.

At the end of the next week, she entered the staff room to splutters of laughter. Half a dozen women stopped and stared at her.

'Want to share the joke?' she asked.

There were embarrassed glances among her workmates. Then Hettie picked up the newspaper they had been leaning over.

'What's the name of that boyfriend of yours?'

Catherine knew from the glee in her voice that it was bad news. Her stomach knotted.

'Frank Pearson, wasn't it?' Hettie goaded. 'From Percy Main. Plays cornet in the Salvation Army band.'

'What if he does?'

'Got himself wed last Saturday.'

Catherine stared in disbelief. The stuffy room seemed to hold its breath. The words buzzed in her ears as if she was about to faint. She struggled not to show her shock, clutching the back of a chair.

'Aye, and that's not all,' Hettie added, with a triumphant look. 'His missus gave birth to a bairn on Monday!'

'Liar!' Catherine cried.

'It's here in black and white,' Hettie said, brandishing the paper. 'Didn't we tell you he was a bad'un?'

Catherine clamped a hand to her mouth and wheeled around. She rushed from the room, not pausing till she reached the toilet. Head spinning, she vomited into the bowl.

Chapter 21

Worn out from a string of sleepless nights, Catherine went storming round to see Father O'Neill.

'I want to become a nun,' she demanded. 'I've thought about it long and hard and it's all I ever wanted to do. I'm not made for marriage, Father.'

The old priest surveyed her from under iron-grey eyebrows and shook his head. 'They wouldn't have you,' he said bluntly.

Catherine flushed. 'Let me try, please, Father. I hate it at Harton.'

'Kitty,' he said firmly, 'I've watched you grow up. I know you well enough to say you're certainly not made for a life of silent obedience and contemplation.'

'But I am!' she protested.

He held up his hand. 'See what I mean?' He allowed himself a half-smile. 'No, Kitty, go away and work hard. I'll have a word with Matron Hatch about you.' With that he dismissed her.

Catherine was still railing at his rejection when she visited William Black Street the following Saturday.

'I'm finished with Jarrow!' she cried at Kate, pacing beside the hearth. 'There's nowt here for me now.'

Her mother shooed her out of the way of the oven door and rammed in a tray of stottie cake. 'You've a grand job at Harton,' Kate puffed, slamming the heavy iron door shut. 'Divn't gan chucking it in 'cos some lad's given you the run-around.'

'I'm sick of the laundry. They make me life a misery – even worse since Frank Pearson . . .' Catherine felt tears of anger sting her eyes again. She had cried all week, astonished that anyone could possess so many tears.

Kate eyed her, hands on hips. 'Why didn't you tell me about this Frank?'

'I would've done in time . . .' Catherine looked morose.

127

Kate let out a long sigh. 'Well, what's done's done.' She wiped her floury hands on her apron. 'A hard day's graft gets rid o' heartache, I always find. Work it out, lass, that's the best remedy.'

Catherine could not help a bleak smile at this homespun advice. It would take more than a day's work to scrub away all her unhappiness.

'That's it, hinny,' Kate encouraged. 'Now get that tea poured and we'll have a cuppa before your grandda wakes up and starts his rantin'.'

As they sat around the worn kitchen table, sipping at hot sweet tea, Catherine told her about pleading to Father O'Neill.

'A *nun*?' Kate spluttered over her teacup. Her eyes went wide, then she burst out laughing. 'A nun!'

'Stop laughin',' Catherine chided.

But Kate could not. She howled and rocked on her chair, until tears rolled down her puffy cheeks. Catherine scraped back her chair, offended.

'Well, if you're going to be like that—'

'Eeh, sit doon, hinny,' Kate cried, wiping away tears with her pinny. 'Don't mind me. That's the best laugh I've had in ages.' She looked at her daughter, her laughter subsiding. 'You have to look on the funny side. I mean, haven't the poor nuns got enough problems? You'd not give them a minute's peace.'

Catherine opened her mouth to protest, then stopped. She let out a snort of amusement. 'Aye, maybes you're right.'

'And you'd hate the clothes.' Kate giggled again. 'How many nuns do you see with high heels and a fancy hat like you?'

Catherine could not help laughing too.

'No, lass,' Kate declared, 'God's got different plans for you, I'm sure of it.'

They smiled at each other and carried on drinking tea until the pot was empty. For once, Kate seemed in no rush to get on with chores. It was good to laugh again, and Catherine went away feeling better. If only it could always be that easy with Kate. Instead, these snatches of time alone when her mother was sober were like breaks in a storm.

As summer came, Catherine's restlessness at her situation grew. Despite the priest's promise, nothing appeared to change at Harton. Davie came home from sea and Kate no longer had time for her. There was money again for whisky, and her mother grew loud and aggressive if Catherine dared to criticise her drinking.

'Hark at Sister Catherine,' Kate would ridicule, 'the first nun in high heels! Don't give me that look. I'll tak a sip in me own home if I want to. You and your twisty face – I've had enough of it!'

On a whim, Catherine went out and had her hair bobbed and permed, in an attempt to make herself feel better. Kate was immediately critical, as if she had done it to spite her.

'Where's all your bonny hair?' she shrieked. 'You look like a lad! And to think of all them hours I spent puttin' in ringlets when you were a bairn.'

Catherine did remember. The humiliation of a spiteful school mistress pulling out her ringlets and yanking her hair into plaits had been a daily source of torture when she was young.

'Well, I'm not a bairn now,' she replied, stalking out before her mother saw how upset she was.

Catherine's only happiness came in escaping for a few hours by bicycle with Lily.

'If you could wish to be somewhere else,' Catherine asked her friend as they picnicked beside a hayrick, 'where would it be?'

Lily shrugged.

'Go on, choose,' Catherine insisted.

'Durham, maybes. Aye, Durham's canny.'

Catherine was disappointed. 'No, somewhere we've never been before. A South Sea island or the heart of London.'

Lily looked anxious. 'Eeh, I wouldn't want to gan anywhere foreign.'

Catherine rolled her eyes. 'I'd like to go somewhere that doesn't smell of the gasworks, where you can see the stars at night, where the sea's clean.'

Lily joined in. 'Aye, as long as it was next to the sea.'

'And the houses are grand and standing in their own gardens,' Catherine enthused.

'And inside toilets,' Lily laughed. 'And canny lads with nice manners.'

'Lads,' Catherine snorted. 'As long as we're together, I don't give tuppence for any lads.'

Shortly afterwards, she went to Matron and declared, 'Me and Lily want to work away. Please could you help us, Matron? I know you sometimes hear of jobs at other institutions.'

To her surprise Matron Hatch did not dismiss her request out of hand. The older woman nodded.

129

'Father O'Neill has been speaking to me about you. I think it might be good for you to get away – but I'm surprised Lily wants to go too.'

'Oh, she does,' Catherine was adamant, 'where I go, she goes.'

Matron nodded. 'Let me look into it.'

A couple of weeks later, just after Catherine's twenty-third birthday, Matron called her in to her office.

'There's a position as head laundress at Tendring in Essex. I think you would have a very good chance. It's smaller than Harton, but there's work for Lily too as a checker. Would you like me to help you apply?'

Catherine nodded quickly. She was unsure where Essex was, but it sounded historic and a little exotic.

Lily was taken aback when told about the vacancies. 'Essex? That sounds very far away.'

'Matron says it's near London – so we'll spend our free time looking round the sights.'

'Still, it's a long way from the Tyne.' Lily was dubious.

'Haway, Lily, it's what we've always wanted – get away from here and see a bit of the world before we're old maids. Maybe you'll find a rich lad down there. Say you'll come if we get offered the jobs, please! I couldn't go on me own.'

Lily agreed. 'Course I wouldn't let you gan on your own.'

Quite unexpectedly, two days later, Catherine ran into Gerald Rolland. The shock of seeing his handsome figure striding towards her left her winded.

'My dear Kitty,' he cried, as if she was the person he most wanted to see in the world. 'How are you? You look so pretty and grown up with your bobbed hair.'

Catherine stood shaking. It was two years since she had seen him, though it seemed a lifetime. He was just as good-looking.

'I'm well, thank you,' she said, trying not to betray her nervousness.

'Would you like to go for tea somewhere?' he offered. 'There's so much I want to ask you.'

Catherine found herself agreeing, the bitter words she had saved for him dying on her lips.

In the corner of a Shields café, she learnt that he had been working away in Middlesbrough.

'But I'm back now,' he smiled. 'I wanted to see you – waited for you.'

She looked him in the eye, her heart hammering. 'Did you marry that other lass?'

He shook his head. 'I don't know what madness came over me to write that letter. I feel so ashamed of it now.' He reached across and took her hands in his. 'It's you I care for, Kitty, no one else. I've thought of you so often, but never dared write after the terrible way I treated you. And being away in Middlesbrough, I could offer you nothing until my return.'

Catherine was unsettled and confused. She ought to hate him, but felt a surge of longing as they touched.

'What do you mean, offer?'

He leant closer. 'Please forgive me for what I did. I want to court you properly this time – start again. There'll be no half-measures – we'll tell everyone.'

'Even your mother?' Catherine challenged.

Gerald's face clouded. 'Mother died a year ago.'

'I'm sorry,' Catherine said hastily, 'I didn't—'

'You weren't to know,' he smiled wistfully. He squeezed her hands tighter. 'But perhaps you'd allow me to meet your family?'

'Third time lucky, you mean?' Catherine jibed.

'I don't blame you for being unsure of me,' Gerald said. 'I just want another chance to prove my love for you. Please, Kitty?'

Catherine turned up at her mother's, head reeling from the encounter. She could not keep it to herself.

John stabbed the fire with the poker. 'That the bugger who never came to your party? Had me sittin' outside like a sentry all afternoon, watching out for him.'

'Trust you to remember that,' Kate snorted, 'when your memory's like a sieve for owt else.'

'He'll have to come here crawling on his knees if he wants my blessin',' John grumbled.

Kate faced her daughter. 'You're not serious about courtin' him again, are you?'

Catherine was surprised at her mother's tone. She thought she would have been relieved that a man as well-to-do as Gerald was now prepared to offer her a future. Past indignities would soon be forgotten if Gerald was to slip a wedding ring on her finger.

'I might be,' Catherine answered defensively. 'I thought I hated him – but as soon as I saw Gerald again, I knew I still cared for him.'

Kate let out a cry of impatience. 'Kitty McMullen, don't be so daft! That man doesn't deserve you.'

'Thought you'd be pleased to have me off your hands,' Catherine retorted.

'Not for the likes of him. Talks through his backside – don't believe a word he tells you.' She marched across the room and took her daughter by the shoulders. 'You've the chance of a good job and a new start down south – you tak it with both hands. Get away from here and mak some'at of yourself.'

Catherine shook her mother off, speechless for a moment. Then she stuttered, 'I might not get the job.'

'You will.' Kate was adamant. 'If not this one then some'at better. Don't settle for a second-class marriage with a man who blows hot and cold like a weathercock.'

Abruptly Catherine laughed. 'I don't think weathercocks blow hot and cold.'

Kate snorted and pushed her away. 'You kna what I mean. We haven't all swallowed dictionaries like you.'

For a week, Catherine went around distractedly, trying to decide what to do. She told herself no choice needed to be made until she heard about the job in Essex. It might come to nothing and then she could pick up with Gerald and see where it led. She knew she still loved him; the way her heart raced when she saw him again told her that.

Matron called for her at the end of the week.

'I'm pleased to say, both you and Lily have been accepted at Tendring.'

Catherine felt a surge of triumph, quickly swamped by doubt. It must have shown on her face.

'Surely you wish to accept?' Matron sounded impatient.

'I – I need to talk it over with Lily first.'

Matron said tersely, 'Have a couple of days to think it over and I'll write to the workhouse on Monday with your decision.'

Catherine went into Shields and wandered through the town, tortured by indecision. She ended up by the boating lake near the promenade, watching children feeding the ducks and courting couples rowing across the water. Seagulls wheeled overhead and a dark-eyed boy selling ice cream winked at her as she walked by. Why was the town looking so dear and familiar just when she had this chance to escape?

She and Gerald could have endless summer days here. How could she possibly want to throw such a future away for an uncertain one in a

132

strange place so far from home? Lily would understand if she called it off. She would probably be relieved. Mrs Hearn had been crying for a month now at the thought of her daughter going away.

Walking back into town, she made her way towards the café where she was to meet Gerald and give him her answer. She glanced in the window and saw he was not there. A familiar sensation of panic rose up inside, her throat stinging with bile. She hung about outside, pretending to look in the shop window next door. Perhaps Kate was right about him.

A moment later, she heard Gerald call her name and turned to see him crossing the street to meet her. A wave of relief shook her. He had not disappointed her after all. Then it struck her. She would always be unsure of him.

'Kitty, sorry to keep you waiting – the trams were full to bursting. Let's go inside.'

'They weren't full,' Catherine contradicted.

'Sorry?'

'The trams. They weren't full. So why were you late?'

'Now don't be silly. What does it matter? I'm here now,' he laughed indulgently, steering her by the elbow.

Her mother's words echoed in her mind. *Kitty McMullen, don't be so daft! That man doesn't deserve you.*

She shook him off.

'It does matter. It all matters! You leave me in the lurch with that nasty cowardly letter – and two years later you turn up like a bad penny and expect me to forget it ever happened. Two years, Gerald! I'm not some toy you can pick up and play with when the mood takes you.'

He gawped at her. 'Of course not.'

'Well, for your information, I'm ganin' down to Essex to work. Me and Lily. Head laundress. So you can shove that in your pipe and smoke it.'

She spun on her heels and marched away. Her heart thumped at her recklessness. Moments later he was chasing her.

'Kitty, come back. Don't be a silly girl. You can't go—'

She picked up her pace. He caught up and tried to grab her hand.

'I want to marry you! That's what I was going to tell you today. I'll ask your grandfather for permission, of course.'

She shook him off. 'You'll ask him nowt. He'll kick you into next week if you so much as darken his door. Now leave off us.'

A tram trundled to a stop right beside them.

133

'I won't leave you – I need you, Kitty. I love you and I know you love me. Remember the times we had at Gilsland?'

'Maybe I do, but I don't trust you as far as I can throw you, Gerald Rolland. So get lost!'

Two workmen jeered from the tram platform.

'Got yoursel' a wildcat there, lad.'

'Don't be hard on him, lass.'

Catherine turned and gave them a mouthful. Then, just as the tram was moving off, she jumped on board. It was the only way of escaping Gerald and his embarrassing entreaties. She had no idea where the tram was going, just that it was taking her away from the pleading, whining man on the pavement.

'Kitty, don't go! I'll change, I promise . . .'

As he receded into the distance, Catherine breathed easy. The heckling men were eyeing her with amusement, but she stared back in defiance. She felt liberated. The world beyond Tyneside beckoned. Instinctively, she knew she had just avoided making the biggest mistake of her life.

'Blows hot and cold as a weathercock!' She laughed out loud.

The men next to her shook their heads as if she were mad.

Two weeks later, the arrangements were made, rail tickets bought and bags packed. Catherine went home for the final night and Aunt Mary and Uncle Alec came round for her farewell tea. Kate fussed about the kitchen, banging down pots and dishes, ordering her family out of the way.

'Sit down and have a minute with the lass,' Davie chided quietly. But Kate ignored him and carried on being busy.

Mary patted the seat next to her. 'Come here, Kitty. I've something for you.' She flourished a box wrapped in green tissue paper and white ribbon.

Catherine was glad of the distraction, unnerved by Kate's frantic bustling. She savoured the moment of pulling the ribbon and carefully unwrapping the paper so it could be reused. Inside the box lay a soft blue woollen shawl. She picked it up and held it to her face, breathing in its new smell.

'It's beautiful, Aunt Mary,' she cried. 'Ta very much.'

Mary smiled with pleasure. 'My Alec says it can be cold as ice down there – winds come straight in from Siberia.'

'Don't be daft!' Kate was scornful. 'She's ganin' to Essex, not Russia.'

'It's true.' Mary was indignant. 'Tell her, Alec.'

Uncle Alec nodded bashfully. 'It's flat and in the winter the winds come whistling in from the east—'

'We don't need a geography lesson,' Kate interrupted. 'Now shift out me way – these dishes are hot.'

'There's no need to be rude,' Mary huffed.

Catherine touched her aunt's arm briefly. 'It's champion. I'll wear it no matter what the weather.'

Swiftly she wrapped it and pushed it out of sight, not wanting the spat between the sisters to escalate. So often in the past, their jealousy of each other had led to arguments and falling out, each knowing how best to rile the other. Soon she would be away from it for good.

John was helped to the table and insisted on sending out for a jug of beer.

'Can't let the lass gan without a toast o' good luck.'

'You can pay for it,' Kate muttered.

'I'll fetch it,' Davie offered quickly to avoid another argument.

After ham soup and stottie cake, washed down by tea and beer, tempers improved. Kate brought out an array of scones, tea bread and cherry cake.

'Me favourite,' Catherine smiled, as Kate placed the cake triumphantly on the table.

'Cut yoursel' a big slice,' her mother ordered. 'If there's owt left over you can have it for the journey.'

The chatter around the table grew in volume as Davie topped up the teacups from a half-bottle of whisky.

'I wrote and told Aunt Sarah I was going,' Catherine said.

'Don't expect her to turn up to see you off.' Mary was dismissive. 'Never gets two minutes to herself with all those lads. But it serves her right for marrying a pitman.'

'Mick's a canny lad,' Kate defended, 'and so are the bairns.'

'Pitmen,' John grunted, 'they're nowt but trouble.'

'She sent me a ten-bob note,' Catherine said.

'Did she?' Mary and Kate chorused.

'See what I mean,' John complained. 'They plead poverty, then hoy their money around like there's no tomorra.'

'Well, there's no risk of that happening round here,' Kate jibed.

'What you say?' John snapped.

Davie intervened. 'Come and sit by the fire, John, and we'll have another drink.'

Catherine helped her mother and aunt clear the table. She glanced at the clock.

'You can't gan to bed yet,' Kate warned, catching her look. 'We'll have a bit singsong when we're done washing the dishes.'

After two hours of John telling tales of Irish heroes, a further jug of beer and Kate's singing, they grew expansive about seeing Catherine off on the train.

'We'll all gan through to Newcastle and see you off,' Kate declared.

'Aye, just like we did for our Jack,' John agreed, 'when he went off to fight the Hun.'

'You weren't here then, were you, Davie?' Mary said.

'No, he was at sea, guarding the likes of you and Alec,' Kate was quick to point out.

'Or at home in Cumbria with his first wife,' Mary said cattily.

'Jack was a grand lad,' Davie said, not rising to the bait.

But Kate grew suddenly tearful. 'Poor Jack. Dying so far from home.'

'Don't start, woman,' John growled.

Kate threw her arms around Catherine. 'Course we'll gan and see you off. We'll all get the train from Tyne Dock – have a drink in the Penny Whistle for Dutch courage on the way.'

Catherine struggled free from her boozy grip. 'I don't want any fuss. And it's early. I'll be off at six. Meeting Lily and her parents at half-past.'

'We'll be there,' Kate promised. 'Can't have strangers seeing you off.'

It was late by the time Mary and Alec left, and Kate and Catherine had cleared up and coaxed John to bed. He was rambling about his own war days, of marching through the heat and dust of Afghanistan.

'Kitty, you try and get him to lie down,' Kate said impatiently. 'You were always best wi' him.'

The parlour, where he slept, smelt of incontinence, and Catherine braced herself as she and Davie hauled him on to the old iron bedstead and pulled off his boots.

John clung to her and began weeping. 'Just like me little Ruth – bonny, bonny lass.'

'Go to sleep, Grandda. I'll write to you from Essex.' Catherine disengaged herself with difficulty.

'Who was Ruth?' Catherine asked, as she closed the door on the wailing man.

Kate shrugged, her eyes bleary. 'He talks a lot o' nonsense, drunk or sober. Most likely there never was a Ruth.'

Catherine could not sleep, dozing and clock-watching through the night on the hard settle. She got up with the dawn, splashing herself in cold water in the scullery. She stoked up the fire, dressed and made a pot of tea. Sitting on the fender, she gazed around the familiar kitchen with its clutter of furniture and smoky walls, wondering when she would do so again. Christmas? Next year? Never? She thought of the times she had sat there contentedly reading a comic, keeping out of the way, only to be shoved, or slapped or shouted at for some forgotten misdemeanour.

In the street outside, she heard footsteps approaching. She went quietly to the door. It was Mr Hearn.

'Lily sent me to help with your case,' he smiled, shiny-faced in the early light.

Catherine had a pang of gratitude for her considerate friend. She hurried back inside, put on her coat and hat and went to her mother's bedroom door. She hesitated with her hand on the handle, listening for any sound that she or Davie were awake. Regular snoring came from beyond the door. She did not want to go in and see the two of them lying in bed together. If Kate woke, she would come to the door red-eyed and reeking of stale whisky, and embarrass Lily's father.

Catherine knocked softly on the door. 'Ta-ra. I'm off.'

Then quickly she stepped away, grabbed her case and rushed for the front door, before anyone had a chance to answer. Closing the door behind her, she strode down the street, eager to get away. Mr Hearn chatted pleasantly, but she said little, glancing around her as they descended the bank into Tyne Dock. They passed the familiar landmarks of the gasworks, Leam Lane, where she was born, and the cavernous, dripping railway arches leaping across to the docks.

At the station there was excited chatter with Lily and her mother. The train came in and Mr Hearn helped them on with their cases. It was only when Lily burst into tears and hugged her parents, that Catherine felt a deep pang of longing and scanned the platform for a sign of her mother. Maybe her feeble knocking might have woken her and she'd come rushing down the hill to wave her away.

But the doors slammed shut and the train jerked into motion without Kate appearing. She and Davie would be sleeping off hangovers until mid-morning, no doubt. As the train picked up speed and took them away from the docks, circling Jarrow and its tightly packed streets, Catherine felt a confusion of triumph and regret.

Suddenly she slammed down the window of the carriage door and stuck her head out. A blast of coal smoke and river smells assaulted her. The houses of the New Buildings flew by in a swirl of steam and were gone. Unexpected tears flooded her eyes. She brushed them away impatiently.

'Goodbye and good riddance, Jarrow,' she shouted out of the window. 'I've had enough of you to last a lifetime!'

'Kitty!' Lily said, shocked by her vehemence.

'It's true,' Catherine said, turning to her friend defiantly. 'I hate this place. I'm never coming back.'

'Don't say that.'

'I mean it. I'm not ever coming back!'

About that time, Kate woke up and found her gone. A half-drunk cup of tea gone cold remained by the hearth.

She went rushing into the bedroom screaming, 'She's gone, Kitty's gone!'

'Calm down, woman,' Davie said, rubbing his eyes.

'She never said goodbye. Why didn't she wake us? She never even said goodbye. I never got a chance to say . . .'

Kate flung herself on the bed and burst into tears of regret.

Chapter 22

Peering from the train window, Catherine gazed at the passing Essex countryside, while Lily dozed in the hot carriage, exhausted by the long journey. Gentle hills and lush woods gave way to fields of ripening corn and barley. At Witham the train stopped amid a sea of poppies. Catherine was reminded of the time she had first seen the blood-red flowers in the countryside beyond Shields. Kate had told her their name, astonished she did not know. But that was before the Great War, when poppies were a symbol of summer and not the dead of Flanders, like Uncle Jack.

Catherine dismissed the unwelcome thought. Flowers bloomed everywhere in this lush land, and glimpses of rippling tiled roofs in market towns whetted her appetite for her new home. The train clattered on to Colchester and the landscape flattened out into a patchwork of green meadows and interlacing streams. Slow herds of dairy cattle migrated towards milking sheds under a cloudless blue sky. Grassland, dykes, windmills and cattle passed to the rhythm of the train, lulling her into a dwam.

At Colchester the carriage emptied and Lily woke up. Two soldiers climbed aboard, smelling of hair oil, and sat down next to them. The younger one winked, making Catherine blush and stare more intently out of the window as they picked up speed.

'Looks nice here, Lily,' she said, scanning the skyline of church spires and timber-beamed houses. 'We can visit on our day off. There are two ruined abbeys and a castle – said so in the guide book I got out the library.'

'As long as we can look round the shops an' all,' Lily yawned, sliding a look at the soldier next to her.

'You girls aren't from round here, are you?' the young man asked with a grin.

'No, we're from South Shields,' Lily said proudly. He looked at her blankly. 'On the Tyne.'

'Where's that then?'

Catherine answered shortly, 'Near Newcastle. Up north.'

The soldier pulled out a packet of Player's and offered them round. The women shook their heads.

'What you come here for?' he asked, lighting up a cigarette.

'Work,' said Lily. 'We're startin' on at Tendring.'

The soldier blew out smoke. 'Never heard of it.'

'It's an institution near Harwich,' Catherine said, wondering at his ignorance.

He shook his head. 'Can't think why you want to work round here. Dull as ditch water.'

'I think it's very pretty,' Catherine said in her most refined voice.

The soldier raised his eyebrows at Lily. 'If you like grass and water.'

Lily smirked.

'So what are you doing here if it's so boring?' Catherine challenged, annoyed at her friend.

'Escaping for a night out in Harwich. Colchester's full of tea shops and old farmers.' He nudged Lily. 'What's your South Shields like then?'

'A grand place,' Lily said. 'Big shops and picture houses and the yards – full of busy.'

'Sounds like my sort of town,' he grinned at her. 'Harwich isn't up to much, but I could show you the sights. Want to join us, girls?'

'No we don't, thank you,' Catherine said at once.

'What about your friend here? She looks like she needs cheering up.'

Catherine saw with alarm that Lily's eyes were filling with tears. Talk of home had upset her.

'She's tired, that's all.' Turning her back on the soldier, she searched for a distraction, cursing the man for reminding Lily of Tyneside. After a while she cried, 'Look at that – a boat stuck in a field!' She pointed at the red-sailed vessel marooned in pastureland on the horizon. 'Must be a barge or something.'

The older soldier beside her spoke for the first time. 'It's a sailing boat. The sea comes all the way inland. Used to be under the sea, that land over there. Call it Little Holland, it's so flat.'

She glanced at him in surprise. 'Fancy that.' His face was serious but his look kindly. Curiosity overcame her and she began asking questions about the area. He told her about the lighthouses and light ships dotted along the treacherous sandbanks, and that Harwich was the final stop of the Great Eastern Railway and had boats to the Continent daily. People still made a living from catching wild fowl in the myriad creeks and waterways, and harvesting oysters. It sounded mysterious and romantic. Catherine felt a shiver of expectation to be going to the lip of England, just a short sail away from the Low Countries and the wide world beyond.

'You want to get yourselves to Clacton-on-Sea,' the younger soldier broke in. 'Nice beach for bathing and a bit of entertainment on the prom this time of year. You can keep the rest of Essex.' He winked at Lily. 'Would you like me to take you to Clacton, Lily my girl?'

'Maybes,' Lily giggled.

Before they pulled into Harwich, the soldier had scribbled his name and address on a torn-off piece of his cigarette packet and pressed it into Lily's hand.

'Let me buy you a drink at the station hotel before you go,' he pressed her. 'That would pep you up.'

Catherine gave Lily a warning look. 'We're being met, thank you.'

The soldier shrugged. 'Never mind, Lily, we'll have that drink in Clacton.' The two men helped them off with their bags, despite Catherine's protestations that they could manage without the help of the army.

'Thought we'd never get rid of them,' she muttered as they left.

'I thought the dark-haired one was canny,' Lily said.

'You shouldn't have encouraged him. You don't know him from Adam.'

'You're the one said we might find rich southern lads down here,' Lily retorted.

'Well, we'll not find them in the barracks at Colchester.' Catherine was dismissive.

Lily gave her a look. 'You're one to talk. Don't think I didn't notice you putting on your posh voice for that other lad. "Ooh, fancy that and fancy this." '

Their arguing was interrupted by a stout man in a tweed jacket waving to them beyond the barrier.

'I'm Mr Stanway, the master,' he greeted them with a firm handshake. 'Vines is laid up with gout – he's the porter – so I'm here to fetch you. Follow me. The car's outside. Missing my game of bridge, don't you know.'

'Sorry, sir,' Catherine said, hurrying after him with her heavy bag.

'Can't be helped. Vines's to blame. Swears he doesn't drink, but he's always bad after fair day. I'd see him out on his ear, but he's related to

141

one of the guardians. Here we are. Climb in. Just push the box of fish over. Mrs Stanway can't live without her rolled herring.'

Squeezed in the back of the battered old Ford, Catherine tried to make conversation but soon gave up. The garrulous master kept it one-sided, throwing out questions but not listening to their answers.

Harwich looked a drab port in the evening gloom, shrouded in a sea mist that chilled after the heat of the train. Through it could be glimpsed a low muddy coastline bound by stone walls. As they meandered inland, the watery landscape turned to marsh caught in a web of wide ditches. Above, the pearly sky was vast and empty. Catherine soon felt queasy from the stench of fish in the box and the twisting country lanes. Glancing at Lily, she saw her friend was sickly pale too.

Winding down the window, Catherine breathed in gulps of damp, salty air. They bounced through small villages, mere straggles of cottages strung out either side of stone and flint churches. Mr Stanway rattled off their names: Little Oakley, Great Oakley, Stones Green, Thorpe-le-Soken. Just after leaving this last village, a wagon appeared in front carrying hay. The driver sat up high in a tall black hat, guiding his horse, and Catherine thought the sight quaint. She was wondering how they were going to get past it on the narrow road, when Mr Stanway picked up speed.

'Careful!' she cried.

The master did not swerve or brake. Heart in mouth, she peered into the fading summer light, but there was nothing there.

'Where did it go?' she gasped.

'Where did what go?' he called over his shoulder.

'The wagon – in front – on the road,' she stuttered.

'Road's been empty for miles,' Mr Stanway snorted.

'But I saw it,' Catherine insisted. 'The driver had this big black hat on . . .'

Lily was giving her a strange look.

'Didn't you see it?'

Lily shook her head.

Mr Stanway grunted. 'Must've seen a ghost. People round here are always claiming they've seen things – the common folk.'

Catherine flushed. 'Was just a shadow, I wouldn't wonder.'

The master continued, oblivious to her embarrassment. 'Course, we've got a very famous ghost in these parts – St Osyth. Killed by the Danes. Still haunts the coast, dressed in white and carrying her head under her arm. Wouldn't like to meet her on a dark night,' he chuckled.

'Priory's worth a visit, though – magnificent gatehouse – near Clacton-on-Sea.'

Lily nudged Catherine. 'Have to go there then, won't we?'

But Catherine was left feeling uneasy by the incident. She had seen the man and his wagon clearly. There was a strange atmosphere about this flat, empty quarter that stole into her bones like the mist at dusk and seemed to bring the past with it.

Her apprehension only increased on their arrival at Tendring. The village was no more than a handful of plain cottages, and a glimpse of a white-washed church surrounded by horse chestnut trees. Driving a further half-mile, they arrived outside a high-walled enclosure and a solid pair of rusting gates. They waited several minutes while Mr Stanway bawled for entry and a hobbling old man in old-fashioned breeches loomed out of the dark with a bunch of keys and let them in.

'Is it always locked at night?' Catherine asked.

'Of course.' The master was brusque. 'No one comes in or out after seven o'clock – or four in winter. There are that many vagrants wandering about these days, we can only take so many.'

'What about visitors?'

'Visitors?' He sounded surprised.

'If we wanted to invite friends . . .'

'You can see them on your day off – every other Saturday. The guardians don't encourage visiting. The inmates can see family members on Wednesday afternoons. But Mrs Stanway will explain all this to you in the morning. I expect you just want to get to your beds now.'

The friends exchanged wary glances as the vast gates clanged behind them, but said nothing. They were too tired to notice much of their surroundings that night, except the chill gloominess of the high-ceilinged gothic building and the starkness of their narrow bedrooms, little more than cubicles, a long corridor apart.

Catherine fell into a fitful sleep and dreamt of runaway wagons hurtling her down to the sea at terrific speed, waking only on the point of drowning. The next morning, she still felt the queasiness of motion from the long journey and the final car ride.

'Miss McMullen?' An elderly woman with a face deeply scored with wrinkles, and wearing a starched cap, knocked on her door and looked in before she answered. 'I'm Mrs Atter. Show you where the dining hall is.'

'Thank you,' Catherine said, hastily buttoning up her cardigan and following. 'Can I call for my friend Lily?'

143

'Miss Hearn's had breakfast.' The woman spoke in a slow, deliberate way, as if she used words sparingly. 'Assistants eat first, then the officers. The mistress wants to see you straight after chapel.'

They passed a dormitory of iron beds with coarse grey blankets where two women were mopping the floor. Yellow light filtered in through dusty screens at the high-up windows and Catherine wondered why they were needed. They turned down another long corridor that overlooked a bare yard. Three old women in faded blue overalls sat on a bench contemplating the worn flagstones.

'Airing yard for the old females,' Mrs Atter said. 'Next one's for girls.'

Catherine stared in surprise as they reached the far end and looked down into an identical yard where a group of young girls was running around in a mass game of skipping. It was the first real sound of life she had heard in this echoing labyrinth of wards and yards.

'Don't they have a separate home for the children? Their own school and that.'

Mrs Atter shook her head. 'Girls this end, boys the other. Idiots go to the asylum at Colchester.'

Breakfast was porridge and tea, but Catherine's stomach was so knotted with apprehension, that she hardly touched hers. She felt she had stepped back fifty years in one night.

Mrs Atter noticed her lack of appetite. 'We get sausages for breakfast twice a week now since inspector came round. And roast dinners Sunday and Thursday.'

Catherine smiled weakly, wondering what they got the rest of the week. At least at Harton they had been well fed. She filed into chapel with the others, too overawed to protest her Catholicism. It smelt pleasantly of polished wood, and someone had put a vase of pink carnations and sweet peas by the vestry door. The chaplain gave a hasty service of prayers and a hymn, then dismissed them to their day's work. She was able only to flash a quick smile of encouragement at Lily as her friend was led away by the relieving officer.

Mrs Stanway was waiting for Catherine. She was a tall, handsome, middle-aged woman with a quick walk, who talked over her shoulder as she hurried out of the building and across a large cobbled drying ground.

'Wash house, drying rooms, laundry.' She pointed at a row of buildings opposite. 'You've met your assistant already, I see.'

'Have I?'

'Mrs Atter.'

'Oh, she didn't say,' Catherine exclaimed.

'She's very experienced – been here since the eighties, when the Kettlewells ran the place – they were the original overseers. Can't say things have changed very much since. But as Mr Stanway says, "If it isn't broken, don't mend it". That's the view of our Board anyway. Inspector shook them up a couple of years back, but things change very slowly in this part of the world.'

'Aren't the County Council responsible for running the institution now?' Catherine asked. 'At home, the guardians are being replaced – since the new law's come in.'

Mrs Stanway gave a snort of laughter. 'As I said, things take time.' She turned in the doorway and gave Catherine a good look over. 'I must say, you're a lot younger than I thought you'd be. You're just a slip of a thing.'

Catherine bristled. 'I've been assistant head laundress for two years in a large city laundry and I'm as strong as an ox.'

The mistress laughed again. 'Good, I like that. You certainly came with a spotless reference. Though it defeats me why you'd want to leave the city for a backwater like this. Why have you come?'

Catherine was taken aback at her directness. 'I – er – wanted a change – to get on – see a bit of the world.'

Mrs Stanway pulled a face. 'A bit is all you'll see.' She saw her dismay. 'Don't listen to me. I come from London and nowhere measures up after you've lived there.'

She showed Catherine into the laundry and introduced her to the staff. It was suffocatingly hot, even that early in the day.

As she was leaving, the mistress turned and asked, 'Is there anything you wish to ask?'

Catherine mustered her courage. 'Is there a Catholic church in the area? I can't miss Mass on a Sunday and I like to make me confession regularly.'

Mrs Stanway said, 'There's a priest in Great Bentley, I believe. But I can't promise to get you there. Won't our chapel do?'

Catherine could just imagine old John fulminating at such a suggestion. 'Lily and I don't mind walking,' she answered.

Her superior gave a dismissive wave. 'I suppose you could borrow the bicycles.'

Catherine felt a flush of relief.

'Oh, by the way,' Mrs Stanway added as an afterthought, 'I'll need to see your birth certificate. Just for the paperwork.'

Catherine froze. 'I – I haven't got one – I mean – I haven't got it with me – didn't bring it.' She was burning under the woman's scrutinising look.

'Well, perhaps you could write home and ask your family to send it. You do have family?'

'Yes, yes, of course,' Catherine stammered. 'Ka— me mother will send it.'

Mrs Stanway stared at her a moment longer, then nodded. 'Good.'

Catherine was left, heart hammering, trying to compose herself enough to listen to Mrs Atter's slow voice over the din of the laundry. The woman must have thought her dim-witted, for she could not concentrate on anything except the thought that she could not produce a birth certificate.

She had never been asked for one until now, and had never wanted to question Kate about it. Did illegitimate offspring have them? Probably not. And if one did exist, what would it say? Father unknown? Born out of wedlock? Or would it give John and Rose's names as her parents, and contradict the information on her application about Kate McDermott being her next of kin? Why had she never asked Kate before?

Catherine was engulfed by waves of panic. She had taken this huge step to escape the shame of her past and start afresh, only to find it catching her up before her new job had even begun. Familiar nausea rose from the pit of her stomach. What was she going to do?

Chapter 23

Catherine dealt with the mistress's request for a birth certificate by ignoring it. From time to time, Mrs Stanway would raise the issue and Catherine would act as if it had totally slipped her mind.

'I'll mention it the next time I write home,' she promised. 'I've been that busy.'

And she had. The workhouse laundry was large and antiquated, the machinery constantly breaking down and needing repair. She tried to befriend her workers, but they were sullenly suspicious of her openness. A mix of country girls who knew nothing of the world beyond the adjacent villages, and the elderly infirm who had lived there half their lives, they struggled to comprehend her northern accent. So used were the old women to institutional life that they never ventured beyond its walls and talked about 'the Queen' as if Victoria had not been dead for nearly thirty years.

Mrs Atter, with whom she clashed daily over how things should be done, did not approve of her attempts at familiarity either.

'They need to know who's boss,' she scolded. 'Give 'em an inch and they'll take a yard. Mrs Kettlewell was never one for mixing the classes.'

Her talk depressed Catherine, for she had grown up with old John's belligerent maxim that no one was any better than the next, no matter to which class they were born. But was that not what she wanted – to be taken for a middle-class woman of standing with a job people looked up to? It was the path she had chosen and she was not going to backtrack now.

Lily had been assigned to the relieving officer, the promised job of checker never materialising. Although Catherine saw little of Lily during the day, they managed to meet up in the evening in the sewing room for a chat over their darning, or a walk around the workhouse gardens if the weather was fine. Lily assisted the relieving officer with the endless stream of unemployed men who came seeking outdoor relief. She wrote their names in the ledger and issued them with tickets that gave them a meal and a night's rest in the casual wards.

In the mornings when the gates swung open, a group of them trudged off down the road to work as labourers for the drainage board, digging ditches and repairing dykes until sundown.

'Come from all over,' Lily told Catherine, 'not just the farm lads from round here. Had one man used to play the organ at the flicks – but the talkies put him out of work. And then you get the lads who haven't had a full week's work since they came back from Flanders.'

It surprised Catherine that there should be so much hardship in the rural south as well as the industrial north. She had imagined the region to be full of picturesque thatched cottages, well-stocked gardens and wealthy country houses; not the drab, crumbling houses with pinched-faced women at their doors she had glimpsed on her day off.

'Flanders,' Catherine sighed, 'and the war's been over ten years or more. Wonder if our Jack would've ended up like that – an out-of-work soldier?'

'Talking of soldiers,' Lily brightened, 'we get next Saturday off. Why don't we meet them lads from the barracks?'

Catherine pulled a face.

'Oh, haway, Kitty,' Lily implored. 'We've not been more than five miles from Tendring in a month. I'm sick of riding round the lanes on the Stanways' old boneshakers. The summer's nearly over. Let's gan to Colchester or Clacton, please!'

'Do we have to meet them lads?' Catherine was reluctant. 'Why can't we go on our own? I wouldn't mind seeing if I could join the library at Colchester.'

'Kitty man, we need a bit fun.' Lily was impatient. 'There's no harm in it if we stick together.'

'What will we tell the Stanways?'

'Nowt,' said Lily. 'Why should they stick their noses in? It's our day off. We're not prisoners.'

At that moment, they heard the jarring clang of the gates banging shut for the night and the jangle of keys in the giant lock. Catherine shivered.

'All right,' she relented, 'you write to that lad Bob. But don't go blabbing it about. That Mrs Atter's always asking sly little questions about me background and that. I don't trust her not to make a song and dance to the mistress.'

Lily was dismissive. 'She's as batty as an old hen, that one.'

'Still,' Catherine warned, 'you could tell her two's two, and she'd make six out of it.'

On the Friday, Lily got a note from Bob in Colchester that he and his mate Alf would meet them on the prom in Clacton-on-Sea at one o'clock, by the bandstand. They borrowed the workhouse bicycles, Lily declaring with a straight face that they were going to visit St Oswald's Priory and look for the headless ghost.

'It's St Osyth,' Catherine snorted in amusement as they cycled out of the gates. 'St Oswald's a northern saint.'

'Same difference,' Lily said. 'The master was too busy giving us the history to notice. We'll just pretend we've been to the priory, of course.'

'Lily Hearn,' Catherine laughed, 'you're going straight to Purgatory for that one!'

'Well, let's hope the day's ganin' to be worth fibbing over,' Lily laughed back, and pedalled faster.

They got lost twice along the maze of lanes, although they could see the coast in the distance like a tempting mirage. A warm southerly breeze buffeted them and butterflies darted out of the swaying grass, while curlews called high above in the dazzling white clouds. They arrived late, hot and breathless.

'We'll never find them in all these crowds,' Lily fretted.

The promenade stretched far along the low crumbling cliffs, looking down on a crowded beach and gaily painted bathing huts.

'Yes we will,' Catherine said, squinting short-sightedly into the distance. 'Look, there's the bandstand.'

Lily smiled quickly, smoothed down her hair and hurried ahead, pushing her bicycle past hordes of day-trippers. Bob grinned when he saw them and stubbed out a cigarette. He was wearing an open-necked shirt, while Alf looked awkward, perspiring in a jacket and tie.

Bob steered them to a café overlooking the front and paid a boy to mind the bicycles for the afternoon. They had ice-cream sodas, and began to relax in the festive air of the small seaside town. Afterwards they strolled along the promenade and watched Harlequin and Columbine performing to the crowds. Bob challenged them to kick off their shoes and stockings and paddle in the sea. Alf looked wary, but when the women raced into the shallow waves, he rolled up his well-pressed trousers and followed.

'Not used to the sea,' he confessed to Catherine. 'Come from Warwickshire.'

Lily shrieked as Bob began to splash them. The women retaliated and soon they were all soaked.

'If old Atter could see you now, Kitty,' Lily giggled.

'She'd need smelling salts to bring her round,' Catherine laughed.

'Who's Atter?' Bob asked, swinging an arm round Lily.

'Holy old wife at Tendring. Thinks we're daughters of the Devil for not ganin' to chapel. We're Catholic, see,' Lily explained. 'Have to cycle to the priest in Great Bentley for confession – and to Mass on Sundays.'

Catherine tensed, waiting for their expressions to change. She had grown up with street fights between Catholics and Protestants. Her grandfather cuffed anyone who spoke favourably of Dissenters. During the war, when rebellion broke out in Ireland, she had been spat at and called a Fenian traitor on her way to church simply for carrying a rosary.

But Bob just laughed and kissed Lily on the cheek. 'What good girls you are,' he teased. 'That halo's blinding me.'

Catherine slid Alf a look. He gave a bashful smile. 'I'm Christian Scientist.'

Bob rolled his eyes. 'Blimey, surrounded by a bunch of Holy Joes. Don't suppose I can tempt any of you to a drink?'

They laughed and Catherine's tension melted. In the end they went for tea and then fish and chips before reclaiming their bicycles.

'Can we see you again?' Bob asked, holding on to Lily's hand.

'Course,' she answered at once. He kissed her on the cheek and made arrangements to see them in a fortnight's time.

Catherine and Alf exchanged looks and an awkward handshake. She liked his gentle seriousness, but experience had made her cautious. He was probably married. She was not going to make a fool of herself or allow herself to be hurt again. Alf would be kept at arm's length.

The warm weather of late summer continued into September. The four met up in Colchester on the next day off, then Wivenhoe at the mouth of the River Colne, a place of boat-building. Crossing the muddy creek in a punt pulled on a rope by a retired mariner, they took a picnic to Mersea Island. Catherine was entranced by the flotilla of houseboats and small yachts that nestled in the lee of the hilly island, and the pewits that scurried across the mudflats.

After the picnic, Bob and Lily went off for a walk and Catherine lay back among the sea lavender, chewing on a long grass, while Alf talked

150

about his family. An older brother had survived the Great War and come back convinced prayer had saved him.

'Doctor said he wouldn't last the night – lost that much blood. Delirious, he was. Had a vision of this figure dressed in a coarse white robe, picked him up and carried him home. Laid him on the bed in our house. Next thing he knows, he's waking up in the field hospital babbling about seeing an angel. Nurses couldn't believe he'd lasted the night. Two days later he's well enough to be moved and on a ship back to England. That's why he became a Christian Scientist. So I did too – always looked up to him.'

Catherine sat up and shaded her eyes from the blinding light that bounced off the sea. A heron rose silently from the reeds.

'Suppose you find the story hard to believe,' Alf said apologetically.

'No,' she assured him. 'When my grandmother was dying, she thought I was her dead daughter come back to her. Kept calling me her angel child. It worried me at the time, but now I see how it must've comforted her.' She looked at Alf. 'Maybe your brother mistook one of the nurses in his fever. But what matters is it gave him the strength to fight back and live. That's still the power of prayer.'

Alf stretched out his hand and covered Catherine's. He left it resting there, warming hers, while they gazed at the rippling ocean and listened to the chittering of reed warblers. She had rarely felt so at peace as in that moment. He did not try to kiss her or spoil the silence between them and she marvelled that it could be like this with a man. The men she had known were demanding, taking from her like leeches – whether it was her grandfather, the men who courted her or the shadowy monster of her childhood with his jade-green eyes and predatory hands.

Catherine shivered and suppressed the memory again, but Alf withdrew his hand, thinking she was warning him off.

'Let's go for a plodge,' she suggested.

He followed her down to the muddy beach and they paddled in the shallows. They emerged with legs dyed blue with the mud and Alf produced a spotless handkerchief to rub them down. Bob and Lily found them laughing and sand-smeared. Catherine scrutinised her friend. She looked flushed and windblown, and firmly hand in hand with Bob. Catherine felt a twinge of uneasiness at what they might have been doing.

They lingered too long over a meal of pie and chips in Wivenhoe and were late back. It was almost dark and they had to rattle the gates for

Vines to come and let them in. He grumbled loudly and the next day saw them hauled in front of the mistress to explain their lateness. Catherine discovered the woman had a temper when crossed.

'We have rules for a purpose. If our staff break them, then what sort of example does that set for the inmates?'

'It won't happen again, miss.' Lily was contrite.

'No it won't,' Mrs Stanway snapped, 'because we'll not lend you our bicycles again. At least not for the rest of the month, until you've learnt your lesson.'

Tears sprang to Lily's eyes. 'But, please, miss, we've arranged to meet—' She stopped herself as Catherine nudged her to be quiet.

'Arranged to meet who?' she asked suspiciously.

'Just friends,' Lily stammered, 'from the army camp.'

'Soldiers?'

Lily looked away mutely.

'This just won't do,' Mrs Stanway reproved. 'The guardians take a dim view of such fraternisation. Can't have my girls bringing the place into disrepute.'

Catherine was indignant. 'We've done nothing shameful. It was our day off and we can go where we like. We're grown women, in case you hadn't noticed.'

The mistress glared at her in astonishment. 'There's no need to be rude. I thought you were quiet girls, but it's not the first time I've had complaints about you. I'm just trying to run an orderly institution. You will not be late back again.'

She dismissed them, but as they were going she called out, 'And, Miss McMullen, you will please provide me with your birth certificate. The clerk is most insistent that he sees it.'

They went to work without the chance to talk it over and by the time Catherine next found Lily alone in the sewing room, her friend was in a deep gloom.

'I don't think I can bear this place if I can't get out to see Bob.'

'You will,' Catherine tried to comfort her. 'It'll blow over by our next day off. Mrs Stanway's not really that bothered – it's just the fuddy-duddy old guardians she's scared of.'

'Why's she ganin' on about your birth certificate, anyway?'

Catherine shrugged evasively. 'I bet old Atter's stirring it up about us. You haven't said anything about me to her, have you?'

'Like what?'

'About me home life,' Catherine said cautiously.

'Not really. Just that you don't have any brothers or sisters. Didn't believe me, of course. "Thought you romans bred like rabbits." ' Lily mimicked the old woman's slow speech.

Catherine felt a jolt of alarm.

'You shouldn't have said that. Don't tell her owt else,' she ordered. 'It's none of her business.'

The moment the words were out, Catherine knew she had spoken too sharply. But it was too late. Lily stomped out of the room, her feelings hurt.

Chapter 24

Harvest came and the workhouse children fought for conkers under the chestnut trees around the church. Then strong south-easterly gales ripped away the tawny leaves and battered the gardens. Catherine and Lily hardly spoke for a fortnight, but when their next day off came round, they agreed to walk to Great Bentley and catch the bus into Colchester together. To Catherine's dismay, Alf was on duty, and she felt awkward tagging along with the other two so took herself off to the library.

So absorbed was she that she arrived too late for the bus back and found a worried Lily waiting for her. They had to flag down a passing farm truck to give them a lift, and ended up walking the last five miles in the dark. They were in deep trouble with Mrs Stanway, who made it plain she did not believe Catherine's story of being in the library all afternoon. The pair were forbidden to leave the grounds for a month.

'Why didn't you keep an eye on the time?' Lily fumed. 'It's not fair, her taking it out on the two of us. I was only late 'cos of you!'

'Sorry,' Catherine said feebly.

'Now I can't gan to see Bob for a month.'

'If Bob's that keen, he can come over here and see you,' Catherine pointed out.

Lily gave her a withering look. 'And do what? Talk to me through the railings in the rain? Don't be daft.'

'Well, I'm in the same boat,' Catherine sighed. 'Can't get over to church or confession for weeks.'

This seemed to rile Lily the more. 'Don't come over all holy with me – I know what you're like with lads. Just 'cos Alf didn't turn up you had to spoil it for me and Bob. Bet you missed the bus on purpose.'

Catherine gawped at her, astonished Lily should think such a thing. But before she could protest, Lily was gone.

For over a week, Catherine kept out of Lily's way, hoping that her anger would fizzle out and they would soon be friends again. But one day, in early October, she found her in tears in the storeroom. Lily shook a letter at her fiercely. 'He's being moved, my Bob. Ganin' to India!'

'India?' Catherine cried, going at once to put an arm round her. 'Oh, Lily...'

But Lily shook her off. 'Now I'll never see him again and it's all your fault!' Her sobbing increased.

Catherine flinched. 'How's it my fault he's going to India?'

'If you hadn't missed the bus, I'd be able to see him Saturday,' Lily wailed. 'Now he's leavin' within the week and I'll not get to kiss him goodbye.'

'Go anyway,' Catherine dared her. 'I'll cover for you – give you money for a taxi.'

'Taxi?' Lily said, startled out of her misery. 'Where we gan to find a taxi round here?'

Catherine looked at her helplessly. 'Why don't you get him to meet you somewhere closer, like Great Bentley?'

Lily was cheered by the suggestion, but after a few days of feverish correspondence, it transpired that Bob would get no time off to come to see her. She sank into depression and Catherine could do nothing to cheer her. Her friend's subdued silence was harder to bear than her previous ranting.

'You can still write to him, keep in touch.'

'I'm no good at letters like you are,' she answered despondently. 'In a month or two he'll have forgotten me.'

So wrapped in misery was Lily, that Catherine did not dare ask her if Alf was being posted abroad too. She had no home address for him and he had not written to tell her of his departure. He left a gentle ache when she thought of him.

Autumn turned to winter and raw winds swept in from the north and east. Catherine wrote to her Uncle Alec to tell him he was right about the weather and how she was thankful for Aunt Mary's shawl. The only news she had from home came from her aunt, for Kate seemed incapable of writing even a note. Mary reported that Davie was back from sea and was doing odd jobs. Kate was borrowing off the neighbours more than ever and John was poorly in bed with a head cold and complaining of pains in his legs.

155

Dull as life had become at Tendring, Catherine was thankful not to be cooped up in William Black Street all winter. Yet the short days and bad weather further curtailed any trips outside the workhouse walls, as if winter was slowly besieging them.

Some November days, the grey mist that seeped in from the marshlands never lifted. These windless days were the coldest Catherine had ever experienced, the damp penetrating her very bones. Mrs Stanway had relented and lent the young women the bicycles once more, but Lily was no longer interested in going about the countryside and the dark came early. She waited in vain for a letter from Bob.

'Maybes he's still at sea,' Catherine tried to comfort, 'and letters take weeks to come from India.'

But Lily refused to be cheered. She went about her work listlessly, throwing accusing looks whenever Catherine was near. 'I hate me life. Hate it here. Wish I'd never left home.'

Occasionally, Catherine would take off into the wind and battle her way to the coast just to get away from the stifling world of Tendring.

The marshlands and desolate empty coast drew her like a siren, yet she found the low, monotonous skyline dreary now. Lines of geese flew over, crying out mournfully, and echoed her own growing unhappiness with Essex. She thought back to the bright days of summer and wondered how the adventure had turned sour so quickly.

Strangely, as Catherine's melancholy deepened, Lily's spirits rallied. She began talking to the other staff again, chattering on about South Shields at Christmas time.

'I'm ganin' home for Christmas,' Lily told Catherine. 'Don't care what it costs, I'm not sittin' round here watching this lot stuffin' themselves with plum puddin' and pretendin' to have a bit fun. Are you comin'?'

Catherine was torn. She did not relish the holidays at Tendring, but neither could she face going home. It would be an admission of defeat. To assuage her guilt, she sent Kate money to pay for Christmas dinner and presents for the family.

On a dark, wintry morning, she walked down to the gates with Lily and helped lift her bag into Vines's truck. The porter held a lantern aloft and her friend looked flushed and happy in the pale light.

'Why don't you come back, Kitty?' she said impulsively. 'There's still time.'

Catherine shook her head. 'You have a grand time and I'll see you in a week. You can tell me all about it.'

Something about Lily's expression made her heart jolt. She grabbed her friend's arm. 'You are coming back, aren't you?'

Lily said nothing, her eyes full of regret.

'You're not, are you?' Catherine whispered.

Lily said, 'I never really wanted to gan away – just did it for you, Kitty. Not sure I can do it twice.'

Catherine was gripped with panic. 'It'll get better – once winter's over. We'll have a good laugh again – gan to Clacton – meet new lads.'

Lily's look hardened and she shook her head. Catherine knew then that she had lost her. Vines coughed and muttered he did not have all day to wait.

'What will you do, Kitty?' Lily asked in sudden concern.

Catherine said defiantly, 'Anything but gan back to Jarrow.'

Briefly, Lily threw her arms about her and they hugged tight. 'Tak care of yoursel',' Lily said, pulling away.

Catherine swallowed her tears, unable to speak. She watched Lily climb into the truck and waved her away. For a long time she stood shivering, peering into the dark at the vanishing taillights, then numbly tramped back up the drive.

Later that day, Mrs Atter cornered her.

'Why you not going home like Miss Hearn?'

'Can't afford to,' Catherine said tersely.

'Don't get on with your mother, I heard.'

'Who told you that?' Catherine was startled.

'Still, it's not surprising in the circumstances,' Mrs Atter said, her eyes narrowed in disapproval. 'In Mrs Kettlewell's day, your sort would never have been taken on. This place isn't what it used to be.'

'I don't know what you mean,' Catherine said in agitation.

'You didn't fool me for a minute,' the woman continued. 'No birth certificate, no brothers or sisters, no talk of a father, gallivanting round the county after men. Tainted with the sin of the mother. I saw it from the beginning.'

Catherine felt faint. 'You've no right to say such things,' she gasped. 'It's a pack of lies!' But even as she said it, she knew her burning cheeks gave her away. She barged past and out of the laundry, aware of the other women staring at her.

Fleeing across the drying yard and into the kitchen garden, she crouched down behind a potting shed and retched into the soil. How many of the workers had overheard Atter's poisonous accusations? Had she gossiped to anyone else already or, worse still, gone with her suspicions to Mrs Stanway? Who had told her such things? Catherine hugged herself in misery. Only Lily knew about her lack of a real father. Only she could have told such things. A sob caught in her throat. *Lily!* How could she have betrayed her?

Catherine howled and wept in hurt and anger that her best friend could have done such a thing. It was petty revenge for losing Bob. But Lily had wronged her far more; the wounds she had inflicted might never heal. Shakily, she got to her feet. Well, she was glad she had gone. Good riddance! She would get on in this world without the likes of Lily Hearn!

Catherine splashed her face with freezing water from the standpipe and went back to the laundry, glaring her defiance. Later that day, she sought out the mistress and told her she wished to transfer to another institution. Mrs Stanway did not try to dissuade her.

'You northern girls are too rebellious for a quiet country place like ours,' she commented. 'You'd do better to find somewhere in the town.'

January came with icy rain and, before the month was out, Catherine had secured a position at the workhouse laundry in Hastings, on the Sussex coast.

A few days before she left, a cheerful letter came from Lily saying she was back working at Harton, and wondering why Catherine had not written to her. Catherine felt a momentary pang for her lost friend, then tore up the letter and threw it on the fire in the dining hall. She would not reply. With bleak satisfaction, she thought how, in a matter of days, she would be living further away from Tyneside than ever – and from those who had let her down.

Chapter 25

1930 – Hastings

'Don't worry, it might never happen,' the woman smiled. Catherine recognised the Irish accent that she had often heard ringing through the streets of Jarrow.

'Beg your pardon?' she asked, startled from her reverie on a park bench. It was too early in the year for boats to be out on the lake, but there were plenty of people walking under the newly budding trees in the mild spring sunshine.

'You look like you're carrying the world on your shoulders – and you're far too young and pretty to be carrying such a burden, Miss McMullen.'

Catherine blushed. 'How do you know my name?'

The woman laughed. 'I'm working at the laundry – have been for a month.'

Catherine squinted up at her. She was a handsome woman of about forty, with wavy red hair under a cloche hat. There were laughter lines around her blue eyes that for a second reminded her of Kate.

'I'm sorry, I don't . . .'

'Don't apologise,' she laughed again. 'You've dozens of women under your command – and you're always rushing around as busy as a bee – and a worker bee at that. I'm glad to see you allow yourself a few minutes off at the end of the day. All work and no play makes for a dull life, don't you think?'

Catherine gawped at her brazenness.

The woman clapped her hands to her face. 'Me and my big mouth. Here you are enjoying a minute's peace and along comes Bridie McKim

159

and spoils it. I'm sorry, Miss McMullen, take no notice of me.' She began to walk away.

Without thinking, Catherine jumped up and called after her, 'No, please, don't go. I didn't mean to be rude.'

Bridie turned and smiled quizzically.

'Miss McKim, did you say?'

'Mrs McKim, if the truth be told – though the saints only know where the Mister is,' she said ruefully. 'Went out for a newspaper five years ago and hasn't been back since. Wouldn't you think he'd be sick of the waiting? And the racing results long out of date.' She laughed at Catherine's shocked expression. 'But you can call me Bridie.'

Catherine abruptly laughed. It sounded strange in her ears. She had not laughed in months. After a moment's hesitation, Catherine put out her hand.

'Miss McMullen,' she replied as they shook hands, then felt foolish because the woman already knew who she was. 'Catherine McMullen,' she added.

She was unsure why she should be telling this to one of her employees, for she had determined on arrival at the Hastings laundry that she would not become overfamiliar with its workers. It had only got her into trouble in the past. Since she had arrived in the seaside town, she had kept to herself, content to explore its hilly streets and quaint harbour and the long stretches of reddish-yellow cliffs alone. She had quickly moved out of the workhouse lodgings and rented a room above a greengrocer's a fifteen-minute walk away.

She already loved Hastings for its smell of the sea and abundance of flowers so early in the year, for its grand hotels and bow-windowed terraces along the promenade. She enjoyed walking through its spacious parks and the tree-lined streets of large villas, snaking up the hill, secluded from onlookers by laurel and yew. Even in February, when winter storms saw the grey, fermenting sea crashing over the pier and promenade railings, she revelled in its gentility. The sea might be comfortingly familiar and the picturesque fishing fleet on the shingle beach remind her of Shields, but the place was a world away from the stench of the Tyne and its blast of hooters and thunder of goods trains.

After a long day's work as head laundress, Catherine walked for miles, up the steep hills that overlooked the sea or along the strand from the fish quay to the bathing pool at St Leonards. She had not thought herself lonely, until now.

'Can I sit myself down a minute?' Bridie asked. Catherine nodded and sat down beside her. 'I know it's none of my business, but you looked that sad when I came by, and you were holding that letter. Is it bad news or something?'

Catherine stared down at the letter crumpled in her left hand. For a moment, Bridie's arrival had taken her mind off its sad contents. She had felt detached from Kate's news, not really believing it.

'Yes,' she admitted. 'Grandda – my grandfather's died. On Maundy Thursday. And there I was on Easter Day, praying for him and not knowing—' She broke off as a sob welled up and choked her. To her embarrassment she wept openly in front of Bridie. But the older woman did not seem abashed. She squeezed Catherine's hand quickly.

'You poor girl. Had he been ill?'

Catherine nodded and fumbled for a handkerchief. Bridie whipped out one of her own. It smelt of lily of the valley, Kate's favourite, which only made Catherine cry harder.

'Maybe it was a blessing for him,' Bridie comforted. 'He'd not be one to linger on in pain, I wouldn't wonder.'

Catherine was startled. 'No, he wouldn't. How did you know?'

Bridie shrugged. 'Men make the worst of patients. I nursed my own father. Was a blessing when he went – just to see his face free of the pain, like a little lad sleeping again.'

Catherine sniffed. 'I feel that bad I never got to see him again. Left home last summer and never went back for Christmas, even though my aunt wrote and told me he was ill. Now I know I should have.'

'And where is home?'

'Jarrow, Tyneside.'

'Well, there you go,' Bridie declared, 'that's the other end of the country. He wouldn't have expected you to go all that way just for a day or two's holiday, now would he?'

Catherine crumpled the letter harder. 'My mother did. Said Grandda lost heart after I went – off his food, showed no interest in anything 'cept when a letter came from me. Blames me for him going downhill so quickly – though she could never stand his guts when he was alive.'

'Does she say all that in the letter?' Bridie asked in concern. 'That's a terrible burden for you, so it is.'

'Not exactly word for word,' Catherine admitted, 'but I can read between the lines.'

'Well, maybe you shouldn't.' Bridie was forthright. 'Maybe your mother's trying to comfort you by saying that your grandfather thought so much of you.'

The thought had not occurred to Catherine and she was reluctant to believe it.

'She wants me to go back for the funeral, but I couldn't possibly. The expense – and the time off work – I've too much to do. And what good would it do? He's dead and gone. I'd be more use lighting candles for him and praying down here.'

She looked at Bridie for reassurance. The woman nodded and patted her hand.

'Of course you would. I'm sure if you write and explain, your mother and father will understand.'

Catherine quickly looked away. The mention of her father made her suddenly anxious. But then it struck her that, to this stranger, she was a normal, respectable woman with an ordinary family. How wonderful it was to be seen in such a light. It made her the more determined not to return to Tyneside and open up all the old wounds of past shame and failure.

'I'll send money, of course,' Catherine brightened, 'help with funeral costs.'

Bridie nodded and murmured about her being generous and thoughtful. Catherine felt a wave of gratitude. Shortly afterwards, Bridie said goodbye and went on her way. Catherine sat on wondering at how she had told this near stranger so much so quickly. She supposed it was because Bridie McKim had been candid about her own circumstances, treating her as if she were a long-lost friend.

As she made her way back to her lodgings, she wondered if she had been too hasty in confiding in the woman. After all, she was one of the laundry workers, and Bridie might be as garrulous as Hettie Brown or Lily for telling others her business. But there was a warmth about the red-headed woman that had reminded her of her grandma, Rose, and attracted her at once. Her pleasant Irish voice had brought back memories of old John's tales and made her think of her grandfather with affection, banishing the numb disbelief at his death.

The thought of Bridie's kindness fortified Catherine to write to Kate, explaining that she would not be coming home for the funeral.

Chapter 26

As summer came, Catherine made the most of the long evenings and fine Sundays to roam the cliff tops and rolling countryside of the South Downs. The regime at Hastings was liberal compared to Harton or Tendring, with more time off. Yet she tried not to make comparisons with the previous summer when she had had Lily as companion, not liking to admit how much she missed her former friend. She felt bad about not replying to Lily's letter and now it seemed too late.

Determined not to dwell on the past, Catherine took swimming lessons and went each evening to the open-air bathing pool at St Leonards, invigorated by the chilly water after the heat and noise of the laundry. At work, she noticed Bridie McKim among the others, with her quick tongue and infectious laughter, and wondered how she could have overlooked the woman before.

Bridie was deferential but friendly, enquiring after her family and the funeral. Catherine kept to herself how Aunt Mary had written in high dudgeon that Kate had squandered on drink half the funeral money that Catherine had sent. Catherine was unsure of the Irish woman, regretting now that she had confided in her so readily. But if she was distant to Bridie, the woman did not seem to mind and continued to amuse her fellow workers when Matron was out of earshot.

One hot night, restless and overtired, Catherine went for a walk in the moonlight. Down the hill, she skirted the hunched silhouette of the ruined castle and passed the entrance to St Clement's Caves. She liked to imagine eighteenth-century smugglers hauling their booty up the narrow lanes of the old town in the dark, and making for the dank caves. She had paid her tourist sixpence to see round them on a crowded Sunday afternoon, but on a starry night she fancied she could see ghosts in the shadows and hear the scrape of their boots as the warm wind raked over the shingle.

Wending her way down the main street past timber-framed houses and the weather-boarded Bull Inn, she breathed in the smell of the sea and pretended she was keeping a tryst with a darkly handsome smuggler down on the shore.

Catherine walked from the harbour along the promenade to the very end of St Leonards resort. Taking off her shoes, she padded across the sand to the water's edge and cooled her feet in the rippling sea. She was startled by laughter, and spun round in alarm. Two figures lay under the promenade wall. In the moonlight she could see them nestling in each other's arms, suppressing giggles. A few yards further on, another couple were stretched out on the sand, and beyond them another. She had stumbled into the midst of courting couples cooling off in the night breeze.

Suddenly, she felt achingly alone. There was no one to put his arms about her and hold her in the dark, to soothe her sleeplessness. She thought of the men she had kissed and held hands with, and wished for one of them now. It was nearly a year since she had lain in the tall reeds on Mersea Island with gentle Alf. She had no idea where he was, but she wished with a passion that he were with her at that moment.

Snatching up her shoes, Catherine hurried from the beach and its lovers, and fled back to her lodgings. She slept badly, but by the next day had determined to change her circumstances. Hastings was where she wanted to stay, so she would look for a flat of her own and fill it with beautiful possessions. If she could not have company then at least she would have comfort. She was earning a good salary and had saved more than enough to make the down payment of a month's rent in advance.

Within a week, Catherine had found a pleasant one-bedroom flat on the ground floor of a large house in Clifton Road. It would be her own place of sanctuary, not a room full of borrowed furniture that reminded her of the tenements of her childhood.

The same week, she joined the local tennis club and went there on Wednesday evenings and Saturday afternoons. To her surprise, she improved rapidly and soon others were asking her to make up foursomes. With her new-found friends she was relaxed and gregarious, and would regale them with anecdotes about the laundry and its eccentric staff. In a game of mixed doubles Catherine met an insurance agent called Maurice.

He started to call on her and take her on sightseeing trips in his toffee-coloured Morris Minor. They went as far afield as Brighton and the fig orchards of West Tarring; took picnics by tranquil rivers where mahogany-red cattle grazed the rich pasture. They visited the Norman castle of Herstmonceux. Maurice would not allow Catherine to pay for anything.

'I could, you know,' she offered. 'I earn a fair salary.'

'Won't hear of it,' Maurice declared. 'You're some girl. Beautiful, talented and rich – just the sort of heiress I'm looking for,' he teased.

Catherine laughed, captivated by his flattery.

Maurice was not keen on walking, preferring to motor about in his prized possession, but he was genial company and she allowed him to choose where they went. As summer wore on, he talked more of what they would do after the tennis season was over, as if it was taken for granted that they would carry on courting. Catherine did everything to please him, even taking out a life insurance policy that he recommended. There was only one thing she would not do.

'Come on, Catherine,' Maurice cajoled at the end of one picnic, as they lay kissing on the edge of a ripe cornfield, 'a little bit more – just for me.' He slipped a hand inside her open blouse and kissed her cleavage.

Her heart began its familiar hammering at his deft touch. 'No, Maurice.' She pushed his head away gently. 'I told you, not that.'

'Come on,' he laughed, 'you don't have to tell everything to your priest. You're a grown woman – I can hear your heart beating, darling. I know you want to.'

He ran a finger up her stockinged leg and squeezed her thigh, pressing himself forward again and kissing her lips. Catherine felt her resolve waver. He excited her and part of her yearned to give in to the sweet longing inside. But always, when she got to this point, the image of Kate copulating with her unknown father forced itself to mind. It made her queasy and fearful. Never, ever, must she make such a stupid ruinous mistake.

She shoved Maurice from her and sat up. 'No! I don't want to – and I do have to tell the priest everything at confession.'

He looked at her with pleading brown eyes. 'I can tell you don't love me – not the way I love you.'

'I do,' Catherine protested, feeling confused.

'I'm mad about you, girl,' Maurice said, holding her face in his hands and covering her with soft kisses like butterflies. 'If you really loved me, you'd show it by making love. That's all we'd be doing, darling, just loving each other. I'll be careful. I've come prepared.'

Catherine felt a surge of alarm. What did he mean by 'prepared'? He must have some sort of contraception. But that was forbidden too. It was a sin akin to murder, the priest said.

'Stop it.' She pushed him away again and scrambled to her feet. 'I want you to take me home, please.' She hated the way she sounded like a whining child.

He looked suddenly annoyed. 'You don't know what you're missing, girl. You and your stuffy religion – it'll stop you being happy – all this guilt and no fun. Well, it's not for me.'

'Don't talk about my religion like that. We Catholics know how to have fun as much as you Protestants – maybe more so,' she answered in agitation. 'But I'll not put my soul at risk just to give you a few minutes' gratification.'

'Is that all you see it as – *my* gratification?' Maurice asked with a wounded look.

'Well, isn't it?'

'Course not. I love you. I've told you enough times, haven't I?'

Catherine looked at him helplessly. 'If you really loved me,' she said quietly, 'you wouldn't push me to make love to you – not until I want to – not until we're—' She broke off in embarrassment.

'What?' Maurice demanded.

'Married,' Catherine whispered hoarsely.

He stared at her, then laughed shortly. 'Oh, marriage.' He said it as if it were of no consequence. 'What an old-fashioned girl you are, after all.'

Catherine reddened. 'What do you mean, after all?'

Maurice picked himself up and straightened out his clothes, adjusted his tie. 'I got the impression at the club that you were – well, you know – one of those girls that was up for a good time.'

'I-I am,' Catherine stuttered.

He glanced at her. 'No, I mean, modern. *Available*.' He stressed the word. 'As a matter of fact, all the chaps at the club thought that. You shouldn't give out such signals, Catherine, if you don't really want it. Get you into real trouble. If I wasn't such a gentleman . . .'

She gawped at him, quite speechless.

'Never mind,' he said brusquely. 'Get in the car and I'll take you home.'

Tears flooded her eyes as she groped to gather up the remains of the picnic. What had she done to earn such a reputation at the tennis

166

club? She had never led anyone on. Maurice, of all people, knew that she was chaste. It was so unfair! She swallowed tears of anger and hurt as she fumbled to close the picnic basket. But she was too upset to speak as Maurice started the car and drove back down to Hastings. She sat feeling wretched, knowing that this brief summer affair was over.

When the car drew up outside her house, Maurice leant over and, for a wild moment, Catherine thought he would kiss her.

'Better do up those buttons,' he said, glancing at her blouse as he opened the passenger door. As she fumbled to do them up, he sat waiting for her to get out, tapping his fingers on the steering wheel and whistling a tune.

She scrambled out and slammed the door, a mumbled thank you dying in her throat. The car roared away, leaving her staring numbly after it. Only later, when she dragged herself into the large bed in the corner of her spacious sitting room, still fully clothed, did she realise she had left her picnic basket in the back of his car.

She would not ask for it back. Catherine could not face the prospect of ever seeing Maurice again. How foolish she would feel, wondering what he might say about her. Perhaps he would pretend they had made love, so as not to lose face, and her reputation would be further tarnished. She buried her burning face in the pillow in anguish over how the men at the tennis club talked about her. Just because she made her own living, had her own flat and relied on no man, they misjudged her. Did her women friends think the same too? Did they gossip about her behind her back, jealous that she was so independent at twenty-four?

Catherine wept through the night, wondering why it was she attracted such men – married men or deceitful, needy men. There must be something wrong with her. She must be to blame – or why did it keep happening? She hit herself with her fists and dug her nails into her flesh. How hateful she was. A bastard inside and out. She would never find happiness with a man, because they would always be able to see through her. No matter how refined her speech or genteel her manners, they would always discover that beneath lurked common, foul-minded Kitty of the New Buildings, Kate's shameful daughter. Kate! Catherine sobbed in desolation. It always came back to Kate.

In the early hours, she was seized by cramps. She doubled up in pain and could not move. By morning her period came. She missed Mass, lying on her bed curled up against the world, listening to the sounds of distant bells, a child's voice singing, footsteps on the pavement passing by.

She dozed and dreamt she was back in Jarrow, ill in bed. The curtain lifted in the breeze and she heard the children playing in the lane, chanting a skipping game. They were calling out her name, but she could not move. Kate was shouting at her to get up and join them, but she was pinned to the prickly mattress and when she tried to call back, no voice came.

'Miss McMullen? Catherine!'

A voice woke her. For a confused moment, she thought it was Grandma Rose, then the pain of remembrance washed over her with renewed force. She lay back and kept quiet. The caller would soon go away. But whoever it was knocked at the door more loudly.

'Miss McMullen! Are you in there?'

A neighbour from the flat upstairs called down. 'What do you want?'

'I'm looking for my friend. Sorry to bother you. But would you know if Catherine McMullen's at home? She wasn't at church this morning and I was worried something was wrong.'

It was Bridie McKim.

'Haven't seen her today. Car dropped her off yesterday afternoon. Maybe she's just having a day off. Curtains are still drawn.'

'So I see. Do you have a key to her flat?' Bridie asked. 'Maybe she's lying in there unconscious.'

Catherine sat up indignantly. What business was it of theirs whether she missed church or took a day off? She would lie dying in bed if she wanted to without them poking their noses in. The neighbour was answering that she did not have a key, but they could always try breaking down the door. Catherine struggled out of bed, still wearing yesterday's clothes and hurriedly straightened out the covers.

But Bridie was cautioning against it.

'No, no, I'll be off. If you happen to see her, tell her Bridie McKim was here – and if she needs anything just to send a message.'

Catherine stood on the other side of the door holding her breath as she listened to Bridie walking down the hallway and closing the front door. A flush of relief was quickly followed by regret. How kind of the woman to notice her absence from St Mary Star-of-the-Sea and to bother calling. Tears stung her tired eyes. No one else in Hastings would have put themselves to such trouble.

Catherine rushed to the large bay window and pulled back the curtain. She rapped hard on the glass.

'Wait, Bridie!' she called. The visitor glanced round, her surprise giving way to a broad smile. Catherine beckoned her back and she waved in acceptance.

'I was sleeping,' Catherine explained sheepishly, as she opened the door.

'Poor lamb,' Bridie said in concern, 'you look terrible – and there I was waking you with my noise. I'll come back later.'

'No, stay,' Catherine insisted. She was sick of her own company and could not bear the thought of being left alone any longer. 'Come in, please. I'll put the kettle on.'

'No, you won't,' Bridie said. 'You'll sit down while I do it.'

To her own amazement, Catherine meekly did as she was told. Bridie pulled back the curtains, letting the sun flood in, then bustled into the small kitchen and made tea while Catherine flopped into a big armchair.

'Cups are in the cupboard over the bath,' Catherine called.

'Don't move, I'll find them,' Bridie called back, humming as she went about the task.

Catherine felt overwhelming relief, just sitting doing nothing, watching the redheaded woman move about the flat taking command. She felt the same snug contentment she remembered from her earliest childhood when she sat between Rose's knees having her hair brushed, while Kate pulled bread from the oven, singing under her breath.

It was a women's world in which she had felt cosy and secure. At no time since had she felt so wrapped around in warmth and contentment as in those earliest days when she had thought Rose her mother and Kate merely a boisterous older sister.

She did not need men – Catherine was struck by the sudden revelation. If men thought so little of her, she could manage without them. As long as there were women like Bridie to remind her of real friendship, she would be content.

'Here, drink this.' Bridie held out a steaming cup of tea. 'Then you can tell your Auntie Bridie all your troubles.'

Catherine took the cup and smiled in gratitude.

Chapter 27

Catherine and Bridie became firm friends. That autumn they spent their free time together, strolling along the promenade arm in arm like school friends, or going to the cinema. Bridie liked to laugh at Charlie Chaplin; Catherine preferred glamorous Mary Pickford.

'I don't see what's so funny about a poor man down on his luck,' Catherine complained. 'I want a story with a happy ending.'

Bridie laughed. 'What a little romantic you are. We'll go and see what you want. I can take Maisie to the flicks when I go home at Christmas. She loves the funny men.'

Maisie was Bridie's twelve-year-old daughter, left in the care of family in Ireland while Bridie sought work in England. She often talked of the day she would have saved up enough money to bring her daughter over too. Catherine already felt sad at the thought of not spending Christmas with her new friend.

'We'll go and see both films,' Catherine declared, 'Chaplin for the matinée and Pickford in the evening, just in case you don't get the chance in Ireland.'

Bridie clapped her hands in delight. 'What a thoughtful girl you are.' She looked at her fondly. 'I wish you were my daughter, so I do.'

'What about Maisie?' Catherine blushed.

Bridie sighed. 'Oh, Maisie. She's a sweet girl, but . . . she's not quite twelve pennies in the shilling, if you get my meaning.'

Catherine did not like to press her further. It was enough that Bridie confided in her, for no one else at the laundry, apart from the motherly matron, Mrs Townsend, knew that Bridie had a child. Once again, Catherine had a confidante, someone to take the place of Lily. But Bridie was worldlier and Catherine could tell her anything and be assured of sympathy. So she told her about the disastrous love affairs with Frank and Gerald on Tyneside, and Maurice in Hastings; of her regret that nothing had come of her friendship with Alf in Essex. The only subject she refused to talk about was Kate, and Bridie did not push her.

Her friend helped her choose furniture for her flat, scouring second-hand shops and auctions for bargains. She bought an antique walnut table and chairs to go in the window, and willow-patterned plates; fancy brass fire irons and a glass-fronted bookcase for her growing collection of books. Catherine would rather skip meals and scrimp on food so that she could afford luxuries for her flat. Yet she was careful with her money, always putting half her salary away each month and choosing her purchases after much thought.

'You have the tastes of a real lady,' Bridie would admire. 'Are you sure you're not the daughter of the Duke of Northumberland?' Catherine knew she was being teased, but on several occasions nearly blurted out that she was indeed the daughter of a gentleman.

When Christmas neared, Catherine grew morose.

'Why don't you go home to your parents?' Bridie suggested. 'Won't they be expecting it? When's the last time you saw them?'

'A year and a half ago,' Catherine answered guiltily.

'Well then, off you go and enjoy yourself. You're too young to be spending your holidays on your own.'

'The Townsends have kindly invited me round for Christmas dinner,' Catherine said, trying to summon enthusiasm.

'They're even older than me,' Bridie protested. 'No, you get yourself up north with your Irish cousins. I bet they know how to celebrate.'

Something in Catherine's expression must have betrayed her dread. Bridie sat down beside her on the seat in the bay window. Outside the wind battered the trees and tugged at the hats of passers-by.

'What's the matter? Is it something I said?'

Catherine shook her head, then abruptly succumbed to tears. Bridie pulled her into her arms and stroked her hair in comfort.

'There, there,' she crooned, 'have a good weep. Tell Auntie Bridie what's upsetting you.'

Haltingly, Catherine began to tell her friend all about Kate and the shame of having no father that hung over her like a black cloud. She told her of Kate's destructive drinking and the fear of growing up in a warring house, where moods could change in an instant and beatings were as common as rainy days.

'My stepfather, Davie, is canny enough,' Catherine conceded, 'but he's weak – can't say no to Kate. When he's home from sea with a bit of money in his pocket, the drinking goes on for days.' She looked at

171

Bridie, willing her to understand. 'You can't imagine what it was like growing up there. I thought I had a real mam and dad and three big sisters and a brother. Then one day, the bairns in the street started picking on me – pushing me around. I pushed them back. Then they said it.' Catherine gulped back tears. ' "You've got no da, you've got no da", on and on like a skipping song. They all knew, and I didn't. Said me mam was Kate. "You've got no da and your mam's a drinker." '

Tears spilt down her face as she forced herself to remember.

'And I ran into the back yard to get away from the horrible chanting – and I looked up and there was Kate staring at me. I was only seven, but I knew that instant it was all true.' Catherine squeezed her eyes shut. 'She'd heard everything. But she was smiling. Standing at the door and smiling. It was the worst moment of me life and yet the stupid woman was smiling, like I should be pleased with the news.' Catherine shuddered. 'I'll never forgive her for that smile – *never*!'

'Hush, hush,' Bridie comforted, rocking her in her arms, 'my poor, darling girl.'

'For years I couldn't bear the thought of her being my mother – still call her Kate like she's my sister.' Catherine looked at her miserably. 'I can't go home. You do see that, don't you?'

'Of course I do. What a terrible burden for such young shoulders.'

'I've just started putting it all behind me,' Catherine went on. 'Since meeting you I've stopped having these terrible nightmares – a man in a black robe chasing me and I can't get away, I'm chained to something and Kate is standing watching in the distance, but she's laughing 'cos she thinks it's all a joke.'

Catherine took the handkerchief Bridie offered. 'Thank you. You always seem to be mopping up my tears.' She tried to smile. 'You're such a good friend, Bridie. More than that. Friend and mother rolled into one – a *real* mother who cares all the time and not just when I've struggled up the hill with a jarful of whisky.'

'That's because I do care,' Bridie said. 'But I wouldn't say no to a drop of sherry. I think we both need one. You sit right there while I fetch a couple of glasses.'

They stoked up the fire and Bridie sat at Catherine's feet while they sipped sherry and ate mince pies that Bridie had brought. Later, they put chestnuts into the embers and ate them piping hot. No more mention was made of Kate or going home to Jarrow, and by the time Bridie came to leave, Catherine felt light-headed with relief that her friend knew her true situation. There would be no more secrets between them.

'I'll miss you,' Catherine said, hugging her fiercely. 'Come back soon, won't you?'

'Like a bad penny,' Bridie grinned, kissing her forehead. 'I hate to leave you on your own – especially now I know what you've been through. If it wasn't for Maisie—'

'I know,' Catherine reassured her quickly. 'You don't have to explain to me. You're doing what a mother should – putting your daughter first. I admire you for it. Wish you were mine.'

Bridie touched her cheek. 'I am yours.'

When she had gone, Catherine went back to the fire and stared into the flickering light. She was drowsy and content. This elegant room, made cosy by long velvet curtains and the yellow glow from a tall reading lamp, was her home. All hers. One day she might have someone with whom to share it.

Bridie left for Ireland in mid-December. Catherine got a postcard of a man with a donkey. 'This is the local taxi!' wrote Bridie. There was no news, but she had added her address.

Catherine wrote back a long letter, full of descriptions of the wintry landscape and news from the laundry. On Christmas Day, she attended Mass in the elegant pebble-dashed Victorian church in the old town, letting her mind wander pleasantly as she gazed into the stone-vaulted roof. Would Bridie be at church at the same time, offering up prayers of thanks to Our Lady that they had found each other?

The Townsends, master and matron of the workhouse, treated her to a huge Christmas dinner of turkey and vegetables, followed by plum pudding and white sauce. Mrs Townsend seemed sorry for her being left on her own and had even wrapped her up a present.

'It's a blue scarf and matching gloves – just your colour, dear,' Mrs Townsend smiled. 'Such a shame you not getting home for Christmas. Perhaps your mother could manage a visit down here when the weather picks up?'

The woman meant well, but Catherine shuddered at the thought of what havoc Kate might wreak in genteel Hastings.

She rushed home and wrote an affectionate letter to Bridie. Matron had been very kind, but how she missed having a real friend at such a time, someone she could laugh with and tell secrets to. In a wave of bonhomie, Catherine rashly added,

I hate to think of you going back to your little cell in the laundry when I'm living in such a palace! When you come back, why

173

don't you share it with me? There's plenty room and you can give me a little towards the rent if you like. We can sort that out later. I'm not doing this out of charity, so don't even think it. I'm asking because it's lonely here without you. You being away so long has made me realise how much I miss your company. We're like soul-mates, you and me. I've never loved any woman the way I love you, Bridie, except maybe Grandma Rose! Write back quickly and tell me what you think. Or better still – *come* back. I can't wait to see you and give you a big, big hug.

All my love,
Catherine

She went and posted it before she changed her mind. The air was sharp, prickling her nose and making her head ache. By the time she got home, her nose had started to bleed heavily and she crawled into bed, feeling suddenly depressed. If Bridie was living with her, there would be someone to take care of her when the bleedings came. How she longed to have someone to look after her. All her life people had expected her to be strong and at their beck and call.

Catherine stayed indoors on Boxing Day, then dragged herself to work the day after. She felt tired and listless.

'You sickening for something?' Matron asked in concern.

Catherine denied it. She could hardly tell her she was missing her friend in Ireland.

Word came a couple of days later from Bridie. Maisie was ill and her return was delayed. Catherine fretted and worried. What if she decided not to come back after all? What if she returned but had to bring Maisie too? There was hardly room for three in the flat. When she had made the offer, it had not occurred to her that Bridie's simple daughter might have to be accommodated too. Finally, Catherine decided that she would be prepared to take Maisie as well, if it guaranteed that Bridie came back.

After a long day at the laundry, in the middle of January, Catherine trudged home in the dark, the pavements frosty and treacherous. When she looked up on the slippery path outside her house, she saw a crack of light between the curtains in her front room. For a moment she puzzled over whether she had left a light on all day. Her heart missed a beat.

As she was fumbling with her key in the lock, the door opened as if by magic. There stood Bridie, smiling face flushed from the fire.

'I used the spare key under the plant pot,' she grinned. 'Got the tea on. Sausages and tatties. You look frozen through. Come in, come in.' Bridie held out her arms.

Catherine hugged her in exultation.

'You came back! Did you get my letter?'

'I did indeed,' Bridie laughed. 'Why do you think I'm here, my darling girl?'

'So you'll stay?' Catherine asked, as her friend helped her out of her coat and hung it on the back of the door.

'As long as you want,' Bridie promised. 'I'm going to look after you from now on.'

Chapter 28

Catherine had never been so happy as in those spring months of 1931. During the day she worked tirelessly at her job, her attention to detail gaining Matron's approval and admiration. In the lengthening evenings, she and Bridie would walk to the end of the pier and watch the fishing boats, or stay indoors listening to their new wireless and cooking.

To Catherine these relaxed moments of companionship were what made her so happy. They reminded her of the rare evenings of her childhood when there had been harmony in the kitchen at William Black Street and she had sat on the warm fender reading while Rose darned, John dozed and Kate gave her the end of the pastry to shape as she wished.

But with Bridie, the evening never ended with an explosion of temper or her in tears. There was much laughter and gossip about the laundry staff and singing along to the wireless. At night, they shared the large bed in the corner, like family, and Bridie snuggled against her back, making her feel safe and secure in the way Kate sometimes had when not reeking of whisky.

When the summer came, Catherine introduced her friend to the tennis club and paid for lessons, ignoring Bridie's protests that she was too old. They went there most weekends and joined in the social activities, the two women proving popular with their repertoire of songs and ready laughter. Catherine treated Maurice and the other men with breezy friendliness as if she had never courted the previous summer, and kept them all at arm's length. With Bridie in tow, she would quash any tittle-tattle that she played fast and loose with men. For above all, Catherine craved to be accepted by her new middle-class friends, and longed for their approval.

At home, in the flat, she did not have to pretend; Bridie knew and accepted everything about her. Catherine bathed in the warmth of the woman's kindness and attention. Even an awkward conversation with Mrs Townsend did not dampen her high spirits.

'I'm not sure it's wise taking Mrs McKim in as your lodger,' Matron warned.

'She's not my lodger – she's my friend,' Catherine answered in surprise.

'Still, it's a very small flat to be sharing with someone – who's – well – not one of your family.'

Catherine bristled. 'It's big enough – and she's much more room than she'd have in the staff block. Anyway, it's good company for me.'

Matron studied her. 'You're a generous young woman. I just don't want to see anyone take advantage of your kindness, that's all.'

Catherine laughed. 'Bridie's not like that. She'd give me the shirt off her back if I asked for it. Really, Mrs Townsend, there's no need for you to worry.'

Afterwards, Catherine pushed the matron's baffling comments to the back of her mind and never mentioned them to her friend, for fear she would be offended. As summer raced by, Bridie made arrangements to visit Maisie in Ireland again.

'I could come with you,' Catherine suggested. 'I've always wanted to visit the place Grandda harked on about all his life.'

But Bridie was evasive. 'Yes, that would be grand – but maybe not this time. I'll not be gone for long and it's such a journey. And we'd not have time to see the sights – just a lot of visiting.'

Catherine was disappointed and wondered if Bridie was embarrassed about her background.

'I'm used to a crowded house, you know. I don't mind if it's not the Ritz.'

But Bridie was stubborn. 'Maisie might be difficult – always demanding my attention. It'd be no holiday for you at all.'

Catherine stalked out of the flat and went for a long walk, hurt and puzzled as to why her friend should not want her to go. It did not matter to her that Maisie was dim-witted or might throw a tantrum; she had coped with much worse on the wards of Harton.

It was dark by the time she returned, and she felt a rush of guilt to see Bridie standing in the street, shaking with cold and looking out for her.

'Come in, little lamb,' Bridie coaxed, 'I've been that worried about you.'

'I'm sorry,' Catherine said, her anger gone.

177

'Not as much as me.'

Bridie fussed over her, plying her with hot tea. It was while they were making friends again, that the older woman came up with the suggestion.

'Why don't you go up to Jarrow while I'm away?'

Catherine stared at her in disbelief.

'I know how you feel,' Bridie went on quickly, 'but you can't go on avoiding your mother for ever.'

'Why not?' Catherine snorted.

'Because it wouldn't be right. Whatever her faults, the woman's not to blame for everything. She never left you in the lurch like your father – she always provided for you, didn't she? You told me yourself, Kate gave up a happy job at the bakery to come home and care for your grandma and you. Isn't it time you went to see her?'

'But I hate Jarrow,' Catherine said in a panic.

'You don't have to go for long,' Bridie reasoned, 'just a few days. Maybe it won't be as bad as you remember.'

'It will be.'

'What about your other relations? Won't your Aunt Mary and Uncle Alec want to see you?'

Catherine shrugged. 'I suppose they might.'

'There you are then. And you never know, your mother might have signed the pledge.'

Catherine gave a short laugh. 'Pigs might fly.'

Yet in the days that followed, she could not get the idea out of her head. It had been over two years since she had been home. Her letters to her mother had become increasingly infrequent and Kate's haphazard replies had been given a cursory glance and thrown on the fire. They usually had a gripe about Mary or a neighbour or the closing of some shop Catherine struggled to remember. She knew nothing about how Kate really was.

Catherine prayed about it and confessed to the priest her reluctance to go home. Like Bridie, Father John urged her to return. She had a duty to go and see that her mother was all right. So she wrote to Kate and told her she would visit at the end of August. A letter came by return, telling her of Kate's delight at the news.

With much trepidation and several sleepless nights before going, Catherine boarded the train for London and then onwards north.

It was late in the day when Catherine reached Tyneside and caught the final train for South Shields. Her heart was thumping with nervousness as the familiar landmarks of the riverside and its cranes trundled into view. As the line curved above Jarrow, she saw the blackened outline of St Paul's and the gantries of Palmer's yards, and felt an unexpected ache. Gazing through the grimy window, she saw a group of men chasing a football on waste ground where a chemical factory used to be.

Alighting at Tyne Dock, she saw with relief that Kate had not come to meet her. It would have been too awkward in front of others trying to find something to say after all this time. She was grateful for the extra time to compose herself.

Nothing seemed to have changed. The same streets and dock warehouses crowded about her and a train thundered overhead as she passed under the massive, echoing arches. Catherine had been drawn to this part of town as a small child. She remembered how she had roamed freely, gazing up at the Arab seamen, who winked at her curiosity.

But as she walked on, something nagged and she tried to pinpoint what was different. Perhaps it was less traffic, or the down-at-heel look of shop fronts. A crowd of children scattered past her like squawking seagulls, their bare feet drumming on the dusty pavement. It struck her that she had not seen children this skinny and sallow in two years. Hastings children had boots and well-fitting clothes.

Her sense of unease grew as she wandered down to the dock gates, only to find them shut and padlocked. Weeds were thriving, undisturbed in the cracked paving. But it was late and the buzzer for the end of work would have long gone. She backtracked and made for the steep climb up the bank to East Jarrow, passing Leam Lane where she had been born. A group of men stood sharing a cigarette outside the Alexandria pub, and she felt a sudden pang of loss for her argumentative old grandfather. This had been one of his favourite drinking haunts and she strained for the sound of his bellowing voice, knowing she was being fanciful.

The men fell silent, watching her go past with her neat suitcase as if it was the most interesting event of their day. It was only when Catherine reached the brow of the bank and saw the solid, sooty rows of the New Buildings ahead that realisation dawned. It was too quiet. Not just the subdued men, but the town and the riverside. Where was the noise of industry – the hooters, the claxons, the sighing and clanking of machinery? The hoot of a far-off train came clear over the distant fields, whereas before it would have been drowned in the clamour of the docks.

Catherine looked about her with new eyes. The huddle of shabby jackets at the street corner were not boys after all. Dozens of men squatted on their haunches in the evening light, playing with children's marbles. Her insides twisted. She knew from Kate that the ironworks had never reopened, but she had no idea things were so bad at the shipyards. Even through the uncertain years after the war, when the steel mills had been mothballed, there was always work to be found at the docks.

Catherine picked up her case and hurried towards William Black Street.

'Hinny!' Kate cried, standing on the doorstep in a faded apron, waving. How much older her mother looked. 'It's our Kitty, come at last,' she shouted to no one in particular. 'Doesn't she look grand?'

Catherine gave a nervous glance round, embarrassed to be spotted by neighbours. A few darted to their doors at the noise and called out a greeting.

'Doesn't she look well, Bessie?' Kate challenged her neighbour. 'I told you she was getting on down south.'

Catherine gave her a beseeching look. 'Let's go inside.'

Kate grabbed her arm and held on to her proudly. 'Bonny frock,' she admired. 'Haway in and let me take a proper look at you.'

Inside, Catherine was overwhelmed by the familiarity of the stuffy kitchen, its dark furniture and old black range.

'Where's the picture of Lord Roberts?' she asked, noticing at once it was missing from above the mantelpiece.

'Sold it,' Kate said with a dismissive wave. 'Always reminded me of old John making us get up in the middle of the night and march around the room. Got rid of the settle an' all, before you ask.'

Catherine saw that the long bench had disappeared from behind the table. 'Where am I going to sleep then?'

'In your grandda's old bed in the parlour, of course.'

Baffled by a sudden surge of tears in her throat, Catherine studied the clippy mat by the hearth.

'Do you remember helping me with that?' Kate asked. 'Your grandda made a song and dance about us using his old jacket that had gone at the elbows – and we had that lilac from the bonny winter coat you always refused to wear.'

Catherine laughed at the memory. 'It was a terrible coat – those big puff sleeves made me look like something from a travelling circus.'

'It cost me a fortune,' Kate protested.

'No it didn't – it came from the church bazaar.'

Kate laughed loudly. 'Trust you to remember.'

It broke the awkwardness between them. Kate pushed Catherine into a seat by the fire and went to fetch a plate of food. She watched as Catherine ate the egg, tinned tomatoes and fried potato that had been keeping warm in the bottom oven.

'Me and Davie have already eaten.' Kate brushed away her attempts to share the food.

Catherine made an effort to finish the plateful, relieved to see there was no sign of the whisky jar. Kate appeared quite sober.

Catherine sat back and looked around. 'Where's Davie? I thought you said he wasn't at sea.'

'Out walkin',' Kate said. 'He's bad with his nerves. Helps clear his head.'

'Nerves?' Catherine repeated in surprise.

'Aye.' Kate looked reflective. 'Hasn't been to sea all year – land doesn't suit him for too long, poor lad.' Suddenly she was looking Catherine full in the face. 'It's bad for the men round here now – yards are closed – there's nowt for them.'

Her mother's face looked suddenly old and drawn in the sepia light from the back window.

Catherine asked anxiously, 'What about you? You're still working, aren't you?'

Kate sighed and shook her head. 'No one wants odd jobs doing when money's tight.'

'You could take in lodgers again, couldn't you? Now Grandda's room's empty.'

A faint smile crossed Kate's lined face. 'It's that peaceful round here without him,' she said quietly, not answering the question.

Catherine would have questioned her further, but Davie appeared at the back door. She was shocked to see how much weight he had lost, his jacket hanging loose and his trousers held up with a thick piece of rope.

'Hello, Kitty,' he smiled. 'It's grand to see you.'

He went and stood behind Kate and she took her husband's hand. 'Isn't she looking bonny – and quite the lady. You should hear the way she talks now – all plums in her mouth.'

Davie rested his other hand casually on his wife's shoulder and Catherine was struck by their easy intimacy.

'Aye, she's looking grand,' Davie nodded.

Shortly afterwards, Catherine said she was tired and retreated to the front room. It smelt musty and unused. There were no rugs on the floor and her shoes echoed over the floorboards. The parlour table and chairs had gone and the fire was empty of fire irons or fender. The bulky iron bed was still in the corner, but the only other piece of furniture was one of the kitchen chairs with a wash jug and bowl balanced on top. Catherine shivered and climbed under the covers with half her clothes still on. If it was this cold in the summer, she could only imagine how icy the winters must be.

The next day, having walked down the bank into Jarrow and seen the large groups of men standing idly round on street corners, she could no longer ignore the obvious. Jarrow was in the grip of a massive slump.

Whenever she had read of such things in the national newspapers at the library in Hastings, she had quickly skimmed over the page. There had always been poverty on Tyneside; it came and went like the tide. But this was different. She had never seen so many out of work, so many children picking over the dross on the railway sidings. The cranes that she had seen from the train were rusting and still, the queues for yesterday's bread long. There was an air of resignation in the stance of the bystanders, their shoulders hunched against the river wind, hands plunged deep into threadbare trouser pockets.

She found Davie shaving on a stool in the back yard with a razor worn thin with years of use. Quietly he answered her questions. There had been strikes and riots down on the quayside caused by disputes between rival seamen desperate for work. Arab sailors who had lived here for years had been deported. The chemical works were closed and Palmer's had gone bankrupt with many workers losing their savings as well as their jobs.

Then he left her speechless with his admission that he and Kate had been forced to apply for dole and means tested by the Social.

'The means test?' Catherine gasped. What an indignity for her hard-working mother.

Davie nodded. 'Had to sell half the furniture before they'd give us a penny,' he said, unable to hide his bitterness.

'Kate never said.'

'She wouldn't – not to you. Too proud. Besides, she wouldn't want to worry you, lass.'

Catherine felt her eyes sting with tears. She thought of her haven in Hastings, with its pleasant furnishings, a vast world away from this dismal existence in Jarrow, but when she tried to raise the matter with Kate, her mother was quick to shrug it off.

'He shouldn't have told you,' she said crossly. 'We're getting by.'

'I can send you money.'

'They'd just tak our dole away if you did, hinny,' Kate said, putting out a hand to touch her. 'I don't want them busybodies coming round here, poking their noses in again.'

'They needn't know,' Catherine said.

Kate snorted. 'One of the gossips round here would sharp tell them.'

Catherine looked so worried, Kate shook her gently. 'It's enough to know you're gettin' on well down south, hinny. That's better than all the tea in China. What I wouldn't give to see this Hastings of yours.'

Catherine looked away, pretending she had not seen the longing in her mother's eyes. She wrote almost daily to Bridie, pouring out her dismay at what she had found. Yet, she took heart from one thing: Kate had never seemed so contented. There was scant food in the pantry and long hours to fill, but her mother was cheerful and sober with no John to bully or deride her. Davie was affectionate and attentive, and Kate basked in his kindness like a cat in sunshine.

'This one thing pleases me,' Catherine wrote to her friend, 'that Kate and Davie are happy together. I've often felt guilty for turning my back and making a life away from Jarrow, away from Kate, but now I see I was right to do it. It's Kate and me that can't make each other happy and it's best we stay apart. I'm glad I came back and you were right to make me, but a week has been long enough. I can't wait to get back to Hastings and be with you again.'

While Catherine was packing her case, Davie appeared in the doorway. Kate was up the street, borrowing sugar for a final cup of tea.

'She'd like nothing better than to pay you a visit, lass,' he said. 'Would do her the world of good to get away for a bit.'

Catherine was flustered. 'But I've got such a small flat – and she couldn't afford the train fare, could she?'

Davie studied her. 'No, but you could.'

Catherine flushed, ashamed of her own reluctance. How could she possibly explain that she had spent two years forging a new life for herself, a new identity, burying her anger and hurt over her mother. A visit from Kate could wreck her new-found peace of mind, let alone her standing in the eyes of her colleagues and friends.

She turned away, unable to meet his look. 'I'll leave money in the caddy,' she mumbled. 'Make sure she spends it wisely.'

Kate came with her to the station. Catherine tried to hurry past the neighbours, but her mother waved and called out to the women at their doorsteps, proudly showing off her well-dressed daughter.

As they walked down the bank, Kate said, 'You never went to see Lily Hearn.'

'No.' Catherine tensed. Several times she had almost set out to go and see her former friend, but her courage had failed.

'Did you two have a falling out?'

Catherine shrugged.

'Canny lass, Lily,' Kate mused. 'Saw her at Easter Mass. Was asking after you.'

Catherine wanted to ask a dozen questions, but they stuck in her throat. It was still too hurtful to think Lily had spread rumours about her at Tendring.

'What's this new friend of yours like?' Kate asked, as they reached the barrier at the station. 'This Bridie lass.'

Catherine smiled. 'Not really a lass – nearer your age than mine.'

Kate's eyebrows arched in surprise. 'Thought you didn't like bossy older women,' she teased.

'Bridie's not bossy, she's a real friend,' Catherine retorted, as she showed her ticket and went through the turnstile. Kate had not bought a ticket for the platform, so could not follow.

When Catherine turned, she realised it was too late to hug her goodbye. Kate stood, her look forlorn.

'I'm glad for you, hinny,' Kate said, her eyes glinting with tears.

Catherine felt wretched with guilt. She had not meant to be hurtful and could not bear the thought of her mother crying at her leaving. The guard was going up the train slamming the doors and there was no time left.

Suddenly Catherine blurted out, 'Maybe you could meet Bridie some day.'

Kate clutched the barrier. 'What do you mean, lass?'

'Come and visit us in Hastings,' Catherine gabbled as she turned to get on the train. She threw her case on board and climbed in. Pulling down the window of the carriage, she leant out and saw her mother's face beaming with delight.

'That'd be grand, Kitty!' she cried over the noise of steam as the train ground into motion.

Catherine smiled back, a warmth flooding through her that took her quite off guard. 'I'll write to you soon,' she promised with a wave.

Kate waved back frantically and, even through the steam, Catherine could see her face was wet with sudden tears. Her mother and Tyne Dock station disappeared in smoke. As Catherine sat back, the first twinge of doubt came. What had she been thinking of, inviting her mother at the last minute when she had spent a week being careful to avoid any such invitation. Kate in Hastings!

Then she thought of Bridie. She would not have to cope with her mother on her own; her friend would be there to stand up to Kate too. They would tackle any difficulties together. Catherine felt a new surge of courage.

Chapter 29

Once back in Hastings, Catherine hoped her mother might forget her rash invitation to visit. Life settled back into its normal routine of busy working day and pleasant evenings at the flat with Bridie. That autumn, Catherine took up painting, joining a life-drawing class for adults. She had not touched a paintbrush since the days of painting cushion covers in Jarrow, but found that she still had an eye for perspective and detail. In a small way, it made her feel connected to her elusive father, whose drawing of Great-Aunt Lizzie's family remained fresh in her memory. She tried to practise on Bridie, but her friend found it impossible to keep still and silent for any length of time.

'You can make it into one of those impressionist paintings,' Bridie teased, when Catherine lost patience with her fidgeting. 'I can't be doing with sitting like a statue. If you want something that doesn't move, paint that banana over there.'

Then a letter came from Kate, reproving her for forgetting her promise.

'Did you not mean it when you asked me to come and see Hastings and meet your friend? I dearly want to come. Write and tell me, lass. I will need a lend of the train fare, but will pay you back when Davie gets work.'

Catherine passed it to Bridie to read.

'What's the harm in a little visit?' Bridie asked. 'You can send her a return ticket, so she can't outstay her welcome. I'd like to meet her.'

'No you wouldn't.'

Bridie pulled a frightening face. 'I want to see what sort of monster produced such a kind and pretty daughter,' she teased.

Catherine laughed and threw a cushion. 'I suppose if it was just for a week . . .'

So in November money for a return ticket was sent, and Catherine relented and suggested a fortnight's holiday. She half expected to hear nothing more, believing her mother would spend the money on Davie and drink. But a letter came the following week with Kate's travel plans and arrival time.

Anxiety kept Catherine awake for days beforehand, and she found herself tired and short-tempered with those around her. Only Bridie understood why. Mrs Townsend was eager to meet her mother and insisted they must all come for Sunday lunch.

'Why did you have to tell her Kate was coming?' Catherine accused her friend.

'Because if she found out afterwards, you'd never hear an end to the woman's questions,' Bridie declared. 'Stop fretting, girl.'

By the time Kate arrived on the Saturday, Catherine was sick with nerves and unable to keep her breakfast down. She felt like a small girl again, brimming with unspoken anxieties. Bridie marched her down to the station, encouraging and bullying her every step.

'Ever thought of joining the army?' Catherine joked morosely. 'You'd be the perfect sergeant.'

'Quiet in the ranks,' Bridie laughed.

Catherine stood shaking at the barrier, imagining Kate staggering off the London train inebriated and shabbily dressed. Or maybe she would not have managed the train changes and been picked up by the police instead.

'Is that her?' Bridie asked. 'The woman in the cloche hat and the purple coat?'

Catherine squinted up the platform. 'Where?'

'You need glasses, girl. The one that's waving at you.' Bridie waved back. 'Doesn't look like a three-headed monster to me.'

For a moment, Catherine saw a neatly dressed middle-aged stranger, with a close-fitting hat, chatting to the porter who was taking her bag. Then she noticed Kate's familiar ambling gait as she walked towards them.

'She's got a limp,' Catherine told Bridie quickly. 'It doesn't mean she's drunk.'

Bridie said nothing, just gave Catherine's arm a squeeze of encouragement. She felt a surge of courage.

Kate came bustling through the barrier. 'This is my daughter, Kitty,' she told the porter proudly. 'She's a manager, you know.' Kate threw her arms around Catherine in a hug of excitement.

Catherine stiffened. Her mother was just showing off in front of the man.

'This is Bridie,' Catherine said, quickly pulling away.

For an instant, the two older women sized each other up, then Bridie held out a hand.

'Pleased to meet you, Mrs McDermott,' Bridie smiled charmingly. 'I've been looking forward to this.'

'Aye, me an' all,' Kate said, shaking her hand.

Catherine noticed she was wearing gloves. Kate must have borrowed them from Mary. There was no smell of alcohol; she was making a real effort. Catherine felt a sudden wave of relief that the visit might go well. Kate slipped an arm through Bridie's as if they were old friends and began to chatter about the journey. Only Catherine seemed to notice the porter standing waiting for a tip.

'Kate – your bag,' she interrupted her mother.

Kate turned in a fluster. 'Eeh, hinny, can you give the lad a penny? He's been that helpful.'

Catherine produced a sixpence from her purse, paid the man and took the bag. She followed the other two, who were deep in conversation again, half relieved that they seemed instantly to like each other, half annoyed at being left to carry Kate's cheap portmanteau.

They took the bus up the hill to Clifton Road and Catherine felt a rush of pride as Kate stood open-mouthed in admiration at her flat.

'It's that grand,' her mother said in awe, as she moved about the main room, touching the furniture and feeling the curtains. When she turned, she had tears in her eyes. 'I'm proud of you, lass.'

'Didn't I say your ma would love it?' Bridie beamed, and rushed about making tea and fussing around them both. 'Catherine has such good taste.'

'Oh, Catherine is it?' Kate teased. 'What happened to my Kitty?'

'Grew up and turned into a beautiful swan,' Bridie joked.

After the evening meal, they sat by the fire and told stories, Kate gossiping about Jarrow neighbours and Bridie about Ireland.

'So you've a daughter an' all?' Kate looked surprised.

'A daughter and a man gone missing,' Bridie said ruefully, 'just like you.'

Kate flushed. 'Kitty has let her tongue go.'

'Don't worry,' Bridie reassured her with a quick hand on her arm, 'I'd not tell a soul. I think you're brave as a lion, keeping your daughter with no man to stand by you. I know how cruel people can be. You're a woman after my own heart.'

188

Kate smiled in gratitude. 'It can't be easy for you, being separated from your Maisie.'

Bridie nodded. 'What I wouldn't give to have her here with me.'

The two women fell into a sympathetic silence.

Catherine rose, uncomfortable at their easy confiding. 'I think we should get some sleep.'

Bridie was up at once. 'Kate, you must share the bed with Catherine. I'll sleep on the couch.'

It was years since Catherine had bedded down with her mother in the feather bed at home. Anxiety gripped, as Kate flopped down beside her. It was ridiculous that she should still feel this way; she was a grown woman, not a child frightened of the night. Yet she wondered if the old nightmares might return, and the ingrained fear of drunken adults.

She had strange half-memories of being woken in the night by tustling and the suppressed cries of Grandma Rose pleading in the next room for John to leave her alone. At other times a dark shadow hovered over them and Kate hissed at someone to leave her be. Not Grandda John this time. Could it be Uncle Jack or a long-forgotten lodger? Catherine fought to overcome such disturbing thoughts. She lay tensed in the dark.

Gradually, she was calmed by the firelight flickering on the ceiling and the sound of a sea wind in the chimney. She grew drowsy listening to Kate's even breathing, the scent of lily of the valley and the warmth of her mother's body strangely comforting.

'Catherine, are you awake?' Bridie whispered.

'Yes,' Catherine murmured.

'It's going to be all right – your mother being here. I know it will.'

Catherine smiled sleepily. 'Umm, hope so.'

Within minutes she was asleep.

The next day they went to Mass at St Mary Star-of-the-Sea in the old town, followed by lunch at the Townsends'. There was one anxious moment when the master offered Kate a sherry, but her mother declined. She shot Catherine a triumphant look as she did so. Conversation rattled around the table and Mrs Townsend was so taken with Kate that she insisted on her paying a visit to the workhouse.

'You'll want to see what a fine job Catherine is making of the laundry.'

'Aye, I would.' Kate looked delighted. 'I brought her up to be hardworking.'

'And what a good job you did of it.' Mrs Townsend was full of praise.

So the next day, Kate was shown around the institution. Catherine was taut with nerves about the visit, praying that her mother did nothing embarrassing or offended any of the staff with her plain speaking. But she need not have worried. Kate appeared on her best behaviour, making everyone laugh and delighting them with breathless compliments.

'It's so much better run than the one back home!' Kate exclaimed. 'More like a holiday camp, if you ask me. Bet you have them queuing round the block to get in.'

'We don't make it that easy for them,' Mrs Townsend protested.

'No, I was just pulling your leg,' Kate said hastily. 'Firm but fair, that's what you are.'

Kate revelled in her new surroundings and was perfectly happy to find her way around town while Catherine and Bridie went to work. Catherine fretted all day that her mother would succumb to old habits and spend the wintry afternoons in a public house. But when they returned home, Kate always had the tea ready and was perfectly sober. The weekend came again and they took her on the bus to Brighton, bought her a new outfit and ate fish and chips near the pier.

Her mother was starry-eyed at the grandeur of the place and the wealth of goods in the shops.

'No one dodging the tick-man round here,' she laughed.

At the end of the fortnight, when her mother was due to go, Catherine felt unexpectedly sad. There had been no sign of the difficult, demanding Kate of old. Her mother had made a special effort to fit in and cause no upset. Most of all, she had got on well with Bridie and the evenings had been full of jokes and laughter. It would be so quiet again once she was gone. Catherine felt depressed at the thought of what her mother would be going back to: a dismal fireside with a morose Davie, if her casual comments were to be believed.

Bridie said, 'Why don't you stay another day or two?'

Kate shook her head. 'Davie wouldn't like it – think I'd run off with another man.' She laughed at Catherine's shocked expression. 'Chance would be a fine thing.'

'Things are all right between you and Davie, aren't they?' Catherine asked.

Kate pulled a face, then laughed. 'Course they are. It's just the thought of ganin' home after such a canny time with you and Bridie.'

'You can come again any time,' Bridie said spontaneously, 'can't she, Catherine?'

Catherine felt irritated at Bridie's rash offer, but the look of expectation on her mother's face made her weaken.

'Course you can,' Catherine promised.

It made it easier saying goodbye to Kate at the station, for she felt guilty at sending her back to a bleak Jarrow and long days of idleness.

'Come in the summer when the days are longer and I can take my holidays,' Catherine suggested.

Kate hugged her tearfully. 'I've had such a canny time. Take care of yoursel', hinny.'

Catherine waved her away, confused by the mix of emotions the disappearing Kate evoked. Relief that it was over without incident, and tears from the rare gesture of her mother's arms pressed around her, for no one's benefit but her own.

Chapter 30

1932

When Kate came back in the summer, which was the next time Catherine saw her, having spent Christmas and Easter in Hastings, she stayed for over a month. Davie had finally found employment, working on a cargo ship plying the Baltic.

'There's nowt for me to go back to,' Kate kept repeating, 'just an empty house.'

Bridie went to Ireland to see Maisie. Catherine would have liked to have gone with her, but she had Kate to look after. Instead, she took a fortnight's holiday and they went for picnics and trips along the coast. Kate was not one for walking for the sake of it: she preferred to sit on the beach, observing and making comments about other people.

'Everyone here has a motor car,' she said in wonder. 'Look at them all! Where can they all be going?'

Catherine laughed. 'The same as those who don't have cars – work, home, on holiday.'

'Do you know what?' Kate said, gazing out over a calm azure sea. 'This is me first summer holiday ever.' She turned to look at her daughter. 'And I'm having the best time of me life, Kitty.'

So when Catherine went back to work, she found it impossible to send her mother home.

'I can get everything shipshape for you – have the dinner on when you come home,' Kate bargained.

'I get dinner at the laundry, remember.'

'Well, the tea then,' Kate said with a pleading look. 'You're that tired when you get in from work. I can look after this place for you. Let me be some use to you, hinny.'

Bridie came back, subdued and resentful at having to leave Maisie again, and was an instant ally of Kate's.

'Let her stay as long as she wants,' Bridie said on a trip to the tennis club. 'She's not a bad cook and she keeps the place spotless.'

Catherine was uncertain. 'But without us around, she'll have too much time on her hands. There'll be nothing to stop her waltzing off to the pub.'

'Has she tried anything since I've been away?'

'No,' Catherine had to admit, 'but . . .'

'But, you're just looking for problems where there aren't any,' Bridie cried. 'You're such a little worry-head. She's desperate to please you; I think you're being too hard on her.'

Catherine was stung. 'I can see how she's got round you. She can be sweetness and light when she wants to, but it won't last.'

Bridie gave her a hooded look. 'I'd give anything to be with my daughter – and Kate's the same. Give her a week or two and see how it goes.'

For the rest of August, Kate played housekeeper, walking to the shops and buying food, which she had ready cooked when they got in from work. Never once did Catherine smell whisky on her breath and she felt guilty at having begrudged her mother the extended holiday.

It was a postcard from Davie that forced the issue of Kate's return. He was back on Tyneside for a fortnight and wanting her home.

'Don't know why he can't manage on his own,' Kate complained. 'I'll no sooner be back and he'll be off to sea again, leaving me all on me own.'

Catherine knew her mother wanted to stay, but she had had enough of sharing the flat. It felt cramped with the couch having to be used as a bed, Kate's sewing cluttering up the table, extra washing strung over the fireplace on wet days. Kate had rearranged the furniture and was forever telling Catherine how things could be done better, ignoring her pleas not to oversalt the food or buy from passing hawkers. She longed for the tranquillity of evenings reading by the fire, just her and Bridie, without Kate's constant chatter and interference. Bridie had been strangely distant with her since returning from Ireland and she wanted to recapture their old friendship.

'You can't stay here for ever,' Catherine pointed out. 'You have to go home sometime.'

They were sitting either side of the fireplace, while Bridie wrote a letter to Maisie at the table. Catherine wished her friend would say something to support her, but she kept quiet.

Kate gave her a mournful look. 'But I feel more at home here than I do back in Jarrow.'

'That's 'cos you've been on holiday,' Catherine protested. 'It's not a picnic all year round. Besides, Davie's your husband and Jarrow's where you live.'

Kate began twisting her hands in her lap. Her veins stood out like ropes on her work-roughened hands. Old hands. She said, 'I don't want to gan back. I hate living on me own – I've never lived on me own. Once Davie's back at sea, I'm frightened of what I might do.' She gave Catherine a beseeching look. 'You know what I'm like when there's no one there to keep the reins on.'

Catherine gulped. 'There's Aunt Mary and Uncle Alec – and all your friends. You wouldn't be on your own. Not like here, where you don't know people.'

'I want to stay,' Kate blurted out. 'Please let me stay!'

Catherine felt panic rise. She stood up and poked the fire, keeping her back to Kate so she could not see the desperation in her mother's eyes. She could not live with her again. Already they were irritating each other, Kate's little jibes getting under her skin, making her feel like an angry child again. Yet, if she sent her back home and Kate started drinking, then it would be all her fault. That's what Kate meant. It was an impossible choice.

'Look at this place,' Catherine said in agitation. 'It's just not big enough for the three of us. There isn't room . . .'

Suddenly, Bridie spoke up. 'We could rent a bigger flat.'

'What?' Catherine spun round to stare at her friend.

'You're on a good salary, Catherine, you could afford it.'

Why was Bridie encouraging Kate's fantasy? Could she not see that her mother would ruin everything for them? Anger choked her. She loved her flat and did not want to move.

'B-but what about Davie?' Catherine fumbled for an excuse.

'What sort of husband is he?' Bridie snorted. 'Away for months on end or moping around like a lost ghost when he's home. That's no way to live for someone as full of life as Kate. He doesn't deserve her.'

Catherine gawped at them both. When had Kate been confiding all this in Bridie?

'But you love Davie, don't you?' she demanded.

Kate sighed. 'He's canny enough – but these past couple of years haven't been a bundle of laughs, I can tell you. Sometimes, he's that drawn into his shell, he never speaks from the minute he gets up till the minute he gans to bed. I end up talking to the walls.'

'But he's still your husband,' Catherine said desperately.

Bridie said fiercely, 'Would you force your ma to go back to a loveless marriage just for appearance's sake? I know all about unhappy marriage and I wouldn't wish it on anyone.' She challenged Catherine with her sharp blue eyes. 'Jarrow has nothing for Kate – you said yourself it's quiet as the grave. How can you send her back to scrimping and the means test?'

Catherine felt tears of frustration well in her eyes. She was not to blame for Jarrow's plight or Kate's stale marriage. She never wanted her mother to marry Davie in the first place! So why was she feeling so guilty? She could not bear Bridie looking at her with such contempt as if she hated her. Unexpectedly, she burst into tears.

Bridie rushed over at once. 'Oh, poor girl, I didn't mean to upset you.' She hugged her tight. 'Here, let me dry your eyes.'

Kate hovered close, touching Catherine's hair with tentative fingers. 'I'll gan back, hinny. Davie and me can manage. I can see there's no room for me here, and I'm sorry for making you cry.'

Catherine felt even more wretched at their sudden kindness. She howled while they fussed and petted her like mother hens. She took Bridie's handkerchief and blew her nose. It was spattered with blood. Dizziness overcame her as more blood poured from her nose. Bridie cried at Kate to fetch cloths from the kitchen while she helped Catherine to the bed. Their voices came and went like bad reception on the wireless. When she lay down the room spun around and made her nauseous.

It was an hour before the bleeding stopped, by which time she was exhausted and past arguing about anything. Catherine fell asleep and woke in the early hours, as a silvery dawn light seeped in around the curtained windows. She felt weak and listless, the wrangling of the previous evening plaguing her thoughts.

Getting up, she went to the window and peered out on the quiet street. Wide pavements, ornate railings, clipped hedges and electric streetlights. It was a world away from the New Buildings in Jarrow. Glancing back at Kate, sleeping in the big bed, she felt a pang of remorse at her selfishness. Her mother looked so peaceful, the lines on her face smoothed away, her mouth half-open like a child's.

'Can't you sleep either?' Bridie whispered, startling her.

'No.'

'Come here, girl, and sit with me.' Bridie made room for her on the couch. 'I'll make us a cup of tea in a minute.' She put an arm about her. 'You're shaking. Are you still feeling ill? I'll fetch the doctor out in the morning.'

'No, I'm all right,' Catherine whispered, grateful for her tenderness. 'I'm sorry about last night. I'll let Kate stay if you think it's the right thing to do. It's just I was looking forward to having the flat to ourselves again.'

'So was I,' Bridie reassured her. 'But if we got a bigger place, we could all get along without being in each other's pockets.'

'I suppose so,' Catherine said resignedly.

'Well, there's no harm in looking, is there?' Bridie encouraged. 'And if we found somewhere you liked, and if it was big enough, then maybe . . .'

'Maybe what?'

'Maybe I could bring Maisie over from Ireland. We could all live together like one big happy family,' Bridie said excitedly.

Catherine finally understood. 'So that's what this is all about. It's Maisie you want, not Kate. Why didn't you tell me before?'

'Because you've already been so good to me,' Bridie said, suddenly tearful. 'I couldn't ask you to dig into your pocket just for my Maisie. She's my responsibility not yours.'

Catherine took Bridie's hand. 'You really miss her, don't you?'

Bridie nodded. 'She's all I can call my own.'

Catherine made up her mind. 'If that's what you really want, then that's what we'll do. We'll go out this weekend and hunt for a bigger flat.'

Bridie threw her arms around her. 'What a darling girl! What a big-hearted darling, darling girl.'

Catherine laughed. She felt flooded with warmth to be able to make someone so happy. Worries over Kate and the cost, or caring for Bridie's young daughter were banished as they hugged each other. She was loved again and that was all that mattered.

Chapter 31

Kate went to Jarrow but wrote twice weekly to ask how plans for her return were progressing. Davie had gone back to sea agreeing that she should live with Catherine while he was away so much. He could take his leave in Hastings.

Catherine felt creeping forboding at Kate coming to live with her, but smothered her doubts and continued to house-hunt to please Bridie. Her friend was skittish at the thought of Maisie being with her again and Catherine's tentative questions were brushed aside.

'Will we need to find her a school?' Catherine asked.

'School?' Bridie laughed. 'She hasn't been to school since I left Ireland. She's not the learning kind.'

'A job then?'

'Maisie's not the kind of girl to hold down a job,' Bridie replied.

'What will she do all day while we're working?' Catherine asked.

'Oh, she can help Kate with the housekeeping. She's a good girl – just needs telling what to do. Your mother will love her.'

So, with pressure coming from both older women, Catherine found a maisonette near the sea front in Laurel Street. At the end of October, Mr Townsend brought round the workhouse van and helped her move her furniture. She handed back the keys to her ground-floor flat with a heavy heart. It had been a happy place that she had made her own. Now she would have to start again, but with two strong-minded women who would want a say in how her home was furnished and run. Still, Catherine clung to the belief that Kate had changed for the better and, anyway, Bridie would protect her from her mother's interference.

Bridie and Catherine set to work spring-cleaning the large flat and ordering extra furniture. Kate and Maisie would have the two small bedrooms, as Bridie thought they needed rooms of their own, while Catherine and Bridie shared the large one. There was a separate bathroom, a kitchen big enough to eat in and a spacious sitting room with a partial view of the promenade and the sea beyond.

'Isn't it a dream place?' Bridie exclaimed. 'Much nicer than Clifton Road. And it's nearer the shops and the beach. Maisie will think she's died and gone to heaven.'

It was arranged that Kate would arrive first and settle in, before Maisie was sent over from Ireland. A nervous Catherine went to meet her mother at the station, with Bridie's words of encouragement ringing in her ears: 'It's the start of a new life for all of us, girl. One happy family, that's what we'll be.'

The carriages of the London train emptied. There was no sign of Kate. Catherine's instant feeling was of relief. Her mother had decided not to come after all. Ridiculous to think she could ever leave Jarrow. But she knew deep down that Kate would come and the next moment there was a commotion at the far end of the train. Bags were being thrown out of the door and a guard was helping a passenger down the step. She heard Kate's laugh. Even at this distance she knew that her mother was drunk.

Catherine hurried up the platform, heart hammering. Kate was talking loudly, the guard placating her, calling for a porter to help.

'There's no need,' Catherine said hastily. 'I'll take her luggage.'

'Here she is,' Kate bellowed, 'my posh daughter, Kitty. Oops, s-sorry, likes to be called Catherine. Bet you thought I was making it up, lad.' She laughed loudly as she stumbled against the guard.

'Steady, ma'am. Let me help you to the barrier.' He shot Catherine an amused look.

'Looked after Kitty for years – now she's ganin' to look after me,' Kate giggled. 'That's fair, isn't it?'

'Sounds fair to me,' the guard answered, winking at Catherine.

She followed behind with Kate's two bags, puce with embarrassment. Swiftly she hailed a taxi and bundled her mother in the back. She did not look capable of walking to the new flat and Catherine feared a scene in public. By the time she had marched her mother up the stairs to the maisonette and staggered up with her heavy bags, Catherine was seething with anger.

She turned on Kate. 'How dare you turn up in such a state?'

'What state?' Kate looked at her blearily.

'Drunk, that's what,' Catherine snapped.

'Just had a little nip,' Kate said, flopping into a chair. 'Keeps the cold out. London's perishing.'

'You promised you wouldn't drink any more,' Catherine accused. 'I wouldn't have agreed to you coming here if I thought you were still hitting the bottle.'

Kate gave a hurt look. 'I was celebratin'. Ta-ra Jarrow, hello Hastings.' She started to hiccup. 'D-on't be cr-oss.'

Catherine gave a sigh of exasperation and strode to the kitchen for a glass of water. By the time she returned, Kate's eyes were closed and her breathing heavy.

'You can't go to sleep here.' Catherine shook her. Kate grunted and slumped further into the chair. Moments later she was snoring loudly.

Bridie came back from the shops to find Catherine sitting at the window her face wet with tears.

'What's wrong, girl?' she asked in concern.

Catherine jerked her head at the sleeping Kate. 'Turned up drunk, didn't she? Same as ever. It's all a big mistake. I should never have let her come.' She covered her face and wept anew.

Bridie put an arm around her. 'She was probably that excited about seeing you. It doesn't mean she's at the drink all the time. Come on, cheer up. We're the bosses here and we'll not let her slip back into bad ways.'

When Kate woke, she was contrite and made an effort to be complimentary about her new home. She hobbled into the kitchen and rolled up her sleeves.

'I'll wash the dishes,' she insisted. 'You two workers put your feet up by the fire.'

'Told you so,' Bridie whispered to Catherine, as she picked up her knitting and settled in a chair. 'Come on, sit down and read something to me.'

Catherine began a new chapter of *Great Expectations*, which they had been reading together. After a while Kate emerged from the kitchen with a fresh pot of tea.

'We'll have this before bed, eh?' she said. 'You carry on readin', hinny. I like to listen to you. She used to do a bit writin' herself, did you know that, Bridie?'

'No, I didn't.' Bridie gave a surprised look.

'Do you still do your writin', Kitty?'

Catherine blushed. 'No, not for ages.' She would feel awkward explaining that she only wrote when she was lonely or unhappy. It was something that had filled in the long evenings at Harton and Tendring.

'Used to scribble away in an old exercise book,' Kate continued. 'Our Jack nicked it for her from a school where he was billeted during the war. Filled every little inch of it, did our Kitty. Whatever happened to it, I wonder.'

'You probably threw it on the fire,' Catherine snorted, secretly astonished her mother had taken such notice.

'I wouldn't have,' Kate protested, 'but maybes old John did. Used it for tapers, more than likely.'

'Well, what a dark horse,' Bridie said in amusement. 'Catherine a writer.'

'Aye, and she wrote this long story for the *Shields Gazette*, but they sent it straight back. And after all that work and paying for that lass Amelia to have it typed up proper like in a book.'

'Bridie doesn't want to hear about all that,' Catherine cried. 'It was just childish—'

'You always had a head for a story, mind,' Kate went on. 'The tales she used to come out with about leprechauns and fairies at the bottom of our lane – and telling all her school friends that I was courtin' Dr Dyer – now that was a fairy story if ever there was one! Her grandda said all her tale-telling would land her in gaol or make her a fortune.'

Bridie and Kate laughed together.

'Well,' said Bridie, 'let's hope it's the fortune, for all our sakes.'

After Kate's arrival, Catherine and Bridie made sure that no alcohol was brought into the house. Kate seemed to settle in easily, busying herself with cleaning the flat and making meals. Every day she walked to the shops, looking for bargains at the butcher's and grocer's. She washed on Mondays, ironed on Tuesdays, baked on Wednesdays, washed the windows Thursdays, scrubbed the kitchen Fridays and baked again on Saturdays.

'See, she's managing just fine without a drink,' Bridie declared one night, after Kate had gone to bed. 'It was high spirits when she first arrived, that's all.'

Only one problem arose those first weeks. Mrs Hind, their widowed neighbour downstairs, complained at Kate hanging out washing in the shared back courtyard.

Mrs Hind waylaid Catherine on her return from work. 'Monday has always been my day, and your mother never takes in the washing line when she's finished. I have to look at her bare line all week.'

Catherine asked Kate to wash on Tuesday or Wednesday instead.

200

'But I've always washed on Mondays,' Kate protested. 'If I leave it till later, all me other jobs get knocked back.'

'Please, Kate,' Catherine pleaded. 'Does it matter?'

'All right for you to say, but I'm the one doing the hard graft. That wife downstairs has only herself to wash for; why can't she shift her day?'

'She goes out other days,' Catherine explained, 'and she's old and set in her ways.'

Kate snorted. 'She might push you around, but she'll not push me.'

Catherine gave up arguing and resigned herself to being lectured by her neighbour every Monday. She had hoped that the widow might have been a companion for Kate, someone with whom to share a cup of tea. But from Mrs Hind's disparaging remarks, Catherine realised the woman thought she was far socially superior to Kate. This irked Catherine, so she left the neighbour to fight her own washing battles with Kate.

'Your mother needs company,' Bridie said, when they discussed the issue. 'It's time for Maisie to come.'

Word was sent to Bridie's sister in Ireland to arrange the ferry crossing. Bridie would meet her at the other end and bring her to Hastings on the train.

'Our first Christmas all together!' Bridie cried in excitement, the day she left to collect her daughter.

'What's she like, this Maisie?' Kate asked, after Bridie had gone.

Catherine shrugged. 'Never met her.'

'You mean she's never been over here in all that time?' Kate exclaimed.

'No, but Bridie's been home to see her often enough,' Catherine defended.

'So what's wrong with her?' Kate persisted.

'Nothing.' Catherine grew impatient. 'She's not very bright, that's all.'

'Feeble-minded, you mean?'

'No! Well, she just needs a bit of looking after.'

'And that's my job, isn't it?' Kate gave her a look. 'That's why your precious Bridie wants me here – to look after her lass, while she gans off to work.'

'You're the one begged to come down here,' Catherine reminded her. 'If it doesn't suit, you can sharp go home.'

Yet Catherine too was apprehensive about the new arrival. How handicapped was Maisie? Would she throw fits or wet the bed or wander around at night like some of the inmates at Harton? Kate was only echoing her own fears. The Stanways at the Essex workhouse had shocked her with their belief that such people should be kept locked up.

'I'd sterilise the lot of them,' the master had declared. 'They'll only bring more mental defectives into the world, given half the chance. Runs in the family, you see.'

Catherine had squirmed at such conversations for it echoed the bigotry she had thought to escape. The Stanways and other adherents of the eugenics society would no doubt condemn her just as harshly for being illegitimate. Her mother's weakness was a moral disease that would taint her too, in their eyes. That was why she had to leave, before they confronted her about it.

As Catherine waited tensely for Bridie to return, she felt ashamed of her unspoken fears.

Chapter 32

It was late when the travellers returned, Catherine and Kate waiting up and struggling to stay awake.

'What a big lass!' Kate blurted out on seeing Bridie's daughter. 'I thought you were just a bairn.'

'Hello, Maisie,' Catherine smiled. 'You must be tired out.'

Maisie clung to her mother, avoiding their eyes. Bridie looked exhausted.

'Don't be shy, girl. Say hello to the nice ladies,' she coaxed. But Maisie hung her head and said nothing.

'I'll fetch the tea,' Kate said quickly.

'Let me take your coat,' Catherine offered. 'Would you like to see your room, Maisie? We've painted it blue, 'cos your mam said that was your favourite colour.'

Maisie looked at her mother as if Catherine had not spoken. 'Milk and two sugar lumps, please.'

'Yes, pet,' Bridie smiled, 'now take off your coat and give it to Catherine.' She helped the girl out of her coat and handed it over. The friends exchanged looks. Bridie said, 'I think Maisie should sleep with me tonight – until she gets used to her new home. You don't mind going in the little room for a night or two, do you?'

'Maisie sleep with you tonight,' Maisie repeated before Catherine had time to answer.

'That's right,' Bridie reassured, 'Catherine won't mind. Now sit with me and drink your tea.'

They sat at the table in the window, slurping tea, while Bridie told them of the journey. Catherine tried not to stare at Maisie the way her mother did. Kate was right, Maisie looked older than her fourteen years. She was large, her body fully grown and her black hair coiled into a bun like a middle-aged woman, though, watching her methodically stir and sip her tea, Catherine saw that her face was fresh-skinned and youthful.

Soon Bridie was ushering her daughter into the main bedroom. Maisie ignored their good nights, then turned in the doorway.

'There are thirty-two steps,' she announced. 'Twenty steps then twelve steps. Thank you for the tea.' Then she went into Catherine's bedroom.

Bridie laughed at their puzzled faces. 'The steps into the flat,' she explained proudly. 'Maisie notices things like that. Wake us in the morning, won't you?'

When the door had closed, Kate said, 'Well, she's a queer one. Not so much as a how-do-you-do, but she's counted the steps to the maisonette. Not sure I can be left with her all day long.'

'You'll get on grand,' Catherine yawned. She was annoyed at the way Bridie had commandeered her bedroom without even asking, but if it helped Maisie settle in then she could hardly complain.

The next day went well, all four of them going to Mass, then returning home for a big breakfast of bacon, eggs and fried bread. The day was wintry but they took Maisie for a walk along the pier, pointing out the harbour and the fishing fleet. When they got home, the girl told them there were sixteen boats in the bay compared to twelve boats at the harbour back in Ireland, one of which belonged to Uncle Michael.

'You'll be a help to me when it comes to countin' up the pennies for shopping,' Kate said with a laugh.

But on Monday morning there was a scene when Bridie left for work. Maisie went to the door and howled like a baby. Kate tried to pull her back, but the girl was strong and pushed her over. Bridie came back and reasoned with her daughter, but by this time she was hysterical. Mrs Hind came to her door, demanding to know what the noise was all about.

'Get her to count the stairs,' Catherine suggested in desperation. 'How many stairs can you see, Maisie?'

The crying subsided a fraction. Maisie peered over the banisters.

'Auntie Kate will count them with you,' Catherine encouraged. 'Go on,' she hissed at her mother.

They left Kate and Maisie walking up and down the stairs, counting out loud.

Each morning, Maisie's protests at her mother's going lessened, until she sat at the table unconcerned and not even calling out goodbye.

Catherine noticed the way the girl began to follow Kate around, and wanted her to fix her hair rather than Bridie.

Kate grumbled, 'I cannot even gan to the privy without her comin' too. She's like me shadow.' But Catherine was sure her mother was secretly pleased that Maisie had taken to her so quickly.

Bridie was less keen on her daughter's transfer of affections.

'She's too old to have her hair put in ringlets,' she complained, when Kate bound Maisie's hair in rags one night.

'She'll look bonny,' Kate contradicted, 'much better than that old maid's bun you make her wear.'

'Look bonny,' Maisie echoed solemnly. 'Sixteen ringlets.'

By December, Catherine insisted that Maisie move out of her bedroom and into her own.

'This is my flat,' she pointed out, when Bridie prevaricated. 'You can squeeze into Maisie's room with her if you want to stay together, but I'm having my own bed back.'

Far from having the tantrum that Bridie predicted, Maisie accepted the move without a murmur.

'I like the blue room,' she announced at breakfast. 'Milk and two sugars. Thank you, Auntie Kate.'

As Christmas drew near, they threw themselves into preparations for their first Christmas together at the new flat. Kate was given extra money to buy ingredients for mince pies and plum pudding. Catherine and Bridie had a happy Saturday afternoon buying presents, and Maisie helped them decorate a tree, though she broke as many baubles as she hung up.

'Watch out, you clumsy lass,' Kate scolded, as Maisie knocked into her when she was carrying a hot tray of pies. Three of them rolled on the floor. Maisie fled to her bedroom.

'It's you should be more careful,' Bridie defended; 'could've given the girl a nasty burn.'

Kate dumped down the remaining pies. 'You make your own Christmas dinner then. I'm not your bloody servant!' She whipped off her apron, hurtled to the door and grabbed her coat on the way out.

'Where you going?' Catherine called after her in alarm.

'None of your business,' Kate shouted as she slammed the door.

Bridie looked baffled. 'What did I say?'

Catherine sighed. 'I'll go after her. She might have money in her pocket.'

She caught up with Kate along the front. A cold sleet splattered over the railings. 'Stop! What's got into you? Bridie was just upset at you shouting at Maisie.'

Kate was about to answer back, then her shoulders slumped and she let go a long sigh.

'I'm sick of Bridie ordering me around like a skivvy as if she's lady muck. And that Maisie,' Kate complained, 'she's canny enough, but it's hard work having her around all day on me own. I cannot gan anywhere without her tappy-lappying along and talking daft.' She gave Catherine a look of desperation. 'Can I not have a little drink this Christmas, a bit fun, hinny?'

Catherine turned away and gazed out over the choppy grey sea. The last thing she wanted was her mother drinking again. Yet she had shouldered the burden of running the house and looking after Maisie with little complaint. It must be lonely at times, with no other friends or neighbours to gossip with or lighten the day. Did she not deserve a celebratory drink just this once?

'Please, Kitty,' Kate pleaded, 'just a little nip on Christmas Day.'

Catherine turned and said, 'Just with Christmas dinner, then.'

To Catherine's surprise, their first Christmas together was a happy one. The day was crisp and clear, the sea pearly blue as they made their way to Mass. Bridie had insisted on staying behind to make the dinner, to give Kate a day off, and Maisie walked contentedly between them, wrapped in a new purple scarf and hat that Catherine had chosen for her.

When they returned, Catherine was puzzled by strange whining and scratching noises behind the bedroom door.

'What you got in there?' she asked suspiciously. 'The turkey escaped?'

Bridie laughed. 'Go on, open the door and let the darling out.'

The moment Catherine did so, a small white-haired terrier came scurrying out, skidding across the linoleum with a bark of excitement. He ran around her legs, then raced around the table, leaping up at Kate.

'Oh, get down!' she shrieked.

Maisie screamed and clapped her hands, which only made him bark louder. Catherine went at once to pet him. 'You're a bonny lad, what's your name?'

'That's for you to decide,' Bridie smiled. 'He's yours. My present to you.'

Catherine gave a cry of delight. 'Mine? That's wonderful!' She crouched down and cuddled the dog, allowing him to lick her face.

'I knew you'd love him,' Bridie grinned. 'Had the Townsends keep him overnight – went and fetched him this morning.'

Catherine laughed as she played with the dog. 'Aren't you a dark horse, keeping a secret like this! It's the best Christmas present I've ever had.'

Kate snorted. 'It's the daftest! This is no place for keepin' dogs – and who's ganin' to look after it while you're at work? Muggins here, that's who.'

Catherine was quick to reassure her. 'I'll take him to work with me – walk him at dinner time.'

She saw the look of fear on Maisie's face. 'Would you like to stroke him?' she asked gently. 'He sounds fierce, but he's a big softy, I can tell.'

'Go on, girl,' Bridie encouraged, leaning forward to pet the dog. 'Like this.'

Maisie crept forward and touched him on his rump. He whipped round and jumped at her, licking her hand. The girl squealed and froze, but he kept jumping and licking. Catherine grabbed him and held him firm.

'Now try,' she said.

Maisie put out a tentative hand and patted his head. The dog stayed still in Catherine's arms. She could feel his heart pounding and felt a surge of love towards the animal, so trusting in her arms. Maisie grew bolder and stroked his wiry coat.

Catherine glanced at her mother, keeping a wary distance. 'Do you want a stroke?'

Kate sniffed. 'Don't give tuppence for dogs – dirty, smelling things.'

Catherine was too entranced by the young dog to mind. She laughed, 'That's what I'll call you, bonny lad. Tuppence.' She put her face next to his. 'A Tuppence worth of love, that's what you are.'

She knew what would sweeten her mother's temper and nodded to Bridie. 'We could open that bottle of sherry now. Toast our new family member.'

Bridie was quick to fetch three glasses and pour out the drinks. Kate's eyes lit at the sight of the bottle, which had been hidden in Catherine and Bridie's bedroom. She finished hers in two swigs and poured herself another without asking.

'I'll get the dinner served,' Bridie said.

'There's no hurry,' said Kate, her expression relaxing as a warm flush crept into her cheeks.

But Catherine nodded in agreement. 'I'll set the table and carve the bird.'

They sat down to a feast of turkey and chestnut stuffing, vegetables and bread sauce. Catherine put the sherry bottle away, but brought out the bottle of beer she had promised Kate. Kate was easily intoxicated, but her mood was merry and the chatter light-hearted as they tucked into the food. Catherine slipped a piece of meat to Tuppence.

'Shouldn't spoil him,' Kate warned. 'He'll be eating off the plates next.'

'She's right,' Bridie said, wagging a finger.

Catherine looked down at the expectant face waiting for more. 'It's his Christmas too,' she said, ignoring their advice and dropping him another shred of turkey.

'Soft as clarts, my lass,' Kate snorted.

'Yes, she is,' Bridie agreed with a warm smile, 'that's why we all love her.'

Catherine blushed and laughed. But, just for a moment, she caught a look in Kate's eye. Was it annoyance or alarm? A glint of anger almost as she looked at Bridie. Then she was swigging at her beer and laughing too.

'Mind you, she wasn't always sweetness and light,' Kate declared. 'Was a right bossy madam with the neighbours' bairns – always wanting to be leader. And the dares she got up to, nearly turned me white-haired, she did. Used to play on the timbers down the Slake – deep as the sea at high tide – if she'd fallen in that would've been it. And there was that lad Billy. Have I ever told you about the time—'

'Stop it, Kate!' Catherine said in sudden agitation. 'Bridie doesn't want to hear all that tittle-tattle from years ago.'

Bridie looked between the two of them, her face alert to the sudden change in mood. Catherine got up abruptly and went to fetch the second bottle of beer she had got in reserve. She put it in front of Kate with a warning look.

'No more stories,' she said lightly. Turning to Bridie she smiled. 'That was a lovely dinner. How about we take Tuppence for a walk before it gets dark?'

'What about the plum puddin'?' Kate cried.

'I'm too full for that just now,' Catherine said. 'Some fresh air will give us an appetite for the rest.'

'That suits me,' Bridie said, getting up quickly.

'Well, me and Maisie will stay and play snap,' Kate announced, 'won't we, hinny?'

'Snap,' Maisie repeated.

Catherine felt relief at the decision. What did it matter if Kate drank all the beer while they were out? It was only for one day in the year.

The two friends enjoyed a chill, bracing walk in the fading light down to the harbour. The warm lights from houses and the sound of a piano being played in an upstairs room gave Catherine a contented feeling, as she hung on to Tuppence's new leather rein and hurried after him.

They paused by the harbour wall. The sea glinted bronze under the wintry setting sun.

'What was all that about a boy called Billy?' Bridie suddenly asked.

Catherine's heart jolted. 'Nothing,' she said dismissively. 'Just a prank that went wrong. Lad fell off the timbers and went into the Slake, nearly drowned. Us other bairns got a good hiding for it. That's all.'

'But it still upsets you?' Bridie said quietly.

Catherine shrugged. 'Haven't thought of it for years. Just don't like the way Kate keeps bringing up the past once she's had a drink inside her. You never know what fanciful tales she's going to come out with.'

Bridie put an arm about her. 'She can say what she likes, it doesn't change a thing. I'll still think the best of you. Even if you were a bossy little madam,' she teased.

'I never was!'

Bridie gave a raucous laugh. 'You couldn't run a laundry if you didn't have a little bit of the bossiness in you.'

Catherine laughed abruptly too. 'No, I suppose you're right.'

Somehow, her friend always managed to make her see the funny side, so her anxiety vanished. Together they returned with the panting dog, who flopped in happy exhaustion by the electric fire.

Drawing the curtains against the dark, they ate the plum pudding and the tea of scones and cake that Kate had baked the day before. Bridie turned on the wireless and they listened to an orchestra while playing cards and drinking tea.

Kate fell asleep by the fire and Catherine read a story to Maisie until they were all too sleepy to stay awake. On her way to bed, Catherine checked to see if the sherry bottle was still hidden at the bottom of her wardrobe. It was there, with half the sherry still untouched. Catherine lay down with Tuppence curled up at her feet, feeling full and drowsily contented. It had turned out to be the best Christmas she could remember for an age.

It was only much later, after Boxing Day and when they were back at work, did she think to check the sherry bottle more closely. Kate had drunk its contents and replaced them with cold tea.

Chapter 33

At first Kate managed to cover up her drinking. Catherine was pleased that her mother seemed to warm to their new dog, Tuppence, and offered to take him for walks in the short January afternoons.

'Makes a purpose of ganin' out,' Kate said. 'And Maisie's taken a shine to him – keeps the lass from under me feet when I'm busy in the kitchen.'

So Catherine walked the boisterous puppy in the dark early mornings and then left him in Kate's care. That winter was a busy one at the workhouse laundry, with an increase in destitute inmates and unemployed vagrants seeking a bed for the night. Catherine and Bridie worked long and hard, happy to return home to one of Kate's hot meals and Tuppence's frantic welcome.

Often Catherine was so exhausted, she went straight to bed after tea, Bridie and Kate vying to make the most fuss over her.

'I'll bring you in a cup of tea, hinny,' Kate offered.

'No, it's rest she needs, not more of your tea.' Bridie was adamant.

'What's wrong with me tea?' Kate bristled.

'It's so strong it'll keep her awake till the small hours.'

'I've always made it like that – the lass likes it that way, don't you, Kitty?'

Catherine felt tired just listening to them. 'I don't need anything, thank you. I just want to sleep.'

'There you are!' Bridie said with satisfaction. 'Leave the girl be. We don't want her wearing herself out and bringing on one of those bleeds.'

'I know more about them than you do,' Kate snorted.

Catherine shot Bridie a pleading look and her friend swallowed a retort.

Suddenly she smiled. 'Of course you do,' Bridie agreed. 'You're her mother, aren't you? We both want what's best for the girl.' She turned to Catherine. 'You get yourself to bed. Kate and I will sit by the fire and

211

finish the pot of tea together and maybe have a wee game of cards. Won't we, Kate?'

Kate was quite disarmed by the sudden charm, and meekly agreed. It occurred to Catherine, as she lay in bed listening to them chatting in the next room, that it suited Bridie to keep in with Kate. How else would Maisie be able to stay with her? If Kate withdrew her co-operation, Maisie would have to go back to Ireland.

So Catherine ignored the small telltale signs that something was wrong at home: a carelessly broken plate blamed on Maisie, scorched ironing, milk put away in the cupboard instead of the pantry. At times Kate seemed absent-minded, but she never smelt of drink, just strongly of lily of the valley given to her for Christmas.

It was a Saturday in February, when Catherine was taking the dog for a walk around the old town with Maisie, that Tuppence pulled her into the doorway of a public house.

'Not in there,' Catherine said, pulling him away. The dog barked at the door. Maisie stood waiting. 'Come on, Tuppence,' Catherine urged, but he barked louder.

Just then the door swung open and a small, stout man in a mustard-coloured waistcoat came out.

'Hello, old fellow,' he chuckled, patting Tuppence fondly. 'Didn't expect you here today. Haven't got your bone.' He glanced up. 'Hello, Maisie.' He gave Catherine a quizzical look. 'You walking the old boy for Kate, are you?'

Catherine gawped at him. 'This is my dog,' she stuttered.

The man looked disbelieving but shrugged. 'Well, you're welcome to come in, miss. Any friend of Tuppence is a friend of mine,' he joked.

Catherine looked at him indignantly. 'I most certainly won't be coming in.' She yanked on the dog's lead and dragged him off down the lane, calling sharply to Maisie to follow.

By the time they got to the harbour wall, she was seething with anger. She turned on Maisie.

'How many times have you been to the Penny Luck with Kate?'

Maisie stared at the fishing boats as if she had not heard.

'Do you go in there with her?' Catherine demanded. When the girl said nothing, Catherine seized her by the arm and shook her. 'Answer me! Do you and Kate go drinking together?'

Maisie met her look, her eyes wide with terror. She pulled away whimpering and began to cry out for her mother. Catherine tried to calm her down.

'I'm sorry, I didn't mean to be cross with you. You haven't done anything wrong. It's Kate I'm mad with.' She stroked the girl's hair as Bridie did to soothe her, but Maisie would not stop wailing.

'Come on,' Catherine said quickly, 'we'll go to the sweetshop on the way home, get some pear drops.' They were Maisie's favourite. The crying subsided a little and Catherine linked arms with the girl and set off briskly.

By the time they reached the sweetshop, Maisie was quiet again. As they drew near to home, Catherine felt sick with dread at confronting her mother.

On the steps, Maisie said between sucks of her sweet, 'Just a wee nip to keep out the cold. A wee nip for Kate and a poke of sweets for Maisie. Our little secret.'

Bridie, who had been out at the hairdresser's, was sitting at the table sewing. Catherine went barging into Kate's bedroom, where she was resting, and began pulling out drawers. Tuppence raced in, barking.

'Where do you hide it?' she demanded, searching through her clothes.

'What you doing?' Kate asked in alarm. 'You've no right—'

'You're drinking again,' Catherine accused, 'buying whisky with my money! How could you? And taking that poor lass into that terrible place, an' all. Not to mention my dog!'

Suddenly she found it, an almost empty half-bottle of whisky, pushed inside a slipper under the bed. She brandished it at Kate.

'How long have you been back on the bottle? I must be green as grass to think you'd got over it. You lied to me – and Bridie. You promised . . .!'

Kate heaved herself off the bed. 'Don't go all holy,' she said scornfully. 'You're hardly little miss perfect with your lady friend here.'

'What's that supposed to mean?' Catherine demanded.

'You and her – grown lasses sharing a bed. It's not natural.' Kate shot Bridie a withering look as she stood behind Catherine, open-mouthed at the argument.

Catherine went puce with indignation. 'You and your filthy mind. *We* used to share a bed, remember? It's no different.'

Kate snapped, 'There's a world of difference. I'm your mam.'

'And that's what Bridie is to me,' Catherine retorted, 'like a mother. So don't bring her into this. You're the one at fault.'

'Oh, am I?' Kate blazed back. 'And is it my fault I'm stuck here on me own all day with daft Maisie and having to clean up after that wild dog?' She shoved Tuppence out of the way. 'You'd never have noticed if the lass hadn't told you. Never says a word all day long, then spills the beans about our little drink.'

Bridie cried, 'You've been taking my girl into pubs? You wicked woman!'

'She enjoys herself,' Kate defended. 'At least the folk in there pay her some attention – more than she gets round here.'

'How dare you?' Bridie raged, barging past Catherine. But Catherine caught her arm.

'No, I'll deal with her, you see to Maisie.'

She could hear the girl whimpering in the background. She pushed Bridie towards the door and shut it behind her. She faced Kate as calmly as she could.

'This can't go on. It's my house you're living in, remember. I'm the one paying for it all, and I'll not have you drinking away my wages like Grandda did yours.'

At this, Kate capitulated, her shoulders sagging in defeat.

'I'm sorry, lass, I cannot help it. I need a little bit of comfort to get me through the day.' She gave a bleak look. 'I'm fifty with nowt to me name. I never see me husband – I'm a fish out of water here, yet I've nowt to gan back for. I need some'at to do, Kitty, not just making the tea for you and your friend. I need to work. I'm better when I'm graftin'. Find me some'at to do, hinny,' she pleaded.

Catherine leant against the door, at a loss as to what to do. A moment ago, she had been ready to throw her mother out, force her back north. She was Davie's problem, not hers. But looking at the forlorn woman hunched on the bed, she knew she could not wash her hands of Kate. She would give her another chance.

'Give me a few days to think it over,' Catherine sighed.

'You'll not send me back to Jarrow?' Kate whispered.

Catherine shook her head.

Kate gave a trembling smile. 'Ta, Kitty, you're a good lass.'

Catherine braced herself. 'But you and Maisie aren't to go anywhere near the Penny Luck again. Promise?'

'Aye,' Kate agreed, wiping her eyes with her sleeve.

Catherine saw from the earnest look on Kate's face that she meant to try, but deep down she doubted whether her mother could ever keep such a promise.

Chapter 34

'Beautiful house, isn't it?' said a woman in passing. 'Shame to see it go to rack and ruin like that.'

Catherine looked round, startled out of her reverie and embarrassed to have been caught peering through the railings at the neglected gardens and house beyond. She had first noticed it on her way to work months ago, when the falling autumn leaves had revealed a red-brick mansion with a quaint turret and large shuttered windows. It looked mysterious and beckoning with its 'For Sale' sign at the gate, as if challenging her to explore further.

'Yes, a shame,' Catherine murmured. 'Surprised no one's bought it yet.'

The woman shook her head. 'My uncle used to deliver tea there,' she confided. 'Belonged to a man who'd made his money in India – had foreign servants, Uncle Vic said. That's the trouble, you see. House that size needs plenty servants and no one wants to do that sort of work now, do they?'

Catherine nodded at the woman and made to move off.

'Course, you could run it as a boarding house, I suppose,' the stranger commented.

Catherine looked at her startled, then realised the woman had not meant her in particular. But all that day at work she could not rid her thoughts of the idea. She was drawn to the place's fading grandeur. The house of a wealthy gentleman. It was crying out to be loved and nurtured back to life. A mansion so similar to the ones in her childish daydreams that it almost seemed as if fate had led her to its gates.

Stop being so fanciful! Such a house was far out of her reach. But a little later she was speculating again as to how many bedrooms it had and how many lodgers it could take. Kate could look after the place and there would be residents to keep her company. It was too far out of the town centre for her to sneak out to the pub as

215

she could now, and Catherine knew she was still nipping into the Penny Luck.

Only yesterday she had found a cough medicine bottle filled with whisky in the kitchen cupboard. When confronted, Kate had denied it was hers and gone into a rant about Bridie, saying she had done it to get her into trouble.

'All lies, you old soak,' Bridie had scoffed, only riling Kate the more.

Catherine knew she had to get her mother away from town and out from under Bridie's feet as soon as possible, if their household was to survive. Before the day was out, she rang the estate agent's office and made an appointment to see The Hurst.

On the Saturday, she took Bridie with her to look around. Catherine was captivated by its sweep of daffodils up the drive and its mature trees that would make it secluded in summer.

'Look, it's got a tennis court,' Bridie exclaimed. 'Think of the tennis parties we could have!'

The agent led them through a series of grand rooms on the ground floor.

'Smells a bit musty,' Catherine said cautiously, peering into the gloom of the drawing room, with its gaping fireplace.

'Just needs a bit of a spring-clean,' Bridie declared.

'Quite so,' said the agent. 'It's been empty for over a year. This is the way to the billiard room.'

'Billiard room?' Bridie squealed. 'More parties!'

'How many rooms altogether?' Catherine gulped, as they followed him back into the hall. Two large china urns with exotic birds still stood either side of the large central staircase.

'Fifteen. It's what you'd expect of a gentleman's residence,' the agent said, ushering them upstairs.

Catherine could imagine how grand it must once have been. It still smelt of faded cigar smoke and vinegar polish, of dried roses. She half expected to see one of the Indian servants dressed in a vivid turban, emerging with a silver tray and tea set. In mounting excitement, she followed the agent, clutching Bridie's arm.

They lost count of the bedrooms. The kitchen was antiquated, with a huge old black range, but there was a separate butler's pantry, a cook's sitting room and a system of bells to call for service, which still worked.

'We can ring for Kate to bring us up tea and toast in the morning,' Bridie joked.

'If you want it poured over your head, you mean,' Catherine snorted.

'Oh, Catherine, it's a dream house, so it is. Maisie will love the gardens – and so will Tuppence. Say you'll buy it!'

Catherine tried to quell her own excitement. There seemed so much work to be done. Panes of glass were missing or broken in half a dozen windows, and at least three of the rooms had pails and saucepans catching drips from the leaking roof.

'And finally, the garden room.' The agent led them into the glass-domed conservatory to the side of the house.

As they entered, a wall of warmth enveloped them and a pungent smell of plants. Some hothouse blooms had survived – someone must have come in to tend them – and they were already flowering in the early spring sunshine. The room led on to the small terrace and a lawn with a sagging tennis net. Beyond was a bank of rhododendrons and mature trees.

For a brief instant, Catherine was reminded of the view from Ravensworth Castle, the sweep of lawns and bushes rolling away from the aristocratic mansion. A Ravensworth in miniature. She blinked hard. A ridiculous comparison, of course, but how she longed to possess such a place! At that moment, she desired it more than anything she had ever wanted before. Kitty McMullen, owner of a gentleman's residence. She would pay for a busload of her old neighbours and school friends to come from Jarrow just to see it! Then there would be no more scoffing and turning up their noses. How they would regret ever excluding her from their games . . .

'Catherine?' Bridie was shaking her arm. 'The gentleman's wanting your opinion.'

The agent was watching her with detached interest. He obviously thought she was wasting his time and could not afford it.

'I want to buy it,' she declared with a defiant look. 'It'll take a few days to get the money in place. Perhaps we could go back to your office to discuss the price?'

The man tried to hide his surprise and nodded quickly. Catherine's heart was hammering at her recklessness. It would take every penny of her savings to put down the deposit and she would have to cash in the insurance policies Maurice had got her to buy. She might be paying off the mortgage with all her salary for evermore, but she would do it.

Bridie was spluttering with delight and gabbling plans all the way down the hill to town.

'Once we've shifted the dirt and given it a splash of paint it'll look like a palace. Everyone will want to stay at The Hurst – we'll get quality folk, so we will. And Kate's used to lodgers. She'll love being the lady of the manor. No time for the drink. And we can get the groceries delivered, so there's no excuse to be popping into town. Oh, girl, we're going to have such a time!'

It took over a month for the finances to be put in place and the sale completed, weeks in which Catherine's nerve almost failed her. She must be quite mad to be saddling herself with a run-down mansion, bargain though it was, wiping out her hard-earned savings that, over the years, she had put by, earning good interest, for 'a rainy day'. She had always been so cautious with money, fearful of being reduced to the plight of those who had no option but to knock on the workhouse door. Now here she was gambling it all on a dream.

But then she thought of how this venture might be the saving of Kate and a new beginning for them all. It was only lowly Kitty of the New Buildings who was afraid of taking on such a place. Catherine McMullen, senior officer of Hastings Poor Law Institute and member of the tennis club, had no such qualms. The Hurst was a fitting home for such a professional woman.

So, just before she turned twenty-seven, Catherine became the sole owner of a home that could have housed half of William Black Street in Jarrow. The day they moved in and set to work scrubbing down walls and floors, Catherine thought of her friend Lily Hearn. So often in the past they'd had conversations about their future dreams, of marrying rich men and living in luxury. She was the only one Catherine had ever confided in about her yearning to discover her father and the privileged world that should have been hers.

As Catherine fell into bed that night, aching all over from the back-breaking cleaning, she knew Lily would have understood her obsession to possess The Hurst. It went beyond a craving for security. It was as if she were fulfilling the destiny that was snatched away from her even before she was born. She was a Pringle-Davies, an owner of property, a respectable middle-class woman. And she had done it all without the help of any man – father or husband.

Chapter 35

It was summer before The Hurst was in any state to open its doors to boarders. The boiler had to be replaced, and Catherine and Bridie scoured the auction rooms for second-hand furniture to furnish the bedrooms. For the first time in over two years Catherine had the luxury of her own bedroom – a beautiful room at the front of the house, with a view over the garden. She slept with the curtains open so that she woke gradually in the early light to the sound of birdsong and watched the dawn filter through the trees. It was the most tranquil part of the day, just her and the birds and sunshine on leaves. But at the end of each month Catherine had nothing left in the bank and she still had to pay the lease on the maisonette in Laurel Street. She sublet it and placed advertisements in the local newspapers for lodgers for The Hurst.

'We can share a room again,' Bridie suggested. 'Then you can rent out that nice one at the front at a higher price.'

Catherine was reluctant to give up the room but Bridie was right. Within two days they had a retired major for the large front bedroom. He brought a battered old trunk and a wind-up gramophone.

'Happy to share my record collection,' said Major Holloway, plonking a box of records in the sitting room. Kate and Bridie rushed to look through them.

'Never heard of half of these,' Kate said in disappointment.

'Opera, my dear lady,' the major chuckled, putting one on the turntable and winding up the brass handle. They sat and listened.

'What was all that about?' Kate said at the end. 'Didn't catch a word of it.'

'The tenor was singing in Italian, dear lady,' said Major Holloway. 'The language of love.'

Kate gave him a dubious look. 'Give me a good north-country song any day,' she sniffed, and went off to make tea.

Over the next few weeks the number of residents grew. A pale, willowy young woman called Dorothy was brought by her parents.

'Needs to be by the sea for the air, doctor says,' her mother explained in hushed tones. 'The air in London's making her ill.' They left in a shiny black Ford, promising to visit every month. Dorothy stood forlornly looking down the drive until Catherine coaxed her back inside with the promise of cherry cake.

Two more came by July: a thin-faced piano tuner and a ventriloquist who talked to himself at mealtimes. They were joined by a retired merchant seaman, who liked to shave in the open-air, a retired cook from a boarding school and a reclusive poet who stayed in his room all day and prowled around the house at night, helping himself to food from the kitchen, to Kate's alarm.

'Scared me out of me wits,' she complained, 'sitting by the stove eating cold stew in the middle of the night.'

'What were you doing up at that hour?' Catherine asked suspiciously.

'Couldn't sleep, that's what,' Kate mumbled. 'You'll have to tell him he can't gan creepin' round like a ghost.'

'I can hardly lock him in his room.'

Kate grumbled. 'They're a queer lot – not workin' lads like we used to have lodging with us.'

Catherine snorted. 'They were just as mixed a bag as these ones. And as long as they're all paying and not harming anyone, doesn't matter what they're like.'

She felt sympathy for the solitary poet, who never seemed to get anything written, for wan Dorothy, whose parents did not visit as promised, and wheezing Mrs Fairy, the retired cook, who hung about the kitchen offering to help, not knowing what to do with retirement. She felt protective towards them and tried to shield them from Kate's impatience and Bridie's teasing.

But it worried Catherine to think Kate might not be able to cope. After all, it was ten years since she had last taken in lodgers. She was snappy and bad-tempered in the mornings when Catherine and Bridie were rushing to work, then full of petty complaints on their return in the evening. Tom, the piano tuner, had left his false teeth in the sink, Mrs Fairy had used up all the sugar in a chocolate cake for Maisie and made the girl sick. Barny, the ventriloquist, had upset Harold, the poet, by practising his noisy monkey routine all morning and Harold was demanding to sleep in the tower.

220

'And I think that Dorothy's got the consumption,' Kate warned, 'coughing all over the place. That's why she's been dumped here. We'll all die of it if you let her stay. Me father and sister Margaret died like that. Terrible business. Lass should be in the sanatorium.'

Catherine, already exhausted by a long hot day at the laundry, had to roll up her sleeves and help with the evening meal, calming tempers and charming the guests and Kate back into good humour.

Only the cheerful major seemed oblivious to Kate's grumbles or the tensions between the other residents. As long as he had music playing on his gramophone he was happy, and turned a deaf ear to those who did not appreciate opera as much as he. Sometimes, Catherine would enjoy sitting in the conservatory on a late summer's evening with Major Holloway listening to Puccini or Verdi and watching the shadows steal across the lawn.

He would talk about his army days in South Africa and the Middle East, until Bridie would come and scold them for staying up late.

'Look at you yawning – big enough to swallow us all. Up to bed this minute, my girl. Major, you can sleep till noon but Miss McMullen must be up with the lark.'

The major blustered with apologies and shut the lid of the gramophone. Catherine thought he was probably frightened of Bridie. Bridie certainly had as little time for him as Kate.

'Shouldn't let him keep you up to all hours,' she fussed as they got into bed.

'He doesn't. I choose to sit in my own garden room and he happens to be there.'

'Only when you are,' Bridie sniffed. 'He's got his sights set on you – and this place, I wouldn't wonder.'

Catherine laughed. 'Don't be silly. He's much too old.'

'And you're much too soft-hearted,' Bridie declared. 'I know he's sometimes late with his rent and what do you do? Not a thing.'

'Only the once,' Catherine protested.

'It'll cause bad feeling if the others get to hear of it.'

'Well, they won't, will they? Not unless you tell them.' Catherine gave her a warning look. 'And what people pay and when they pay it is my concern.'

'Well, that's gratitude for you!' Bridie cried. 'And after I've worked my hands to the bone helping get this place nice for you. I'm just an unpaid maid in your eyes!'

Catherine was quick to placate her. 'Of course you're not. You're my best friend,' she insisted. 'This is your home as much as mine.'

Bridie was soon mollified, but after that, Catherine was careful to avoid being left alone with the major. For some reason Bridie seemed jealous of the genial man and Catherine did not want to upset her friend. But soon her worries over Kate overshadowed any arguments over the major.

Her mother's behaviour was becoming increasingly erratic. Some days she was full of a manic energy, cleaning windows at six in the morning and singing at the top of her voice; on others she was listless and bad-tempered, and Catherine had to shake her awake.

'They're all waiting for their breakfast,' Catherine cried.

'You get it,' Kate mumbled, and buried her head under the covers.

Catherine left in exasperation, knowing that she would have to serve breakfast and be late for work. Mrs Fairy came to the rescue.

'Leave it to me,' the old cook offered. 'I can whip up some scrambled eggs and young Maisie can help me.'

Catherine gratefully accepted, even though she knew Kate would be indignant about it later in the day.

As she walked to work with Bridie, her friend abruptly said, 'I'm sure Kate's drinking again. The way she's acting.'

Catherine was shocked by the suggestion. Yet Bridie was only voicing her own unspoken fear.

'I haven't seen her at it, have you?' Catherine countered.

'She's sly – drinking after we've all gone to bed, I reckon. That's why she's like a bear with a sore head some mornings.'

'But she can't be,' Catherine said wildly. 'She doesn't go out – I know that from Mrs Fairy. She hasn't set foot in a pub since we moved. And I don't give her any money.'

Bridie just shrugged.

Catherine's heart sank. 'Oh, Bridie, I hope you're wrong. I don't know what I'd do if she started all that again.'

Unexpectedly, while Catherine was trying to work out how to confront her mother, Davie turned up on leave. At first, she welcomed his arrival. Kate's humour improved and Davie was eager to help out doing odd jobs around the house. There was so much to be done: rotten window frames to replace, roof tiles to fix, gutters to clean. But after a week, Kate grew impatient.

'He's not here to mend your palace,' she complained, 'he's here to see me. Haway, Davie lad, I'm ganin' to show you the sights of Hastings.'

Catherine felt leaden. She knew just what sights her mother had in mind. She tried to warn Davie.

'She's promised me she's off the drink. Please don't let her start again – don't give her any money.' But even as she pleaded with her stepfather, she knew he was not strong enough to keep Kate in check. By the way he looked at Kate, Catherine knew Davie still idolised his wife and would do anything to keep her happy.

'I'm only here another week,' he said with an apologetic glance. 'A week won't make a difference.'

But by the end of Davie's leave, Kate was in defiant mood. The day he left, Catherine found her openly swigging whisky from a teacup in the kitchen. Catherine seized it from her and dashed the dregs into the sink.

'Where's the rest of it?' Catherine demanded angrily.

'Drunk it,' Kate slurred. 'And why not? Me Davie's gone; was drowning me sorrows. He's the only one who cares.'

'The only one who'll buy you drink, you mean,' Catherine said impatiently. 'Well, the party's over.' She faced her mother. 'There's to be no more of it, do you hear?'

Suddenly Kate burst into tears. 'I cannot bear it,' she sobbed. 'Me own daughter hates me. You just want a skivvy, that's all.'

'That's not true,' Catherine said, trying to keep her temper. 'I've given you a home, haven't I? This place is costing me a fortune, but I did it for you. You're the one wanted a job to do, remember?'

'They all hate me,' Kate whimpered. 'Look down their posh noses. And you're just the same now.' She got up, swaying. 'I'll gan back to Jarrow. I'll gan now.' She took a few unsteady steps towards the door, banging into the kitchen table. Kate clutched her hip in pain.

Catherine reached out. 'Don't talk daft. You're going to bed to sleep it off.'

Kate tried to push her away, but Catherine was stronger and marched her to the door. Mrs Fairy was in the corridor and came to help.

'Banged her hip on the table,' Catherine said briskly. 'She's going to lie down for a bit.'

The stout cook asked no questions as she helped get Kate up the stairs and into her bedroom. Afterwards the woman said, 'I'll help with the Sunday tea. Let her sleep it off.'

Catherine smiled gratefully. 'Thanks, but I can't keep relying on you to come to the rescue.'

'Why not? Cooking's been my life, dearie,' Mrs Fairy beamed.

'Well, I'll deduct some of your rent this month,' Catherine offered quickly. The older woman gave a shrug of agreement. No doubt Bridie would scold her for her readiness to reduce the cook's rent, but the arrangement was only fair.

Catherine added more awkwardly, 'And, Mrs Fairy, could you keep an eye on my mother – let me know if she – er – gets herself in a similar state again?'

Mrs Fairy nodded. She was a Methodist and had texts on her bedroom wall urging temperance and godliness. She would be an ally in controlling Kate.

But as the autumn wore on, Catherine's worst fears were confirmed. 'She drinks rum with Mr Wilkie in the summerhouse,' Mrs Fairy reported.

Catherine gawped in amazement. The retired merchant seaman was a keen gardener and was out in all weathers sweeping up leaves and clearing the flowerbeds.

'She takes him out a cup of tea mid-afternoon,' Mrs Fairy continued, 'and doesn't come back in for an hour. Leaves Maisie to mind the fire and the stove on her own. And that's not all. She's ordering alcohol with the groceries. Couldn't work out where she was hiding it, till I came across a bottle of vodka in the drying room – down behind the pipes.'

'With the groceries?' Catherine cried in disbelief. 'But I pay the bills. There's never been any charge for vodka.'

'Must have it down as something else,' the old cook suggested.

Catherine went straight to her desk and riffled through the bills. When she looked closer, some of the amounts seemed excessive. One week there was a huge weight of flour ordered, the next enough boot polish to wax the footwear of a regiment. More recently there seemed to have been a large volume of cleaning gumption ordered twice weekly.

A telephone call to the grocer's confirmed that two bottles of whisky or vodka a week had been added to the bill in the guise of other groceries, under instruction from Mrs McDermott.

'Sorry, missus,' the clerk apologised, 'but she said it was in case some of the teetotal residents signed for the packages and got offended. Said it was for medicinal purposes.'

Catherine gave him short shrift. 'In future you are to ignore any requests from Mrs McDermott. Either Mrs McKim or I will be ringing in the orders from now on. If there's any alcohol delivered here again, I shall take my business elsewhere.'

She told Bridie the whole story that night. 'What shall I do? I don't trust her. And I can't ask Mrs Fairy to watch her all hours of the day. She's already helping out in the kitchen more than she should, Kate's getting that unreliable with the meals.'

'You're right,' Bridie agreed. 'She can't be trusted. Leaving my Maisie to put coal on the fire – she could have us up in flames.' Bridie was indignant. 'The only answer is for one of us to be here all the time.'

Catherine was dismayed. 'But I can't. We need every penny of my salary to keep this roof over our heads.'

'Then it'll have to be me,' Bridie said in resignation. 'The money we save on Kate's drinking will probably cover the loss of my wages,' she added with a weak laugh.

When they confronted Kate, she went on the attack.

'It's all lies! Me and Wilkie drink tea, that's all. That fat old cook, sticking her nose in – she's just jealous 'cos he's friendly with me and not her.'

'I know how you're getting it,' Catherine said. 'I've spoken to the grocer.'

Kate flushed. ''Twas just the odd half-bottle now and then. For me aches and pains. Am I not allowed a bit medicine? You work us that hard.'

'Well, it won't be necessary from now on,' Catherine told her sharply. 'Bridie's giving up her job to help you run The Hurst. She's in charge from now on – and that includes the ordering.'

Kate banged her fist on the kitchen table, making Maisie jump.

'That's not fair! This is my job.'

'It's too much for you,' Catherine said, trying to keep calm.

'That's right,' Bridie smiled. 'It's a huge weight on your shoulders. Together we'll get on grand – make this the best boarding house in Hastings, eh?'

Kate glared at them. 'You're both against me, the pair of you. You want me out.'

'No we don't—'

'Aye, you do. *She* wants me out!' Kate jabbed a finger at Bridie. 'Wants you all for hersel'. Pretends to be all sweetness and light, till your back's turned.'

'Stop it,' Catherine ordered. 'There's no need to be nasty to Bridie. It's my decision. I want her here to keep an eye on things – and I want you to stop drinking.'

Kate clenched her fists, her face contorted suddenly into a mask of hate. Catherine stepped backwards, fearful that her mother would hit

225

her. Maddened, Kate whirled round, picked up a pretty milk jug from the table and dashed it on to the stone hearth. Maisie screamed as it shattered into a dozen shards.

With a roar of anger, Kate barged past them and stormed from the room, slamming the door behind her so that the windows shook. Catherine clutched the back of a chair, her heart pounding with fear and relief.

Maisie began to wail, 'Auntie Kate's angry with Maisie.'

'No, pet,' Catherine tried to reassure her, 'just with me.'

Bridie cuddled her daughter. 'There's no need for tears, girl. It's all right. Auntie Kate's in a mood. It'll blow over like the rain.' She went to Catherine and hugged her. 'Don't worry, I'll sort your mother out.'

Catherine could not stop shaking. 'This is what it was always like,' she whispered, 'rages and fighting. That's what I came here to get away from. I can't stand all that again.' She gave Bridie a desperate look.

'You won't have to,' Bridie said stoutly. 'I'll see to that.' She kissed Catherine on the forehead like a child. 'Didn't I say I'd take care of you?'

'Yes,' Catherine said, feeling comforted.

'And I always will,' Bridie promised.

Chapter 36

For a time, tempers settled down at The Hurst and Bridie did seem to manage Kate. With a combination of breezy charm and bullying, the Irish woman won Kate's co-operation. Together they were conspirators in thwarting Mrs Fairy's interference in the kitchen. Bridie resented the woman for fussing over Maisie and relaying gossip to Catherine.

'Miss McMullen doesn't need to be bothered with petty problems, Mrs Fairy,' Catherine overheard her friend say one day. 'Me and Mrs McDermott are in charge here, so don't you worry about a thing. Off you go and enjoy a walk to the park while the weather holds.'

Catherine was thankful for Bridie's firm hand. She had enough to cope with at work with turnover of staff and taking on the laundering of a nearby children's home. It was a relief to come home and find the evening meal ready and not be in fear of what else she might find. Often, she was so tired she ate swiftly and went straight to bed. Later, Bridie would come up with a cup of cocoa and relay the gossip of the day to make Catherine laugh. If there was any trouble with Kate, Bridie kept it to herself.

'Sober as a judge,' Bridie laughed, when Catherine asked.

Kate did appear to be off the drink. With Catherine she was wary, keeping out of her way as if she feared another outburst. Only occasionally did Kate let slip a reproachful remark.

When making pastry one evening and supervising Maisie's cutting, she said to the girl, 'Used to do this with Kitty once upon a time. Made pastry-men together. Long ago, before she got too grand for such things.' She shot Catherine a look. 'Not that she'd remember.'

Catherine was stung. 'Course I remember.'

Kate's look was disbelieving.

'I do,' Catherine insisted. 'There was only ever enough pastry left over for one and a half men. You used to say he'd lost his leg in the Boer War.'

A half-smile flickered across Kate's flushed face, then she turned to Maisie. 'See, she only ever remembers the bad things – never enough pastry for madam. Listen to Kitty, you'd think she'd had the worst childhood in the world. She should've had a taste of mine.'

Catherine had left before Kate saw the tears of hurt welling in her eyes and thought she had got the better of her.

Christmas came and most of the residents went to spend it with relations. Only the major, Harold the poet and Mrs Fairy stayed. Catherine was looking forward to a quiet, cosy holiday, when Davie hove back from sea.

'Got a month's leave,' he grinned. 'I can have a proper go at fixing that roof this time.'

But the winds were too wild and Kate forbade him to clamber on any ladders. Torrential rain set in for days and leaks sprung in half a dozen new places. Harold's bed was soaked and he had to move out of the turret into a lower room, which caused him to resume his night rambles. Kate and Davie went out on Christmas Eve morning to fetch chestnuts to roast on the fire and did not return until dark.

They came back drunk, Kate singing at the top of her voice and Davie swirling her around the kitchen in a crazy dance and laughing at nothing in particular. She ordered the major to carry in his gramophone and put on one of his two dance records. Every time it ended, Kate would lurch over to wind it up again.

Mrs Fairy stalked out in disapproval, but Kate was oblivious. She pulled Maisie up and made her dance too. Catherine watched nervously, but Bridie winked at her.

'It's Christmas, she's doing no harm,' her friend whispered, as Kate burst into song again.

Catherine went off to serve supper to the three remaining lodgers, the sound of her mother's raucous singing carrying along the corridor.

'Tomorrow we'll have a nice Christmas dinner all together,' Catherine smiled, hiding her dismay.

'Sounds like some have celebrated enough already,' Mrs Fairy sniffed.

Major Holloway chuckled. 'Like a bit of song and dance my-self, now and again.' He looked shyly at Catherine. 'In fact, there's a dance on at The Imperial on Boxing Day. Wondered if you'd like to go?'

Catherine's spirits lifted. She had not been dancing for so long. The Hurst had consumed all her energies.

'How kind,' she smiled. 'I'll ask Bridie if she'd like to come too.'

His smile faltered. 'Course, Mrs McKim's most welcome,' he mumbled, and dropped his gaze.

Catherine hid her amusement at his invitation. She had no intention of becoming romantically attached to the old soldier. Bridie would be a perfect chaperone.

Christmas Day came. Catherine, Bridie and Maisie trooped off to Mass, unable to rouse Kate or Davie from sleep. When they returned, Kate was bustling about the kitchen, red-eyed but defiantly cheerful. Davie stamped in from the wet with a full hod for the kitchen fire. The damp coal hissed and spat as he shovelled it on.

'You get yourselves along to the sitting room,' Kate ordered. 'I'll see to the dinner.' She refused any help, so Catherine went to join the other guests in a glass of ginger wine. As a Christmas present to each other, she and Bridie had decided on a second-hand piano. It had been delivered in a downpour the day before and Tom Hobbs had tuned it before catching a train to his sister's in London.

Catherine had told Bridie about her disastrous lessons as a girl and her half-hearted attempt to play again while courting Gerald Rolland. But Bridie played a bit and insisted Catherine would love it if she just let herself try. While they sipped drinks in front of a crackling fire, Bridie opened the lid and began to play a jaunty music-hall tune. Then, to the surprise of everyone, Harold stepped forward.

'I'd like to play,' he said simply. He sat flexing his fingers then bent over the keys. After a hesitant start, he began to play 'Greensleeves'. After once through, Harold began to sing the song too. Catherine was amazed at his clear, tuneful voice. She had never heard him sing in the six months he had lived there.

Bridie clapped in delight. 'What talent! You're a dark horse, so you are. Play us another one, Mr Harold.'

He smiled boyishly under his mop of fair hair and played 'Linden Lee'. The others gathered around him and sang along. They were almost finished when the door banged open. Catherine turned to see her mother standing white-faced in the doorway, staring.

Harold finished and the last notes died away. Bridie clapped. Kate limped across the room, her hand outstretched towards Harold, mouthing something. As she reached him, he turned and she stopped abruptly, dropping her hand.

'I thought – it sounded – you looked—' she mumbled in confusion.

229

Catherine stepped round quickly and took her by the arm. 'Doesn't Mr Harold play well, Kate?'

'Mr Harold? Yes . . .'

Her mother looked on the verge of tears.

'Why don't you sit down a minute?' Catherine said in alarm. The last thing she wanted was a scene in front of the residents. 'I'll get you a sip of ginger wine.' It was non-alcoholic, so even Mrs Fairy could not disapprove.

But Kate waved her away, seeming to take control of herself again.

'Whose piano is it?' she demanded.

Bridie said brightly, 'It's ours. Me and Catherine bought it for Christmas. Isn't it just the grandest thing?'

Kate gave Catherine a hard look. 'You've bought a piano?'

Catherine nodded, feeling like a child again under her mother's glare. 'It was Bridie's idea.'

Kate snorted. 'Aye, it would be. No doubt you'll play for her like you never played for me.'

With that, she turned and made for the door, calling, 'Dinner's ready when you've finished your little singsong.'

An awkwardness settled on the group and Harold quietly shut the piano lid. Catherine was annoyed with her mother for spoiling the moment, yet felt a prick of guilt about the piano. Kate had been so keen for her to learn the instrument and play it for a living, but Catherine had resented the pressure and been fearful of the mounting debt of unpaid lessons and payments. It had ended in failure and the humiliation of Kate's piano being repossessed.

Through Christmas lunch, Catherine watched her mother warily for signs of a storm brewing, but Kate's strange mood seemed to have passed. Once they were all full to the brim with turkey and plum pudding, it was Kate who suggested they return to the fire and a singsong around the piano.

'My father used to play "Linden Lee",' she told Harold as she propped herself on a chair by the piano. 'It's one of the few things I remember about him. Will you play it again for me?'

She sang along with tears in her eyes and Catherine felt pity for her mother. It explained her agitated state earlier. Harold's music had conjured up a strong memory of Kate's real father, a man she could hardly recall. Catherine felt a bitter-sweet longing for her own unknown father. Perhaps he had played the piano or sung such songs. She would never know and Kate would never tell her.

Mrs Fairy went for a nap, the major dozed by the fire and Catherine and Bridie went for a walk before the light faded. By the time they returned it was dark and they could see Kate and Davie illuminated in the sitting-room window, swigging from cups and singing, Harold still banging away at the piano.

'Bet that's not tea they're drinking,' Catherine muttered.

Bridie took her arm. 'Don't say anything today. It'll only spoil things. Plenty time to sober her up before the other lodgers come back.'

Catherine sighed. 'Suppose you're right. It's just, whenever Davie's around she drinks like there's no tomorrow.'

'It's 'cos he's there to stand up for her. She knows she can push her luck when her man's around,' Bridie answered. 'You should put him off coming here so much.'

Catherine tried to curb Kate's boisterousness by bringing in tea and fruit cake, and suggesting a game of cards. But her mother ignored her and carried on singing, bullying Harold to keep playing. Eventually he got up.

'I can't play any more,' he announced, and left for the sanctuary of his own room.

'We'll get the major's gramophone then,' Kate cried, and sent Davie to fetch it from the kitchen.

She ordered Davie and the major to push back the furniture and roll up the carpet so they could dance. Mrs Fairy stalked out and Catherine gave up trying to organise a game of whist. She helped Maisie with a game of patience, then left the others dancing and went early to bed.

'There she goes, Miss Misery Guts,' Kate shouted after her. 'Doesn't know how to enjoy herself.'

For a long time Catherine lay in the chilly bedroom listening to her mother's raucous singing, stung by the taunt that she was joyless. Could it be true? As a child she had been happy to stand on the fender and sing for the family. On feast days and Hogmanays she had stayed up late at the houses of cousins or friends and joined in the celebrations.

But a part of her had always held back, frightened that the evening would spin out of control. It might end in a fight or fire irons being hurled across the room. She had to stay awake, be ever vigilant or something would happen to Kate. Predatory hands might come for her in the night, seek her mother out while she lay unconscious with drink.

Once more, Catherine had a vivid memory of a dark shadow looming over the feather bed that she had once shared with Kate in Jarrow. A man was pulling at her mother, breathing hard, cursing and pleading.

'Gerr-off her,' Catherine said in fright. 'Leave our Kate alone!'

But the man ignored her and went on pawing at Kate's prone body, bending over her and breathing his staleness over them both.

'Wake up, Kate,' Catherine whimpered, until finally her mother stirred. Befuddled confusion quickly turned to panic, as Kate tried to push the man off her. She hissed at him and struck out. There was tussling and swearing, then Kate was out of bed and groping for the door. With a blast of cold air she was gone. The back door banged and Catherine heard her feet slapping across the backyard into the privy.

She was left, crouching under the covers, heart hammering while the dark man swayed above her. She held her breath, waiting for him to move, until her lungs nearly burst. Finally he went and she was left shaking in the bed, all alone. She kept awake, waiting and waiting for Kate to return and warm up the space beside her. But she never came. Catherine lay for the rest of the night, listening out for noises, for her mother's return or the thud of the man's big feet and praying, praying for the dawn . . .

Remembering the menace of it now, Catherine lay once again sweating with fear, yet shaking with cold. This was how celebrations ended. Just the sound of her mother's singing and the whisky-fuelled laughter was enough to set her insides churning. How could she ever explain this? Not even fun-loving Bridie would understand. Her friend had stayed below; she thought Catherine was spoiling the fun too. Burying down under the covers, Catherine wished she could share in their light-heartedness.

Boxing Day broke with pale sunshine and a sea becalmed after days of storms. Catherine's spirits lifted at once to see the light glinting through the bare branches, and she determined to put the upsets of the previous day behind her.

She got up and went to cook breakfast for everyone. In the kitchen she found empty whisky and rum bottles on the hearth. The sitting room was littered with dirty glasses and plates, and none of the furniture had been pulled back into place. She was annoyed to think that Bridie would leave everything in such a state. As she set to, Mrs Fairy came wheezing through the door, tutting at the mess.

'I'm sorry—' Catherine began.

'Not your doing,' the old lady replied, and helped her clear up.

Kate and Davie did not appear for breakfast. Bridie sat bleary-eyed, drinking large cupfuls of tea. Sensing Catherine's disapproval, she made no mention of the night before, but talked of the major's plan to take them to the hotel dance that evening.

'Proper dance band,' Bridie enthused, 'and supper served halfway through. I think you should wear that green dress we bought in the sale – with the velvet collar and cuffs. They'll be queuing up to fill your dance card, with you dressed like a princess.'

Catherine laughed, eager at the thought of getting dressed up. The lodgers would begin to return after Boxing Day, so she was going to make the most of her trip out.

She hardly saw Kate or Davie during the day. They disappeared out at lunchtime and only came back as the threesome were on the point of leaving for the dance at The Imperial. Maisie was rushing about feeling their dresses and twirling her own pleated woollen skirt.

Mrs Fairy said, 'Let them go, dearie. We'll have ourselves a bite of supper and a game of snap.'

Kate just stared at them with glassy eyes and said nothing. Catherine picked up her coat and let Major Holloway put it on, eager to be gone. She could not read her mother's mood. Maudlin or belligerent? Certainly not the desperate cheerfulness of Christmas night.

As soon as they got to the hotel, glittering with lights and warmth, Catherine forgot about Kate's look and determined to enjoy every minute of the evening. She danced with the major several times and another man she knew from the tennis club. He invited them over to share a supper table with several others.

They teased her good-naturedly. 'Well, if it isn't the lady of the manor!'

'Where have you been hiding all year?'

'We've missed you, darling.'

Catherine laughed and joked with them about life at The Hurst, and promised she would play more tennis come 1934. She was enjoying herself so much that she hardly noticed how quiet Bridie had become, sitting at her side. It was only when her friend complained of a headache and rose to leave that she realised something was wrong.

'No, you stay and enjoy yourself,' Bridie said, pressing fingers to her brow. 'I'll make my own way home.'

Catherine got up in concern and followed her. 'You can't go back on your own – it's too dark. Can't you just stay a little longer? I've promised the next dance to the major.'

Bridie closed her eyes and shook her head. 'A walk in the fresh air might clear it.'

Catherine sighed. 'No, don't worry, we'll come back now. I'm sure Major Holloway will understand.'

She returned to say goodbye to her friends. As she crossed the ballroom with the major to rejoin Bridie, he murmured, 'You shouldn't let her get her own way all the time. Runs rings round you.'

'Who?' Catherine asked, startled.

'Mrs McKim, of course. Got to show her who's boss. Otherwise you'll have a dog's life.'

Catherine flushed. 'I-I don't know what you're on about.'

His look was pitying. 'No, my dear lady, I don't think you do.'

Baffled by his words, Catherine dismissed them. He was just disappointed at having to go early.

Back at the house, Bridie seemed to revive with a cup of tea. The major excused himself, waving aside Catherine's attempts to thank him for the evening. The house was quiet, with no sign of anyone else still up. They took their tea into the sitting room, lit only by a flickering fire.

With a start, Catherine saw a figure rise up from an armchair in the bay window.

'What a fright!' she gasped.

'S-so the love-birds are back, eh?' Kate's voice was slurred.

Catherine huffed with impatience. 'If you mean me and the major, we—'

'The major?' Kate laughed harshly. 'No, not him.' She staggered forward and knocked over a small drinks table.

Catherine fumbled to switch on the standard lamp before something got broken. Light fell in a pool around them. Kate clutched a chair to steady herself, her face blotchy and hair dishevelled. She was very drunk.

'That one there!' she snarled, pointing a finger at Bridie. 'She's your love-bird.'

'Kate, sit down and stop your daft talk,' Catherine said, trying to steer her to a seat. 'How much have you had to drink?'

'Not enough,' Kate cried, throwing off her daughter's hand. She barged forward to the piano. Catherine saw a row of bottles arranged along the lid. Kate picked one up and took a swig straight from it. It splashed down her chin.

'I hope you've not marked the wood,' Catherine said indignantly.

'Why should I care about your bloody piano?' Kate said savagely. 'You never cared about mine! My little nest egg – all spent on you. Everything on you. Scrimpin' and savin' for lessons. Payin' wi' owt I had – makin' pies for the teacher – jus' for my Kitty. Threw it all back in me face.'

Catherine answered back. 'The piano wasn't paid for – it was taken away. How could I have gone on playing?'

'You never tried,' Kate accused. 'Just to spite me.'

'You never asked me if I wanted to learn in the first place. Would have saved us all a lot of bother if you had.'

'You hate me, don't you? Always have done,' Kate cried. 'I can see it in your eyes – those damned eyes of his!' She swung towards the piano again and seized a bottle in both hands. She took a swig from one and then the other.

'Stop it, Kate—'

'This is what I'm like,' Kate laughed mirthlessly, 'this is yer mother. Not good enough for you.' She poured whisky into her mouth. It splashed down her front. 'A whore and a drunk, that's what your grandda called me. That's what I am.'

Catherine watched in horror as she did the same with the brandy. Suddenly Bridie moved from beside the fire and wrestled the bottles out of Kate's hands.

'Enough,' she decreed. 'Do you want to kill yourself?'

Kate fought back for them, staggered and lost her balance. She fell to the floor, raging.

'You'd like that, wouldn't you? Kill mesel'. I'll do it! Then you two whores can be together.' She picked herself up, panting for breath, her eyes wild.

'Don't say such things,' Catherine cried in disgust.

'It's true,' Kate shouted. 'Actin' all holy to the priest – puttin' on airs for your lodgers. But I know what you're really like – worse than me – you and that creature!' She spat out the words. 'Sharin' a bed. What d'you do in it, eh?'

Catherine was livid. She bunched her fists. 'How dare you! We do nothing but sleep – not like you when we used to share a bed!'

Bridie said, 'Don't, Catherine, you're making it worse.'

But she was too upset to stop. 'Was it with me grandda or one of the lodgers?'

Kate gasped in shock. For a moment they stared at each other, numbed by the hateful words. Then Kate's face contorted in fury. In a flash, she seized one of Davie's hobnailed boots, left on the hearth, and raised it above her head. With a scream of rage, she hurled it straight at Catherine's head.

In that split second, Bridie shoved Catherine. The boot caught Catherine on the side of the head as she turned away. Stunned, she gripped her ear, the pain flaring. Bridie had her arms around her in seconds.

'Are you all right? Let me look. My God, you're bleeding. Come to the kitchen, I'll clean it up.'

Catherine was too shocked to cry.

Bridie steered her from the room. 'You're all right, pet lamb . . .'

Behind them, through ringing ears, Catherine could hear her mother sobbing.

Chapter 37

The next morning, Bridie tried to persuade Catherine to stay in bed.

'You rest,' her friend urged. 'I'll ring Mrs Townsend, tell her you're sick.'

Catherine was tempted. Her head throbbed and she dreaded facing the world, especially Kate. But she knew if she did not, then it would be twice as hard later. She had hardly slept, kept awake by dwelling on their terrible row and the hatred on her mother's face. Her feelings for Kate went beyond resentment and anger; now she feared her mother too. How could they carry on living under the same roof?

She struggled out of bed, feeling weak and nauseous. For the sake of the residents, she must carry on as if nothing had happened. Carefully, she combed her hair over the cut on her ear and dabbed on extra foundation to cover up the bruising to her cheekbone, wincing at the pain.

There was no sign of Kate in the kitchen. With Bridie's help, Catherine made a hasty breakfast and left it in the dining room for the guests to help themselves.

All day, she worried over what to do, but as she was preparing to drag herself home, she saw Bridie waiting for her outside the laundry gates.

'It's all calmed down,' Bridie reported cheerfully. 'Dorothy and Mr Hobbs are back and Kate's been making up the beds. Tail between her legs and can't do enough to help.'

Catherine said indignantly, 'She can't just pretend last night didn't happen. The things she said to me—'

'She was very drunk. She won't remember half she said – and probably never meant it.'

'How can you defend her after the things she said about us?' Catherine accused.

Bridie shrugged, but Catherine was still filled with disgust at her mother's poisonous words. 'Well, I can't forgive her. She could have killed me with that boot. I don't feel safe in my own house any more.' Catherine gripped her arms tensely, willing Bridie to take her side.

Bridie touched her shoulder in sympathy. 'It's up to you, of course. But she's still your mother. You can't just throw her out on the street.' She gave Catherine a wry look. 'I think it'll all blow over – once that useless husband of hers clears off to sea.'

Catherine returned with a heavy heart. She could see no way out of the situation. Kate stood pasty-faced by the kitchen range, hands shaking as she poured Catherine a cup of tea.

'Sorry, Kitty,' she mumbled, handing over the cup.

Catherine was still too upset to speak. She busied herself for the rest of the evening, serving supper and chatting to the returned guests, hiding her unhappiness behind a cheerful mask.

It was Davie who waylaid her on the landing on the way to bed.

'Kitty, can I have a word?'

She nodded warily.

'Kate's feeling that bad about what she did – tossing me boot at you. She went too far.'

'She always goes too far,' Catherine said in agitation. 'I can't trust her. What if she took against one of the lodgers? You'll have to take her back, Davie. I can't cope with her drinking.'

Davie gave her a desperate look. 'I can't. We've nowhere to go.' He put his callused hands on her shoulders. 'You've no idea what it's like back in Jarrow – ten times worse than when you last saw it. There's hardly a man in work. It's a ghost town. Don't send her back to that, Kitty. It'll kill her.'

Catherine shrugged off his hold.

'She's doing a good job of trying that here – the way she's drinking.'

Davie struggled to say something. With alarm, Catherine saw tears welling in his eyes. He gulped. 'Give her another chance, Kitty.'

'The Hurst was to be her last chance,' Catherine protested.

'Please! Just one more. You're the only one can save her.'

She stood at a loss, the burden of his hopes pressing on her so hard she found it difficult to breathe.

Finally she whispered, 'She can stay.'

'Kitty, thanks! You're a lass in a million—'

'But you have to promise me one thing,' Catherine interrupted, steeling herself to tell him. 'You have to keep away from here. You being on leave – it brings out the worst in her.'

Davie gave her a long pained look. She knew how much it hurt him, but coping with the two of them together was beyond her.

'That's Bridie talking,' he said dully.

'No, it's me.' Catherine was firm. 'Do I have your promise? You won't visit till Kate's proved she's off the drink for good.'

'Aye,' he said hoarsely, and turned away.

It was the last word they exchanged before he left The Hurst two days later.

The new year, 1934, was hardly underway, when Catherine was regretting her weakness in letting Kate stay. On the surface, her mother appeared normal, busying herself around the house and calling out cheerily to the guests. But there was a glint in her eye when she looked at Catherine that made the young woman nervous. Kate was seething at Davie's forced departure and resentful at the watchful eye kept on her drinking.

Despite Bridie being around the house and Mrs Fairy spying for Catherine, Kate was still managing to get hold of alcohol, though Catherine was baffled as to how. She could find no trace of it, but Kate's mood seesawed and she was constantly staggering into furniture and breaking things as if inebriated. When challenged, she would laugh manically, or curse Catherine foully and burst into tears.

Then there was a series of strange incidents. Tom Hobbs went to tune the piano one day and found two of the internal hammers had been snapped off. The following week the door handle of his room was smeared in jam and the contents of his chamber pot spilt on his bedside rug.

'Someone's got it in for me,' he complained.

Catherine confronted her mother. 'Are you picking on Mr Hobbs for some reason?'

Kate gave her a wounded look. 'What on earth for?'

'To get back at me about the piano,' Catherine accused.

Kate shook her head and walked off. A few days later there was jam on the piano tuner's door again.

'I've found other lodgings,' he told Catherine at the end of the month. She tried to placate him, but his mind was made up and he left.

Other bizarre happenings occurred throughout the spring. A mouse-trap was found in the ventriloquist's bed, soap was put in the butter dish at breakfast. By Easter, three more residents had gone.

'Why are you doing all this?' Catherine cried at her mother.

'Doing what?' Kate sniggered like a child.

'Picking on the residents. They've done nothing to you.'

'Don't know what you mean.'

Catherine wanted to shake her till her teeth rattled, but did not trust herself to touch her. 'We'll have no business left if you don't stop your carry-on.'

Kate grew openly abusive to Catherine in front of the household.

'A bossy little bitch she was as a bairn,' Kate announced in the dining room one day when Catherine had asked her to fill up the salt. 'And she's just the same – for all her posh ways. I could tell you a few tales about our Kitty that would make your hair stand on end.'

Bridie intervened. 'Kate, the guests are waiting for the salt. You can keep your tales for another time.' She steered Kate towards the door.

'Gerr-off us,' Kate snarled, turning on her. 'You're just as bad. Dirty, filthy things you get up to—'

Bridie shoved her through the door and banged it shut behind them. Kate's muffled shouting and swearing could still be heard, as Bridie dragged her down the corridor. Catherine was left, puce-faced with humiliation, not knowing what to say.

The major cleared his throat. 'Soup doesn't need salt. Perfectly good as it is.' He bent to eat. Catherine felt tears prick her eyes as she shot him a grateful look. After an awkward pause, the others began eating.

Mealtimes became a battleground and Catherine dreaded them, not knowing what prank her mother would try, or what foul-mouthed ranting would ruin the conversation. She was a bundle of taut nerves during the day, but the long nights were even worse. She could not sleep, tossing and turning in the bed. Although there were now spare bedrooms, Catherine could not face the dark on her own. She was plagued with fearful memories of long ago: the hurtful teasing of playmates, her grandfather wielding the fire poker, Kate beating her for playing at the forbidden Slake. In the depth of the night she dwelled on her failure with men. *You're a bastard inside and out!* – the words of a neighbour rang in her head again and again. That was why men did not want her. She was tainted, unworthy. She would always be Kate's unwanted child.

When Catherine did fall asleep, she was caught in a web of recurring nightmares. The black-hooded priest was always walking towards her, about to envelop her in his darkness, never showing his face. In the dream, she escaped into a room that turned out to be the old bedroom at William Black Street. Kate was in the bed, laughing at her. The noise would give them away. She picked up the pillow and covered Kate's face, trying to stifle the laughter, just for a minute. She kept pressing on the pillow, but the tall black figure always found her. *She's dead, dead*, his voice would echo. Then she was sobbing by a corpse laid out in the parlour, fluids dripping from the trestle into a bucket. Terrified and alone, Catherine dared herself to look at the face. But it wasn't Kate, it was Grandma Rose.

Catherine woke from these nightmares crying out and bathed in sweat. Bridie grew tired of being woken and trying to soothe her.

'Perhaps you should see the doctor,' Bridie yawned in exhaustion. 'You're worn out – we both are.'

'And tell him what? That I dream about smothering me mother with a pillow!'

'Well, if she's the cause of all this, it's time she went. I've lost all patience with the woman. She throws our help back in our faces. It's as if she's daring us to put her out.'

Catherine buried her face in her hands. Bridie was right. Kate seemed constantly to be spoiling for a fight. Catherine was fraught with trying to avoid one, bottling up her anger like steam in a pressure-cooker. What really frightened her was the growing urge inside to harm Kate, to unleash that anger. What kind of appalling person was she?

It was the shame that engulfed her after such dreaming that made Catherine carry on putting up with Kate's increasing madness.

Early summer came and the only residents left were the major, Mrs Fairy and Dorothy, who seemed impervious to practical joking. In desperation, Catherine and Bridie went round the local hotels and asked if they had any overflow of customers. She put up a notice on the church board and in shop windows.

A trickle of summer visitors came, but none of them stayed more than a few days. The beds were not made properly, the hot water ran cold, the puddings tasted salty or the soups sweet. Then a French woman came to stay on a painting holiday.

She was charming and cultured, and Catherine took to her at once. After the evening meal they would sit in the conservatory and talk about books, Catherine trying out her rudimentary French that she had learnt in her Harton days. Madame Clevy introduced her to French writers such as Voltaire and Flaubert, lending her books in translation. She could play tennis and it spurred Catherine on to cut the lawn and hold a tennis party, inviting friends from the club.

All that sunny Saturday afternoon they played in the secluded garden at The Hurst, and sat about on rugs or lounged in deck chairs. Kate came and went, puffing in the heat and joking with guests. Catherine was pleased to see her making an effort to be friendly.

At tea time, Catherine went inside to carry out a tray of drinks.

'Let me help you,' Madame Clevy insisted, and followed her into the kitchen.

The door was open into the butler's pantry. Kate was swigging from a bottle. Catherine froze. Her mother saw them, calmly put the stopper back in and placed it under the sink with the cleaning materials.

She came out swaggering. 'Well, well, caught you both together, haven't I? Kitty and her little French sweetheart.'

'Pardon?' Madame Clevy looked puzzled.

Kate lurched towards them. Catherine caught a strong whiff of spirits.

'Wanted a little bit of a kiss and cuddle in the pantry, eh?' Kate cackled.

'Shut up!' Catherine ordered, blushing hotly.

'Well, you're wasting your time, madame,' Kate said loudly. 'She's already spoken for. Bridie's her little companion. Lady in the bedchamber.'

'Keep your voice down,' Catherine hissed. She took the French woman by the elbow and pulled her towards the door. 'I'm so sorry, she's not herself.'

'Drunk, you mean?' Kate came after them, grabbing at Catherine. 'Yes, I am. It's me only pleasure in this bloody place! Too busy with your fancy friends to care about me. Never cared about me. I might as well be dead, for all the notice you take. Hate me, don't you? *Don't you?*' she screamed.

Catherine shook her off, her heart thudding in agitation. 'Keep away from me! Don't you dare come back out in such a state, or I'll never forgive you.'

She hurried away, stuttering apologies to Madame Clevy. Outside, Bridie saw at once she was upset.

'Is it Kate?' she asked. Catherine nodded.

'Let me deal with her,' Bridie said, and went inside.

Ten minutes later, she reappeared with the tea tray, smiling. Passing Catherine she murmured, 'Locked her in the pantry.'

Catherine gasped. Kate was probably drinking herself unconscious. Insides knotting, Catherine forced a smile and set about pouring tea. The afternoon was ruined and she could not wait for people to leave, fearful of Kate breaking out and making a scene.

242

Bridie cut the cherry cake and handed it round. Madame Clevy took a bite, then cried out. She held her jaw.

'What's wrong?' Bridie asked.

'Something hard – my tooth,' she gabbled.

Catherine grabbed her plate and pulled something out of the cake. It was a small hammer from the piano.

'How on earth did that get there?' said Joyce, one of her tennis friends.

Catherine knew if she answered she would burst into tears. Her mother was spiteful and hateful! She would not stop until she had driven away all her lodgers, all her friends. It was the final straw.

She banged down the plate and strode back into the house. She was going to give Kate such an earful! She would kick her out on to the street, there and then. To hell with what the neighbours thought! Her mother could beg in the gutter, for all she cared.

As she marched into the kitchen, she heard Bridie hurrying behind her.

'Catherine, don't do anything hasty—'

'Just try and stop me,' Catherine cried.

She rushed to the pantry, turned the key and wrenched the door open. Kate was sprawled on the floor, an empty bottle lying beside her. She was deadly pale and motionless. Fear clawed at Catherine's stomach.

'Is she breathing?' Bridie whispered.

Catherine stood, too paralysed to move. Bridie pushed her aside and bent down, putting an ear to Kate's mouth. A long moment passed. *Don't let her die like this!*

'She's breathing, but it's shallow,' Bridie said at last. 'Best call out the doctor.'

Catherine let out a long breath.

Bridie picked up the bottle and sniffed it. 'Mary Mother! She's been drinking meths.'

Catherine stared at the crumpled body, the greying, dishevelled hair across a once-pretty face. All the fury and fear of moments before dissolved.

'Oh, Kate,' she whispered, bending to touch her hair. 'Oh, our Kate!'

Chapter 38

Kate was nursed in bed for several days. The doctor told her she might have done irreparable harm to her stomach and liver from her drinking. Time would tell. When Kate asked if she could have a tot of brandy for medicinal purposes, Catherine was filled with disgust. Her mother seemed bent on self-destruction. But she would not allow Kate to wreck life at The Hurst too.

Once Kate was up and about again, meddling in the running of the household, Catherine screwed up her courage to confront her.

'I'm making arrangements for you to live elsewhere. The tenants in our old maisonette are moving out at the end of the month. You can move back there.'

Kate gawped at her in disbelief. 'You're hoying me out?'

Catherine swallowed. 'I'm providing you with a roof over your head. It's more than you deserve after all this carry-on.'

'All on me own?' Kate said in a fluster. 'How will I manage?'

'By taking in your own lodgers. I've talked it over with Bridie. We're getting a joiner to put in a couple of false walls so you can have extra rooms. You'll have to pay your own way; I can't afford to run two places. Specially with business so bad at The Hurst,' Catherine added pointedly.

Kate said stubbornly, 'And what if I refuse to go?'

Catherine held her look. 'Then you'll have to go back north. I'm not having you living at The Hurst any longer.'

Kate stormed out of the room.

Later, she was contrite and begged Catherine to let her stay. 'I never meant any of those things I said about you and Bridie. I don't believe them – I just can't bear you seeing her as your mam, and not me!' But, encouraged by Bridie, Catherine held firm and went ahead with the alterations to the flat in Laurel Street. In September, she scraped enough money together to cover the first month's bills and placed an advertisement in the newspaper for custom.

When the first two enquirers paid over a week's rent, Catherine ordered her mother to pack.

'I'll see her settled in,' Bridie insisted. 'I don't trust you not to change your mind at the last minute. A few tears from Kate and you'll have her back to The Hurst in a trice.'

So Catherine and Kate exchanged a strained goodbye in the kitchen. Catherine went off to work and felt miserable all day, haunted by her mother's reproachful look. She worried whether Kate had thrown a tantrum with Bridie about going and whether her lodgers had turned up.

On her return, Bridie assured her. 'She's fine and dandy. Putting on a show for the new boarders. Long may it last.'

Catherine was full of doubt that it would. Each day she dreaded finding that Kate had returned, drunk and in debt and demanding her ungrateful daughter to take her in. But the days passed and she did not hear from her.

'Maybe I should go down and see how she's managing,' Catherine fretted.

'Leave her be,' Bridie said impatiently. 'It's what you wanted, isn't it?'

'Yes, but—'

'Then stop fussing. Kate'll manage. She'll do it just to spite you.'

At the end of the month, Catherine came home from work to find Bridie grinning like a Cheshire cat at the kitchen table. She pushed an envelope towards her.

'Have a look in there.'

Inside were two ten-shilling notes and a scrawled message: 'Here's the money I had a lend of. I have got four lodgers. Hope you are well. Kate.'

Catherine looked over in amazement. 'She's doing better than we are!'

Bridie laughed. 'Didn't I tell you? She's out to prove herself to you. So you can stop worrying – you've done the right thing by her.'

Catherine smiled in relief. 'Not that she'll see it that way.'

Bridie came over and hugged her. 'Oh, but isn't it grand without her? Just you, me and Maisie. Promise me you'll not take her back. I couldn't bear to see you fading away with the worry again.'

'Oh, I promise,' Catherine said. 'Never again.'

245

Winter came, and Catherine and Bridie gradually built up the numbers at The Hurst once more. The roof needed constant repairs and it was a struggle to keep the damp and mould at bay during the cold wet months. The house devoured money like an insatiable beast, and often Catherine wondered why she had bought such a monstrous place.

'You worry too much about things,' Bridie would chide.

'And you don't worry enough,' Catherine retorted on discovering a new patch of crumbling wall in the tower room.

Bridie, she discovered, was as haphazard in her housekeeping as Kate. She never seemed to be able to keep within the weekly budget, and dismissed Catherine's attempts to curb her spending with a shrug and a laugh as if it were a joke. To her friend's annoyance, Catherine offered the loyal Mrs Fairy free board and lodging if she would help with the cooking and housekeeping.

'I can manage fine without that woman huffing and puffing down my neck!'

'I thought you'd be pleased with the extra help,' Catherine said.

'You don't trust me, do you?' Bridie reproached.

'It's too big a job for you to run everything on your own. And Mrs Fairy's good with Maisie.'

Bridie was moody for weeks afterwards and Catherine had to tread carefully. Casual comments could be taken as criticism; the slightest attention to Mrs Fairy was seen as favouritism. But at least she did not have to worry about her unstable mother screaming in front of the guests or causing chaos. She was so relieved that the battles with Kate were over that the odd tiff with Bridie was nothing in comparison.

Months went by without Catherine seeing or hearing from her mother. The lease on the maisonette had been assigned over to Kate, and Catherine took the lack of news to mean that her mother was coping.

'Bad news travels fast,' Bridie reminded her. 'If she wants you she knows where to find you.'

So, with no encouragement from Bridie, Catherine did not make an effort to keep in contact.

As Christmas approached and Catherine wondered what to do about Kate, Bridie said, 'She'll have Davie for company. Spare us a Christmas like last year!'

Catherine shuddered to think of it. Instead, she sent her mother money in a card. It made her feel less guilty at having a quiet Christmas at The Hurst. There was no sign of Kate at Mass, but a note came in the new year to wish her well.

It was well into 1935 before she had further news of her mother.

'Didn't I run into her down on the seafront buying fish!' Bridie reported. 'Maisie saw her first. Weight's dropped off her.'

Catherine's stomach twisted. 'Is she all right?'

'Right as rain,' Bridie assured. 'Got six lodgers and proud of it.'

'Good,' Catherine said, her throat feeling tight.

'Asking after you,' Bridie continued. 'Says to come for your tea one night. Bring Maisie – have a game of snap. I told her how busy you were and not to expect it.'

Catherine was grateful. She did not want to visit. She was happy to think that her mother was managing without her but did not want to see her. She had striven hard for peace of mind since the previous terrible year. It had completely drained her of emotion. Once again there was equilibrium in her life. To re-establish contact with Kate would destroy all that.

Catherine said, 'Maisie could go on her own – or you could take her.'

Bridie shrugged and the subject was dropped.

With spring blossom and the fresh green of early summer leaves, Catherine's spirits rose. She felt filled with a new energy and optimism. Whenever she had doubts about The Hurst, she only had to go out into its garden to chase them away. She would walk among its trees, touching the rough bark and stand under their shade, mesmerised by the flickering, filtering light. Breathing in the scent of flowers and damp grass after a shower was better than any expensive perfume. For snatched moments, Catherine felt more at peace there than at any time in her life.

But such times were rare, for she continued to work hard at the laundry and when she came back home, the chores of the boarding house went on until bedtime. As summer wore on, all her plans to hold tennis parties unravelled. There never seemed enough time. She and Bridie played together on occasional Saturday afternoons, challenging some of the lodgers to games of doubles.

Catherine was surprised Bridie did not seem to mind the lack of social contact.

'It must be dull for you, being stuck here all week long,' Catherine said. 'We should make more effort to get out.'

247

Bridie pinched her cheek. 'Don't worry about me – I love it here. I've got you and Maisie and a beautiful home. What more could I want?'

Still, as the year waned, Catherine felt an increasing need for contact outside the enclosed world of laundry and boarding house. She yearned for more time for reading and learning. She almost envied those far-off days at Harton when she had spent her free time devouring books from the library. When was the last time she had spent a whole evening reading?

The days shortened and they could no longer play tennis or sit in the garden of an evening. Confined to the house in bad weather, Bridie and Mrs Fairy began to bicker again and pour out their grievances to Catherine on her return from work. Each strove to win control in the kitchen.

One evening, when Catherine was returning from work wondering what petty wrangling she would find, she spotted a poster in a newsagent's window. Fencing lessons. She stopped and studied it. One hour a week at a gym in Harcourt Street. For an instant she held a ridiculous thought of herself wielding a sword like one of the Three Musketeers. Madame Clevy had introduced her to the novel by Dumas and she had been captivated by the swashbuckling tale.

She laughed at the idea, dismissed it and walked home. That night Bridie was in a mood over a burnt cheese sauce that had been left on the stove and ruined a pan. She blamed Mrs Fairy, who indignantly denied it.

'You can't leave a sauce and go off for a bath,' the old cook scolded.

'I left it on the hearth,' Bridie cried.

'You left it on top.'

'Oh, go boil your head in a bucket!' Bridie flounced out and gave no further help with the evening meal.

The following day Catherine went down to the gym in Harcourt Street and signed up for fencing lessons with a wiry ex-actor called Mr Gascoigne. Bridie was flabbergasted.

'Fencing? You mean sword fighting?'

'Yes.' Catherine laughed at her impulsiveness.

'But why?'

Catherine shrugged. She could hardly tell her it was to vent her irritation at the squabbling between the women at The Hurst. 'It'll keep me fit and trim.'

'There's not an ounce of spare flesh on you, girl,' Bridie exclaimed.

'And who is this Mr Gascoigne? He might be one of these men you hear about who lure young women up to their rooms and murder them!'

Catherine laughed dismissively, 'He's as small as a mouse – I'd get the better of him any day.'

After Catherine had been for a couple of weeks and come to no harm, Bridie accepted the situation.

'Suppose it'll come in handy if Kate ever comes after you with a carving knife,' she joked bleakly.

Catherine laughed uncomfortably. She did not like to admit that she rid herself of her pent-up aggression against Kate when she parried and lunged for her opponent. But she grew to enjoy her weekly sessions at the gym with the nimble and talkative tutor, and the assortment of other fencers. For an hour a week she concentrated on something physical, channelling her frustrations into the point of her épée and emptying her mind of everything else.

Harcourt Street was towards the sea front and, walking home, Catherine passed near the end of Laurel Street. One December night when the moon was so bright it lit the rooftops in silvery light, Catherine was gripped by a powerful memory. She and Kate had been walking up the bank to East Jarrow after a rare day out on a charabanc trip, when suddenly her mother had grabbed her hand.

'Haway, let's race the moon!' Kate had cried, and yanked her along so fast that her feet had left the ground as if she were flying. It was so unexpected and exhilarating, that for a moment she had been over-whelmed by a surge of love.

Catherine stopped in the cold air and gasped for breath. She had not thought of the incident for years. Kate had spoken with such warmth about her real father, William Fawcett, playing the same game when she was small, that Catherine had been emboldened to ask about her own mysterious father. It had spoilt the moment. Kate had grown angry and told her never to mention him again. He was never coming back. He was dead.

Catherine's heart hammered at the bitter-sweet memory; one instant so close, the next at loggerheads. She looked up at the dazzling moon and it seemed to flood her with courage. Without giving herself time to think it over, she turned abruptly right and retraced her steps to her mother's maisonette.

Kate gasped when she opened the door. 'You look familiar. Do I know you from somewhere?' Catherine's courage withered at the sarcasm, but Kate quickly pulled her in. 'Don't stand there letting all the heat out – haway in.'

She led her into the kitchen. Somewhere a radio was playing. Washing was strewn overhead, the room smelt of pies and damp clothes, but somehow it was homely.

'Can't stop long,' Catherine said awkwardly.

Kate poured her out a stewed cup of tea from the pot. 'Sit down, lass, you're makin' me nervous.'

Catherine sipped gingerly. She had forgotten how strong Kate made it.

'Business going all right?'

'Champion,' Kate said with a defiant look. 'I hear you're employing Mrs Fairy these days. Saw her at the market – full of it, she was. Bet that doesn't suit Bridie.'

Catherine said, 'They get on fine.'

Kate snorted and changed the subject. She chattered on about her own lodgers and about Davie, who had sent her a postcard from Cape Town.

'He'll not be back till next year,' Kate said matter-of-factly. 'And you, lass, what have you been doing?'

'Just the same,' Catherine said, standing up. Then she added, 'I've taken up fencing.'

'What do you mean, fencing?' Kate looked baffled.

'Épée – sword play.'

Kate burst into laughter. 'Eeh, hinny, I thought you meant mending folks's garden fences!'

Catherine could not help smiling as she made for the door. Kate followed her.

'Fencing. Fancy that.'

A tall man with a towel round his shoulders emerged from the bathroom. Quick as a flash, Kate said, 'Mr Soulsby, this is my daughter, Kitty. She's a champion fencer, don't you know?'

The man gave a startled nod in Catherine's direction and bolted down the corridor.

'You shouldn't have said that,' Catherine said in embarrassment. 'It's not true.'

'Will be one day. Come again, won't you, lass,' Kate insisted.

Catherine promised she would and headed quickly down the stairs. Glancing back at the outside door, she saw her mother still at the stairwell watching her go.

Catherine hurried home, relieved the ordeal was over, yet strangely glad she had gone. Ten minutes together was probably as much as they could manage without an argument, so she would keep her visits occasional and brief.

That Christmas, Catherine called on Kate with a hamper of food and a pretty woollen cardigan.

'When will I get to wear a fancy cardy?' Kate said ungraciously. 'No one asks me anywhere.'

Catherine knew her mother was trying to shame her into inviting her to The Hurst for Christmas, but she resisted. She had promised Bridie never to share Christmas with Kate again. Besides, this year Harold, the poet, had come back, reassured that 'mad Mrs McDermott' had left. She would not have him upset either.

Through the spring of the following year, Catherine continued to make the odd duty visit to her mother on her way home from fencing lessons. Usually, she chose not to tell Bridie, for her friend only nagged her about spending time there rather than at The Hurst. Catherine and Kate talked about the death of old King George, who had once come to visit South Shields during the Great War.

'You were that excited to see him,' Kate recalled. 'Put old John in a black mood, making all that fuss over royalty.'

' "To Hell with kings and generals – and up with the Pope." ' Catherine laughed as she recalled her grandfather's words.

Kate was suddenly glum. 'Got a letter from our Mary last week. Alec's out of work and he's taken poorly bad – never was a strong man. Says there's more shops closed in Jarrow than open. Where will it end, eh?'

Catherine felt uncomfortable, as she always did when talk turned to the deepening poverty on Tyneside.

'What about cousin Alec?' She swallowed. 'He'll have finished his apprenticeship by now.'

Kate sighed. 'There's no call for joiners at the yards. But he's lucky to get gardening work over Cleadon way. Doesn't pay much, but it's a job. Mary doesn't know what they'd do without him.'

Suddenly Catherine was angry. 'What a waste! Lads like Alec serving their time, learning the job – then out on the dole as soon as their apprenticeship's finished. It's a crying shame. And what do the politicians do about it? Sit around their clubs in London doing nothing! Everyone deserves the right to work and keep their family.'

Kate's eyes glittered. 'By, you've a Geordie heart after all. Me father used to talk like that about the working man, so your Grandma Rose used to say.'

It was the one thing that mother and daughter could agree on: work was the life-blood of a person, of a community. For all her hankering after a life of leisure in her daydreams, Catherine knew she would go mad if she had nothing to do.

Catherine was quietly impressed with her mother's success in making her own living without her or Davie's help. Kate thrived on being busy as much as she did. Yet Catherine was always half in dread at these visits in case her mother had slipped back into her destructive drinking.

That June, Catherine turned thirty. As her birthday approached, she grew gloomy. Bridie overheard her talking to the dog.

'Life's passing me by, Tuppence. What have I got to show for it? This big leaky house and you, eh?'

'That's no way to talk!' Bridie scolded. 'You've a good job and a fine business – and friends that think the world of you. What more do you want?'

Catherine blushed. 'Sorry, I didn't mean . . .'

'What you need is a party,' Bridie declared.

'I don't want everyone to know my age,' Catherine protested.

'We don't have to tell them. It'll just be a summer party for all our friends.'

Catherine was soon persuaded. It fell on a Saturday, so they planned a lunch party with tennis afterwards. She kept away from Kate's, fearful that if her mother heard about a party she would turn up uninvited and make a spectacle of herself. Bridie and Maisie bought new outfits, while Catherine made do with last summer's dress. The money saved was quietly sent to Aunt Mary.

The day was a success, with breezy sunshine. Friends came from the tennis club, church and her fencing class, as well as the Townsends and several of the lodgers. There was birthday cake at tea time, but no mention of her age.

As she was leaving Mrs Townsend said, 'Sorry not to see your mother. Is she unwell?'

Catherine flushed. She had kept from her employer just how difficult the situation had been two years ago and why Kate had to leave. 'No, she's fine. Full of busy.'

A friend from church joined in. 'Yes, she must be with that new place she's taken on.'

Catherine stared at the woman. 'I beg your pardon?'

'The house in Maritime Place – big terrace. Bumped into her at the shops. Full of it, she was. Eight lodgers. But you'll know all that, of course.'

Catherine stammered, 'Oh, y-yes.'

That night she told Bridie. 'Fancy her moving without telling us. I felt foolish not knowing.'

Bridie yawned. 'Well, you haven't been to see her for ages.'

'Still, she could have sent a change of address. She said nothing in the birthday card. And a house in Maritime Place! How can she afford that?'

'That's her affair. One thing's for sure, though – she'll be cock-a-hoop that she's upsides with you and your eight lodgers.'

When Catherine finally tracked down her mother's new home, she was amazed. It was a substantial boarding house near the sea front.

'One of the lodgers is a decorator – got me some paint on the cheap,' Kate said proudly as she showed off the house.

The rooms were spartan but clean enough, and the upstairs sitting room had an attractive bay window with a partial view of the sea. Catherine felt a stab of envy for the airy room full of light.

'It's nice,' she admitted. 'But how can you afford it?'

'None of your business,' Kate said tartly.

'You can't come running to me if you get into debt.' Catherine was brusque. 'I've got no spare.'

'I can pay me own way,' Kate snapped. 'Don't need your charity.'

'Good. And you could've told me you'd moved.'

'You never bothered calling. Had to do it all mesel'.'

'And who was it got you started in Laurel Street?' Catherine cried indignantly. 'Not that you once thanked me.'

'Thanks for nowt! You hoyed me out.'

'If you're going to be like that, I'll not bother coming.'

'And if you're ganin' to twist your face, better that you divint!'

Catherine marched out, vowing never to visit again. Her ungrateful mother could do what she wanted; she refused to worry about her.

Later, when Bridie had calmed her down with hot tea and reassurances, Catherine felt a twinge of shame for her outburst. She had not meant to be churlish about Kate's new lodging house, but her mother's crowing over her had riled her so. After all she had put up with, the least Kate could have done was let her know where she had gone.

She was struck by a sudden memory. Catherine was playing around the lamppost in William Black Street with the other children. It was misty. She was smaller than most of them. They must have just moved from Leam Lane. Out of the mist came a tall woman in a pale lilac dress and a matching hat. Her oval face was flushed, eyes wide, skin translucent. Catherine gazed up at her, thinking how beautiful she was.

As soon as the woman set eyes on her, she rushed forward and grabbed her arms, shaking her hard. Catherine gasped in shock, realising it was Kate.

'You little bugger! Where've you been? I thought you were dead! Don't you ever do that to me again, do you hear?'

All the air was trapped in Catherine's throat. She had no idea why her big sister was so angry, just that her grip was hurting her arms. Usually she looked forward to the rare visits home because Kate always brought treats from the baker's where she worked. But now she was really angry with her for something she had done. The next minute, Kate was dragging her down the street, demanding to know where her house was. As soon as they got there, a furious row erupted with their parents . . .

Catherine shook off the memory. It was from a time before she discovered that Rose and John were her grandparents and Kate her mother. The great betrayal. They had moved house to escape the rumours without telling Kate, and she had come frantically looking for them. Years later, Kate had still been furious about it and blamed it on her.

Catherine stifled her pity. Kate had been just as petty not telling her of the move to Maritime Place. As usual she was behaving like a wayward child.

It was autumn before Catherine forced herself to go and check on her mother. Bridie told her to let sleeping dogs lie, but a sense of duty got the better of her. She would call on her way to fencing so she could not stay more than a few minutes.

'Haway in!' Kate beamed at the unexpected visit, making Catherine feel worse.

'Can't stay – I've got a lesson.'

'I've that much to tell you, lass.' Kate ignored her excuse and pulled her inside. She made for the stairs. 'I've a pot of tea brewing in the sittin' room. One of me lodgers likes to take tea there while he's studyin'.'

'The kitchen will do,' Catherine said in dismay. 'I haven't time for tea.'

'Don't be daft. It won't take a minute.' Kate gave her a proud look. 'He's a *teacher* at the Grammar School.'

'Who is?'

'Me new lodger. Got a degree at Oxford University. Fancy that, eh? One of my lads with a degree! Wait till you meet him.'

Catherine's heart sank. 'I don't want to meet him – I've just come for a minute to see you.'

'Told him me daughter was well read, an' all. Think he thought I'd made you up – you not coming round here. You'll just come upstairs for a minute. Rude not to.' Kate went ahead, panting up the steep stairs.

Catherine gripped the banisters in irritation. Her mother was determined to show off in front of this tiresome teacher. She followed her into the sitting room, scowling and impatient.

'This is me daughter, Kitty, I was tellin' you about,' Kate said breathlessly.

Low autumn sun was flooding the room. For a moment Catherine was dazzled and could not see to whom she was talking. There was a movement in the bay window and a slim man stepped forward from behind the table. The light caught his face, boyish and bespectacled. He looked far too young to be a teacher, more like a head boy.

'This is Mr Cookson,' Kate announced. 'He teaches mathematics.'

The young teacher hesitated.

Catherine felt his awkwardness. 'I'm just on my way to a fencing lesson,' she said, 'thought I'd call by.'

He regarded her silently, hands in pockets. Books lay open on the table beside him.

'But you're studying. Mustn't interrupt,' she said hastily. 'I didn't want to come up.'

'Mr Cookson doesn't mind,' Kate said grandly. 'We always stop for a cup of tea about now.'

'Well, I can't,' Catherine said in a panic. The way he was staring at her was unnerving. 'Got to go.'

Quite suddenly, he stepped towards her and held out his hand.

'Tom,' he said in a deep voice that belied his slight frame. 'Pleased to meet you.'

Catherine hesitated.

'Where're your manners, lass?' Kate said. 'Gan on, he won't bite!'

She stepped to meet him and took his hand. It was smooth and warm – an academic's hand. He held on to hers firmly. Close up, his eyes through the glinting spectacles were a warm brown, his mouth sensual.

'Do you fence?' she demanded.

His thick eyebrows raised in surprise. 'N-no. I'm afraid I don't.'

She pulled away. What on earth had possessed her to ask such an absurd question?

'It doesn't matter.' She spun round and strode to the door. 'I'll see myself out,' she gabbled. 'Goodbye.'

'Kitty!' Kate cried.

Hot with embarrassment at making such a fool of herself, Catherine fled down the stairs and out of the house.

Chapter 39

'What in the world is the matter?' Bridie asked. 'The Hound of the Baskervilles been chasing you?'

Catherine caught her breath. 'No, nothing's the matter.'

Bridie gave her a curious look. 'Then why are you back so early?'

'Early?'

'You're not usually back from fencing till after eight – and it's just turned six.'

'Fencing!' Catherine clapped her hands to her face. 'I quite forgot.'

Bridie was baffled. 'But that's why you went out.'

'Yes, it was.' Catherine burst out laughing.

'If I didn't know you better, I'd say you'd been drinking,' Bridie declared.

'No, really I haven't,' Catherine said, flopping on to a kitchen chair.

'Spill the beans, girl,' Bridie ordered.

Catherine glanced at Mrs Fairy and Maisie, but they were deep in a game of snap at the table.

'I went to see Kate.'

Bridie gasped. 'She upset you? She's back on the drink?'

'No,' Catherine said hastily, 'nothing like that.'

'Well, something must've happened to make you run back here like a rabbit!'

Catherine felt foolish. 'She was showing off – wanting me to meet one of her lodgers just 'cos he's a teacher. I didn't want to meet him but she made me. And . . .'

'And?'

'Made a fool of myself. I was a bit rude to the poor man. Then I ran out.'

Bridie was watching her intently. Catherine could feel herself blushing.

'Doesn't sound like anything to get in a stew about,' said Bridie.

'No.' Catherine cringed anew to think of her strange behaviour. If she hadn't been so annoyed with Kate, dragging her to meet the shy teacher, she might have greeted him with more courtesy and poise.

'What was he like?' Bridie asked.

'Very young – looked more like a schoolboy – probably his first job.'

'Too young for you then,' Bridie said bluntly.

Catherine gave her a startled look. 'Oh, of course – I didn't mean – I'm not the least bit interested—'

Bridie abruptly laughed. 'Listen to you! Skittish as a kitten. Kate'll be pleased she got you in such a tizzy over one of her precious lodgers.'

It was too late to go back for her fencing lesson and Catherine cursed her forgetfulness. Panic had made her head for home. By the next day, she could not believe her stupidity. She was cross with Kate for the embarrassing encounter and herself for missing her precious fencing lesson. What did it matter if some maths teacher thought her rude or odd? She would probably never see him again.

It was Saturday tea time when the timid Dorothy came to find her. Catherine was mending a chair in the chilly billiard room, which was now a glorified storeroom.

'Miss McMullen – there's a man at the door.'

Catherine pushed hair out of her eyes. 'Can't Bridie see to him? I'm busy, pet.'

Dorothy looked anxious. 'He asked for you.'

'Who is it?'

The pale girl bit her lip. 'Sorry, I didn't ask. I've never seen him before.'

Catherine sighed. It was probably some salesman who had got hold of her name. She marched through to the front entrance.

'Hello, Kitty.' It was Tom Cookson standing on the doorstep, hands in pockets.

Catherine stared at him open-mouthed. He was dressed casually in an open-necked shirt and tweed jacket, looking even more like a young student.

'I hope you don't mind me calling. I was passing by – Mrs McDermott mentioned where you lived.'

'Oh.' Catherine was speechless.

'But I can see you're busy.' He stepped back, looking less sure. 'Unless you greet all your guests with a hammer.'

Catherine glanced down and saw she still clutched the tool. 'Goodness! No, of course not.' She plonked it quickly on the porch table. What a sight she must look, in an old pair of trousers and her hair in a mess. She pushed back her wavy fringe. 'Please, come in.'

Tom hesitated. 'I'd like to, but your mother will have tea on the table in twenty minutes, and I'll be in trouble if I'm not back.'

Catherine was disappointed at such timidity, then saw from his sudden smile it was part in jest.

'Yes, you will be,' she smiled back. 'Another time perhaps.'

'Well,' Tom said, clearing his throat, 'there's a Carole Lombard film on at the Odeon this evening. I wondered if you'd like to go.'

Catherine's eyes widened in surprise. How did he know she idolised Lombard, even tried to copy her dreamy hairstyle?

'Go with you?' she asked.

'Well, yes.' He looked so young and uncertain after the bravado of asking, that she wanted to throw her arms about him in reassurance.

'Of course I'd like to go,' she said quickly. 'What time?'

His lean face brightened. 'Seven thirty.'

Catherine nodded. 'I'll meet you in the foyer just after seven.'

'You will?' He stood there grinning foolishly.

'Yes,' Catherine said a touch impatiently.

'Good.'

He walked off down the drive, hands in pockets, whistling. Catherine wondered if she was mad going to meet him. Bridie would certainly think so.

She did not tell her friend until it was nearly time to go. Bridie gawped as she appeared downstairs in her favourite blue dress and high heels.

'Not going dancing with the major, are you?'

'No, the pictures.' Catherine hurriedly put on her coat.

'With Major Holloway?' Bridie cried in disbelief.

'With Mr Cookson.'

Bridie came after her to the door. 'Who the devil is Mr Cookson? You're not going to meet a stranger on your own? Why didn't you tell me?'

'He only asked me two hours ago,' Catherine answered with an apologetic shrug.

'I better come with you,' Bridie said at once. 'Give me a minute to change.'

'No, Bridie.' Catherine was firm. 'I can look after myself. I'm thirty, for heaven's sake – and bigger than him!'

She opened the door and hurried into the dark.

'You never told me who he was,' Bridie called after her, 'or where you met him.'

'Tell you later,' Catherine answered, and quickened her pace.

She knew from the light thrown on the driveway that her friend watched her till she disappeared from sight. She felt bad for springing such a surprise on Bridie, but it was tinged with excitement at her daring. Why shouldn't she go out to the pictures with a young man? She couldn't remember the last time someone had asked her. Bridie and she had gone so often when their friendship was new, and now she missed such outings.

Tom Cookson was a stranger in Hastings and probably lonely. Once he found friends he wouldn't need to ask an old spinster like her. She would take advantage of the offer while she could.

He was waiting for her, dressed in a smart suit and tie, hair smoothed down. On catching sight of her, his serious face broke into a smile and she felt a small flutter inside. He had made an effort for her and she was flattered.

'Bought you chocolates,' he said bashfully, holding out a box. 'Mrs McDermott said you liked them.'

'You told Kate you were meeting me?' Catherine said in alarm.

'Shouldn't I have?'

Catherine knew it would cause Kate amusement to think of her thirty-year-old daughter meeting her youthful lodger, but she didn't care. She would endure teasing from her mother just to see a Carole Lombard film.

'Doesn't matter,' she smiled quickly and accepted the chocolates. 'Thanks, this is a real treat.'

Tom had bought good seats in the balcony. As they settled in and ate chocolates, they swapped questions. Tom had come straight from university in Oxford into his first job at Hastings Grammar School. He loved his subject. The pupils were great. Essex was where he came from.

'I worked in Essex for a short time,' Catherine said.

'I know. Your mother said you didn't like it.'

Catherine blushed. 'I wouldn't say that—'

'Too flat for you northerners,' Tom suggested.

'Let's just say, I prefer it here.'

Tom nodded. 'So do I.'

She looked at him in astonishment. 'But you've only just moved here.'

'Yes,' he agreed, 'but I can already tell I'm going to be happy.'

'Go on.' Catherine was intrigued. 'Give me examples.'

'Walking the Downs – the light on the sea – my job.' He paused. 'Getting away from my noisy family – and the snobs at Oxford who look down their noses at scholarship boys.' He looked at her. 'I like the people I've met.'

Catherine's heart quickened. He spoke as she felt. Could it be that he was running away from his past too – forging a new identity in this pleasant coastal town?

Before she could ask him any more, the lights went down and the Pathé news came on. Catherine froze, a chocolate halfway to her mouth, at the sight of scores of shabbily dressed men marching in the rain behind banners.

'The Jarrow Marchers have reached Bradford, where they enjoyed their first hot bath,' said the commentary. 'The mayor turned out to greet them, and donations of food have been pouring in for the foot-sore men. Two medical students are on hand to treat those blisters and a walking barber to keep them looking trim. They've come a long way from home – but they've got even further to go before reaching London and handing in their petition to the Prime Minister, Mr Baldwin . . .'

Catherine put back the chocolate, her appetite soured by the sight of their gaunt faces. If her eyes weren't blurred with tears she might see one that she recognised – men from the New Buildings or the dock gates. Men so desperate for work that they were prepared to march hundreds of miles to London to shame the government into action. Her people. She was filled with a fierce pride, and yet this news spoilt everything. How could she sit back and enjoy a silly romantic film when she knew the marchers would be bedding down on a hard hall floor, clothes damp and stinking, their hungry families left behind to worry and fend for themselves? She could imagine it all too vividly.

The main film began, but she was dangerously close to bursting into tears. She might move to the other end of the country but she could never shake off her past. It would always catch up with her when she least expected it.

Just then, she felt a warm hand cover hers. Tom took her hand and squeezed it gently, as if he guessed her misery. He said nothing, just gave her his shy smile and then turned to watch the film. She let her hand rest in his for several minutes.

After the film, Tom asked, 'Can I walk you home?'

Catherine felt touched. 'It's a long time since a lad's asked me that,' she smiled. 'But it's quite out of your way.'

'I like walking.'

'All right,' Catherine agreed.

As they walked through the dark, chilly streets they talked about films, which led on to books. She thought to show off her reading knowledge, only to discover that his was far greater. Not only did he know the classics of English literature, but was well read in philosophy, poetry and drama.

'Didn't know mathematicians read that much!' she cried with envy.

'Always had my head buried in a book,' he said sheepishly, 'when Mother thought I should've been helping with my younger brothers and sisters.'

'You were lucky to have books,' Catherine said, thinking how she had had to make do with penny comics and the rare book from a lodger.

Reaching The Hurst gates, Catherine said on impulse, 'Come inside for a cup of cocoa – warm you up before your trek down the hill.'

'Thank you,' Tom agreed at once.

Bridie was waiting up for her in the kitchen. She looked startled at Tom's presence.

Catherine introduced them, then hurried to boil up some milk.

'So how did you meet?' Bridie asked.

'Through Mrs McDermott,' Tom answered. 'I'm in digs there.'

Bridie exclaimed, 'Oh, you must be the schoolboy!' Catherine shot her a look, but she went on, 'That's what Catherine calls you. And you a teacher! Still, it must be grand for the boys to have someone near their own age.'

Tom reddened.

'Don't listen to her.' Catherine tried to laugh it off. 'Bridie can be such a tease.'

Tom smiled uncertainly. 'Kitty says you come from Ireland?'

'Oh, Kitty, is it?' Bridie crowed. 'And what else has Kitty been saying about me?'

'Nothing,' he said.

Her smile died. 'Well, that's a surprise – seeing as we've been best of friends for six years or more. There's nothing she doesn't know about me – or me about her.'

The brittle look in her blue eyes made Catherine nervous.

'Tom and I are going to take our cocoa into the sitting room,' Catherine said, messily stirring the hot drinks. 'You look tired – there's no need to wait up any longer.' She plonked the mugs on a tray with a plate of biscuits and nodded at Tom to follow.

'It's been nice meeting you, Mrs McKim,' he said.

Bridie ignored him. 'I'll see you upstairs later, Catherine,' she called after them.

Catherine hid her irritation at the woman's rudeness. Thankfully, the sitting room was empty. Putting on the standard lamp and stoking up the fire, she put the tray down on the hearth and flopped beside it.

Tom was studying the collection of books in the glass-fronted case.

'Trollope! Have you read the Barsetshire novels?'

Catherine shook her head. 'Just the one you can see.'

'I'll lend them to you,' he enthused. 'They're such a good picture of Anglican life.'

'I wouldn't know, I'm Roman Catholic.' She looked at him, wondering if she would catch that look of disdain.

He came over and squatted down beside her, his face thoughtful. 'My father was a verger – but he died when I was a baby. I sometimes wonder what my life would have been like had he lived.'

Catherine held her breath, waiting for him to go on.

'Mother married again. I have a big family and nothing to complain about – but it doesn't stop me thinking . . . I would like to have known him. I feel different from the others.'

'Yes!' Catherine agreed. 'Different – that's it. I've a stepfather too. Never knew my real one. It's like you're standing in a painting but it's only half finished – part of it's missing – and you can never see the full picture no matter how hard you try.'

'Is that why your mother drinks – to try and forget?'

'Drinks?' Catherine flushed. 'She doesn't any more!'

'Sorry,' Tom said hastily, 'I shouldn't have said—'

Catherine put out a hand quickly and touched him. 'No, it's me that's sorry. Oh, it's no surprise, but I get so angry. Just when I think she's off it for good . . .! It's me who'll have to pick up the pieces again when she drinks herself into debt. She nearly ruined me here—' She stopped, appalled that she had said so much. Tears stung her eyes. 'What must you think of me, with a mother like that?'

Tom took her hand and raised it to his lips, kissing it gently. 'I think you're the most amazing woman I've ever met – so strong and full of life. You're beautiful and clever and I could go on listening to your voice all night long.'

Catherine gazed at him in astonishment. What an extraordinary young man he was. Didn't look like he would say boo to a goose, but could flatter as well as any of the worldly-wise men who had deceived her in the past. Yet she could see from his earnest expression and kind eyes that he meant every word of it.

Impulsively, she leant towards him and kissed him on the lips. His mouth was firm and warm, and the contact sent a shiver right through her. When she pulled away, she was shaking. Neither of them knew what to say.

'Look, we've let the cocoa get cold,' she said, pushing a mug towards him and hiding behind her own. 'Tell me more about Trollope.'

They sat by the fire late into the night, discussing literature and history, arguing about religion and social justice. Tom was a liberal and devoutly Anglican; Catherine believed working people were enslaved by bigotry and ignorance as much as by the bosses.

'There's no one more cruel than the bigot,' Catherine declared, 'whether gossiping neighbour or fire-brand priest.'

'But all your priests – even the kind ones – believe Protestants like me are going to Hell.'

'I know, but that doesn't mean I do.'

'So why do you follow what the priests tell you?' he challenged.

'Guilt,' Catherine admitted. 'I'm not as religious as I was back home – but I can't stop going. It's a part of who I am, even though I don't agree with all they teach.'

She had never had such a conversation with anyone before, least of all a man. Catherine was excited and stirred by it. There were so many things she wanted to know and discuss. She hid her disappointment when Tom finally stretched his cramped legs and made to leave.

'Can we do this again next Saturday?' he asked as she showed him out.

'I'd like that,' Catherine smiled.

'Perhaps we could have tea out before the film?'

'Yes, let's.'

It took her a long time that night to get to sleep. Her mind buzzed with their talk.

In the morning she was exhausted and Bridie critical.

'Don't know what the guests must think of you, staying up all hours with that boy!'

'He's not a boy,' Catherine said irritably.

'He is compared to you. It's not seemly.'

'We just talked. He's an interesting man.'

'You don't want to go getting a reputation,' Bridie warned darkly.

Catherine went for a walk to escape. Down at the harbour she watched the waves crashing on to the beach. What would Father John say to her courting an Anglican? What would her grandda have thought? Even Kate might not be best pleased. She felt the sudden weight of tradition pressing down, her mother's voice telling her not to start something that would only end in trouble or more heartbreak.

Then she thought of Tom's deep brown compassionate eyes watching her in the firelight and felt again a tug in her heart. It was worth the risk. Something had flickered into life deep within her the previous evening – something newborn – and she was determined to nurture it.

Chapter 40

1937

Catherine and Tom's friendship developed quickly. She was impatient for the weekends when they were off work and could meet. Tom had school commitments, including helping with the scouts, so often she was reduced to writing him letters brimming with questions and ideas for them to discuss. To her amazed delight, he seemed just as eager to be in her company, despite the ridicule and jealousy of Bridie and Kate.

Through the winter they would escape on walks along the cliff paths to Fairlight Glen and its lovers' seat, or inland to the ruined church of St Helen's and picnic in the shelter of its overgrown tower. They kissed, but to Catherine's relief, Tom never pushed her further as other men had tried to do. As spring came, they ventured further afield across the Brede Valley. They talked of the books Tom lent her, of the civil war in Spain, of the abdication of the king.

Catherine was as shocked by King Edward's sudden departure as most of the country.

'But to give up *everything* for that Wallis Simpson – to have to leave his country, his family – it's a terrible business. He had duties to his country. How could he do it?'

Tom looked at her and said, 'He loves her and he can't manage without her. It's as simple as that.'

Catherine shook her head vigorously. 'It's a rare man gives up all that power and privilege over one woman – and a twice-divorced woman at that! I don't understand it.'

'I do,' Tom said quietly.

She studied him. 'But everything was against them – his family, the Prime Minister, the Church. How could he stand up to such pressure?'

266

Tom shrugged. 'His need for her was stronger.'

'It won't last,' Catherine said, suddenly depressed by the subject. Tom looked away and she wondered if he was thinking about their situation too.

She had expected opposition to her deepening relationship with Tom, but not the degree of jealousy and spitefulness that their courtship had unleashed. Bridie did all she could to stop her going out; developing sudden headaches and ailments, arranging for the priest to call when she was due to meet Tom or letting jobs pile up and demanding Catherine's help.

To Tom's face she was downright rude, always referring to him as 'the schoolboy' and never using his name.

'Doesn't it bother you that Catherine's taller?' she would jibe. 'Most men would be.' Or, 'How much younger *are* you? Is it six or seven years? She usually likes them older.'

Tom never rose to her baiting, just answered her with a strained smile. This infuriated Bridie.

'Don't know what you see in him,' she fulminated at Catherine late at night. 'Hardly strings two words together. A puny little man, that's what he is.'

'He's a good sportsman,' Catherine defended, 'and a good talker – when he's given half a chance. Why can't you be civil to him? It doesn't cost anything!'

Then Bridie would change tack. 'Darling girl, don't get upset. I'm just trying to stop you making a fool of yourself over this little man. He's not strong enough for you, Catherine. You're too full of life. Believe me, if I thought he would make you happy, I'd be the first to give you my blessing. And it's not just me – people are talking.'

'What people?' Catherine demanded.

Bridie looked sorrowful. 'The guests – our friends – they can see you're not suited. And the ones from church! You know Father John doesn't approve. And that nun from the convent you like to chat to – she was round here the other day asking questions.'

'Sister Marguerite?' Catherine asked, baffled. 'Why?'

'Wanted to know if it was true you were courting a Protestant.'

'How did she know?' Catherine reddened.

'People talk.'

'Yes, I bet they do,' Catherine said with a glare. 'It's you stirring up trouble, isn't it? It's no business of Sister Marguerite's or the priest's who I go out with!'

'That's not how Father John sees it. You're endangering your mortal soul, carrying on with a Protestant, that's what he and the nuns at the convent think.' Bridie held out her arms. 'Poor darling girl. It's just your bad luck to fall in love with an Anglican. You could never marry him. You do see that, don't you?'

While Bridie's opposition was relentless at home, Kate was being difficult too. Catherine suspected that Tom did not report half of what went on, but he let slip the odd comment. Kate's drinking was on the increase again. She had asked him for his rent early and a loan to pay the gas bill. Letters that Catherine had sent had not been received.

When she went round to Maritime Place, there was an air of neglect. The rooms were dusty and washing-up was piled high in the sink. One time she caught Tom washing his own sheets in the bath.

'What's the meaning of this?' Catherine stormed into the kitchen to find Kate nursing a cup of tea. 'Since when have the lodgers had to do their own washing?'

Kate waved a hand. 'That fussy little man. Said I'd wash them tomorra.'

'Tomorrow's Friday. You always wash on Mondays,' Catherine snapped. 'You'll lose your business if you carry on like this. And don't expect me to bail you out again.'

Kate gave her a bleak unfocused look.

'No, you don't care what happens to me. You'll gan off with your fancy boy and leave me to rot. I'll end up in that workhouse of yours and then you'll be sorry.'

'So that's what this is all about – me and Tom? You can't bear the thought of us being happy. You'd rather have me at your beck and call for ever than see me settled with a decent man!'

' 'S not true.' Kate got up, swaying. 'Always done what's best for you. You cannot marry him – he's not one of us – be a sin. Saving you from makin' a big mistake.'

'You're drunk,' Catherine said in disgust, grabbing the cup from Kate. She sniffed it. 'It's more whisky than tea.'

'Give it back!' Kate cried, lunging forward. 'My house, I'll do as I please.'

As they grappled over the cup, Tom walked in.

'Please, don't fight,' he said with a look of horror.

The cup dropped between them and smashed on the unswept floor, splashing Catherine's best shoes.

'Now look what you've done,' Kate accused them both.

268

Tom bent down and began to pick up the pieces.

'You'll have to buy me a new one,' Kate ordered. 'Wouldn't have been arguing if it hadn't been for you, Tom Cookson. Everything was champion till you came.'

Catherine waited for Tom to answer back, give Kate a mouthful. If she had been spoken to like that, she'd be marching out of the lodgings there and then. But Tom said nothing, just carried on sweeping up the mess.

Suddenly Catherine was angry with him. 'Stop, Tom! Let her do it.'

He looked up puzzled. 'I don't mind—'

'Well, you should do!' she blazed. 'Why do you put up with it? You let her treat you like dirt. Bridie's right: you're not man enough. How can I expect you to stand up for me if you won't even stand up for yourself!'

Catherine stormed out of the house. Later, after she had calmed down, she was filled with remorse at her outburst. Tom did not deserve her sharp tongue; she was hateful for taking out her frustration with Kate and Bridie on him.

She wrote him a note of apology, but heard nothing back. She felt wretched all week.

It was May, and Tom had started coaching cricket. On Saturday afternoons he umpired games. Catherine went along to the school grounds and hung about outside, summoning the courage to go in.

She slipped in the gates behind a couple of schoolboys and followed them. Standing under a large canopy of cherry blossom away from the other spectators she observed the game. Tom was umpiring at one end, serious with concentration. She sat in the grass and watched. This was where he was happy, she could see that. The tranquillity and order of the cricket pitch, the athleticism and endeavour of young people. Tom looked at one with the scene. When they broke for tea, she saw how he smiled and chatted to the boys and how they gravitated towards him. He was their role model.

Catherine felt a deep pang of longing and regret. How could she compete with this other world? She was too ill-educated to fit into his circle of academics. And what could she offer him? A life of turmoil among those who resented him for being young and intellectual, for not being Catholic. Catherine walked away, tears stinging her eyes.

'Kitty!'

She turned at the gate, heart leaping at the sound of Tom's voice.

'You came to watch.' He smiled quizzically.

'I wanted to say sorry,' Catherine said, swallowing tears.

'I thought you'd had enough of me, when you didn't answer my telephone calls.'

'What calls?' Catherine asked.

'Bridie took them.'

'Oh, Bridie!' Catherine said crossly. 'She never said.'

'No, I was stupid to think she would.' Tom looked forlorn.

Catherine stepped towards him. 'No, you're too trusting,' she corrected. 'You always think the best of folk – that's your trouble.'

'Is there any hope for us, Kitty?' he asked quietly.

Catherine threw her arms around him. 'Yes, yes there is. You must believe it.'

Stubbornly, they went on seeing each other throughout the summer term. It provoked Bridie into open war on Tom. She put about a rumour that Catherine was seeking to make her and Maisie homeless, in order to move Tom in. Some of the lodgers were openly disapproving, believing Bridie rather than Catherine, who was seldom there to defend herself. Bridie embarrassed Tom with tales of Catherine attracting married men. 'Always goes for the unsuitable ones – can't help herself. It's me who keeps her on the straight and narrow. Has she told you the scandal she caused at the tennis club?'

When Tom asked her about Maurice, Catherine forced out of him what Bridie had said. She was furious and hurt at the attempts to ruin her reputation.

'Maurice wasn't married – and the other men resented me for being successful and a woman.'

Tom insisted it made no difference, but Catherine knew once doubts were sown it was difficult not to dwell on them. Catherine hardly trusted herself to speak to Bridie and made up a bed in the billiard room rather than be near her at night. She was not going to let her ruin things with Tom.

Visits from the priest and nuns from the convent became ever more frequent as Bridie whipped up opposition to Catherine's consorting with a non-Catholic. But when none of this put a stop to the romance, Bridie set aside her resentment of Kate, and went to enlist her help in wrecking it.

'We can't have Catherine throwing away her career and independence for a pipsqueak like him,' Bridie declared. 'She wants me out of the house, I'm sure of it. She'd throw me and Maisie on to the street for that man.'

'It's the same for me,' Kate fretted, her fear fuelled by Bridie's alarmist words. 'Doesn't care what happens. Said she'll not support me any longer – and I'm having trouble managing such a big place. All I need is a little help with the bills. It's not much to ask.'

'It's up to you to put him off,' Bridie challenged. 'Only you can tell him things about Catherine – show him she would never fit in at his posh school. If you do, I'll make sure Catherine stumps up the money you need.'

The next time Catherine was out with Tom at a school concert, he was unusually subdued. Walking home, she tried to discover what troubled him.

'Is it something I've said?'

'No, it's nothing.'

'Yes it is. Talk to me Tom. Has Kate been at you again?'

His look gave him away.

'Tell me,' she pleaded.

He stopped and stared back at the sea, rattling the change in his pockets in agitation.

'She told me about – about you not having a father.'

Catherine felt punched in the stomach. She could hardly breathe. It was the one thing she had kept from Tom, fearing it would mar his love for her. How could Kate have done such a thing? The look on Tom's face told her how shocked and disappointed he was. He was a devout man of strong principles. How he must despise her now!

'She had no right,' Catherine rasped. 'You must hate me.'

Tom swung round. 'No, of course I don't. It doesn't matter to me how you were born.'

'It must do,' Catherine said in confusion. 'That's why you've been so quiet all night. You can hardly bring yourself to speak to me.' She began to walk on. Tom came after her.

'Stop, Kitty, it's not that.' He pulled her round. 'I feel so sorry for you – I understand now all your hatred of bigotry. It must have been terrible. Why didn't you tell me? I thought there was nothing we couldn't say to each other.'

'I didn't want you to look at me like others do,' Catherine said, 'the ones who know. I didn't want you to look down on me – pity me!'

Tom dropped his hold.

271

'What else did my interfering mother tell you? How many failed love affairs I've had?' His silence and wary look frightened her. 'She did, didn't she? Well, you hardly get to my age without having been out with other men. Not that any of them wanted me except for one thing. But that's what people expect from bastards!'

'Stop it!' he said. 'Don't say such things.' He clenched his fists. 'The only one pitying you round here is yourself!'

'Well, at least I know what you really think of me.' Catherine was stung.

'Listen for once, Kitty!' he demanded. She had never seen him so angry. 'I know why your mother says such things – to try and put me off you. She's been against me from the start – sees me as a threat because I love you as much as she does.'

'She doesn't love me!' Catherine cried indignantly.

'Yes she does and you're blind if you can't see it. She can't bear the thought of losing you to me. She's a frightened old woman, lashing out. She needs you, Kitty.'

Panic gripped Catherine; she felt faint. 'But I need you.'

'Do you?' he challenged, his look fierce.

'Yes, I do!'

He seized her hands. 'Then marry me.'

'Marry?' she gasped.

'Yes, before they drive us apart for good.'

Catherine stood, clutching his hands, head reeling with the idea. She heard Father John's censorious words about jeopardising her soul; she saw Bridie's face contorted in hatred; Kate wailing at her desertion.

She looked in desperation at Tom's eager face. 'W-would you – could you convert to being a Catholic?' she whispered. 'Father John and Sister Marguerite say it's impossible for me to marry an Anglican.'

'We could get married in a registry office,' Tom said wildly.

Catherine shook her head. 'I couldn't marry if it wasn't in church, you know that. To me we wouldn't be married.'

Tom pushed her hands away and plunged his into his pockets. His face looked resigned.

'I couldn't give up my faith, Kitty,' he said quietly, 'and I wouldn't expect you to give up yours.'

She looked at him, stunned. He was as good as saying it was over. They had come to an impasse that neither was strong enough to overcome. She felt sick with misery, yet even in that moment it was tinged with relief. To go on would have been purgatory, falling deeper in love with a man she could never marry. Better that it stopped now before her heart was torn in two.

'Then I don't think we should see each other again,' Catherine said, her calmness belying her inner turmoil.

Tom's lean face was tense with regret. He seemed about to say something, then stopped.

'Yes, you're right,' he nodded. 'Goodbye, Kitty.'

He turned away and walked into the gloom. Catherine stood looking after him, gulping back the sob in her throat, the cry that would call him back. But she remained as still as stone, watching the man she loved walk out of her life.

Only later, in the middle of the night out in the garden, did she curl up under an oak tree and weep out her sorrow.

Chapter 41

Catherine buried her hurt and plunged herself into work. She spent long days at the laundry, not hurrying home, and when she did so, took a notebook into the garden and wrote. On wet evenings she huddled in the leaking summerhouse. She filled notebook after notebook with stories and characters that transported her far from the drudgery and disappointments of real life.

Bridie fussed around her, now that Tom was no longer calling.

'You're tired out, come inside,' she would coax. 'I've made you a hot cup of cocoa. You'll ruin your eyes, scribbling in the dark.'

But Catherine was still angry with Bridie for her part in spoiling the relationship with Tom. She would not be comforted. She spoke as little as possible and kept out of Bridie's way. When one of the lodgers left, Catherine moved from the billiard room into the small spare room rather than go back to sharing with the older woman. There was no solace in being told that she and Tom were incompatible, even if it were true.

She avoided Kate even more, refusing to call at Maritime Place for fear of running into Tom. She was furious with Kate for telling Tom too much about their past, and could not forgive her. Catherine neither knew nor cared how her mother was coping.

Yet, as the summer wore on, Catherine came to the painful conclusion that Bridie and her mother had probably been right. She and Tom were complete opposites: she was extrovert and impulsive, he cautious and shy. She was older and worldly-wise, he young and idealistic. He was an Oxford scholar, intellectual and well read, while her education had stopped at thirteen. The more she knew him, the more ignorant she felt.

Above all, Tom was Church of England and she Catholic to her very core. The two were not supposed to mix. Hers was the true faith, as the priest and nuns kept reminding her. If Tom was not prepared to convert then there was no future for them, however strongly they might be attracted.

For a short time, Catherine stopped going to church, resentful of her situation. She railed against a God that would cast good men like Tom into the flames of Hell. But Sister Marguerite continued to visit. She was putting her own soul at risk by avoiding confession and absolution, the nun worried.

While Catherine wrestled with her spiritual dilemma, another crisis erupted. A distraught Kate came round to The Hurst to seek her out.

'It's Davie,' she sobbed, her face puffy and tear-stained.

'What's happened?' Catherine said in alarm.

'Has he had an accident?' Bridie asked.

Kate shook her head. She held out a letter with a trembling hand. Catherine took it and read the brief note. Her concern turned swiftly to annoyance.

'What's bad about this? He's got a job working on a Shields ferry – and what's more, he wants you back.'

'I cannot!' Kate cried. 'Me home's down here now. I don't want to gan back to Jarrow.'

'Well, write and tell him so.' Bridie was blunt.

Kate looked at Catherine warily, twisting her hands in her lap. 'The thing is, there's another reason – I can't afford to gan back.'

Catherine sighed. 'I'll pay your train fare if that's what's worrying you.'

'It's not just that,' Kate said, on the verge of tears again. 'I'm owing a bit on the house – got behind on the payments.'

'How behind?' Catherine demanded, her heart sinking.

'Couple of months – and the gas bill's due and they're threatening to cut me electric off.' Her look was pleading. 'I need a bit money to tide me over – till I find a couple more lodgers. It's been quiet over the summer. But I'll sharp pay it back, I promise.'

Catherine eyed her mother, unable to hide her contempt. 'Your promises aren't worth a pinch of salt.'

Instead of lashing back, Kate's face crumpled. 'I know,' she whispered. 'I'm sorry, Kitty.'

Bridie patted her shoulder. 'Maybe it's for the best if you go back north. At least Davie can put a roof over your head.'

Kate shot her a bitter look. Once she had thought her an ally, but the Irish woman had usurped her place in Catherine's affections. Bridie no longer had a use for her.

275

'Bridie's right,' Catherine said. 'You've got no choice.'

'Please, hinny, don't send me away,' Kate begged.

'This isn't my doing!' Catherine gave her mother a hard look. 'I'll bail you out one last time, but it's on one condition – you go back to Davie.'

Kate bowed her head. 'But what about me lodgers? I'd feel bad, putting them out.'

Catherine tensed.

'How many do you have?' Bridie asked.

'Two,' Kate answered, almost inaudibly.

'Two in the whole of that big house?' Catherine cried in disbelief. 'No wonder you're up to your neck in debt.'

Kate lifted her head defiantly. 'And there's Tom Cookson – said he'd come back after the summer holidays.'

Catherine reddened at his name.

'Where is he?' Bridie asked, glancing between them.

'Gone travelling on the Continent. Said there was nowt to keep him in Hastings.'

Catherine swallowed. 'We can take your lodgers in here if they can't find anywhere else.'

Bridie was suspicious. 'But what about the schoolboy? What if he comes back to Hastings?'

Catherine answered briskly, 'He can take his chances like the rest of the lodgers. I really couldn't care.'

A week later, Catherine received a letter from Davie too. He was tired of living in lodgings apart from Kate. She was his wife and he wanted her back to look after him. He was proud to have found the Shields job when so many were idle. He knew Kate would be pleased so it worried him that he'd heard nothing from her.

Catherine went straight round to her mother's, any half-doubts about making her leave Hastings gone.

'If you haven't written to Davie, you'll do it right this minute,' she ordered. 'He's worried about you.'

Kate snorted. 'Worried he's got no housekeeper, more like.'

Catherine did not know why things had soured between her mother and stepfather, and it was none of her business. She stood over her while Kate wrote a letter back, telling him she would be home by the end of August. Before she left, she spoke to the two lodgers, offering them accommodation at The Hurst, paid Kate's overdue bills and agreed to dispose of the lease as soon as she could.

276

Kate looked stunned by her quick businesslike handling of the mess. She did not try to argue or prevaricate with Catherine, who reminded her of Rose when faced with a crisis. Kate thought how her mother would have handled the situation with just as much tough-minded fairness as Catherine.

A week later, a one-way ticket was bought, and Catherine arrived in a taxi to pick up Kate and her two bags of belongings. Bridie had offered to come too, believing Catherine might weaken at the last minute and allow her mother to stay.

'I won't change my mind.' Catherine was resolute. 'I can't wait for her to be gone.'

Kate sat in the taxi, white-faced and sober, clutching a handbag. They rode all the way in silence.

At the station, Catherine bought a platform ticket to make sure she got Kate and her possessions on to the train. Kate, who had been mute since being collected, suddenly burst into tears at the carriage steps. She turned and threw her arms around her daughter.

'I-I'm so s-sorry, Kitty!' she wept. 'It's all a mistake. I didn't mean to spoil things for you and your teacher. I'll never stand in your way again. Just please don't send me away. I cannot bear to gan away from you!'

Catherine was horrified at the clinging, wailing woman. She looked around in embarrassment at the other boarding passengers.

'Don't, Kate,' she hissed. 'You're making a fool of yourself.'

Kate cried louder, 'I don't care – I want to stay! Please take me back – I'll never tak another drink – I'll do anything you want. You're all I've got. *Please*, Kitty!'

Catherine was overcome by her mother's desperate last-minute plea. For a moment she held on to her, in a self-conscious hug. Kate shook in her arms, her tears soaking her collar.

The guard came by. 'You'll have to get on board now, ma'am. Sorry, but the train's leaving.'

With a huge effort of will, Catherine pulled away from her mother. 'Come on, you have to go, it's all arranged. There's no going back on it.' She pushed Kate towards the carriage, forcing her up the steps. 'It'll be all right once you get there.'

Kate turned and gave her such a look of desolation that Catherine almost relented. But the guard came back and she had just enough time to heave the bags on board before he slammed the door shut. She watched her mother standing hunched and crying in the empty carriage. She looked so old and utterly dejected. The whistle shrieked.

The train jolted forward and Kate swayed, almost losing her balance. Who would look after her now? Catherine was flooded with guilt. She wanted to wrench the door open again and pull her mother off. But she clenched her hands and resisted the urge, fighting back her own tears. She waved Kate away.

Moments later, her mother was out of view and the train was picking up speed. Catherine stood for a long time, peering through the smoke of the departing train at the place where her mother had been. She had severed the cord between them for the last time, and it ached as if it had been physical.

Catherine went for a long walk along the cliffs above Hastings, gulping in sea air to try to stem her sense of failure. Finally, the buffeting breeze brought her to her senses.

Kate had Davie to look after her. Here, her mother was out of her depth, incapable of fending for herself. Catherine's own relationship with her was in shreds and she could do no more for Kate here.

As Catherine turned for home and the job of picking up the pieces of her life again, she clung to the belief that her mother was a survivor. She had done the best thing by Kate in sending her home to Davie and her family. One day she would see that.

Chapter 42

It was a shock to open the door to Tom, one September evening. Catherine knew he would probably call – there was a box of books cleared from his room to collect. Even so, her heart thumped to see him standing there lean and suntanned under a Panama hat, with a battered suitcase at his feet.

'Hello, Kitty,' he said, removing his hat. 'I know it's late, but I got this message at the school . . .'

She stared at him, ridiculously tongue-tied, her insides doing somersaults. He was as handsome as she had remembered.

Tom ploughed on, 'You see, I don't have anywhere to stay. Your mother's place is closed and they said at the school to call here. What's happened to Mrs McDermott?'

'She's gone,' Catherine said, finding her voice. 'Back to Jarrow – her husband's got work. I said I'd take in any of her lodgers who needed it. Mr Parish is here. And there's your box of books – you'll want those, of course.'

Tom eyed her warily. 'I know this is awkward for both of us, but if you have a room spare I'd take it. Just till I find somewhere else. I'll keep out of your way.'

Catherine's heart twisted at the bittersweet thought of having him so close yet untouchable. She waved a hand at him. 'Not awkward at all,' she said briskly, 'not for me. There's a room at the back of the house you can have.'

Tom hesitated. 'Won't Mrs McKim mind me being here?'

Catherine hid her disquiet. 'Bridie's in Ireland – taken Maisie on holiday. Anyway, it's up to me who I take in as lodgers. It is my house, after all.'

Tom blushed. She had not meant to sound so brusque, but she did not trust herself not to betray the surge of tenderness she felt towards him.

Just at that moment, Tuppence came bounding out of the trees from chasing rabbits and rushed up to Tom. The dog ran round him excitedly, barking a welcome.

'Get down, Tuppence!' Catherine cried.

But Tom bent to greet him with the same enthusiasm. 'Hello, old boy. How've you been? Yes, I've missed you too.'

'Tuppence, that's enough,' Catherine said, calling the dog to her side. 'Why don't you join the other guests in the sitting room while I get your room ready, Mr Cookson?'

Tom shot her a look. 'Thank you – Miss McMullen.'

Aware he was probably teasing her, she marched quickly ahead of him so he could not see her blushing.

Tom settled into The Hurst without any fuss and, like Catherine, was out all day at work. In the evenings he would disappear to his room to mark books, and his light was often on late at night when Catherine went out to walk the dog. She wondered what he was thinking and could only guess at his feelings. He was pleasant and civil to her like he was with the other lodgers but she had to assume his infatuation with her had passed. Catherine, though, was tortured by having him under her roof, sick with longing for their old intimacy. How had she ever imagined the arrangement would work?

Then Bridie came back from Ireland.

'How long has *he* been here? As soon as my back's turned he's got his feet under the table!'

'Don't be daft,' Catherine defended. 'He's not interested in me any more, and he's treated the same as all the others.'

Bridie scowled. 'I'm not fooled by all this "yes Mr Cookson, no Miss McMullen". I can see the way he looks at you.'

Catherine made for the door. It was pointless arguing: Bridie was set against Tom, whatever he did. How peaceful the household had been with Mrs Fairy in charge and an obliging girl, Rita, from the town to help.

'Don't turn your back on me, girl! When's he going to find other lodgings?'

'That's up to him,' Catherine replied, and slammed the door behind her.

It was not long before Bridie was stirring up trouble. She cut Tom out of the conversation at meal times and, behind Catherine's back, spread rumours that his intentions towards her were far from honourable.

'Tried it on with her last spring. She sent him away with a flea in his ear, but he's back again. Course, she shouldn't have let him stay here, but that's Catherine, far too soft for her own good. I don't trust him. It's obvious he's after her money and a big house. Always the quiet ones you've got to watch,' she added darkly.

Only Major Holloway ridiculed the idea.

'Utter nonsense! Tom's a first-rate chap. Plays a good straight bat. Miss McMullen has nothing to fear from *him*.'

All through the winter, Bridie attempted to oust the young teacher. If Catherine spoke up for him, it only made things worse. Bridie's jealousy and suspicion that Catherine had taken up with Tom again only increased. Nothing had happened between them, but Bridie was unbelieving. What perplexed Catherine was why Tom put up with the insults and remained at The Hurst. She admired him for the way he quietly stood up to Bridie and refused to be provoked. But he would not take it for ever. The thought of him leaving was unbearable, yet she would not lay bare her feelings when he had done nothing to encourage her.

The Christmas holidays came and Tom made arrangements to spend it with his family in Essex. He searched for Catherine and found her in the summerhouse, rug around her knees, huddled over a notebook.

'What are you doing?' he asked in surprise.

'Writing,' Catherine said bashfully, pushing the notebook under the rug. Her heart hammered to be suddenly alone with him.

'What sort of writing?'

'Stories,' she flushed.

'C-could I read one of them?'

She gawped. No one had ever asked to read anything of hers, ever. The idea quite unnerved her.

'Oh, no! They're not for anyone to read. I-I just do them for myself.'

Tom nodded. 'Sorry – I didn't mean to be rude.'

'No, you weren't,' she said hastily. Catherine watched his warm breath cloud the icy air. How could she keep him there long enough to tell him how she felt? Perhaps he had come to declare his love at last? Her spirits leapt. 'Is there something you came to ask?'

Tom cleared his throat. 'I think it best if I find somewhere else after Christmas.'

Catherine gasped as if winded. 'Why? Is it Bridie?'

Tom looked uncomfortable. 'I know Mrs McKim doesn't like me – I'd put up with that just to stay here – but I think I'm causing you too much embarrassment. I foolishly thought . . .'

Catherine's heart pounded. She was losing him. 'Thought what?'

'It doesn't matter now.' Tom shrugged. 'I'll leave my books at school over the holiday, so you can relet the room straight away.' He gave his quick bashful smile that tore at her heart. 'Take care – Kitty.'

'No, don't go!' She sprang to her feet. 'I don't want you to go.'

He stopped and stared. 'What do you want?'

Catherine reached out to him. 'I want you, Tom,' she cried. 'I want you so much.'

In an instant he had his arms about her, holding her tight. 'Oh God, Kitty. You don't know how much I've wanted to hear you say that!' He kissed her firmly on the lips.

'I've missed you,' she said, half crying, half laughing in relief. 'You've no idea how much.'

'I thought you didn't care for me – that last spring was just a passing phase,' Tom confessed. 'That's why I was going. It was too hard being in love with you – being near you – and thinking you felt nothing.'

'It was the same for me! How could you not see how much I wanted you? I've been going mad not telling you.'

They kissed again, a long tender kiss that made warmth flood through her.

When they pulled away, she felt light-headed.

Tom asked, 'What about Mrs McKim?'

Catherine looked around guiltily, as if Bridie was watching. Then she shrugged off her unease. If Tom loved her as much as she did him, they would find a way of dealing with the difficulty.

'Leave her to me,' Catherine assured him. 'I'll talk her round.'

Catherine's plan to tackle Bridie about Tom was sent awry by a bout of bleeding over Christmas. The doctor was called and diagnosed overwork.

'It's a nervous condition, triggered by stressful situations,' he pronounced.

Catherine was sceptical, but happy to take to bed for several days. Bridie insisted on nursing her night and day.

'Anything you want, you just tell Auntie Bridie. Nothing's too much trouble, you know that, dear girl.'

Catherine felt ashamed of the dark, resentful thoughts she had been harbouring towards the woman. When faced with a crisis like this, there was no one more tender and kind than her Irish friend.

At New Year, she sat wrapped in blankets by a roaring fire – with Bridie and Maisie feeding her chocolates, and Tuppence resting his head in her lap – wondering what to do. She felt beholden to Bridie.

Then she thought of Tom and felt a familiar ache. How she wanted him! She hungered for physical companionship, for his world of knowledge and respectability. Catherine felt a shiver at the thought of being intimate with Tom. It excited yet unnerved her in a way she did not understand. Having him under the same roof would make it increasingly difficult to resist. But to make the same mistake as Kate had frightened her even more. She smothered her lustful thoughts.

Just before Tom returned, Catherine faced up to Bridie.

'I want you to be nicer to Tom Cookson. It's upsetting the way you pick on him in front of the others.'

Bridie snorted. 'Not upsetting enough obviously – the wretched little man is still here.'

'Don't talk like that,' Catherine reproved. 'He's done nothing to you and I'll not put up with the way you treat him. This is his home in Hastings.'

Bridie shot her a keen-eyed look. 'I knew it. He's after you again, isn't he?'

The aggression in Bridie's voice made Catherine suddenly wary. 'He's a friend – but I'll not be questioned about it as if I've done something wrong, do you hear?'

Bridie said nothing more as she slammed out of the room.

Although delighted to see Tom return, Catherine had to caution him when they snatched a moment alone.

'We can't let her know we're courting again – not yet. She'll just make things difficult for the both of us. But we can meet up away from here – especially when the days get longer. We can go for walks.'

Tom looked at her in disappointment. 'You said you were going to tell her.'

'I was ill over the holidays and she was so kind to me – I couldn't be too hard on her.'

'Ill?' Tom asked in concern. 'How ill?'

Catherine was evasive. 'Just overtired. I get heavy nosebleeds when I'm run down.'

Tom touched her face. 'My poor Kitty. I wish I'd been here to take care of you.'

Catherine seized his hand, kissing it quickly. 'Me too. I've really missed you.'

Tom abided by Catherine's ruling that they would show nothing of their feelings in front of the household, but it grew increasingly difficult for both of them. They had stolen moments on Saturday afternoons when they walked the quiet country lanes. Tom would take a book and read to her, while Catherine sat with her head on his shoulder and drank in his words. They would kiss and joke about having to sneak about at their age. Somehow it heightened the excitement of their romance, yet Catherine was fearful of Bridie finding out, knowing how cruel she would be to Tom. More and more, Catherine contemplated getting rid of Bridie. But she could not afford to set her up in another boarding house like Kate, and it would seem like a betrayal of their former friendship. Above all, Catherine felt responsible for Maisie and could never make her homeless.

The summer term came and Tom became restless.

'We know how we feel about each other. Isn't it time we did something about it? We could get engaged – worry about marriage later.'

'Not yet,' Catherine panicked. 'It wouldn't look right with you living under the same roof. You'd have to move out and then we'd hardly see each other. I couldn't bear that. It works better this way – and it won't be for ever.'

Tom gave her a rueful look. 'How long, Kitty? I love you and want to be with you.'

'Soon,' Catherine promised.

Bridie was growing suspicious of the number of times they were out at the same time. One afternoon she got Dorothy to follow them and report back where they went. That night, Bridie confronted Catherine in her bedroom.

'How long have you been sneaking around with the schoolboy?' she demanded. 'And don't deny it. Dorothy saw you.'

Catherine faced her. 'I don't deny it. Tom and I are courting.'

Bridie went puce. She marched forward and seized Catherine by the arms. 'You silly little fool! Can't you see he's a nasty little gold-digger. He only wants you for what you can give him.'

Catherine was stung. 'That's not true! Tom doesn't need my money. It's me who needs him. He has ten times more to offer.'

'Like what?' Bridie was scathing. 'A handful of books. I can buy you those.'

'It's not what he can buy,' Catherine exclaimed, trying to shake her off. 'I want him for who he is. He makes me feel like the most special person in the world. I love him.'

'What about me?' Bridie cried, gripping her harder. 'Haven't I been your best friend? Who was the one cheered you up when you were new and lonely in Hastings? We were so happy together. And I was the one had to deal with Kate's tantrums. I did it all for you, Catherine, I did everything for you!'

Catherine felt a flicker of fear at the anger in Bridie's intense blue eyes. She gently pulled away.

'I know you did. I'm still your friend. Loving Tom doesn't change that.'

'It changes everything!' Bridie screamed. 'He'll take you away from me. You'll throw me out. I'll die if you try and get rid of me, I swear it!'

'I'm not going to throw you out,' Catherine insisted. 'I couldn't run this place without you. There's always a job here for you as long as you want it.'

Bridie gave her such a look that Catherine thought she would strike her.

'*Job?*' She spat out the word. 'Is that how little you care for me? I'm just your bloody housekeeper!'

Catherine stepped back. 'Keep your voice down. Everyone will hear—'

'Let them,' Bridie shouted. 'Let them hear how you've used me. You want to cast me off like an old shirt now you've no further use for me! What's the schoolboy got that I haven't got?' She began to sob uncontrollably.

'You're being ridiculous,' Catherine said in agitation. 'It's not a matter of one or the other.'

'Yes it is,' Bridie said, tears coursing down her angry red face. 'It's me or him.'

Catherine stood holding her look. 'Then it's Tom,' she said decisively.

Bridie shrieked as if she'd been burnt.

'You can't, you can't! The priest won't let you. You'd have to live in sin and you'd never do that, I know you. You could never marry that man!'

'We'll face that when the time's right,' Catherine insisted. 'Now will you please leave my room?'

Bridie looked at her wild-eyed. 'Please don't make me go. I love you too. I love you more than he ever could!'

She was so distraught, Catherine was terrified the woman would attack her.

'I'm not going to throw you out. Not if you calm down and leave my room now.'

Bridie glared at her and Catherine held her breath, trying not to betray her fear. The moment passed and Bridie stormed from the room. Catherine sank on to the bed, shaking violently. Never had she guessed that Bridie was capable of such hysteria, such jealousy over her. She was behaving like a possessed lover.

Catherine's stomach turned over. Surely Bridie did not see her in that light? They had been friends, more like mother and daughter. But Bridie had spoken of loving her more than Tom ever could. If Bridie saw herself as a spurned partner, however far-fetched that was, then she really had something to fear. Catherine clamped her hands over her mouth to stop herself crying.

The next day, she caught up with Tom as he walked down the street towards school and told him of the dreadful scene. Tom's face broke into a smile of relief.

'Don't worry. It's finally out in the open. Now we can get on with our courtship.'

'How can we? I'm frightened of her,' Catherine exclaimed, 'frightened of what she might do to us – to herself!'

Tom unexpectedly grabbed her hand. 'She's playing games – manipulating your feelings. Don't let her do it, Kitty. She'll ruin everything if you let her.'

The next days were tense. Bridie's mood was volatile: protective and mothering one moment, threatening and sarcastic the next.

It was the major who intervened to lighten the atmosphere in the house.

'There's a dance on at the Calais on Saturday night. Why don't we go – you, Tom and myself?'

Catherine agreed at once. But when the evening came, Bridie sent Maisie to fetch her as she was getting ready. Maisie was upset that her mother was ill. Catherine rushed to her room to find Bridie retching into a basin, her hair damp and stuck to her flushed face. Catherine felt her head: it was burning hot. The room was unbearably stuffy, as if the electric fire had been on.

'You've a fever – I'll call the doctor.'

'No,' Bridie whispered. 'I don't want a doctor. I want you to look after me.'

Catherine caught sight of a hot-water bottle on the bed. It was the middle of summer. Bridie's fever was manufactured. She did not try to hide her irritation. 'Maisie will run you a cool bath and get you to bed. Mrs Fairy can keep an eye on you while I'm out.'

'You can't go and leave me,' Bridie wailed. 'Please don't leave me.'

'I'm going out with Tom and the major. It's just for the evening. I'm not running away. There's no need to make this fuss.'

Bridie grabbed on to her. 'No, don't go! If you care anything for me you won't go.'

'Oh, Bridie,' Catherine entreated. 'I don't love you in that way. You must know that?'

Bridie screamed, 'I'll kill myself! I swear I'll kill myself if you go with him!'

Catherine shrank from her, appalled. 'Don't be daft. Of course you wouldn't.'

'I would!' Bridie lunged for a metal button hook on the dressing table and jabbed it at her wrist.

'Stop it,' Catherine cried, wrestling it away from her. Bridie screamed incoherently. Maisie backed against the door, whimpering in fright.

'All right,' Catherine panted. 'I won't go out – not tonight. Please calm down. Maisie, it's all right, pet. Nothing's going to happen to your mother.' She looked at Bridie. What had she done to reduce this vivacious woman to the shaking wreck in front of her? She must be partly to blame.

Catherine put out a hand. 'Lie down, you're all done in.' She went to the door.

'Where are you going?' Bridie said in panic.

'To tell the major I won't be going with them,' Catherine said in a flat voice.

'Thank you,' Bridie said tearfully.

She found the men waiting in the hallway, dressed smartly in dinner jackets, the major wearing his Boer War medals. Tom looked so handsome, Catherine's heart twisted.

'You're not ready,' he said in dismay.

'No. I'm not coming. I'm sorry – Bridie's not well – she has a fever.'

'Fever be damned!' Major Holloway barked. 'The woman's leading you a dance.'

Catherine looked at them pleadingly and dropped her voice. 'She's threatening to kill herself. She's in such a state, I daren't leave her.'

The major shook his head. 'You shouldn't let her get the upper hand like this. She'll rule your life for ever.'

But it was the look on Tom's face that turned her cold. He stared at her with a mixture of anger and disappointment. If he had ordered her there and then to go with him, she might have. But he turned away from her without a word, his back stiff with rejection, and walked out of the house.

Chapter 43

That night, Catherine dozed in a chair in Bridie's room. She could not sleep for fear of what Bridie might do and could not rid her mind of the angry look on Tom's face. Bridie finally slept and Catherine listened out for the return of the men.

After midnight she heard the key in the door and whispered good nights on the stair. She wanted to rush out and apologise, but when she moved across the creaking boards, Bridie stirred. She could not risk a scene this late at night. So she let the footsteps pass, and sat awake, wondering with whom Tom had danced.

The next morning, Catherine brought Bridie breakfast in bed and told her to rest. The woman looked haggard and contrite.

'I know the Devil gets into me when I think I'm going to lose you,' she confessed. 'I'm sorry, girl. I don't mean to cause you trouble. Please forgive me.'

Catherine nodded, her heart heavy. She was only just beginning to see how obsessive was Bridie's love. It was more stifling than Kate's need for her.

Downstairs, Mrs Fairy helped her serve out bacon and eggs. The major told her pointedly what a good dance she had missed. There was no sign of Tom.

'Mr Cookson's gone to communion,' Mrs Fairy said. 'Taken a picnic – said he'd be out all day.'

Catherine's unease grew. Summer Sunday afternoons were times they managed a walk together. She needed to talk to him. She spent the day in the garden, weeding vigorously, unable to settle to writing or reading. By the end she was aching and exhausted. Pausing to sit in the warm summerhouse on her way back to the house, she promptly fell asleep.

She was woken by a gentle shake of the shoulder. Tom's deep brown eyes were looking straight into hers.

'Tom!' she cried in startled relief. She reached her arms around his neck but he pulled away. 'You're cross with me, I know,' Catherine said quickly, seeing his stern look, 'but I had no choice last night. I've never seen her in such a state. I really think she would have done some harm.'

Tom stood watching her, his face taut. 'Maybe you're right,' he said quietly, 'but I can't go on like this, Kitty. Nobody's happy. There's a bad feeling about the house – you could cut it with a knife.'

'What am I supposed to do?' Catherine asked desperately.

His look did not waver. 'Choose between us. Either Bridie goes or I go.'

Catherine gulped. 'But I can't just hoy her out – not with Maisie as well.'

He was suddenly angry. 'Then you've made your decision. I think it's the wrong one. Bridie's like a leech on your back – she'll never let you be your own woman like I would – but it's your choice.'

'It's not my choice!' Catherine protested. 'I don't want to be tied to Bridie's apron strings any more. It's suffocating living with her. But what can I do?'

'You could help find her another lodging house – like you did for your mother,' Tom challenged.

'I've thought of that,' Catherine insisted, 'but I can't afford to.'

'It's not impossible.' Tom was adamant. 'But you've got to want it to happen, Kitty, really want it. For you and me. And I don't think deep down you really do.'

He turned away. Catherine was filled with panic. She knew that this time he would not come back. He was too hurt, and there was a stubbornness under the shy exterior, a firmness of purpose to match her own.

'I do want it!' she cried, jumping up after him and grabbing his arm. 'More than anything I want us to be together.' She shook him to try to make him understand. 'But you've got to help me deal with Bridie. After last night, I think she might be capable of anything.'

Tom seized her to him and held her tight. 'I'll be here to face her with you.'

Catherine clung on. 'Then together we'll be strong.'

Before she said anything to Bridie, Catherine went to the bank and asked about a loan. She could not raise enough to buy Bridie out. She had managed to build up another insurance policy, but again the cash value was not enough. It caused another argument with Tom.

'If you can't afford to set her up in business, she'll just have to go back to work,' he said, losing patience. 'There's plenty of it around now – new armaments factories opening up by the day.'

'No.' Catherine was firm. 'I'll think of something else. She gave up her job to help me with The Hurst. She's used to this life now – and she's put a lot into the place. It wouldn't be fair.'

Catherine had another reason she could not share with Tom. Only she knew just how intense and dangerous was Bridie's love for her. She had seen it in the wildness of her eyes the night she had threatened to kill herself. Catherine knew from her own confused feelings for Kate how love could seesaw with hate. If Bridie's love was spurned, the backlash of hate could be deadly. She must do all she could to give Bridie a decent alternative.

It was while walking in the garden in the early hours of the morning, unable to sleep, that the idea came. She looked up at the dark canopy of trees and back across the damp sweep of lawns. This was her greatest asset, the land beneath her feet. Builders would snap up the chance of putting a modern villa on such a site. With the money she could buy Bridie a boarding house of her own.

Catherine's heart was sore at the very thought. But it was the answer she had been praying for. Armed with this new proposal, she braced herself to put it to Bridie.

As predicted, Bridie exploded with rage. Catherine was heartless and spiteful, a betrayer of loyal friends. Then there were tears and pleadings. For Maisie's sake let them stay. She would not stop her going out with Tom if that's what she really wanted.

But Catherine, strengthened by Tom's quiet presence, went ahead with the sale of two-thirds of the garden. Even suicide threats and malicious slandering did not sway her.

'You ungrateful woman!' Catherine finally snapped. 'I'm nearly bankrupting myself to set you up in your own place! How dare you tell my guests that I'm throwing you and Maisie out? I'm being more than fair – and after all you've said and done to Tom.'

Any mention of Tom brought a string of invective from Bridie.

'You're making a big mistake throwing your life away for such a man. It won't last. He'll bore you to death. In ten years' time he'll go off with a younger woman. Then you'll regret getting rid of the only real friend you've ever had.'

Catherine locked herself in her bedroom at night, ignoring Bridie's nightly tirades or pitiful wailing at her door. It was a terrible few weeks, while she searched for a house she could afford. The world at large was at odds with itself too, seeming to mirror the poisonous atmosphere at The Hurst. Hitler's storm-troopers had marched into Czechoslovakia, his imperial ambitions growing. The fascists in Spain were gaining the upper hand. The fear of another Great War was brewing and nobody seemed certain of what to do.

Catherine bullied Bridie into going to see a boarding house in St Leonards. It was more than she had wanted to pay, but she knew Bridie would like it, set as it was in a street they had admired on long-ago promenades around the resort.

After the contract was signed, Bridie fell into sullen acceptance. She spoke to Catherine only through the other guests.

'Ask her whether she wants the fire on tonight.' Or, 'Tell her I'm taking Tuppence for a walk with Maisie.'

Embarrassing though this was, it was preferable to the weeks of emotional outbursts. But Catherine had not foreseen the consequences of Bridie's insidious remarks. When it came for her and Maisie to move out, five of her lodgers gave their notice too.

'She's taking all my custom!' Catherine wailed at Tom. 'They think I'm to blame for it all. It's so unfair!'

Tom wrapped strong arms about her. 'You've still got me and the major – and sweet Dorothy. We'll soon build up the numbers again.'

It was the way he included himself in tackling the future that gave Catherine the courage to get through the final days of Bridie's presence. A van was hired to take furniture to the new house. Bridie loaded up extra pieces that had not been agreed on, but Catherine let them go.

On the day of departure, Catherine returned from the bathroom to find Bridie in her room searching through drawers. She had amassed a pile of trinkets, handkerchiefs and scarves.

'What are you doing?'

Bridie flicked her a look and carried on rummaging. 'Taking back what's mine.'

'But you gave me those things,' Catherine protested.

'I gave them to a different Catherine – a caring girl I used to know.'

Catherine was indignant. 'Please don't go through my things.'

Bridie's look was disdainful. 'Don't worry – I'm returning everything you gave me.' She picked up a bag and emptied it on to the bed. Out fell clothes, hair combs and jewellery. Savagely, she stuffed in the reclaimed presents. Catherine gripped her dressing gown about her, biting back bitter words.

Bridie advanced towards her. 'The only things I've kept are the letters,' she said with suppressed fury.

'Letters?'

Bridie's face lit with triumph. 'Don't pretend you've forgotten. All those letters you wrote to me when I was in Ireland telling me how much you loved me, how much you missed me – inviting me to live with you. *Love letters*, Catherine! I couldn't throw those away now, could I? Wonder what your precious schoolboy would make of them?'

Catherine looked at her in horror, struggling to remember. She had written to Bridie once or twice when she was lonely in Hastings – and on a visit to Jarrow telling her what she was doing. They were far from love letters. Perhaps overaffectionate in retrospect, but then she had been young and hungry for friendship after falling out with Lily.

'They weren't love letters,' she protested.

'Yes they were – full of passion – better than anything you've written to the schoolboy, I bet.'

'Don't say that!'

Bridie's look softened. 'Oh, girl, how have we come to this?' Abruptly she dropped the bag and threw her arms about Catherine. 'I don't want to hurt you – I want to stay with you! Change your mind. We can rent out the other place. It's not too late.'

Catherine could hardly bear to be touched by her. Bridie felt her tense and slowly pulled away. Her blue eyes were brimming with tears. She spoke so quietly that Catherine struggled to hear.

'If I can't have you, he never will – I'll make sure of that.'

Before Catherine could ask her what she meant, Bridie was barging past her with her bag of possessions and out of the room.

Shaken by the encounter, Catherine skipped breakfast and went off early to work without further goodbyes. She left a ten-shilling note in an envelope for Maisie and kissed the sleepy girl goodbye in the kitchen.

'You can come back any time to visit,' Catherine assured her, 'and help me walk Tuppence.'

All day at the laundry she felt faint with lack of food and sleep, but was too anxious to eat. Returning home that evening, her battered spirits lifted to see Tom coming out to greet her. Bridie would be gone with most of her business, but at least there would be peace and quiet at The Hurst.

Tom kissed her openly, but something about his guarded look made her stop.

'What is it? Surely she's not still here?'

Tom shook his head. A muscle throbbed in his tense face as he spoke.

'She's taken Tuppence.'

Catherine looked at him in bewilderment.

'It's all right. I'll go over there and fetch him back. She's just being spiteful to the last. Told Mrs Fairy that the dog was hers since she'd bought him – and that Maisie couldn't live without him.'

It was too much for Catherine. She crumpled against him and broke down weeping. Tuppence was like a child to her, full of unquestioning love. Tom hugged and comforted her with soft kisses, steering her back to the house. She could hardly bear to walk in the door with no dog bounding out to meet her.

But Tom was resolute. He'd go over that very evening, if that's what Catherine wanted.

'Why would she do such a thing?' Catherine kept asking, quite at a loss.

Mrs Fairy shook her head in disbelief. 'She was acting that strange when she left, I think she just did it on the spur of the moment.' She pressed Catherine to eat her soup while it was hot.

They ate in subdued silence, then Mrs Fairy said, 'She left a message for you – not that it makes a ha'pence of sense. Said before you came demanding the dog back, think about the letters.'

Catherine let her spoon clatter in the bowl. Mrs Fairy shrugged.

'That's what she said – "Tell her it's the dog or the letters." '

Catherine stared at her bowl. How Bridie must hate her with a vengeance to make such a demand. Damn the letters! Let Bridie show them; Tom would see them as naïvely passionate, and still love her.

'What does she mean, Kitty?' he asked.

His troubled face made Catherine decide. She would put him through no further worry or humiliation at Bridie's hand. Catherine shook her head. 'Means nothing. Let Maisie keep Tuppence. He'll help her settle in.'

Tom looked baffled, but let the matter drop. He was so happy to be free of Bridie's relentless bullying that Catherine's sadness over Tuppence soon lifted. For the first time they could sit and chat and laugh together without glancing over their shoulders. Tom was shaking off his shyness, his confidence increasing in their growing love.

Catherine's exhaustion after the turmoil of the summer lessened. She revelled in his company and did not care if the priest or anyone else disapproved. She was deeply in love.

At times, she was so happy, that she almost forgot about Bridie's existence.

Chapter 44

1939

Catherine, Tom and Major Holloway sat tensely around the wireless, listening to the King's broadcast confirming the country was at war.

'We can only do the right as we see the right, and reverently commit our cause to God.'

Tom turned it off. Outside it was a beautiful sunny September evening. They sat in silence for several minutes, then the major shook his head.

'I never thought I'd see another war in my lifetime. The war-to-end-all-wars, they said.' He gave out a long sigh. 'I'm too old to fight. What will you do, Tom?'

Catherine was startled. She was thinking back to the first day of the Great War when, as a child, she had rushed outside to see if they were being invaded. Her grandfather had laughed at her foolishness. She had not thought of Tom enlisting.

'You won't go and join up, surely?' she cried. 'They'll still need teachers.'

Tom regarded her with troubled eyes. 'If I'm called up . . .' He shrugged.

She went to bed that night full of foreboding. Their strangely tranquil year together was over. It was months ago that Catherine had given in her notice at the laundry. Tired out from trying to juggle her job with running The Hurst, she had decided to concentrate on building up her business once more.

Money had been tight, but with the help of Tom, Mrs Fairy and Rita, she had attracted new custom and begun to make The Hurst viable again. She had bumped into Bridie twice; once in church at Christmas and once outside the cinema. The woman had been more like her old self, breezy and full of chatter as if the past rows and recriminations had never been.

'I'm doing grand – turning away business, so I am,' she declared. 'Hear you've given up work at the laundry. Wasn't I always telling you to do that? You look younger by years!'

Catherine remembered her saying no such thing, but let it pass. She waited for Bridie to question her about Tom, but she didn't. Nor did she say a word of thanks for the gift of the boarding house that was giving her such a good living. Catherine refrained from a caustic reminder.

'Come round and see me and Maisie,' Bridie encouraged. 'I miss our chats.'

Catherine ignored the invitation and did not mention it to Tom.

The one incident that disturbed their peaceful existence was an emotional letter from Kate in the spring. Davie had been killed in an accident – fallen off the quayside returning to his ship and drowned. By the time the letter arrived the funeral was over. Catherine wrote her mother a long sympathetic letter, but stopped short of inviting her back to Hastings. She was not going to risk anyone coming between her and Tom again.

When she heard nothing back from Kate, she wrote to Aunt Mary for news. Her aunt was quick to write back with the gossip. Davie had been drunk. They'd rowed over something. He'd stormed off to his ship and never returned. Body washed up in the Slake two days later weighed down with whisky bottles. Maybe he'd meant to step off the staithes, maybe he hadn't . . . Whichever it was, Kate was blaming herself.

Catherine discussed it with Tom. 'I thought he was working the ferries?'

'Perhaps he'd decided to go back to sea,' Tom suggested. 'Poor man. Poor Kate.'

They looked at each other for a long time, but neither voiced what the other was thinking. Take Kate back and she'd be meddling in their lives just as before. Instead, Catherine sent money that she could scarcely afford. She heard nothing back for a month until a card came on her thirty-third birthday wishing her well. Kate had moved to a flat in Chaloner's Lane and had a cleaning job at a doctor's surgery. Catherine was thankful that her prayers had been answered.

As for Tom, somehow the talk of marriage had slipped into the background. They were living quite happily under the same roof, sharing meals and conversation, going to films and concerts, reading to each other by the fireside like an old married couple. All that was missing was sharing each other's bed.

When she allowed herself to think about it, a wave of panic rose up inside. It reminded her of painful confessions to Father O'Neill as a growing woman. Sexual thoughts were sinful, he scolded, and she had come away feeling dirty. She was the product of sin and she must be doubly virtuous to make up for her bad beginning.

Yet Catherine knew that Tom would not wait for ever to marry her. She had witnessed his slow-burning impatience over Bridie. These days, she felt it in his kisses. Now that the country was at war with Germany, the future was thrown into uncertainty. There was a spate of marriages that warm September as the town filled up with uniformed soldiers and sailors. Some of Tom's pupils enlisted.

Tom raised the subject of marriage again. 'We could have a quiet ceremony. Half our neighbours and friends think we're either secretly married or living in sin anyway,' he teased.

Catherine blushed. 'Don't joke about it!'

'Well, then?'

'We'll see,' Catherine put him off. 'The war could be over soon – and then we could do things properly.'

But the news turned grim as ship after ship was sunk by German U-boats and supplies from abroad were disrupted. One day local officials came to The Hurst and asked to look around. Shortly afterwards Catherine received a letter.

'I have to get rid of my lodgers,' she told Tom gloomily. 'They're sending a group of blind veterans from London – say it's not safe for them there.'

'And you're to look after them?' Tom queried.

Catherine nodded. She put out a hand. 'You'll stay, won't you? I'll make sure there's room for you.'

Mrs Fairy remained to help, despite her advanced age. Catherine said a tearful farewell to Major Holloway, who was moving to smaller digs in the town. 'Invite me to the wedding,' he whispered loudly.

Dorothy cried and clung on to Catherine when her mother came to collect her, and they promised to stay in touch.

When the men arrived from London, Catherine got a shock. As well as blind, they were mostly old and infirm.

'I can't manage them all!' she protested to the staff who delivered them. 'They need proper nursing.'

'You'll just have to try,' they told her bluntly. 'There's a war on.'

With the help of Rita and Mrs Fairy, and Tom in the evenings, Catherine threw her energies into caring for the displaced men. They had stories from the Great War that made her weep. Others had been blinded in accidents at work. Some were incontinent, one was senile, two suffered from nerves, all were disorientated by the move. But she was amazed at their patience with her rudimentary nursing skills and humbled by their cheerfulness. It helped her to soldier on with the job without complaint.

Early in 1940, Bridie erupted into her life again. On a chilly spring day, she appeared on the doorstep dressed in army uniform, holding Tuppence on a lead.

Catherine leapt at Tuppence and hugged him in joy as the dog licked her in return.

'And do I get a welcome like that?' Bridie cried.

Catherine looked at her warily. 'Hello, Bridie. What brings you here?'

'Let me in and I'll tell you.'

Sitting at the kitchen table drinking tea, Bridie spoke.

'Joined up. Maisie's gone back to my sister in Ireland. Don't want her here if the Jerries are going to invade.' She pulled out a revolver and placed it on the table. 'Look, I get my own gun.'

Catherine stared at it in horror. 'Put it away!'

Bridie laughed, picking up the weapon and caressing it.

Mrs Fairy sniffed in disapproval. 'What about the boarding house Catherine bought you?' she asked pointedly.

Bridie's look was dismissive. 'If we win the war and it's still standing – and I'm still alive – I'll go back to it.' She turned back to Catherine. 'What's happened to your lodgers? Place smells like a hospital.'

Catherine grimaced. 'That's near enough what it is. Had to take men from a blind asylum in London.'

'So you've had to get rid of the schoolboy?' Bridie said with glee.

Catherine reddened. 'No, Tom's still here.'

Bridie showed sudden alarm. 'Not married, though?'

Catherine did not answer. Bridie gave a short laugh.

'Can't imagine what Father John has to say about you living out of wedlock with that man.'

'We're not,' Catherine said indignantly.

Mrs Fairy warned, 'I think you should leave before Mr Cookson gets back and finds you here.'

Bridie snorted. 'Don't think I'm frightened of that little mouse.' She looked knowingly at Catherine as she pocketed the gun. 'It's him who should be in fear and trembling of me.'

Catherine's insides jolted. She stood up. She would not be intimidated. 'I wish you good luck in the army,' she said stiffly.

'We can still see each other,' Bridie said. 'The training barracks are only twenty minutes away.'

Catherine remained silent as they walked to the door. Tuppence padded beside them. Abruptly Bridie held out the leash.

'I can't have him with me – he's yours.'

'Mine?' Catherine cried, breaking into a grin of delight. 'Oh, thank you, Bridie!'

Swiftly Bridie leant towards Catherine and kissed her on the lips. 'Goodbye, my darling girl.' She ran down the steps, leaving Catherine gasping.

Behind, Tom was walking up the drive. He stopped and stared at Bridie. Catherine thought for one crazed moment that Bridie might pull her gun and shoot Tom. But she passed him without exchanging a word. Tom hurried towards the house and a bounding Tuppence. The dog jumped up to greet him. Catherine could not speak for the pounding in her chest, relief engulfing her after stark fear. While Tom was distracted fondling the dog, she forced herself to calm down.

'What was she doing here?' he asked suspiciously.

'Came to give Tuppence back. She's joined up.' Catherine tried to hide the trembling in her voice. Had Tom seen the kiss on the doorstep?

'So she's leaving the town.' Tom's look brightened.

'Not yet – the barracks are on the outskirts.'

He tensed. 'No doubt she'll be calling here on her days off.'

Catherine felt uneasy. She could not rid her mind of Bridie showing off her revolver. Tom walked past her without a kiss of welcome, Tuppence padding behind him.

The atmosphere between them was strained all evening. Finally, when all the men had been settled in their rooms, Catherine confronted him.

'I didn't invite Bridie here, so why are you punishing me for it?'

Tom eyed her. 'She'll always be here – coming between us. I can see that now. You can go months without seeing her, but the minute you do, you're a different person. It's like she has some sort of hold over you. What is it between you and that woman, Kitty?'

Catherine went hot. 'There's nothing between us!'

Tom shook his head in disbelief. 'That's why you won't marry me. All those excuses about the priest – it's not him – it's Bridie McKim. If she says you're not to marry me then you won't.'

'That's not true,' Catherine protested.

Tom's look was disbelieving.

'No! I'm frightened of her. She came here today with a gun, Tom, making threats. I'm scared of what she might do to you.'

'Don't be melodramatic.'

'I'm not. You've no idea how jealous she can be.' Catherine was desperate for him to understand. Should she tell him about the letters?

He said in a low voice, 'I think you're scared of being happy. You're scared of letting go and trusting a future you can't control. Just because your mother made a mess of love and marriage, doesn't mean that you will, Kitty.' He looked at her with regret. 'It's such a waste. We would have been happy together. I know I'll never find another love like ours.'

Catherine stared at him in panic. 'Don't talk like that, as if it's all over. We've still got each other – we *are* together, Tom.'

'Not for much longer. The school's being evacuated – inland to St Albans.'

Catherine's heart thumped. 'When?' she whispered.

'Two weeks,' he said flatly. 'I'll be gone in two weeks.'

That night, she found it impossible to sleep. Getting up, she slipped outside into the midsummer night. Despite the blackout, it was only half dark, a faint blush of light illuminating the sighing trees. Perhaps she was foolish to be out on such a night that might bring enemy bombers, but she was too restless. Catherine sat under her favourite oak that had not been bulldozed by the builder. The half-built villa on the sold-off grounds stood gaunt as a ruin. Next to it, The Hurst's massive gothic bulk was like a sleeping beast.

Catherine pressed her back into the rough shelter of the tree. The future was so uncertain now: rumours of defeat in Belgium and Holland were rife. British troops were in retreat and it was said that the smoke and fire from German bombing could be seen and heard from the Kent coast. Invasion, so unthinkable a year ago, now seemed a terrifying possibility. And here they were, sitting on the edge of England. If France was to fall . . .

Soon Tom would be gone for good. She and her patients might be evacuated too. The Hurst might be bombed and all her years of toil here would be for nothing. How ridiculous she had been, holding so much store by wealth and possessions. It all seemed so petty when there were others fighting for their lives just a short way across the English Channel.

None of it matters. Only love and being loved.

She sat up abruptly. The branches of the oak rustled in the night wind. It was as if the tree had spoken. She pressed her hands to its gnarled bark and felt comforted. This oak had seen people and wars come and go, but had still remained. She was suffused with courage and renewed determination.

'Please be here when I come back,' Catherine whispered and kissed its cold roughness.

She went back to bed, resolved what to do.

Catherine was woken by Rita banging on her door. She had slept in late. With a start she leapt out of bed, fumbling for her clothes. Opening the blind, she saw Tom walking off down the drive. She had missed him at breakfast.

In a panic, she rushed for the stairs, ignoring Rita's complaints about helping lift one of the men. Her hair a riot of unbrushed curls and her clothes half-buttoned, she dashed out of the front door and down the steps.

'Tom!' she cried. He was at the gate and did not turn round. 'Stop, Tom!' she yelled louder, racing after him. Just as he turned into the street, he caught sight of her. He stared at her half-dressed state in alarm.

'Tom,' she panted, 'wait. I've something to say. About yesterday and Bridie.'

'Not now, Kitty,' he said in exasperation.

'She's not the least bit important,' she ploughed on. 'None of this is.' She waved at the house behind. 'Only one thing matters. You and me. You're all I care about, Tom Cookson.'

She faced him, eyes welling up with tears.

'Oh, Kitty,' he said, his voice full of sadness, 'why have you waited all this time to say it? It's too late. I have to go away and there's nothing I can do about it now.'

Catherine started to shake. She could barely speak. She knew if she let this moment go, she would regret it for the rest of her life. She cared nothing for the people walking past them, staring in curiosity. It was just her and Tom on the pavement, and their future hanging on a thread.

'Saturday,' she croaked. 'What are you doing on Saturday?'

He frowned. 'Lessons in the morning, cricket match in the afternoon. You know all that.'

'Let's get married,' she blurted out, 'on Saturday – before cricket.'

He gawped at her. 'Married? You really want to marry me?'

Catherine nodded and gulped back tears.

'Even if it's not in church?' he asked.

'Anywhere. Just as long as we can be together.' She held out her arms.

'Oh, Kitty!' he said, his face breaking into a grin. He grabbed her to him and kissed her full on the lips in front of a startled passer-by.

'We'll do it then?' Catherine gasped in excitement.

'Yes.' Tom was adamant. 'I might even cancel the cricket.'

She laughed and hugged him again, wondering why it had taken her so long to see where happiness lay.

Chapter 45

Catherine and Tom were to be married quietly on Saturday, 1 June in St Mary Star-of-the-Sea. Father John relented at the final hour, agreeing to marry the couple if Tom promised to bring their children up in the Catholic faith. Catherine had gone to the priest threatening to marry in the registry office and, seeing how determined she was, her priest had come up with the compromise.

Their friend Major Holloway was to give her away and the Townsends and a colleague of Tom's were invited as witnesses. It was too rushed to alert anyone else. Tom sent a letter to his mother and Kate was notified by telegram. With war-time travel difficult there was no possibility of them attending.

'It doesn't matter,' Tom said, happy to avoid a fuss. 'Just making you Mrs Cookson is all I care about.'

Catherine's heart swelled at his words. At last she would have a name to call her own, untainted by the past. But right up until the day, she was tense with fear. Tom did not know that she had also begged Kate to send her birth certificate. Catherine did not know whether her mother would even send it, for in it her shameful illegitimacy would be written for all to see.

But the certificate arrived on the Friday with Kate's blessing. Catherine was stunned when she read it. Kate had recorded herself as Mrs Davies and the father as Alexander Davies, Commission Agent. She sat down, winded at the bare-faced lie. Kate must have risked imprisonment to pass herself off as a married woman. But to what gain? And why had her mother never mentioned it to her before now? To think of the lengths she had gone to not to produce her birth certificate in the past! She could have lost her job at Tendring because of it.

Oh, Kate! Catherine thought of her mother with a mixture of anger and admiration. How strange it was to think of herself as Catherine

Davies. She touched her father's name on the faded document. But he was as elusive as ever. Catherine Davies was as fictitious as this piece of paper and she was as eager to be rid of her as she was Kitty McMullen.

The day of the wedding, Catherine dressed in her best dress and high heels. Hot day though it was, she put on the fur stole Tom had bought her as a wedding present, determined to feel her most glamorous, despite the low-key event. Tom went off to teach the morning's lessons and meet her at the church.

All morning, she was tense with anxiety that somehow Bridie would get to hear of the wedding and try to stop it. She imagined her storming to the house and taking her captive, or blocking the steps to the church waving the love letters in her face. Bridie would get there ahead of her and shoot Tom dead at the door.

'Get this down you.' Mrs Fairy pushed a teaspoon of brandy into her mouth. 'You're shaking like a leaf. Need a bit colour in your cheeks for your wedding day.'

'I still don't believe it's going to happen,' Catherine confided in the old cook. 'I'm frightened something—'

Mrs Fairy gave her shoulder a squeeze.

'Stop worrying for once and enjoy yourself. It's a day to remember for the rest of your life.'

As she spoke, the doorbell went. Catherine jumped.

'I'll go,' Mrs Fairy said firmly, and lumbered out of the room.

Catherine stood in the passageway listening to the raised voices. Her heart banged in shock. It was Bridie.

'I must speak to her – let me in!'

'She's not here.'

'I know she is. I've been watching the house. She's not left it. I just want to speak to her. You can't stop me!'

Catherine heard them tussle and shout, Mrs Fairy panting. She must not cower like a coward while Bridie got the better of the old woman. She was going to be married. She had nothing to fear. Catherine marched down the hallway to the door.

'It's all right, Mrs Fairy.' Catherine launched herself between them and pushed Bridie off. 'Why are you here, Bridie?' She gave her most challenging look while her insides turned to water.

Bridie was dressed in uniform, her red hair tied back, accentuating her high cheekbones and blazing blue eyes. She looked wild, beautiful, mad.

'Tell me you're not going to marry him – that little runt.'

'I'm marrying Tom,' Catherine said sharply. 'You can wish me well or not, I really don't care. But you'll not stop me.'

Bridie seized hold of her and shook her hard. 'I will. I've got those letters with me. And I've got my gun.'

'I'm going to ring for the police,' Mrs Fairy wheezed in agitation.

'She's lying,' Catherine said in disdain. 'Don't let her frighten you.'

Maddened by her calmness, Bridie fumbled for her revolver. She shook it unsteadily. Catherine jerked backwards.

'Mrs Fairy, get inside and bolt the door behind you!' When the woman hesitated, Catherine shoved her inside. 'Do as I say!'

She faced Bridie, trying to mask her terror. 'I'm going now and I want you to stand out of my way.'

Bridie's eyes glinted with furious tears. 'I won't let him have you. He's not worthy of your love.' She waved the gun.

'Tom is worth ten of me,' Catherine said quietly. 'Shooting me won't stop me loving him. I'll always be his, whether you let us marry today or not. I'll never be yours, Bridie. Not in the way you want. Never.'

She held her breath. Bridie looked at her with such hatred that Catherine knew she was going to die. Here she was, standing in the sunshine, dressed up to the nines, half an hour from being married and her best friend was going to shoot her. It all seemed so ridiculous, so pointless, so darkly funny. But Catherine knew if she laughed at that instant, Bridie would fire the gun.

Nothing happened. They held each other's look. Bridie still gripped the revolver but with less conviction.

Slowly, Catherine walked forward. Their shoulders brushed as she passed. Down the steps. Her heart boomed like a bass drum. Surely Bridie must hear her fear, smell it on her person? She kept putting one foot in front of the other, hardly daring to breathe. She was halfway down the drive and still alive. If Bridie shot her in the back from this range, she might survive. Her steps quickened. From here she could run into the street and scream for help. At the gate, she wondered if Bridie could shoot after all. Perhaps there were no bullets in the gun. Perhaps she had never been issued with bullets and it was all a bluff.

Turning into the street, Catherine began to run, not daring to look back. She ran, sobbing with relief until her lungs were fit to burst. Slowing, she walked through the town, mingling with strangers, dabbing at her tear-stained face, trying to compose her shattered nerves.

She was five minutes late. Tom was at the top of the church steps anxiously looking out for her. She gave him a huge smile.

'Aren't you supposed to be inside?' she panted.

'Thought you'd changed your mind,' he said with a bashful grin.

'Wild horses wouldn't keep me away.' Her laughter was strained. *Not even wild soldiers*.

The service was brief, almost hurried. Father John could not hide his awkwardness in having to marry Catherine to an Anglican. Although Tom showed no signs of being offended, Catherine felt annoyed and hurt on his behalf. What should have been a high moment of fulfilment was reduced to a gabble of words and a hasty blessing.

Perhaps it was because of her overwrought state, but it was easier to blame the priest for the joyless service. Still, Catherine put on a brave face for the others and pretended that all was well. At last it was over. She was married to Tom. Bridie had not stopped them. She would never be alone again. They came out of the church grinning at Major Holloway's box camera, arm in arm. Catherine was touched to see some of Tom's pupils had turned up to wish them well.

Her dread returned at the thought of what they might find at The Hurst. The guests were to share a sandwich lunch before the Townsends took the newlyweds to the station. Tom had booked a brief honeymoon, with a couple of nights in London and a visit to his family in Essex.

Thankfully, all was calm at the house. Mrs Fairy whispered to her that Bridie had sat on the steps crying her eyes out for ten minutes, refused a cup of tea and then left.

'I was all for ringing the police, but she promised she never intended to harm you. Told her to clear off and not come back.' Mrs Fairy patted her hand. 'Still, you'll be leaving Hastings soon and you'll not have to worry about her again.'

Tom wanted to know what they were gossiping about. Catherine swung her arm possessively through his.

'Nothing my husband needs to know about,' she joked, delighting in making him blush.

She was glad when it was time to catch the train and wave their friends away. They sat close, holding hands, revelling in being alone together at last. Tom had arranged a theatre trip for the evening and Catherine felt light-headed at the thought of parading round the big city on the arm of her handsome new husband.

But halfway to the capital, the train stopped at a crowded station. Scores of bedraggled soldiers squeezed on. Their clothes were damp, their exhausted faces unshaven. A strange smell hung about them of sweat and dirt and smoke. Catherine clutched Tom's hand tighter, fearful of what it might mean. The train finally pulled away, but the crowded carriage was eerily silent. One man caught her staring at him.

'Where have you come from?' Catherine whispered.

'France,' he said. She waited for him to say more but he didn't.

She felt compelled to ask, 'Is it very – bad?'

He hung his head, too overcome to speak.

An older man next to him said wearily, 'Were lucky to get out. Jerries everywhere. Took us days to get to the coast. That many refugees on the road.' His eyes looked haunted. 'Killing the lot – every bugger in their way – even the bairns. Bloody mass murder.' He didn't apologise for his language. Catherine recognised his accent as North-Eastern, possibly Sunderland.

Her eyes stung with tears; she felt overwhelmed by what these men must have been through. Glancing around she saw how some of them were bandaged, their uniforms torn. They were still in shock at their defeat and utterly spent. Anything she said would be quite inadequate.

'You're – very – brave lads,' she whispered.

The older soldier studied her a moment, then shook his head. 'No lass, not us. It's the lads we left behind covering our backs are the brave ones.'

She saw the glint of tears in his eyes and looked away, fearful of bursting into tears at their plight. The next time she glanced over, he was asleep on a comrade's shoulder. No one spoke again. She exchanged silent looks with Tom and felt his discomfort. Did he feel guilt at sitting there among men his own age who had narrowly escaped death while they had been marrying? It left the pair of them subdued that evening.

London felt edgy. It was teeming with people in uniform, boarded-up buildings and queues outside food shops. There was a desperate gaiety about the theatregoers that jarred after the train journey. Newspaper billboards confirmed the stark news that the evacuation of troops from Dunkirk had begun.

Their landlady pointed out the tube station they should go to should the sirens go off.

'Thinking of shutting up the place and going to stay with my sister in Worthing,' she told them glumly. 'You'll likely be my last customers till this war's done with.'

They retreated to their dingy room, infected by the woman's gloominess.

'Let's go to bed,' Tom beckoned.

Catherine looked anxiously at the faded green counterpane that Tom was turning back. He caught her look.

'I'll change in the bathroom down the hall if you like.'

Catherine nodded, her nervousness mounting. She had pushed the thought of the wedding night to the back of her mind. That morning she had doubted she'd live long enough to see it. Then the soldiers on the train had occupied her thoughts, filling her with an unnamed dread. But now the moment had come: the consummation, sex. She had worried over it for years. But there was no need. She was married and nothing she did would be sordid or dirty. So why was she gripped by such overwhelming panic that she felt physically sick?

Hurriedly, she stripped off while Tom was out of the room and threw on her nightdress. She climbed between the sheets, which were chilly and damp-smelling despite it being June. Catherine turned off the light and plunged the blacked-out room into pitch darkness. Tom came back, fumbling and clattering into furniture.

'Where are you?' He banged into the bed.

Catherine would have laughed if she didn't have her hand clamped over her mouth to stop the nausea. Tom clambered in and reached for her in the dark. She froze at his touch.

'What's wrong? Are you cold?' He began to rub her shoulders. 'I'll soon have you warmed up.'

Catherine had a violent flash of memory. She was sitting on a man's knee and he was jiggling her up and down, whispering in her ear. He was a friend of Kate's. But her mother was not there. She was too small for her legs to reach the ground and they flapped out in front of her like a doll's. They were alone. His words were strange and frightening and she wanted her mother to come back and stop the jiggling and the talking.

Catherine swallowed the bile in her throat at the memory. It was Tom whispering in her ear now, not the man from long ago who smelt of whisky and hair oil and stale sweat. Danny. That was the man's name.

'Kitty, you're shaking. It'll be all right, I promise. I won't hurt you.'

Catherine's stomach heaved. Tom's words. Or were they Danny's? Suddenly, she remembered how it ended. She was eight years old again and running into the backyard to get away from him. Danny came after her, telling her to be quiet and not to wake her grandda or grandma. He caught her halfway to the dry closet and wrapped big strong arms about her.

'*Kitty, you're shaking. I'm not going to hurt you.*'

He pushed her against the brick wall. Then he was caressing her trembling limbs with one hand, the other over her mouth so she could not cry out. A big, clammy hand that smelled of the docks.

'*I'll get you ready for bed, eh? Help your mammy. It's our own little game.*'

He pulled at her knickers. She had never played this before, didn't want to now. Wanted him to take his hands away more than anything in the world. He unbuttoned his trousers.

'*Look, Kitty.*'

She didn't want to look. She screwed her eyes shut. But she had seen the thing and still saw it even with her eyes closed. She whimpered in fear. Vomit rose in her throat. She gagged behind his foul hand. She would drown in her own sick. She hated this game. Kate and Grandma Rose would be cross if she puked down her newly starched pinafore.

Then someone was yanking Danny backwards and roaring like a bull. Pushed aside, she fell on to the cold cobbles and banged her hip. Grandda was screaming obscenities over them and beating Danny with the fire-poker like he was a lump of clinker. Screaming and beating and yelling . . .

Catherine lurched for the side of the bed in the tiny London boarding house and vomited on to the thin rug.

'Kitty!' Tom cried in concern, swiftly turning on a rickety side lamp. He stroked her head. 'Darling, you should have said you weren't feeling well. Perhaps it's something you've eaten.'

Catherine retched and cried in misery. How could she possibly explain it was nothing to do with food. A twenty-six-year-old memory had reared up the moment he had tried to touch her intimately, and spoilt everything. Danny. Some lodger her mother had been allowed to court because he was Irish and Catholic and 'kind to the bairn'.

'*Sit on his knee, Kitty. Why won't you sit on his knee? Danny's bought you a twist of sweets.*'

Kate's horrible man. But Kate had not been there to protect her. She was probably out buying whisky in the 'grey hen' for her and Danny to drink. How was it that all her troubles led their way back to her mother?

'I'm sorry,' Catherine sobbed, as Tom wiped up the mess. 'I've ruined our wedding night.' She watched him roll up the rug and put it outside the door.

He came and sat on the edge of the bed, but did not try to touch her.

'It doesn't matter,' he said tiredly. 'We've got a lifetime together. One night makes no difference. I've got you for ever, that's what counts with me.'

Catherine put out her hand and grasped his tightly. 'You're such a kind man,' she whispered.

The next day, they both put on a cheerful face and went out sightseeing. But the news sweeping the city was doom-laden. There was fierce fighting on French soil. Many of the ships sent to rescue the British Expeditionary Force were being sunk. Thousands were trapped with their backs to the sea. Paris was being bombed.

They went to a matinée and saw *Gone with the Wind*. For a couple of delicious hours, Catherine lost herself in the dramatic love story and cried when headstrong Scarlett O'Hara was abandoned by Rhett Butler. The actor Clark Gable was one of her heartthrobs. Afterwards, Tom took her for a meal, but the restaurant closed early and there was nothing for it but to return to the boarding house.

This time, Catherine steeled herself for the marriage bed, determined to get the deed over with. Again Tom changed in the bathroom, but came back to find her waiting with a side light on.

They kissed and held each other, then Tom whispered, 'Do you want . . .?'

'I'm ready,' she agreed tensely.

He caressed her gently, hesitantly, as if it was all new to him too. Suddenly it dawned on Catherine.

'You haven't done this before either, have you?' she blurted out.

Tom stopped. She saw him blush in the dim light. Catherine giggled. Somehow it made it easier. Neither had expectations of the other. She stroked his lean, sinewy back.

'Haway then, let's have a go,' she smiled.

He bent and kissed her, a long tender kiss, while they touched and explored each other's bodies. Catherine found it unexpectedly pleasant. She would have been quite happy if that had been it. But she knew there had to be something more. When the moment came, she tensed and cried out in pain. Tom faltered, so she stifled any noise and clung to his strong back. The bed creaked rhythmically, reminding her of the strange sounds she had sometimes heard coming from her grandparents' room – after Rose's protests had failed.

Tom gave a small grunt, sighed and relaxed back. Catherine lay, wondering if that was it. When he leant over to turn out the light, she realised it was over. They were properly husband and wife. She felt a surge of triumph. Lying in the dark, she could not help a smile of satisfaction. Though she was baffled as to why people made such a thing about sex. Books and films had led her to believe it was something special, something irresistible. Instead it was messy and uncomfortable and faintly comical. Perhaps it would improve.

She sought Tom's hand in the dark and held it. She loved this man. She wanted him with her for ever.

She slept deeply, dreaming about Tom being one of the Dunkirk soldiers. He was on a train and she was trying to reach it, but the crowds on the station kept pushing her back. He beckoned frantically for her to follow, but the train left without her and she was alone, crying and waving.

She woke with a shudder, to find Tom with his arms around her, stroking her hair.

'It was a bad dream, Kitty,' he soothed. 'Just a bad dream.'

Catherine allowed herself to be comforted. How could she tell him that often her bad dreams were premonitions of things to come?

Chapter 46

Catherine sat at the window of their small flat and gazed out at the September sunset, reluctant to turn on a light and draw the blinds. Ferocious bombing over London seemed the new tactic of the Luftwaffe rather than dog-fights with the RAF over the Channel. Not for the first time, she wondered at the decision to evacuate to St Albans. They were more likely to be attacked here. On still nights they could hear the explosions over London and see the far-away glow of a city on fire.

'Come away from the window,' Tom urged, pulling down the blackout.

She felt drained, unable to move from the chair. He put a hand on her forehead.

'Are you feeling unwell again? You haven't had another nosebleed?' His look was anxious.

She shook her head. 'No. I'm just tired. Though I don't know why. I worked for hours on end in Hastings and never felt like this. It's more tiring doing nothing,' she laughed.

Tom gave her a wary look. It was the one thing they had argued over since their marriage in June: the lack of a job for Catherine. He thought she would welcome having a much smaller place to care for, after the back-breaking work at The Hurst. And there were social duties as a teacher's wife to keep her occupied even in wartime. But once their small flat was unpacked and organised, Catherine balked at the long hours waiting for Tom to return. Queuing with a ration book at the grocer's was the main event of her day. She longed for activity.

A lot of Tom's colleagues these days were elderly bachelors, brought out of retirement to replace younger men already called up. Catherine held a couple of dinner parties, but felt overawed by their conversation and classical education. One in particular, an English teacher called Forbes, seemed to delight in putting her down. The only time he spoke to her directly was to ask for tips on how to get stains out of his shirts.

313

'You worked in a laundry, didn't you, my dear?'

Catherine wished she could think of a witty remark to put him in his place, but could only blush and mumble about the cleaning powers of vinegar. She yearned to be able to hold her own in conversation with such men. She had no confidant of her own – except for Tom. Catherine revelled in her husband's company and had never been so happy. But the hours when he was not there were long and lonely.

At times, she missed the fug of The Hurst kitchen with Mrs Fairy and Rita bustling about, and guests wandering in for a biscuit or to borrow the scissors. Her old house had been requisitioned and occupied by army officers; Mrs Fairy was being kept on to make their breakfast and Rita was working in a factory. Farewells had been tearful, Catherine far more upset at leaving The Hurst than she ever would have predicted.

Although she would never dare say so to Tom, Catherine regretted the terrible falling out with Bridie. How she wished for the company of the Bridie she had first known, before she had grown jealous and manipulative and bullying.

A card from her former friend had followed them to St Albans via the school, wishing her a happy marriage and that one day they would be reunited in Hastings. Catherine had destroyed the card and not written back; to do so would have felt disloyal to Tom.

If only she had had Tuppence's boisterous company to keep her occupied, but dogs were not allowed in their lodgings. It had been a terrible wrench giving the dog away to the Townsends.

Bored and guilty that she was doing nothing towards the war effort, Catherine had gone for a job in a munitions factory without telling Tom. He had been dismayed, but said nothing until she rapidly developed breathing problems and lethargy. She was brought home in an ambulance one day, bleeding profusely from her tongue and nose, and Tom had put a stop to the job.

The doctor had ordered bed rest. A further repercussion was their continued avoidance of sex. They had not made love since their short honeymoon in London. Their abstinence had not been deliberate. Tom had come down with a heavy bout of flu after their visit to his family in Essex. The packing up and moving to St Albans had left them both too tired. Her frequent bleeding and increasing nausea had so concerned Tom that he treated her like a china doll, not daring to touch her or press her into lovemaking. This suited Catherine, yet she felt guilty at their lack of intimacy for Tom's sake. If only she could explain about her trauma as a child, he would see that the fault was not theirs. But she was too ashamed to speak of it.

Somewhere, far off, a siren wailed. Tom took her hand and led her to the fireside.

'I'll make us a pot of tea. You just sit there. Tomorrow,' he gave her a stern look, 'you're going back to see the doctor.'

Catherine protested. 'I don't need a doctor – I need something to do.'

He studied her. 'What about your writing? You've got some great stories – they just need a bit of polishing up.'

Catherine considered the suggestion. She had not felt the need to write since their marriage. Her pile of exercise books languished in the airing cupboard and only Tom had been allowed to read them.

'Or education,' he persisted. 'Now's your chance to read all the books you ever wanted. You can treat it like a job. There's a library two streets away. Why don't you join it?'

Catherine felt a quick flare of interest. To read for improvement and not mere enjoyment would give her a purpose. She would rekindle her old thirst for learning that had been smothered by years of overwork and coping with Kate and Bridie.

'Yes,' she agreed excitedly. 'What a good idea.' She imagined herself holding forth at table, with Mr Forbes nodding in admiration.

When Tom came back with the tea, she said, 'You can draw up a list of books I should be reading. I want to be able to talk about books you've read. I've so much catching-up to do.'

He gave her a tender smile and poured the tea.

The next day Catherine came back from the library with a full quota of books. She set herself a target of a book a day, starting with Socrates and Chaucer. She would work her way through Shakespeare, the Enlightenment, Romantics and up to modern writers. Sitting at the upstairs window of their flat and opening a new book gave her a thrill of expectation, like a child opening a Christmas present. She could lose herself for hours in the pages of these books, only realising the time when Tom came tramping up the stairs for tea.

The evenings were spent questioning Tom about what she had read, demanding explanations of passages she had not understood. She was drawn to the teachings of the ancient Greek philosophers that held great store by truth and love. How much easier to follow such teachings than the guilt-ridden, judgemental faith to which she was harnessed.

On their arrival in St Albans she had persuaded Tom to go with her to the Catholic church, secretly hoping it might encourage him to convert. But the visiting missionary priest had railed against those not in the true faith, promising them Hell and Damnation. Catherine had squirmed in her seat, ashamed and embarrassed, wondering if Tom would walk out. He hadn't, but the next week went quietly to early communion at the local Anglican church.

Despite Catherine's new absorption in books, her fragile health continued to worry Tom. She was too thin, too tired, too often sick, he fretted. Finally, to keep him happy she made an appointment at the local surgery. A young woman doctor examined her. She diagnosed anaemia.

'And you're also pregnant,' she smiled.

Catherine stared at her. Pregnant? She shook her head in disbelief.

'I-I can't be. I'm not.'

'You've missed your periods, you're being sick every morning,' the doctor said breezily. 'You're going to have a baby.'

'But I haven't . . .' Catherine stopped, reddening in confusion. She could not tell this stranger that she had not made love with her husband for over three months – and then only the once.

The doctor gave her a keen look. 'Is there a problem? You are married, aren't you?'

Catherine jumped to her feet, offended. 'Of course I'm married,' she glared. 'But I'm not expecting.'

As she made for the door, the doctor said, 'Come back next month and we'll see which one of us is right.'

Catherine went home quite flustered. Tom coaxed out of her what the doctor had said.

'But you might be, Kitty,' he smiled shyly. 'It is just possible.'

Catherine flushed. 'She's too young to be a doctor. I don't trust her judgement. I'll go and see someone else.'

Tom's puzzled look made her feel ashamed. Why should it unnerve her so much to think she might be carrying a baby? Wasn't it what all newly married couples wanted to hear? The priests would approve. Tom's kindly mother and boisterous family would be pleased. Even Kate might fuss over a new baby.

Catherine could not name her fear. Perhaps it was because it proved to the world that she had had sex. Perhaps it was the dangers of labour and the horror of giving birth that frightened her most. Whichever, she was not ready to be a mother. She wanted to go on having Tom to

316

herself, having time for her reading, being in charge of her own life, not that of some terrifying, squalling infant.

The second doctor she saw was a naval doctor newly out of retirement. Of course she wasn't pregnant. She had bowel trouble, acute constipation. He gave her a strong emetic to flush through her problems.

'French stuff, you know. Can't get it now the war's on. Clear you out in a jiffy.'

Catherine went home in relief and drank the medicine. For three days she suffered vomiting and diarrhoea, so severe that she could hardly crawl between the bed and the bathroom. Tom stayed off work to nurse her, beside himself with worry.

'What on earth did that man give you?' he demanded.

Catherine, too ill to care, thought she was dying. At the end of the week, when she was well enough again to sit up in bed and eat a little soup, the doctor reappeared. He examined her briefly and gruffly admitted, 'Sorry, Mrs Cookson. We both got it wrong. You're going to have a baby. I'd say you're about four months into the pregnancy.' He cleared his throat. 'Don't take any more of that medicine I gave you.'

By the look on Tom's face, Catherine thought he would throw the bottle of medicine after the retreating doctor. He came back and took her hand.

'I'm wrapping you up in cotton wool for the next five months, Mrs Cookson,' he declared.

She felt weak and tearful. Now that she had to face the truth of her pregnancy, Catherine was suddenly seized with worry about taking the emetic.

'Do you think I've damaged the baby?' she whispered. 'I've never been so sick in all my life. What if I've harmed it?'

Tom squeezed her hand. 'No, don't think like that. The baby'll be fine. You just need feeding up and plenty of rest.'

'Kiss me,' she said, a wave of affection flooding through her.

He leant over and tenderly brushed her lips.

'Our first baby,' he smiled. 'I'm so happy I could dance down the street.'

Catherine laughed at the thought of her shy husband doing anything so extrovert. His enthusiasm gave her courage. There was nothing to fear in having this baby. If Tom was so keen on having a family, then she would be too. She would do anything to make him as happy as he made her.

'Go and get your dancing shoes on, then,' she teased. 'This I have to see.'

He laughed and kissed her again.

Once Catherine got used to the idea, she began to relax and enjoy the thought of their baby growing inside her. She delighted in the fuss that Tom made of her and his attempts to get hold of extra rationed meat to build up her strength. The sickness passed, but she continued to feel tired. Anything mildly strenuous, such as carrying books from the library, could bring on haemorrhaging from the nose and mouth.

Tom insisted on fetching her reading and much of the shopping. Catherine spent the autumn cocooned in the flat, being pampered and loved. Her optimism for the future grew with the baby. The imminent threat of invasion that had hung over the country for months receded a little. The heroics of the RAF had decimated Hitler's air force and the bravery of the navy to keep supply lines open had helped thwart a Nazi overthrow – at least for the winter.

Catherine dared to hope for a less dangerous future into which her baby could be born. She began to write short stories and verse for her unborn child, imagining the day when she could read them aloud to a child snuggled in her lap. By the end of October, her 'bump' was still small but she could feel the baby kicking strongly inside her, turning restlessly. If Tom was there, she would quickly put his hand over the movement and watch the look of awe spread across his face. They laughed with nervous excitement. She and Tom played endless make-believe games.

'We'll call her Catherine after you,' he said. 'Catherine the Great – an empress with beauty and brains.'

'It's a boy, he's already batting for his country,' Catherine joked. 'He'll be sporty and handsome like his father. William. That would suit.'

'I like John.'

'No,' Catherine cried, 'he might be bad-tempered like my grandda.'

Tom chuckled. 'David then. A small man like me against an uncertain world – Goliath.'

Catherine laughed. 'Yes, small, but with a lion's heart – and a clever mind. He'll go to Oxford like you, of course. David, that's perfect.'

Then in November a note arrived from Tyneside telling Catherine that her mother was seriously ill.

'Who's it from?' Tom asked. 'It's not signed.'

Catherine was just as perplexed. 'It's not Aunt Mary's writing . . .'

'Some busybody.' Tom was suspicious.

'But what if it's true?' Catherine fretted. 'I'll have to go to her. I couldn't bear the thought of her dying alone and me not getting to see her. The last time – I was that sharp—'

'Kitty, you can't travel all that way in your condition. You're not strong enough. Think of the baby.'

'I am thinking of the baby,' Catherine said in distress. 'I haven't told Kate yet. She might die and never know she had a grandbairn. She has a right to know.' Suddenly she burst into tears.

At once Tom was contrite, hugging her close. 'I didn't mean to upset you.'

Catherine tried to explain. 'I still feel so guilty – leaving her to fend for herself after Davie died. Now I'm going to be a mother myself – I want to make it up with her before it's too late.'

'I understand,' Tom assured her. 'We'll ring Mary and find out what's going on.'

But the lines were down and Tom failed to get through. This only heightened Catherine's anxiety. He could do nothing to put his wife's mind at ease or dissuade her from attempting the long journey north.

'I'm coming with you,' he insisted. 'I'll beg two days' compassionate leave.'

After hours of delays on freezing station platforms, they rattled north in an overcrowded train. Because of the lateness, they travelled during the blackout, plunged in darkness all the way. Catherine felt jumpy and ill, the baby fluttering in her womb as if sensing her disquiet.

They arrived in Gateshead in the middle of the night and dozed in a waiting room until the early morning train could take them to Tyne Dock. It was still dark when they reached Kate's flat in Chaloner Lane and hammered on her door. Tom gripped his wife's arm in support, as she swayed with fatigue and worry.

A bleary-eyed Kate came down the stairs to answer the frantic knocking. Catherine threw herself at her mother and burst into tears.

'You're alive!' she sobbed.

'By all the saints! What you doing here, hinny?'

'Let us in, please, Mrs McDermott,' Tom said wearily.

She led them up the narrow staircase and into her small living room, Catherine gabbling incoherently about the letter. Kate fetched her a glass of water and a blanket.

'Just had a bad cold,' she said in bemusement. 'Nowt to call the undertaker for. You shouldn't have worried.'

Catherine's relief turned quickly to annoyance. 'Then why would someone write such a thing?'

'Bet it's that wife downstairs sticking her nose in. Thinks I spend too long in the drink shop with her man. Not that I do,' Kate added hastily. 'Maybes she thought if you were around you'd put a stop to it.' Her mother looked sheepish. 'Sorry, hinny. By, but it's grand to see you!'

Catherine sank back and closed her eyes. She felt terrible. It was Tom who broke the news about the baby.

'A bairn!' Kate gasped in delight. 'That's champion. I'll come and help when your time comes,' she said eagerly. 'Eeh, a grandbairn! Wait till I tell our Mary.' She brushed away a tear.

At Tom's insistence, they put Catherine to bed. She slept fitfully, unused to the clanking and hooting from the docks. Every time a train rumbled by, the house shook and the windows rattled. She got up at tea time, listless and out of sorts. Kate looked better than she had seen her in years. With liquor harder to come by and work to keep her occupied, her mother was as brisk and bossy as ever.

Catherine felt resentful at having rushed north on false pretences. She half suspected Kate might have concocted the letter herself, just to get attention. Well, she wouldn't do it again – not once the baby was born – and she'd resist her mother's plans to take over her home and baby.

'Tom's going to help me at the birth,' Catherine declared, startling both her husband and mother. 'There's no need for you to be there.'

Kate was scandalised. 'You cannot have him there! Lads don't bring out bairns.'

'Doctors do it all the time,' Catherine pointed out.

Kate blustered. 'Aye, but they're different. It's bad luck to have a man in the house.'

'I don't believe in all that superstitious nonsense,' Catherine said crossly.

They left early the next day, Kate fussing over Catherine and scolding Tom for allowing her daughter to make the journey.

'She looks worse than I do,' Kate tutted. 'You'll need me when the time comes. Be sure to let me know. Tak care of yoursel', hinny.'

As usual, Tom did not complain about Kate's brusque treatment, which made Catherine feel all the more guilty for having dragged them both to Tyneside.

'You shouldn't let her speak to you like that,' she said, as they embarked on the slow journey home. 'Why can't you stand up for yourself more?'

He looked unperturbed. 'She's never going to change her mind about me. I took her precious daughter away. I don't mind what she says to me. It's you that matters.'

'Oh, stop being so bloody reasonable!' Catherine cried.

They travelled back in silence, Catherine feeling awful for taking out her anger on Tom when the whole situation was her fault. But she was too wretched to try to make amends.

Back home, she retreated to bed and Tom went back to work. He brought her a small bunch of flowers as a peace offering, but they made her sneeze violently and brought on a nosebleed. Tom was mortified and Catherine's protests that he was not to blame fell on deaf ears.

For his sake, she tried to galvanise herself out of bed and have tea ready for him when he came home. She sat by the small fire, depressed by the shortening days and a nagging anxiety that she could not articulate.

That late November evening, watching Tom marking books at the table, she covered her swollen belly and knew what it was. The baby wasn't moving. She jolted. How long had it been still? A day? Two days? Longer? She tried to think calmly. She had felt movement on the journey south – small, squeezing sensations as if the baby were curling up to hibernate for winter. But nothing much since. Not the strong kicks of before.

Catherine pressed her hands hard on her stomach, willing her baby to move. Was she being fanciful, or did it feel smaller, a hard round ball under her trembling hands? She must have cried out, for Tom looked up startled. Without asking, he came to her at once and put his large warm hands over hers.

She gazed at him in fear.

'Something's wrong,' she gasped. 'I can't feel . . .'

Tom rushed out of the house without stopping to put on his coat. Catherine sat hunched in the chair, forbidding her mind to think of anything until his return. He came back twenty minutes later with a doctor she'd never seen before.

He was cheerful and reassuring as they helped her to bed. He looked more troubled after an examination.

'There's still a heartbeat, though it's not very strong. It might be best if we have you moved to hospital, Mrs Cookson.'

321

'Hospital?' Panic choked her. She clung to Tom's arm. Maternity hospital to her meant long, humiliating, public rows of beds in dismal workhouse wards. Tom would not be allowed to be there. She would be all alone. Fear overwhelmed her.

'What would they do?' Tom asked, equally anxious.

The doctor looked pitying. 'It might be necessary to induce the baby.'

'Make it come?' Tom queried. The man nodded.

'No!' Catherine cried. 'It's too early. The baby's not ready. I'm only six months gone.'

Tom hushed her and looked to the doctor for advice.

He tried a smile of reassurance. 'Listen, we'll do nothing tonight. You stay still in bed and rest. I'll come back in the morning and we'll make a decision then.'

He left to the eerie sound of the air-raid siren, the first since their return from Tyneside. Tom lay on the bed and held her.

'You're not moving anywhere for any sirens.' He kissed her. 'The three of us'll stay together or go together.'

Catherine buried her face in his chest.

The raid was a false alarm and the all-clear sounded late that night. By then she was past sleeping. Sometime in the early hours, she felt moisture trickle between her legs. For a moment she thought she had wet herself, then worried it might be blood. She lay, not daring to move, wishing for the morning to come.

When Tom woke he berated her. 'Why didn't you wake me?' He went rushing off for the doctor again.

This time there was no cheery banter.

'I'm afraid your waters have broken, Mrs Cookson.'

'What does that mean?' she asked in bewilderment.

'It means your labour has started.'

Catherine let out a whimper. 'But it can't survive at six months, can it? It's not a proper baby.'

'If we can get you to hospital, it might be possible to delay the birth. But I'm sorry to say the chances aren't good. The heartbeat is very weak.'

Tom said very calmly, 'Wouldn't it be better if she stays still in her own bed? If there was a midwife to help me, I could look after her.'

The doctor eyed him in surprise. Eventually he nodded.

'It's as good a plan as any – if you're not squeamish, Mr Cookson.'

'She's my wife,' Tom said proudly. 'I'd do anything for her.'

322

Catherine was too overcome to speak, humbled by Tom's devotion and grateful at not having the trauma of being uprooted to a lonely hospital bed.

Later in the day, Mrs Hume arrived to oversee the birth. She was a widow who liked to talk about her son at sea, dodging the hazards in the Atlantic convoys. Her hearty chatter grated on Catherine's nerves. Tom sensed this and kept the woman at bay in the sitting room, supplied with endless cups of tea.

'Nothing much we can do until the baby decides to come,' she said, launching into a description of a long arduous birth she had attended the previous week.

By the end of the day, the situation had not changed and Tom sent her home. For a week, Catherine lay in a twilight world, waiting. Mrs Hume and Tom took it in turns to be at the flat, Catherine insisting that he went back to work. She could see by the tired creases around his eyes and his tense mouth that he was finding their state of limbo unbearable. At least his lessons would keep his mind distracted for a short while.

On the eighth day, Mrs Hume lost patience.

'There's not a flicker of life, Mrs Cookson. It's time we got on with getting it out.'

Distraught and ill as she felt, Catherine did not believe her baby was dead.

'I can feel it,' she said in distress.

'But you've said there's been no movement for days.' Mrs Hume was blunt. 'You'll make yourself really sick if you don't expel that baby.'

When Tom came home, Catherine heard her say, 'I'll not have your wife's death on my hands.'

After that, Mrs Hume set to work, giving her a draught of bitter liquid to drink and pummelling Catherine's womb to hasten the labour. Late that night, exhausted and sore, Catherine felt the first real pangs of pain seize her body. She cried out and Tom came running into the room.

'I think it's coming. Help me, Tom. I'm scared.'

He wiped her face and neck with a damp cloth and spoke to her soothingly. She had nothing to fear; he'd talked it over a dozen times with the midwife and knew what to do.

She gripped his hand when the next labour pain swept through her body. It was like an iron fist squeezing her insides and she stifled a yell.

'Scream if you want to, Kitty,' Tom ordered.

'I – don't – want – to – wake – that woman,' she panted.

'She'll not come near you,' Tom said with feeling. 'You can wake the whole bloody street – it doesn't matter a bit.'

Catherine writhed and groaned through the early hours of the morning. She prayed for it all to be over, prayed that she would not have to look at the creature that was taking so long to leave her womb. It would be half formed, a freak of nature, a lumpen mass of flesh. Tom would have to wrap it up quickly and take it away. It was the one useful task the garrulous Mrs Hume could have done for them. But she was still snoring on their sofa.

Suddenly, Catherine felt a rushing sensation between her legs, like letting go on a slide. It couldn't be stopped.

'This is it,' she whispered weakly.

Tom held her hand tight. 'Push, Kitty!'

All at once, the baby was slipping out of her. Tom let go of her to catch it. She felt instant relief as the strange pressure subsided. Her whole body throbbed and shook. She squeezed her eyes shut. It was over. She knew without looking the baby was dead. Sometime in the dark hours she had felt it fade away.

'Look, Kitty,' Tom said in a hushed voice. 'You were right. He's a boy.'

Catherine's heart lurched. She could not look. He was perverse to make her. But the next moment, he was thrusting something into her arms.

'Don't be frightened – look at him,' Tom said, his voice full of wonder. 'Our baby son.'

Catherine opened her eyes. A tiny slippery figure, still covered in mucus and blood, lay nestled between them. She gasped in surprise. He was perfectly formed – a miniature version of Tom, with his lean head and long feet and expressive hands. Tentatively she touched him, wondering at his neat fingers, his little bud of a mouth. He lay with his eyes closed as if peacefully sleeping, his body still warm.

'He's beautiful,' she whispered. 'I never thought . . .'

She heard a strange noise, half yelp, half groan. Looking up, she saw the tears coursing down Tom's harrowed face. The sight of it tore at her heart. In that instant, Catherine realised the enormity of what they had lost. Their son. A real flesh-and-blood person, not the figment of their guessing games. She gazed at the sweet baby in her arms and felt winded by the first violent pain of grief. Not only had he died, but all the years of life ahead of him that they should have

324

shared together were gone too. She hugged him close, not wanting to ever let go.

Just then, Mrs Hume appeared at the door blinking sleepily. She looked confused at the sight of Catherine cradling the baby as if it lived. But Tom's sobbing told the truth.

'Poor things, let me take it away,' she said, bustling in quickly.

Catherine faced her in defiance. For that brief moment she was a mother.

'He's a boy, Mrs Hume,' she said proudly. 'And we've called him David.'

Chapter 47

Catherine refused to let the midwife take her baby away until the priest had been. She wrapped David in her bed shawl and cradled his cooling body. The rancid smell of the afterbirth burning on the sitting-room fire made her want to vomit. Tom, unshaven and bleary-eyed, came back with Father Shay, the elderly priest at St Michael's.

He was kind and concerned, saying a prayer over Catherine and her lifeless son. Mrs Hume hovered in the doorway, sighing in disapproval and muttering about it being unnatural to make such a fuss over a stillborn.

'I want him christened, Father,' Catherine croaked. 'He must go to Heaven.'

The priest looked sorrowful and shook his head.

'I can't christen a child that's never lived.'

Catherine stared at him in confusion. 'But he did—' She could not find the words to describe how very real her son had been. He had grown and moved and lived inside her.

'If it had lived a few hours . . .' He spread his hands in apology.

Tom said very quietly, 'Will *he* be allowed a Christian burial?'

Father Shay looked uncomfortable. 'I'm sorry, but if he's not christened he can't be buried in sacred ground.'

Tom looked at Catherine in distress. She gripped David in desperation.

'Where then?' she demanded. 'What will they do with him?'

At that moment, Mrs Hume bustled past the embarrassed priest.

'You mustn't upset yourself over such things,' she said, reaching for the bundle in Catherine's arms. 'It's just not meant to be.' Swiftly she pulled the dead baby away and carried it from the room.

Tom followed her out. The priest turned to go.

'Tell me!' Catherine cried hoarsely. 'Where will she take him?'

'The body will be put in a common grave,' Father Shay said.

'Like a heathen,' Catherine said, beginning to shake. 'What about his soul? Where will that go? Stuck in Purgatory for ever and ever!'

'You mustn't dwell on it, Mrs Cookson,' he said. 'God takes care of his own.'

She struggled to sit up. 'But he's not God's – he hasn't been christened. If the Church thinks he never existed, then he doesn't have a soul. That's what you think, isn't it? My baby has no soul!'

Alarmed, the priest said, 'You must accept God's will.' He hurried from the room.

Tom came back to find Catherine clinging to the bed covers, trembling and sobbing. He went to her and held her tight. For minutes they hugged and wept, beyond speech. Finally, Tom pulled away.

'Mrs Hume said you must wash and then rest. She'll call back later to see you.'

Catherine looked at him, wondering how he could talk about such mundane things as washing and sleeping. She did not care if she never washed again.

'Did you kiss him?' she asked abruptly.

Tom looked haggard. He shook his head.

Catherine gulped. 'Neither did I. We didn't kiss him. That woman took him so quickly.' Tears began to stream down her face once more. 'I never got to kiss him goodbye!'

Catherine remembered little of the following days. They were a fog of pain. She was physically exhausted and mentally in torment. In the long sleepless nights, she searched around for someone or something to blame for her son's death.

The naval doctor had weakened her and damaged the baby with his brutal emetic. The wild-goose chase to Tyneside had brought on the premature labour. Kate was to blame. If her mother hadn't caught a cold, if she hadn't provoked a jealous neighbour with her drinking, if she had been a more responsible mother . . .

Mrs Hume was a terrible midwife, doing nothing until it was too late, then punching her insides and cutting off the life-breath of her struggling son. Even Tom did not escape her fevered attempt to find a scapegoat. He should have listened to the doctor who wanted to send her to hospital. Perhaps there might have been a chance of saving David there. Tom should have insisted.

Round and round she argued in her head. But every time she came back to the one guilty thought. She, more than anyone, had killed her baby. If she had believed the first doctor that she was pregnant she would have taken more care. It was she who took the emetic – eagerly. She was the one who had stubbornly insisted on trekking up to Jarrow and it was she who did not want to go into hospital to save her child.

But Catherine had not thought of him as a child then. She had had no conception of what she carried in her womb. Pregnancy and birth had been shrouded in terrible secrecy; her mind swaddled in ignorance. All she knew from Kate was that pregnancy was shameful and birth was torture.

Her eyes had been opened too late. Nothing had prepared her for the startling joy of holding a fully formed human being in her arms. Nobody had told her what a miracle it was. She had been utterly surprised by the fierce, possessive love that had welled up inside at the sight and touch of her baby son.

David. David. *David*.

Catherine grew to believe she was not worthy of such a gift. If she had been a better person it would not have happened. She was wicked and sinful. Yet, even as she punished herself for the stillbirth, she turned her back on the Church and its judgement.

Even when she was well enough to leave the flat and walk short distances, she avoided confession and Mass. She would not answer the door in case it was the priest. She cut herself off from the old comforting prayers to Our Lady.

'Why should her son be born alive and not mine?' she railed at Tom. 'What would have happened if Jesus had been stillborn?'

He looked at her, shocked. But she could not stop.

'Where would his soul have gone?' she demanded. 'Let the priests answer that!'

Tom could not answer her torrent of questions either. He moved around the flat, subdued and wary of her. It seemed to Catherine he could not get away quick enough in the mornings and stayed long hours at school.

She began to resent his work and the way he had slipped back into it as if nothing had happened. He had dozens of boys to call his own – he did not need their David. He thought bringing her tea and biscuits in bed before he left was all the comfort she needed. She wanted to talk about their baby, but he could not bring himself to mention his name. She needed him there to protect her from callers and neighbours, but he was never there when they came.

Catherine dreaded going out for fear of seeing women pushing prams. She froze at the sight of babies bundled up in shawls and woollen bonnets. She held her breath and hurried past shop windows displaying baby clothes and booties. Nausea engulfed her when she saw a heavily pregnant woman lumbering across the street.

Tom watched her in mounting concern, wretched that he could not comfort her. Anything he suggested she dismissed with hurtful looks.

'Why don't you go to the library today?'

'I can't read any more – it gives me a headache.'

'A walk in the park, then?'

'I hate the park. It's full of mothers with prams.'

'Your writing. That's something you could do here in the flat.'

'I can't write! What could I possibly want to write about now?'

Catherine looked at him in misery. How could she explain that the thought of picking up a pencil again made her physically sick? The last thing she had been working on was a story for David. It was half written. If she opened the exercise book, it would be lying there waiting for a happy ending.

Tom stopped making suggestions. By the Christmas holidays, he was hardly speaking at all. They were invited to Essex to stay with his family. His mother had written to say she was sorry about the 'miscarriage'. Kate had also asked them north for Christmas, but Catherine could not face going back there. It would remind her too painfully of the dreadful November journey, and Kate would be tearful and morose about her lost grandchild. She would rather go somewhere that held no reminders of when she was pregnant, so agreed on Essex.

Catherine avoided all the end-of-term activities: the Christmas play, the carol service, the staff party. Tom's look was reproachful but she was incapable of putting on a brave face. One choir boy singing about angels or one merry teacher talking about their children and she would burst into tears. Tom went on his own and did not tell her about them on his return.

On Christmas Eve, they packed a small suitcase and a bag of presents and set off for Grays in Essex. London was chaotic with people on leave trying to catch trains and evacuees returning home for the brief holiday. Slowly they made their way down the Thames towards the massive docks at Tilbury. The river was crowded with shipping, the low-lying riverside etched with chalk quarries and industry. There was a bustle about it that reminded Catherine of Tyneside, though the accents made her think she was in a different country.

Christmas in the Cooksons' small terraced house passed quickly enough and Tom's mother did her best to make Catherine feel one of the family. Catherine stood in the cramped kitchen peeling potatoes, half listening to the chatter of Tom's sisters, both of whom were courting. One brother was away in the navy – Egypt, they thought. The youngest was out kicking a ball in the wet back lane.

Tom kept peering in anxiously to see if she was all right. Catherine relaxed and ate more than she had in weeks, grateful for their friendly warmth. The small glass of sherry, specially hoarded for the occasion, made her light-headed and comfortably detached. After lunch she went to lie down while Tom went for a walk with his sisters.

When Catherine got up she could hear voices and laughter downstairs. His mother had mentioned some cousins were calling for tea to see them. She walked in and was halfway across the room to Tom when she stopped.

A dark-haired young woman was sitting by the fire, joggling a baby on her knee. The baby was gazing about with large eyes, a fist in his mouth, dribbling and making little noises. Catherine was transfixed.

'This is cousin Betty,' Tom's mother said, 'and little Winston. Come and sit down, Kitty.'

The young cousin smiled. The only empty seat was next to her. Catherine looked at Tom in panic. He smiled at her tensely. She went and sat down, shrinking into her seat, heart pounding. The room was overpoweringly stuffy, her palms sweaty.

The conversation resumed. It was all about baby Winston, what a good appetite he had and how he was nearly sitting up by himself. One of the sisters offered Catherine a cup of tea. She nodded, feeling faint.

'Perhaps you'd like to have a hold of the baby first?' the senior Mrs Cookson asked.

Catherine gawped. She could not mean it. But Tom's mother was smiling at her in encouragement and nodding.

'Course you can,' Betty said, holding the baby out to her. Winston sensed the handing over and began to grizzle. Betty joggled him up and down and waited for Catherine to take him.

She sat paralysed. The thought of touching the child made bile flood her throat. She swallowed and tried to speak. Everyone was looking at her now, willing her to hold the baby. What did they think? That nursing someone else's baby boy would make up for the absence of her own?

330

What torture! No one had made any mention of David, not one word. Now they were behaving as if she and Tom had never had a baby at all. How could they?

'No, I don't want to . . .' she mumbled.

As she sat frozen, Tom abruptly stepped forward.

'I'll take him,' he said, fumbling for the boy. He took the baby gingerly, as if he were made of porcelain. Gripping him awkwardly to his chest, Winston instantly began to cry.

'Rock him,' Tom's mother said. 'They like movement.'

'He likes to look over your shoulder,' Betty advised.

Winston bawled louder. The noise seared Catherine like a branding iron. They had never heard David cry. She would have given the world to hear it. It was more than she could bear, watching Tom holding the baby, struggling to stop the wailing.

She sprang out of her seat and rushed for the door, knocking over someone's cup of tea on the carpet.

'Sorry,' she gabbled, but did not stop. She raced from the room.

Behind, she could hear Mrs Cookson say in an offended voice, 'There was no need for that. Thought it might help the girl to have a little cuddle.'

Catherine fled out of the house. It was already dark outside and she stumbled around in the pitch-black. Tom found her at the end of the street, shivering and weeping in a boarded-up doorway.

'H-how could you h-hold him?' she accused. 'And your m-mother – so cruel!'

She tried to shake him off when he put an arm around her. But he persisted.

'She thought she was helping – she doesn't understand.'

'No, she doesn't,' Catherine said bitterly. 'Nobody does.'

'I do,' Tom said gently.

Catherine said hotly, 'No you don't – or you wouldn't have been able to touch Winston.'

Tom dropped his hold. She could not see his expression but saw him stiffen.

'Do you think I wanted to?' he demanded. 'I dreaded it as much as you – but I took him so you didn't have to. I did it for you, Kitty, no one else. I'd do anything to make things better, make you smile again. You've no idea how lonely it's been.'

Catherine lashed out. 'Lonely for you! You've got your job, your colleagues, your precious boys. What have I got? Nothing! Just emptiness – a big gaping hole – and arms that ache 'cos I've got no baby to hold! You've no idea how that feels.'

'Yes, I do,' Tom cried, seizing hold of her. 'You're not the only one suffering. I miss him every waking minute. I think of him all the time – what he might have looked like at two, three, twenty-three. I imagine him sitting at the back of my class, putting his hand up to answer a question, gazing at me through spectacles like mine.' His voice trembled. 'I lie awake at night in our bed and can't sleep, because I can't get the picture out of my mind of you holding him in that very same bed.'

Catherine gasped in pain. She clutched at him.

'Say it,' she whispered, 'say his name. Call him by his *name*.'

A sob caught in Tom's throat. 'David,' he rasped, '*David*.'

Instantly their arms went round each other.

'I'm sorry,' Catherine cried. 'I'm so sorry.'

They clung together in the icy drizzle, weeping. Gradually, the pain that oppressed them eased a little in each other's arms.

Back in St Albans, one cold January day, Catherine set out for the cemetery where she believed David was buried. She had badgered the priest and the parish for information. It was starting to snow and the day was darkening though it was just past noon.

She roamed around the large graveyard, glancing at the headstones. There would be nothing to mark her baby's grave. He would have been bundled into a parish grave like a pauper. Still, she could not rest until she knew under which mound of black earth he lay.

Eventually she came across the sexton, who was chatting to one of the gravediggers. Catherine gave them the rough date of burial.

'A stillborn boy. Cookson. Father Shay said he was here.'

The two men looked at her in surprise. They fell silent while they thought about it. The sexton shook his head.

'There's been a few babies from the workhouse . . .'

'No,' Catherine was adamant, 'he wasn't one of those.'

'I remember,' the gravedigger suddenly said, 'tiny baby in early December. Sure the name was Cookson.'

Catherine's heart thumped. 'Do you remember where he was put?'

The man nodded. 'Yes, over there. We buried him along with an old woman from the workhouse. Remember thinking, well at least he's got company, poor little mite.'

Catherine's eyes stung with tears. 'Can you show me?'

332

The gravedigger took her to an unmarked grave, touched her shoulder and left her alone.

Catherine squatted down and fingered the frozen earth under its thin blanket of snow. She was strangely comforted to think of David being laid beside an elderly woman; a surrogate grandmother. A Rose McMullen to cradle him in death. He would never be alone.

When the spring came, she would return and put flowers here for the two of them. Catherine stood up, stiff and cold in the raw air and walked away.

Halfway home, on an impulse, she turned in to the library. For the rest of the afternoon she sat in its warmth and read a history book. When it was time to leave, she spotted a notice for drawing lessons. After a moment's hesitation, she wrote down the details. Somehow, she would find a way out of the tunnel of grief that entombed her.

Today was the first day she had glimpsed a chink of light.

Chapter 48

'It's marvellous,' Tom said in admiration when Catherine showed him her sketch of St Alban's cathedral. 'The texture of the stone – the detail – it's so alive.'

She smiled at him in triumph. The life classes at the art school had not lasted long. She had felt inferior to the young students, and unable to draw people. Her attempt to draw a small child to illustrate one of her short stories had ended in failure, but she had an eye for intricate detail. Catherine's charcoal sketches of buildings were good and she was proud at being self-taught.

Tom looked at her fondly. 'If only you'd had the chance I've had – won a scholarship to grammar school and had the best of teachers. You've so much talent.'

Catherine laughed. 'And you look at me through rose-tinted spectacles.'

'Maybe after the war you could have a proper training,' he enthused. 'You must keep it up, Kitty.'

Tom was quick to boast of Catherine's new-found ability to his colleagues and made her show her sketches when they came to the house. Even Mr Forbes was impressed.

'You could have these printed up as Christmas cards,' he suggested, 'sell them round the town.'

Catherine was entranced by the idea and heady from the English teacher's approval. Recklessly, she asked him to take a look at some of her short stories too.

'I'd be grateful if you'd read some of them – see if they're fit for publication. I was thinking of illustrating one or two.'

Mr Forbes showed surprise but agreed to take them away to read over the summer holidays.

Then Tom received his call-up papers and Catherine was thrown into panic. He was to enlist with the RAF. Several tense days followed with

Catherine imagining him being sent abroad to train. She'd heard of men going to South Africa or Canada. How could she possibly cope here on her own? And flying was the most dangerous of occupations.

Tom came home despondent. 'I failed the medical. I'll get a desk job.'

Catherine flung her arms around him in relief. 'Thank the saints!'

'It's hardly heroic,' he said glumly, unhooking her arms.

'Maybe not – but you'll still be needed, whatever it is. And I'm coming with you, even if it's John O'Groats.'

They spent the school holiday going on walks and picnics, visiting the Cooksons and packing up their flat. Tom was appointed an instructor and left for his first post in Leicester. Catherine was to follow and find lodgings once his initial training was over. Just before she left, a parcel arrived returning her notebooks.

Eagerly, she unfolded the enclosed letter from Mr Forbes. It was brief and brutal in its advice. The stories were so badly written, so ungrammatical that they were virtually unreadable. It would be most unwise to send them to a publisher. Art was another matter. She might certainly have a future there – and one that could fit in with her husband's vocation. He wished them both the best of luck.

Catherine crumpled up the letter in disgust. How dare he pour such scorn on her work. Tom thought her stories were good. But then Tom was hopelessly biased and would say anything to keep her happy. Perhaps her stories *were* unpublishable. She looked accusingly at the pile of dog-eared exercise books. They would only take up room in her suitcase and be shoved in another cupboard to lie unread.

Tight-lipped, Catherine began tearing up the books and throwing them into the empty fire grate. She lit a match and put a taper to the mass of paper. Grimly, she watched several years of work disappear in a roar of flame and turn quickly to hot ashes. Why did she need to escape into a fantastical world of lords and ladies? She had Tom and her art. She would have to be content with the real world and the adventure of starting again in a new place.

It was not long before Tom was posted to Lincolnshire. Catherine packed up their belongings once more and followed. All she could find was a tiny bedsitting room at the back of a terraced house in Sleaford. The landlady was mean, cutting off the electricity at nine in the evening through the winter and rationing the toilet paper. To Catherine's embarrassment, she had to walk through the kitchen where the family congregated to get to the lavatory. They always stopped talking and stared at her when she went, so she would wait until she was desperate.

But her urge to go grew more frequent and she soon suspected why. With long winter nights in a darkened room, she and Tom had resumed lovemaking. The more practice they had, the more pleasurable she found it.

The spring and early summer brought fresh bombing raids over London and the South-East, and a new campaign was launched to get women out of their homes and into factories to help with the war effort.

'It can't be me this year,' she told Tom bashfully in June. 'I think I'm expecting again.'

He hugged her in joy.

'I was hoping!' he admitted, and kissed her tenderly.

Cautiously, they began to make plans about moving to bigger lodgings once the baby came. By the end of the summer, Catherine allowed herself to hope that this time all would go well. She started writing children's stories again and short verse.

As the days began to shorten, Tom came home to say he was being posted to Hereford, on the other side of the country.

'It's near Wales,' he said, 'supposed to be a lovely cathedral town. The camp is a few miles out – but I can cycle. Be a nice place to bring up a family.'

Catherine put on a show of being pleased, but was secretly dismayed at yet another move. She felt tired just thinking of it, packing up and having to find new accommodation. She hated the thought of being without Tom, even for a short time.

There was no time to dwell on it, for Tom had to catch a train four days later. Catherine waved him away at the station and walked home feeling bereft and ill at ease.

The next day she woke to find the bed sheets soaked in blood. In the first moments of disbelief she thought she must have cut herself, but there was no pain. In a panic, she rushed for the landlady, who was preparing to go on holiday.

'Will you ring for the doctor,' Catherine pleaded, feeling faint. She saw the woman's reluctance. 'I'll pay you back.'

The doctor was called. 'You're probably miscarrying. All you can do is stay in bed and lie still. Nature will work its course.'

Catherine stared at him numbly. 'You mean I'll lose the baby?'

He shrugged. 'It looks likely. Is there anyone I can contact for you?'

Catherine's ears rang as if she was hearing his words in a dream. A terrible, nightmarish dream.

'My husband,' she whispered. 'He's gone to RAF Madley. I don't know how to reach him . . .'

'Maybe best to see what happens first,' the doctor suggested. 'I'll call round in the morning.'

She sank back, consumed with fear, listening to the doctor telling the landlady.

'I can't nurse her,' she said indignantly. 'I'm going on holiday tomorrow.'

Catherine closed her eyes and wept as quietly as she could. The night was interminable. She hardly dared move, but even lying still she could feel herself haemorrhaging. In the dark hours, stabbing pains increased as her hopes died. The next day, the doctor confirmed her worst fears. She had miscarried.

'But I still feel like it's there,' Catherine sobbed. 'I'm still in pain.'

He examined her again. 'You'll need to go to hospital for an operation. Not all of the placenta has come away. I'll arrange an ambulance.'

Catherine was ferried to Grantham hospital and put into blissful oblivion by a general anaesthetic. She woke to the sound of babies crying and for one disorientating moment could remember nothing of what had happened. Then it came flooding back in an all-consuming wave of pain. Their second baby was gone.

A nurse came to tell her that they had tried to contact her husband, but had not been able to get through.

'Good,' Catherine said miserably. She didn't want him to see her like this, didn't want him to get the news down a crackly telephone line, hurrying between classes. 'I'll tell him myself.'

Weak and grief-stricken though she was, Catherine could not bear to stay in the busy hospital within earshot of the maternity ward. She discharged herself against the wishes of the doctors. All that drove her on was the thought of getting to Hereford as quickly as possible and joining Tom.

The moment he saw her face at the station, he knew. She fell into his arms and wept. Tom struggled to find words of comfort, but could hardly speak. It was too cruel for it to happen all over again.

They found rooms in the market town, and for Tom's sake, Catherine tried to rally her broken spirits. But she spent long lonely hours once more questioning why such a tragedy should have befallen them. She went back to the Catholic Church. Why, she asked the local priest, had she lost two babies?

'Have you ever thought it's God's punishment for marrying out of the faith?' he asked her sternly.

Catherine was deeply wounded by the accusation and could not rid her mind of it.

'What sort of God would do that?' she cried at Tom. 'Not a loving God!'

'It's irrational,' Tom said impatiently, furious at the priest for his wife's distress. 'What nonsense to think God would kill our babies out of spite. You're not to take any notice of such superstitious dogma.'

Catherine knew he was right, yet part of her responded in fear to the priest's censure. If she was good from now on, went to confession and attended church regularly, she might earn forgiveness. She might win the chance of another child. She struggled to reconcile these two warring parts of her. At home with Tom, she was questioning and critical of many aspects of Catholicism. On Sundays she went to Mass and found her senses stirred by the beauty and mystery of the service, at home with its unchanging familiarity.

She made friends with Sister Teresa from the local convent. They would walk in the enclosed garden under the bare trees and talk.

' "Come to me all you who are heavy laden, and I will give you rest",' the nun quoted. 'Now they're not the words of a cruel God, are they?'

Catherine sighed. 'Then maybe it's the Church at fault, not letting you think your own thoughts. You can do any amount of sinning and be forgiven with a couple of Hail Marys, but you're not allowed to question. Why can't we talk directly to God like the Protestants do, instead of through the priests? It's like we can't be trusted.'

'You must be more humble,' Sister Teresa said gently. 'The priests are there to help us – and the Pope is God's holy representative on Earth.'

'The Pope's just another man,' Catherine snorted.

If this shocked the serene nun, she did not show it and Catherine continued to visit her throughout the following year. She felt guilty at her lack of war work. As a married woman without children she had received call-up papers early in 1942, but had promptly failed the medical. Catherine was suffering regular nosebleeds that left her weak and anaemic.

'Tom doesn't want me to do factory work either – says I'm not fit enough,' she confided in Sister Teresa. 'But I feel so useless when everyone else around me is being busy. Like here at the convent,' she waved her hands at the garden, 'you've dug up every spare inch to grow food.' She looked despairingly at her friend. 'If I'm never to be a mother, what *am* I supposed to do?'

The nun stood for a moment, gazing into the distance. Catherine envied her poise and stillness.

'You have a beautiful spirit, Catherine,' she said quietly. 'You will give beauty back to the world, whatever it is you finally choose to do.' She smiled, slipping an arm through hers. 'And goodness knows, we need it in this world of make-do-and-mend! Maybe it's time to take up your drawing again.'

Encouraged, Catherine found a renewed interest in art. She went around Hereford sketching its old buildings. Remembering Mr Forbes's advice, she took her pictures to a local printer and costed out putting them on cards. Impressed, the printer helped her sell them in shops around the town and she made a small profit. Word spread and Catherine was asked to do some small commercial jobs, scaling up illustrations for a magazine and copying photographs for postcards. The head of the art school got to see her work and offered her an exhibition. Here she met a Dutch painter and his wife who invited her to watch him at his studio whenever she wanted.

While Tom was away at the camp from half-six in the morning until six at night, Catherine found refuge in the attic studio of the van der Meershes, with its smell of oil paints and turpentine. In its peaceful surroundings she watched intently as he painted vivid colours on to a large canvas. Before long she had bought some brushes and paints of her own and began to experiment at their bedroom window, while her landlady's daughter plonked away on the piano downstairs.

One day, feeling lonely without Tom, Catherine slipped into the sitting room and lifted the lid on the piano. She played a few tentative notes. Finding a book of music on the stand, she flicked through it and found an old familiar song, 'The Waters of Tyne'. Stumbling over the keys, she worked through the tune.

It conjured up a time long ago, when the McMullens had gathered around someone's piano and sang. It was probably a neighbour's, and it may have been Christmas. All she recalled was sitting between Grandma Rose's knees, enjoying the music and someone's sweet voice. Her big sister Kate. Or so she had thought at the time.

She felt a brief flutter of happiness to think she could remember a time of simple pleasure and innocence, before life was poisoned by illegitimacy and Kate's slide into alcoholism. Catherine held on to that feeling in the months that followed. She took piano lessons and sat for exams, thinking defiantly how her mother was not there to call her ungrateful or hurl hobnailed boots at her head.

When 1944 came, and the surprise D-Day landings with the Allies pushing back into France, Tom was restless.

'I wish I was part of the action,' he said enviously, 'doing something to make a difference.'

'I thought you liked teaching?' Catherine was surprised.

'Not this job. It's so tedious – the same lessons over and over again. And the young lads are here one minute and gone the next – never a chance to get to know them.'

It worried Catherine that he thought life with her too dull. One night she woke to find the bed beside her empty and cold. She found him sitting in the small garden under a bright moon, his eyes closed and face drawn.

'Tom, what is it?'

'A headache that's all – couldn't sleep. Didn't mean to wake you.'

She sat on the bench beside him, shivering in her dressing gown.

'What sort of headache? Can I get you something?'

He shook his head and winced with pain. 'Please go back to bed, Kitty. No point both of us losing sleep.'

She went, but lay for the rest of the night wide awake and fretful. What if he were really ill? A headache one day, dead the next. Or maybe it was just an excuse, and he didn't want her company. What if he was bored with his life and decided to up and leave her? If this invasion of France was the beginning of the end of war, perhaps Tom was looking beyond it to a new life without her. Their marriage must be such a disappointment to him: their mediocre lovemaking and still no family to show for it, her sickly health and panic attacks about losing her faith. Catherine scrambled out of bed, sank to her knees and prayed that Tom would not leave her.

Shortly afterwards, she was pregnant again and Tom's strange mood lifted. Her prayers had been answered. She had been right to go back to church for now her faithfulness was rewarded. Only one event checked her soaring spirits that autumn: her friend van der Meersh died unexpectedly. Not only did she miss his quiet encouragement and example, but also the warm haven of his attic studio.

She tried to recreate its tranquillity in their cramped bedroom, but could not. The smell of paints brought on Tom's headaches and the landlady complained at the mess. Besides, Catherine hated being confined to the one room for hours on end. Going to the studio had been a welcome escape from its confines and somewhere to fill in the endless hours of Tom's absence.

Instead, Catherine haunted the tea rooms of Hereford, making a cup last an hour, as well as the library where she sat and worked on her drawings. She had more cards printed, which sold well in the local shops that Christmas, making up for the wartime shortage of traditional cards.

With the approach of Christmas she was feeling more settled. Tom had agreed, after much persuasion, to go with her to Mass. They were busily wrapping up presents for each other in reused paper kept from the previous year, when Catherine grabbed at the table.

'I feel faint—' she said, standing up. A moment later she was doubled up on the floor, clutching her stomach.

This time the haemorrhaging was massive and swift. Tom fled to the telephone downstairs and summoned an ambulance. Catherine was carried, half conscious, from the house, and hurried to hospital. She bled so profusely and was left so weakened that the doctor took aside a stunned Tom.

'If you hadn't acted quickly, we might have lost her,' he told him. 'Your wife's health is very delicate. She shouldn't attempt any more pregnancies.'

In the new year, when Catherine was back home and lying recuperating in bed, Tom raised the subject.

'They said you weren't to have any more babies, Kitty.'

She looked at him with lifeless, dark-ringed eyes, her face drained of all colour. She nodded. 'They told me too,' she whispered. 'I'm so sorry.'

He took her hand quickly. 'It's not your fault.'

'But I know how much you want children,' she said in a flat, defeated voice. 'And now I can't give you any.'

He saw the glint of fresh tears. 'I love you, Kitty Cookson. We've still got each other,' he insisted. 'That's what I want most of all. And it doesn't mean we can't – ' he struggled to find a delicate way of putting it – 'I mean, we can take precautions, can't we?'

She looked at him uncomprehendingly. He blushed furiously.

'Not yet, of course. When you're fit enough. The doctor can advise us on what kind of contraception—'

'Contraception?' Catherine gasped.

'We can still be husband and wife,' he mumbled.

'But I c-can't,' she stuttered, suddenly agitated. 'It's forbidden. Stopping babies like that is a sin.'

Tom dropped her hand in dismay. 'After all you've been through, you're still more afraid of that wretched priest than protecting your own life.'

'No I'm not,' she said, stung by the truth. 'And if you cared about me, you'd leave me alone rather than thinking about your own satisfaction!'

Tom stood up abruptly. 'If that's what you want, then I won't touch you.' At the door he glanced back. 'I just want to comfort you, Kitty, that's all.'

He left for work and Catherine lay, head spinning. The walls seemed to be moving, shapes conjuring themselves out of the patterned wallpaper, faces coming to leer at her, chattering voices filling her head. She was useless, a failure, a bastard inside and out. Sinful. She'd go to Hell for marrying a Protestant. It was Tom's fault. Her babies were screaming in Purgatory because of him, because of her. Kate's face stared at her from the ceiling, Kate's raucous laughter filled the room. She was bad seed of a bad woman. Blood will out. Her babies stood no chance coming from her infected womb. She wasn't really married – not a proper marriage – so her babies were doomed. Better to die in the womb than to suffer the same shame that she had suffered . . .

Catherine pressed her hands over her ears and screamed for the voices to stop. But they grew louder, began to curse and swear. They were like her own voice, once again thick with dialect, peppered with foul language like Grandda John's. She buried her head under the covers, praying for them to stop.

Eventually, after a supreme effort of will, she staggered from the bed and got dressed. Unsteady and light-headed, she wrapped herself in coat, hat and scarf and went in search of Father Logan. In the dark of the confessional she poured out her torment about her dead babies and how she must not have any more.

'But I'm still a wife,' she said hoarsely. 'I still have a duty, don't I? How can I without – without using contraception? That would be a greater sin, wouldn't it?'

She waited, dry-mouthed for the voice behind the grille to answer.

'Your husband is Protestant, isn't he?'

Catherine braced herself for another lecture on the wrongfulness of mixed marriage. 'Yes,' she swallowed.

'Then let him do the sinning,' Father Logan advised.

'What do you mean?'

'If he takes the precautions, then the sin is not yours and you have not put your mortal soul at risk.'

Catherine was flabbergasted. What hypocrisy! She was beset with a huge moral dilemma, drowning in doubts, and he was reducing it to a child's game of who to blame. She was too upset and angry to speak. Leaving the church, she wandered around the town in a daze, outraged at what the priest had suggested. It was all nonsense. God didn't exist. She was seized by a wild aggression, like a caged animal. God, the Church, the priests had all betrayed her. It was as shattering as the moment she had discovered as a seven-year-old that Rose and John had lied about being her parents.

Catherine collided with a woman who was turning into a chemist's shop.

'Sorry,' Catherine said, only half aware of what she was doing.

The woman put the brake on her pram and left it in the doorway. Catherine stared into it. A swaddled baby lay under a mound of blankets, his tiny features just visible under a knitted bonnet. A button nose, rosebud lips, closed eyelids so new and fragile that the veins showed. A beautiful sleeping newborn.

Catherine put out a hand and touched the blanket. He was hers for the taking. All she had to do was reach out and pull him to her. She yearned to hold him with every fibre of her being. She deserved him. There was nothing else in her life to fill the gaping black hole inside. God would not punish her because God wasn't there.

Catherine glanced into the shop. The woman had her back to her. She probably had half a dozen other children at school, at home. She did not need this one like Catherine did – would thank her for taking him off her hands. Her heart began to palpitate. Do it now, a voice said. *Now.* Her arms ached at the thought of holding him. Her fingers flexed over the blanket.

'Excuse me,' the woman spoke behind her.

Catherine looked round startled. The mother gave her a wary look and took hold of the pram's handle possessively.

'I was – just – looking . . .' Catherine mumbled, snatching back her hands and bunching them at her sides.

343

The woman nodded and pushed her baby briskly up the street, glancing back once with a curious look. Catherine stood gasping for breath, horrified at what she had nearly done. Would she have run away with the baby? Would she have smothered it to death? She felt she was capable of anything. There was nothing to stop her, no beliefs to hold her back. She wanted to run to the sanctuary of the church and throw herself at the feet of the statue of the Virgin Mary and plead for help. But if there was no God there was no Holy Family, no Our Lady to offer forgiveness and comfort.

Nausea engulfed her. Catherine staggered into an alleyway and vomited into the gutter.

She did not tell Tom about her urge to snatch the baby, only about her anger at Father Logan.

'I've lost all faith,' she declared. Yet when Tom reached for her at night in bed, she shrank away. She could not bear for him to touch her. Abstinence was the only way to gain peace of mind.

Tom searched for a way to stop her withdrawing into a twilight world of accusing voices and hallucinations.

'I've been to see the priest,' he told her one spring day.

'Why?' she asked in suspicion.

'To ask for instruction,' he said diffidently. 'I'm thinking of converting to Catholicism.'

'What on earth for?' Catherine asked, appalled.

'So we can go to church together,' he said, looking suddenly unsure. 'I want to help you through this, Kitty.'

She blazed at him, 'Help me? You stupid man! You've waited all this time – till I've lost all belief – and now you think converting will make the slightest bit of difference? Well it won't, so don't even bother!'

He flinched as if she'd hit him.

'I'm trying to help,' he said losing patience, 'I'm doing it because I love you.'

'Do you?' she challenged. 'Is that why you stay away at the camp till late at night? Maybe you've got a fancy woman up there – one who'll sleep with you and give you brats. Then you can leave me for good.'

He stared at her as if she were a stranger. But that's how she felt. She did not know from where such hateful words came. They bubbled up from some deep cesspool inside her, poisoning her sickly marriage.

Tom said, 'If you won't let me help you, then someone else must. I want you to go back to the doctor. You're not well, Kitty.'

344

'Not well?' she laughed harshly. 'That's the understatement of the bloody year. Of course I'm not well. I'm in Hell! I hate living here – I hate this room – I hate being here with you! I don't love you any more, Tom!'

He left. That evening he didn't return. She stayed up all night waiting and worrying, her rage turning to panic. By the time he came home the following evening, she was in a sweat of anxiety.

'I slept up at the camp – thought I'd be doing you a favour,' he said, tired out.

Catherine threw her arms round him. 'I was so worried. I thought you were dead. I didn't mean any of those things I said. Don't leave me, Tom. Promise me!'

He pulled away, unable to hide his irritation.

'I'm not going to leave you.' His voice was dull, resigned.

As news came of the Nazi surrender in Europe and the country erupted in celebration, Catherine forced herself to join in. She put on a desperate show of being happy and threw a party for some of Tom's workmates. His friends teased Tom for keeping his vivacious wife hidden away.

'No wonder you never wanted to live at the camp,' one joked.

Catherine laughed and joked with them, and that night encouraged Tom to make love.

But when the morning came and he was gone to work, Catherine's depression descended more heavily than ever. She was seized anew by a host of fears. Fear of dying, fear of Tom leaving, fear of Kate, fear of having no father, fear of drunkards, fear of God, fear of no God, fear of the black-robed priest who haunted her dreams, fear of hands that smelled of the docks, fear of going mad, fear of getting out of bed.

She stared at the room and once again it was filling with faces and voices that swore and screamed at her to get out of bed. She tried and could not move. Her legs were as heavy and useless as iron weights.

She cried out for Tom, even though she knew he was far away in camp. She wept and whimpered like a child, calling out for her mother. Eventually Mrs Bright, the landlady, came, scolding her for making such a racket.

'It's all that partying till late at night,' she said in disapproval.

'I can't move,' Catherine said helplessly.

The woman gave her a sceptical look. 'Sleep it off, I say. I'll bring you a cup of tea. But no more noise. Mr Bright's trying to sleep before his nightshift.'

Catherine lay all day, tortured by the voices. Memories from her childhood flashed in front of her eyes like a flickering film. She was climbing the steps to Bella's house, dressed in a fresh pinafore and new hair ribbons. She's knocking at the door but nobody hears. After a long time, Bella comes to the door with all their other friends crowding about, laughing and pointing.

'*You can't come in – you've got no da . . .*'

The words rang around her head like the Angelus bell.

Then Catherine saw herself down at Jarrow Slake, bobbing from timber to timber on the oily tide, playing a game of dare.

'*Dare you to jump to that one, Billy,*' she taunts a smaller boy.

She's full of anger because the other children won't play with her any more. They say she's a bully, too rough by half. She feels like a firework ready to go off. Danny, the Irish lodger, has gone, but she knows it's her fault. Kate hates her for it. Danny was going to be her da. The idea made her sick. She has no da. *She has no da!* Roughly, she pushes scrawny Billy into the water.

'*Jump, you little waster!*' He misses the next plank and splashes into the brackish water. He comes up spluttering and thrashing for help. The other children won't play with her; she's not good enough for them, their parents say. She can't go to their parties. But Kate says she'll get her own back one day, just see if she doesn't.

She'll have her revenge now. Billy the cry-baby will pay for all the hurt. She's got power over him, at least. It flashes through her mind in the seconds it takes Billy to scream. She's full of a red-hot feeling. She pushes Billy's head under the water again. His hands are waving as if in goodbye.

Hands seize her and shove her away. Billy is being hauled from the water by a big man in hoggers and work boots.

'*You nearly drowned him, you evil little bitch!*'

Catherine clings to the bank, horrified. In an instant, she's scrambling up it and running away from the furious man and the gasping, sobbing boy . . .

In the claustrophobic bedroom in Hereford, Catherine lay pinned in terror. For years she had denied the truth, too ashamed to think of it. Kate had beaten her when she'd found out. It was what she deserved. She had tried to drown an innocent boy. She was wicked to the core. No wonder God had taken away her babies – she wasn't fit to keep them. She was a danger to children. Catherine was filled with fear to think how close she had come to stealing a baby that winter.

346

'Help me!' she screamed to the pulsating room.

Trying to raise herself up, she caught sight of herself in the spotted mirror above the washstand. Kate's puffy, drink-sodden face stared back at her. Catherine put her hands to her face and the woman in the mirror did the same. Who *was she*? She did not know any more. Some husk that looked like her mother. Her real self had done a flit, vanished away. Maybe she had never been a real person.

Tom came back to find her sweating and cowering under the covers. The doctor was called and she was taken to hospital. A few days later, when she could walk a few shaky steps, she agreed to see a psychiatrist.

She could not talk to Tom. They moved around each other like strangers in a silent film, while all the time her head burst with arguing, angry voices. After a week, she agreed to be admitted to St Mary's mental asylum. She could no longer run from her past; it was time to turn around and face up to it.

Chapter 49

It could have been five days, five weeks, a life-time that she had been at St Mary's; Catherine had no concept of time inside the large gothic asylum. It had echoing corridors and high-ceilinged wards that reminded her all too painfully of workhouse hospitals. In the next bed was a widow who would not speak, and on the other side a young woman who thought she was a film star. Every morning she packed her bag and sat waiting for someone to come and take her to the film set.

During the day Catherine sat in a chair staring out at the leafy grounds, picking at a piece of needlework they had given her to do. At night she was kept awake by her own whirling thoughts and the crying of others. But the days she grew to dread were the ones she was taken down the stone steps to the basement for electro-convulsive therapy. She sat waiting her turn on a wooden bench in a dingy corridor like a pupil awaiting punishment. It was next to a lavatory that stank of urine and Catherine would have to clamp a hand over her mouth to stop herself being sick on the stone floor.

By the time her turn came to be strapped to the hard bed by the white-coated medical staff and hit by the glare of harsh light, she was rigid with fear. White tiles, the clank of metal instruments, the bite of leather straps, the sinister hum of machinery all compounded her terror. Was this what Nazi torture chambers looked and smelled like? Stark, clinically clean, devoid of human touch.

Next, something hard and bruising was clamped to her head. A rushing sound filled her ears as the shock of electricity pulsated through her, drowning out her thoughts, lifting her body, possessing her. For a second, everything was the colour red. Then it was blackness, oblivion.

Once Catherine knew what awaited her in the white-tiled theatre, she would alternately sweat and shake as she queued on the bench. While her fellow inmates sat in silent resignation, Catherine fought back nausea, convinced that she had stumbled into a living Hell.

The treatment was gradually robbing her of thought, of emotion, of memory. Afterwards she could not recall what day it was, what she had eaten for breakfast or what her grandmother's name was. Gradually, details would come back to her. But some things did not. She found it hard to remember large chunks of her school years or the names of her classmates that she had once summoned as easily as her own.

Sometimes this forgetfulness was welcome. There was so much in her past she wished to obliterate. It was comforting to sit in a fog of confusion, unable to concentrate on the simplest tasks, her thoughts cocooned. But the fog robbed her of feeling. She felt no strong emotion for anything or anyone. She woke, dressed, ate, walked and sat. She didn't smile, laugh, cry or love.

At times she felt so detached that she struggled to remember who and where she was.

'Mr Cookson's here to see you,' the nurse told her one evening.

Catherine stared at her blankly. Who was Mr Cookson?

'Your husband,' she prompted, 'he's come to visit.'

Husband. What a strange word. What did it mean? What did husbands do? She did not have the will or energy to find out.

'Shall I tell him you're too tired tonight?' the nurse suggested. 'He can come again tomorrow.'

Catherine nodded. It did not seem to have anything to do with her. The nurse and the husband could sort it out between them.

Later, in the middle of the night Catherine came wide awake. The husband was Tom. Tom had come to see her. He would have cycled miles only to be turned away again. She could visualise Tom on a bicycle, pounding along narrow lanes, whistling. It was like watching a film of another life. How strange to think of a world other than her own going on somewhere else.

Sometimes Tom would arrive and sit with Catherine in silence the whole visit. He had given up trying to tell her about his work or current affairs, such as the build-up to a general election. She showed no interest, hardly seemed to notice that he was there. She was even less inclined to tell him what was happening to her in the hospital. He only gleaned that from questioning the staff. She was having regular electric shock treatment.

Watching his once lively wife, sitting lank-haired and pinch-faced, Tom feared that she would never recover. Gone were their long conversations on literature and ethics, gone was her sudden infectious laugh and wry northern humour, gone the feeling of her arms around

349

him in bed. After a month of cycling to the asylum every evening after a long day at camp, Tom almost gave up going.

His presence made no difference, perhaps even harmed her recovery. She looked at him with suspicion or not at all. Then came the day that Catherine refused to see him. It was terrifying to think he might have lost his Kitty for good. The relief of not having a depressed and volatile wife to return to at night had been short-lived. Lying in their bed alone was a desolate experience. A life without her vibrant, loving nature was a life without colour or warmth. A life in monochrome.

He must remind himself of the woman he had fallen in love with the instant he saw and heard her in Kate's lodging house. She was the real Catherine, not the bitter, raging, hurtful woman who had told him she no longer loved him. His Kitty was ill – lost in a black storm of depression – and he must not abandon her as others had done.

Tom forced himself back the following day. At once he found a different Catherine waiting for him. She was slow and weak on her feet, but there was a glimmer in her sad eyes.

'Would you like to walk in the garden?' Catherine asked.

'Very much,' he smiled, holding out his arm.

After a moment's hesitation, she took it and clung on to it for the short walk along the drive.

'They tell me I've been here five weeks,' Catherine said.

'Nearly,' Tom agreed. 'It's a very short time really. You've been through so much, Kitty. You must give yourself all the time you need to get better. I'll be based at Madley for some time yet.'

She stopped and clutched his arm. 'No! I have to get out of here. I know what they're doing – making me fit for nothing but life inside. I've seen it happen before – in the workhouse. You get to the stage where you can't cope outside even if they let you free. There's a woman on the ward been here for fifty years – *fifty years* – and she won't even leave the building. Hardly knows there's been a war on – can't see why she's had no banana and custard for five years. I'll end up like her if I stop any longer.'

Tom was astounded at the torrent of words, but worried at her agitation.

'No you won't – not after a mere month.'

'I will.' Catherine was adamant. 'They can't make me stay. I want to come home, Tom. Help me come home.'

His eyes filled with tears at her sudden appeal. It was the first time she had used his name in over a month.

'Course I will,' he reassured.

It was arranged with the doctors that Catherine would have a day out to Hereford that Saturday. If all went well they would consider a longer spell at home. She screwed up her courage to face the outside world, getting up early to dress and arrange her hair as meticulously as possible. Tom met the bus she came on but could tell straight away she was in distress.

Catherine did not want to go to their lodgings, afraid of the faces and voices that might still lurk in its walls. Neither did she want to sit quietly in a church where her doubts and disbelief might swamp her. So they tried a café, but it was too crowded, and Catherine kept looking towards the door as if she would flee at any moment. Her cup of tea half drunk, she rushed into the street, Tom pursuing. She was trembling all over, her hands sweating in their gloves, her face clammy and grey. When Tom tried to hold her, she went rigid and couldn't breathe.

He took her back to the hospital in a taxi, explaining about her panic attack. Greatly dispirited, he left.

The next day Catherine forced herself to walk the length of the driveway and peer beyond its gates. She breathed in the warm scented air, the smell of cut grass, listened to the chatter of wood pigeons. These were small pleasures she could learn to enjoy again. The world beyond the asylum walls need not be so terrifying. The fresh air made her feel heady and she reached and steadied herself against a large tree. An oak.

In an instant she was back at The Hurst, pressing her back into the comforting strength of her favourite oak. How could she have forgotten that tree? It glowed like a talisman in her mind. Something good to cling on to, something to which to return.

From that moment, Catherine was convinced that she must get back to The Hurst. Hereford held too much pain. Even if it meant being separated from Tom, she would go. Only there, in the shabby familiar surroundings of the creaking house and its beautiful garden would she have peace of mind. There she could recapture the feeling of being in love with Tom, of feeling passion for books and for life. The war was over; the soldiers who were billeted there would be moving out. Mrs Fairy was now in a nursing home, but even without the old cook's help, she would reclaim The Hurst. While she nurtured it back into a home, it would nurse her back to life.

On Tom's next visit she told of her plan and brushed aside his concerns.

'Someone should be there to help you,' he said. 'Can't you wait till I get demobbed?'

'No. I'm not staying here any longer – and I can't bear the thought of being in Hereford either. The Hurst is our home, Tom. It's the only place I can think of where I'll have a chance of getting better – where we'll have a chance of piecing our marriage back together.'

Tom reddened at her blunt words. But she was right. Their marriage had been shattered by the upheavals of war, the loss of their babies and Catherine's breakdown. He did not know if they could ever live peacefully together, or whether the wounds went too deep. Only time would tell.

'I can try and get down at weekends, I suppose,' he said doubtfully. 'But I'd be happier if you weren't alone. Perhaps your mother could come – just for a short while?'

She gave him a furious look. '*Kate?* After all she's done to me – to us! I can't believe you'd even suggest it. That woman's been the cause of all my grief. If there's one thing I'm sure of, it's that she'll never live with me again.'

A week later, Catherine signed herself out of St Mary's and Tom travelled with her back to Hastings. A neighbour who held the keys had assured them that the house was empty and largely unscathed. They found that the tower had been damaged by an incendiary bomb and the conservatory had fallen in, but the rest was still standing. Inside, though, was a scene of decay and squalor. Wallpaper hung off the damp walls, carpets had been ripped up and wooden joists gaped through holes in the plaster.

As they crept cautiously upstairs, Catherine was assailed by the overpowering smell of stale urine. She gagged and for a nightmarish moment thought she was back in the subterranean passageway outside the ECT theatre. It was proof she was mad and should never have been let out. She gripped the banisters and cried out for Tom.

'That smell – can you smell it?'

Tom soon discovered the source. The bedrooms had been left with chamber pots full to the brim. The soldiers had left in such a hurry they had not bothered to empty them.

'I'll do it,' Tom said in distaste. 'You go and see if they've left us a kettle.'

They spent the weekend attempting to make the kitchen and a bedroom habitable. Before Tom returned to Hereford, he told Catherine that his mother would be arriving to help out for a couple of weeks.

Catherine's protests were half-hearted. Now that she was back in the vast empty house, she was afraid of being left alone to her thoughts. The company of the practical and friendly Mrs Cookson would be ten times more welcome than her own mother's.

On their final night together, Catherine and Tom made love. It had not been planned and both were surprised at their wish to come together and be intimate. They lay holding each other in the quiet of their musty bedroom, listening to the evening call of birds through a broken window. For the first time in many weeks, Catherine felt a twinge of contentment. Perhaps they had a future after all.

Mrs Cookson arrived and helped her daughter-in-law tackle the huge task of making The Hurst habitable again. They cleaned, scrubbed and painted. They mended furniture, washed and ironed curtains, took carpets out and beat them. It was exhausting work that left Catherine aching and hardly able to climb the stairs at night. She tried to hide her nosebleeds from her worried mother-in-law, laughing off her attempts to make her rest.

'I've had them for years. Doctors tell me it's my nervous nature brings them on,' Catherine said wryly. 'It might as well be to do with the weather forecast – cold windy day, nosebleeds light and variable.'

What Catherine could not tell Tom's mother was that work was her reason for living. Hard graft kept the demons in her head at bay and rendered her so tired that she fell asleep as soon as she lay down at night. Work – hard physical work – and sleep. This was all she wanted.

When Mrs Cookson had to go home to her own family, Catherine felt bereft. She had enjoyed their easy companionship around the kitchen table and on rare ventures to the shops. Only the presence of the older woman had stopped her running in a panic from the sight of a queue or a busy store.

But it was more than just the fear of being left alone that preoccupied Catherine. It was the creeping knowledge that she was pregnant again. She could hardly believe it. One night of lovemaking with Tom had happened so quickly and unexpectedly that they had not even raised the question of prevention.

It filled her with dread and excitement. She was nearly forty. Surely this was her last chance of becoming a mother. It was a final gift from an absent God whom she had rejected. But she dared not hope. She knew if she lost this fourth child, she would fall back into the pit of madness. Catherine doubted she could climb out a second time.

She almost confided in Mrs Cookson, but didn't. The loss of her babies was something they had never discussed, and Catherine was still awkward about that unhappy Christmas when she had fled from her mother-in-law's house rather than hold baby Winston.

Tom was due at the end of the following week. She would wait and tell him. A letter arrived from Kate asking if she could come and stay. Catherine threw it on the fire. The next one was more reproachful. She had not seen her for the whole of the war. They would be company for each other while Tom was away. Catherine tore it up, wondering crossly if it was Tom or his mother who had written to Kate. How else did she know of their circumstances?

She was sweeping up the first pile of autumn leaves when she felt it starting. A twinge of pain and the gushing of blood. As Catherine hurried inside, she was struck by her own lack of surprise. She had been waiting for the dread moment, knew deep down she would miscarry. Women like her did not deserve to have babies.

Catherine lined the bed with newspaper and crawled under the covers. She was not as far gone as the last time and by morning the bleeding had stopped. Numbly, she bundled up the paper and sheets and took them outside. Along with yesterday's leaves she made a bonfire and lit the lot. She watched it smoulder then ignite, the flames licking higher, the smell pinching her nostrils.

Back in the house, she pulled out drawings from the bedside cabinet, scraps of notebook with poems that she did not remember writing. She seized a bundle of letters from Tom and Kate, tore photographs out of an album, of Bridie and Maisie when they'd first moved to The Hurst. She took them and threw them all on the bonfire. A savage triumph lit inside to see her life go up in flames – her past and her future.

It did not last. She wandered back into the empty house. She ought to bathe and change, ring the doctor or tell someone what had happened. But a heavy listlessness weighed her down. She could hardly be bothered to climb the stairs or write a note to Tom explaining why she was leaving him. Yet there was nothing else left to do.

After sitting on the staircase for an hour or more, she forced herself to move. She found a half-drunk bottle of rum left by one of the soldiers and took it upstairs. Rummaging around in the bedroom she collected up her supply of tranquillisers and sleeping pills.

Catherine went into the bathroom, locked the door, then unlocked it. There was no point in making it difficult for the police or whoever found her to remove her body. If she'd had an ounce of energy left she would have run a hot bath and lain in it drinking the rum with her wrists cut. But that seemed too much effort. She would shovel down the drugs and be done with it.

Pouring herself a glass of water, Catherine swallowed the first pill.

Chapter 50

'*I love you Kitty Cookson.*' The words were so strong and clear, Catherine swung round, expecting to see Tom standing behind her. She could feel him in the bathroom with her.

'Tom . . .?' She gripped the basin. There was no one there. She stared at herself in the mirror. Who was that emaciated woman with the lacklustre hair that stared back? She looked fifty or more. Yet the eyes were those of a perplexed little girl. How could Tom possibly love such a pathetic creature?

'*I love you . . . we've still got each other, that's what I want most of all.*'

Catherine felt her legs go weak. Her dry eyes stung with tears. She looked down at the handful of tablets ready to take her to oblivion or the Devil. What was she doing? How could she let Tom walk in and find her rotting on the bathroom floor, a scrawled note on the dressing table explaining nothing?

Tom of the warm brown eyes and the shy smile; her studious, conscientious, loyal friend. Her diffident lover. Maybe he would choose to leave her anyway. But she knew in that split second that she did not want to lose him. Abruptly, Catherine scooped up the pills and threw them into the toilet bowl. She yanked on the chain and watched them swirl away. With it came the first choking sob and tears.

Howling, she stumbled out of the bathroom, down the stairs and out of the house. It had started to rain. She rushed into the garden, making for the sanctuary of the oak tree. Cold rain whipped at her face as she fell into the wet leaves around the tree trunk. She wept out her misery, amazed that she could still cry. Even as the pain consumed her, she knew it was proof that she was alive, still alive.

Catherine sat shaking and frozen without the first idea how she was going to get through the rest of the day, let alone the next day and the day after that. However she managed she would have to do it herself, without the help of her husband or the numbing relief of drugs. She pressed into the tree, doubting if she had enough courage.

'*Work it out, lass.*'

The words went through her like an electric shock. Kate's words. Her mother's recipe for overcoming grief or hardship. Of course it was the answer. But Catherine had tried that, brought herself to a standstill and probably miscarried because of the gruelling housework she had made herself do. That's what Kate meant by work.

Yet Catherine had her own cure for a sore heart. Writing. If she could only bring herself to begin writing again . . .

She scrambled on to numb feet and hobbled back indoors. That night she could not face it. She banked up the fire in the kitchen and lay down on the hearth rug with a blanket and slept fitfully.

In the early morning, Catherine brewed a pot of tea and went in search of paper. Tearing out some blank pages from old cookbooks of Mrs Fairy's she took them to the kitchen table. Hands trembling, she picked up a pencil used for shopping lists. She felt nauseous. Holding it reminded her of being pregnant with David. Catherine rushed to the sink and threw up.

For the rest of the day she gave up and walked and walked around the garden, tiring herself out. For a second night she slept on the kitchen floor. In the morning, she tried again. *Just write anything – no one's going to read it*. This time the advice seemed to be her own.

She sat staring at her idle hands, listening to rain spatter down the chimney and hiss on to the fire. Just like in 10 William Black Street. If she closed her eyes she could hear the rustle of Grandda's newspaper, the slam of the oven door, Kate humming as she pounded pastry with a rolling pin. She could smell the cinders, the rising dough.

Catherine picked up the pencil and began to write. At the end of two hours she had filled six pages and was amazed to find it was already midday. She made more tea, ate two biscuits and went back to her writing. That night, she ventured up to her bedroom and read over her scrawled pages. It was a near perfect recreation of the kitchen in East Jarrow. She could see it, smell it, taste it.

Over the next few days, Catherine thought about places and people in her childhood that she had tried to forget for years. Eccentric lodgers, bad-tempered shopkeepers, the kind pawnbroker who sensed her shame at having to bring in her family's belongings. Picking over dross along the railway track, running through the scary dripping arches by the docks, gasping in wonder at a sea of red poppies in a field above

Shields. Someone grasping her hand and pulling her off her feet as they flew along, chasing the moon. Kate's hand.

She pushed the uncomfortable thought from her mind. She had come too far, spent too much energy trying to rid herself of Kate's influence to think kindly of her now. She was Catherine Cookson, wife of an Oxford graduate. There was no going back.

Catherine put away her descriptions of Tyneside. They were too vivid and disturbing. But they had given her a taste for writing again and she set herself the gruelling task of writing ten, twelve, sometimes fourteen hours a day.

Tom was demobbed early in 1946 and took up his post as maths teacher at the grammar school once more. They settled into a quiet routine: teaching, scouts and cricket coaching for him; writing, housework and gardening for her. Tom was full of admiration for the way Catherine battled her bouts of depression with a rigorous regime at her desk, often sitting up into the early hours, filling pages of script.

She tried plays but they were wooden and lifeless. She tried poems but they were sentimental and gushing. Joining a writers' circle, she tentatively tested out her short stories and came home bruised and oversensitive at their criticisms. Tom tried to help with her grammar, but they argued and fell out about it.

'I can't write like that,' Catherine protested. 'It knocks all the stuffing out of my characters.'

'You can't send them to magazines with that many spelling mistakes,' Tom said impatiently. 'And half the sentences aren't proper sentences.'

Catherine stopped showing him her work; she would do it her own way or not at all. Determined to prove to Tom she could succeed, she sent off a short story every week. After a year, they had all been returned. She carried on sending them out. Each time a large brown envelope was sent back, she would march into the garden and vigorously attack the weeds, battling her sense of failure.

She and Tom existed under the same roof, yet were distant. It was like having a lodger in the house again, Catherine thought bleakly. Too scared of pregnancy, they had stopped making love. They shared the same bed, but often Catherine stayed up half the night writing or she would wake in the early hours to find Tom sitting upright on a chair, nursing a migraine.

Outwardly, they put on a happy front. He was dedicated to his teaching and his pupils. Catherine forced herself to attend school functions to support him and invited boys back for tea after matches. She made a fuss of them and understood why Tom was so attached to the lively youngsters. Yet she could not help resenting the attention he lavished on them and the long hours he spent away from The Hurst. If only they had had their own family . . .

One summer afternoon, Catherine set out to join Tom at a school cricket match. He would be umpiring and she would have to sit and make light conversation with the other wives. She did not feel at all sociable. A short story had been returned that morning. Maybe she should give up and go back to her painting, be a lady of leisure, the type of wife that would suit Tom.

As she walked into town in a new summer dress, her resentment grew. Why did a wife always have to bend her life to her husband's? Why did Tom have the luck of a proper education and not her? She knew she could be a writer, if only she had some guidance. But Tom was a man of numbers and facts; he did not understand the compulsion within her to write.

By the time she had reached the town centre, Catherine was seething with aggression. Walking past some workmen mending a wall, she felt an overwhelming urge to pick up one of the loose bricks and hurl it through the shop window opposite. She stopped and stared at a brick. Her fists clenched as she fought down the desire to throw it and break something.

'Want to take the brick home, love?' one of the builders teased.

Catherine blushed and turned in confusion. She rushed home, appalled to think how her anger had so nearly overtaken her. She wasn't safe to be out on the streets. Back at The Hurst, she stripped off her fine clothes and pulled on her gardening trousers and shirt. Halfway through digging up a bucketful of carrots, she heard footsteps coming up the drive. Turning, she gasped in surprise.

'Bridie?'

The red-haired woman strode towards her and gave her a hug. 'Catherine, you're so thin. Thought you were a scarecrow standing there! That husband of yours not looking after you?'

Catherine grimaced, but said nothing. It was so strange seeing Bridie after all this time. She had long stopped feeling angry towards her. If she felt anything it was probably pity.

'Well, aren't you going to offer me a cup of tea or do I have to make my own?' Bridie teased.

Catherine nodded and led the way inside. While she fumbled with the tea caddy and warmed the pot, Bridie told her about her years in the army.

'I've been back running the boarding house for the past two years.' She watched Catherine over the rim of her cup. 'I'm sorry you can't have children.'

Catherine jolted. 'Who told you that?'

'I get the odd letter from Kate. She told me you've had a hard time – I know about the mental hospital.'

Catherine snapped. 'I was in a nursing home for my nerves, that's all.'

Bridie gave her a disbelieving look. 'I'm sorry all the same. If I'd known I would have come to see you – tried to help. Obviously that husband of yours is next to useless.'

Catherine knew she should defend Tom, but suddenly her lips were trembling. She put down her cup and burst into tears. Bridie was round the table in an instant, hugging her in comfort.

'Have a good cry, girl,' she crooned. 'Bridie will take care of you. I can see how unhappy you are. I knew that man would bring you nothing but heartache.'

Catherine was sobbing so hard she could not speak.

'Listen,' Bridie said softly, 'I came to tell you I'm selling up the business and going back to Ireland. Why don't you come with me? We'll have enough to start our own place over there. You, me and Maisie, just like old times. I'm the only one who's ever really understood you, Catherine, loved you for who you are. You'll never be happy as a schoolmaster's wife, always taking second place. You're better than that, much better. Come away with me, girl!'

Catherine's head spun at the idea. To run away from the drabness of post-war Hastings, from the loneliness of endless solitary hours at The Hurst, from the guilt of failing Tom as a wife – all this was suddenly possible. Bridie was offering escape.

Before Catherine could answer, the front door banged shut and steps came hurrying down the corridor. Tom burst into the kitchen.

'What's happened?' he said breathless. 'You didn't come—'

Bridie stood up but kept her hands on Catherine's shoulders.

'What are you doing here?' he asked suspiciously.

'Your wife's at the end of her tether,' Bridie said, her look contemptuous. 'Look what you've done to her.'

'Kitty,' Tom rushed forward, 'what's wrong?'

'You're what's wrong,' Bridie answered at once. 'She's sick and tired of you. I've asked her to go to Ireland with me. She needs someone to take proper care of her.'

Tom gazed at Catherine, stupefied.

'Is it true?' he demanded. 'Tell me you wouldn't go with that woman.'

'If she's any sense she will,' Bridie cried. 'At least I know how to love her.'

'Love her?' Tom shouted. 'You nearly drove her mad.'

'No, that's what you did!' Bridie accused.

Catherine jumped to her feet. 'Stop it, both of you! I can speak for myself.' She glared at them. 'I don't know what I want to do, I just know I'm not happy. Stop fighting over me like I'm some possession. Neither of you knows the real me.' She faced Tom. 'Bridie wants me to be like Maisie – a helpless little girl she can take care of – and you want a middle-class wife who can entertain and not show you up in front of your educated friends. But I'm neither of those things. I'm Kitty McMullen – Kate's bastard daughter. I feel emotions that no refined lady should feel – anger and passion and hatred. I learnt them on the streets of Jarrow. I understand badness 'cos I've seen and heard it – lived it. I'm not a fit wife for you, Tom,' she cried. 'I've spent half my life trying to be someone I'm not – and it's nearly destroyed me!'

Catherine rushed past him and fled outside. She walked for ages, her direction aimless. What a destructive person she was! She destroyed those who loved her. Yet, with each step she grew more certain that what she had shouted at Tom was the truth. Catherine Cookson, the well-spoken wife of the school teacher, was a myth. Her painfully learnt speech and manners and lofty attempts to improve herself were a veneer. Strip them away and she was still the same wild and frightened child she had always been.

Evening came before Catherine made her weary way home. To her relief Bridie had gone. She saw a light on in the bedroom and went up to face Tom. He was sitting on the bed, a packed suitcase beside him. On seeing her, he got up and closed the lid.

'I was waiting for you to come back before I left,' he said, his voice cold.

'What are you doing?' Catherine stared in alarm.

'Leaving you, Kitty. It's what you want, isn't it? You and Bridie.'

'Me and Bridie? Don't be daft. I was never going to go with her.'

He turned and fixed her with angry eyes. 'That's not what she thinks. You've made it perfectly plain you don't love me. And now I know you loved that woman all the time. How often have you seen her behind my back? What a fool I've been to think I could make you happy.' He yanked the case off the bed.

'Stop it, Tom. You're frightening me. I don't know what you're talking about. Today's the first time I've set eyes on Bridie since we got married.'

'I don't believe you,' he glared. 'Bridie said you've never stopped loving each other.'

Catherine cried, 'And you'd rather believe her than me, would you?'

Tom pulled a bundle from his jacket pocket. His voice shook with anger. 'I believe these!' He thrust them at Catherine. A pile of letters; her letters to Bridie. A grenade lobbed into their midst by a departing Bridie, to blow their marriage to smithereens. Did Bridie think by destroying Tom's love, she would have no other option but to go running to her? *If I can't have you – he never will – I'll make sure of that.*

Catherine grabbed Tom's arm as he pushed past. 'These don't mean what you think they mean,' she gabbled. 'They were written years ago. I was lonely—'

'And in love with her,' Tom said savagely.

'No! I don't know. More star-struck than in love – like a girl's crush on someone older. She gave me love and encouragement that I had never had from Kate, and at a time I really needed it.' Catherine's look was pleading. 'But I stopped loving her years ago. It's you I love, Tom, *you.*'

He looked at her bewildered. 'Then what was all that about not wanting to be my wife?'

'I do. But not the way it is now.'

'Then how?' he shouted. 'What is it you want, Kitty?'

'I need to be my own person, Tom, not just your wife. But I'm frightened that's not the woman you want to be married to.'

He dropped the suitcase, his look desolate. 'All I've ever wanted was you, Kitty. Not a posh Mrs Cookson. I'm not ashamed of who you are or where you come from. I love you for it. Can't you see that? I love Kitty McMullen from Jarrow. I love Kate's daughter.'

Catherine's throat choked with tears. She reached out and their arms went around each other. Warmth flooded her like a benediction.

'That's the best thing anyone's ever said to me,' she whispered. 'I love you, Tom. I love you so much it hurts. Please forgive me?'

His answering hug told her he did.

Chapter 51

After the crisis over Bridie, Tom and Catherine grew closer. They talked and read together in the evenings, they gardened side by side. After an operation to remove half Catherine's womb, they resumed lovemaking. Most of all, Tom encouraged her to write about what she knew. He discovered her descriptions of her grandparents' kitchen and the places of her childhood.

'You've got something here,' he said excitedly. 'Write about Jarrow and Shields, Kitty.'

So Catherine wrote. Every day of the year she wrote. Eventually the scores of pages took the shape of a novel. A story about a beautiful woman nearly ruined by having an illegitimate daughter came pouring out. Except her heroine, Kate Hannigan, was saved by marriage to an honourable man. Through a speaker at the writers' circle, Catherine secured an agent and shortly afterwards, to her amazed delight, it was accepted for publication.

She resisted the desire to run into the streets and scream out the news. Once in print, a proud Tom mentioned it to anyone who would listen – from his colleagues to the local butcher. Some people, having read it, looked at her askance.

' "A bit too brutal for a romance, don't you think?" ' Catherine mimicked a member of the writers' group to Tom. She laughed shortly. 'I'm not writing romance – I'm writing about real people, warts and all.'

Catherine wrote on. Her follow-up novel was rejected and she sank into depression, questioning if she should continue with such gritty subject matter. Tom wouldn't hear of her changing course.

'You're right and the publishers are wrong,' he insisted. 'Keep at it.'

At times, the old depression took hold and she wandered around the empty house bereft of ideas. One day, alone at The Hurst, she cried out angrily, 'If there's anything there, give me a story!'

Within an hour, one had come to her, so clear and complete that Catherine was shaken to the core. Had it come from deep within or was Our Lady still watching over her, despite her lapsed faith? She worked on it night and day. The following year, *The Fifteen Streets* was published; a year after that, *Colour Blind*. Exiled though she was from Tyneside, the place had never seemed more vivid and alive to her. She wrote about the Edwardian streets she remembered, but was happy to revisit them only in her mind.

Strangely, Catherine was thinking about Kate when a letter came from Aunt Mary.

She ran to meet Tom on his way home from school. 'Kate's ill,' she told him in agitation. 'Our Mary says she's – she's – dying.'

'You must go and see her,' Tom said at once. 'If you don't, you'll never forgive yourself.'

'But what will I say to her after all this time?' Catherine asked helplessly.

'You've never been stuck for words before,' Tom said drily.

She held his hand. 'Please will you come with me?'

A week later, they were travelling north along the same route as when Catherine had been carrying David. She tried not to think of it. When smoky Tyneside hove into view, Catherine felt her heart lurch. Was it nerves or something deeper? Walking from the station into the narrow streets of Tyne Dock to Kate's flat, her eyes prickled at the familiar accents and the faded awnings over shops she knew. Feeling tearful, she gripped Tom's arm for support.

Aunt Mary let them in. When Catherine saw her mother lying in bed, her bloated face creasing into a smile at her appearance, she burst into tears.

'Haway, hinny and stop your noise,' Kate chided. 'I'm not dead yet.'

Catherine sat down before her knees buckled. Her mother looked so old and helpless, not a threat at all. The gloomy room smelled of decay. She should have brought flowers to brighten it. Why had she not thought to buy any?

Tom, seeing his wife overcome with emotion, chatted to Kate about the journey. When he asked her about herself, Kate waved at him dismissively.

'Doctor's making too much of a fuss. Tell me about Kitty's books.'

Later, as Kate slept, Mary told them bluntly, 'She's got cancer. It's in her liver. Dropsy and heart trouble too. Doctor says it's likely she won't last more than three months – maybes six.'

364

Catherine swallowed. 'Can't they operate?'

Mary shook her head. 'Too far gone. She's puffed up like a balloon. Doesn't complain much, but you can tell she's in pain.'

'What can we do?' Catherine asked.

'Doctor says she should be somewhere more healthy – where the air's cleaner. Nowt can cure her, but at least it would help her breathing. She gets that short of breath, can't make it down the stairs any longer. And I'm too old to be running up here all day to see to her.'

Catherine looked at Tom. His eyes were full of compassion.

'She could come and stay with us,' he said quietly.

Catherine was filled with gratitude. Despite Kate's past treatment of him, Tom was willing to forgive and take her in. Catherine knew in her heart that that was what they should do – offer the dying Kate a home – but she did not have the courage to do it without him.

She touched his face gently. 'Thank you.'

Kate visibly revived at the news, but the doctor was dubious she could make the long journey. In the end, she was taken by ambulance to the station and put on a sleeper to London using the luggage hoist. When Mary cried, Kate told her not to be so soft.

In London, she was hoisted into another ambulance across the city to the Hastings train, where a third ambulance awaited. After a gruelling night and day of travel, Catherine and Tom got Kate safely to The Hurst.

They brought down a bed and put it in the cook's sitting room.

'You'll get the warmth from the kitchen in here,' Catherine told her, tucking her in. 'Tom's heating you up a bowl of soup.'

Kate grabbed feebly at her arm. Her eyes glittered.

'Ta for doing this, hinny,' she croaked.

Catherine shrugged awkwardly. 'It's Tom you should thank – it was his idea.'

'Aye, but it's your doing.' Kate's chin wobbled. 'Oh lass, I've come home!'

Kate did not die as soon as expected.

'It's your skill as a nurse has kept her alive,' Tom said.

'Her sheer bloody-mindedness,' Catherine joked.

After a year, Kate was able to take short walks around the garden and help with the cooking. She lost her bloated look and stayed sober, for there was no one to buy her drink. Yet keeping The Hurst running, looking after Kate and trying to write was proving too much for Catherine. Her own health was deteriorating again.

Tom took the decision that they should move to somewhere more manageable. When they discovered a charming mock-Tudor villa with a sunny garden, Catherine found it easier to leave her old home than she had imagined.

'It's just bricks and mortar, nowt else,' Kate said, excited about the move.

She chose a room on the ground floor with a view on to the garden through French windows. Once they were settled in, Tom came home with a frisky terrier.

'Been abandoned in the school yard – no one wants it.'

Catherine patted it in sympathy. 'How could no one want you, eh?' She fell instantly and besottedly in love with the noisy, affectionate dog. He raced around the house like an irrepressible child, which was what he became in Catherine's eyes. They called him Bill for no particular reason and even Kate spoilt him with titbits from the table.

At times, Catherine balked at being so tied to her mother. She and Tom hardly ever went out alone, for Kate could not reach the bathroom without help and they feared she would fall if left unattended. Gradually she began to fade again, but rather than accept her restrictions she railed against them, growing more crotchety by the day. Catherine relented and allowed her mother a glass of beer at night to ease the pain.

Some days, Kate would sit happily in a chair, slowly reading one of Catherine's books, Bill lying in her lap. *Maggie Rowan* and *A Grand Man* had recently been published. On others she could not rise from bed, and snapped at Catherine about the food or being left for more than ten minutes.

The doctor warned Catherine to prepare herself for her mother's death.

'I could arrange for nursing care – give you a break,' he suggested.

'No.' Catherine was adamant. 'I'll nurse her myself. She'll only give some poor nurse the run-around.'

But her sense of obligation was not her only reason for wanting to nurse her mother. As Kate's life ebbed away, so did the secrets of her past. If Catherine stayed close, the dying woman might let slip something about her father. Catherine still yearned to find out anything about this shadowy figure – fill in the pieces of herself that had been missing all her life. She wanted to hear the truth from Kate, not just second-hand gossip from Aunt Mary or Great-Aunt Lizzie.

One late September day, when the garden was gleaming bronze in the sunlight, Catherine found her mother in bed, crying over her book *Colour Blind*.

'How did you know?' Kate whispered. 'About our Jack.'

'Know what?' Catherine looked at her puzzled.

'He was just like this man in the book – the way he tret me. But you were too young to know.'

Catherine stared in shock. The character in her novel forced himself on his sister. Surely her Uncle Jack had not been like that? She remembered him as shy and timid with girls. But Kate's face told a different story. The old memory resurfaced: waking in bed beside Kate, a figure looming over them with a waft of whisky, a struggle, whispered wrangling, Kate breaking free and fleeing to the safety of the privy. Uncle Jack. She must have known it all along, for there it was in her book.

'Why did you not say anything to Grandma or Grandda?'

Kate's laugh was bitter. 'Who would've believed me? He was Rose's blue-eyed boy. I was the one would've been blamed – Kate the slut – for leadin' him astray.'

Catherine sat on the bed, her heart heavy. 'Tell me about those days,' she asked gently, 'and the time before I was born.'

Kate brusquely brushed away tears. 'You don't want to hear about all that.'

'I do,' Catherine insisted. 'Whatever you say won't go beyond these four walls, I promise. Not even to Tom. But I need to know, Kate. I'd rather know my father was a bad'un than know nothing.'

For long minutes they sat in silence and Catherine feared her mother would remain stubbornly mute. Then suddenly she began to speak, her voice reflective.

'I first met him at Ravensworth – saw him with Lady Emma – then out riding. He stopped to pick up the raspberries I'd dropped – made me eat one.' Her faded eyes shone, her tone almost girlish. 'So handsome in his riding clothes – hair all chestnut waves like a lion's mane and eyes that looked right inside me. Your eyes.' Kate looked fondly.

Catherine sat holding her breath while her mother spoke of the growing romance with Alexander, a coal agent's adopted son who came often to the estate and courted her.

367

'Am I like him in any other way?' she dared ask. 'Great-Aunt Lizzie said he was an artist.'

Kate looked startled, then nodded. 'He was, though he liked to draw people, not buildings. That's what interested him – ordinary lads and lasses. Went all over the estate drawing them at work.' She paused, her hands moving in agitation over the covers. 'And some'at else. He used to have nosebleeds like yours – bad ones. But I could never tell Dr Dyer for the shame of it. Didn't like to think he had owt to do with you – wouldn't think about him – not after he'd turned his back on us and left me to face the music on me own.'

'So you never saw him again? Perhaps if he'd seen you face to face – seen you carrying me – he might have done something for us.' Catherine was desperate to believe the best of her absent father.

Kate gave her a look of such pity that her stomach turned over.

'He did come back to see me,' she said sadly. 'Thought he'd come to fetch us from Leam Lane, but he threw money at me and your grandma and waltzed off. Never saw him again. Was like living in a tomb in that terrible house – those weeks before you were born.' Her face was harrowed. 'Always hoped he'd change his mind, even afterwards. That's why I put his name on your birth certificate and lied about being Mrs Davies. Could've gone to gaol, but it was all I could give you – a decent name.'

Catherine swallowed. 'So when you told me he was dead – when I was a bairn – you didn't know about him dying in Sweden?'

'No, that was to stop your questions. You always had a head too full of fancy notions and a gob full of questions. But I didn't know till years later when Davie said he'd seen his gravestone.' Her voice was flat. 'It was only then I gave up on Alexander and married Davie.'

'But he might just have said that to get you to marry him,' Catherine said indignantly. 'Have you ever thought of that?'

Kate closed her eyes tight shut as if the pain was too great. 'Aye,' she whispered. 'That's what we were arguing about the night Davie went missin'. It was a terrible row. We'd both had one too many. I said I didn't believe Alexander was really dead – that he'd only said it to make me forget him. I said some terrible things – that I never should've married him – that Alexander was the only man I'd ever loved.'

Kate was almost whispering now and Catherine had to lean closer.

'And – and then he told me. Not only had Alexander died all those years ago, but the gravestone was put there by his loving wife, Polly.' A sob caught in her throat. 'I knew then it was true. Your father had been

368

engaged to some posh woman – one of the gentry – when he was still seeing me. I was daft enough to hope he might choose me over her – I was that in love with him and thought he was too. Well, Polly was the lass's name. I could have waited all me life, but Alexander would never have come back even if he'd lived.' Kate shuddered. 'I told Davie to get out and never come back – even though I knew he was tellin' the truth. But it hurt too much, hinny. Then poor Davie—'

Catherine reached across quickly and squeezed her mother's hand. She was filled with a sense of loss, not just for herself but for the young Kate who had been treated so callously.

That afternoon, as the sun dipped behind the trees, Kate talked of the birth and how she had been banished by her parents to work in Chester-le-Street while they brought Catherine up as their own.

'Was to save face, I had to give you up,' Kate said bitterly. 'My punishment was to work to keep you and not be allowed to be a mam. Was just a servant, nowt else, after you were born. Old John said I was lucky he hadn't kicked me on to the street like the whore I was.' Tears brimmed in her sunken eyes. 'Wouldn't even let me pick you up for a cuddle when I came home.'

Tears filled Catherine's throat. She thought of how she still yearned to hold her baby David after all this time. How cruel was Kate's punishment – a mother's love stifled at birth.

On impulse, Catherine reached across the bed and gathered Kate into her arms. Wordlessly they held on to each other, while her mother cried into her hair.

Eventually, Kate sobbed, 'I've been a terrible mother – a wicked woman to you, Kitty!'

Catherine thought of all the pain and hurt of their fraught relationship. At times she had hated her mother more than anything else in the world, but she knew there was nothing to be gained from speaking her anger. Kate must be allowed to die in peace. Catherine summoned up words of forgiveness.

'No you haven't,' she gulped. 'The only person you've really hurt all these years is you. It's not your fault what happened, so stop blaming yourself.'

Kate lay back quietly weeping. 'Don't leave me, Kitty.'

Catherine stayed with her mother till she fell asleep. That night she went to bed drained and slept straight away. For the next couple of days, Kate slipped in and out of consciousness, always seeming to settle when Catherine came near. On the third morning, Catherine noticed a difference in Kate's breathing. It was shallow and fast, like marbles in her throat.

Her mother lay with her eyes closed, but when Catherine tried to leave the room, her hand moved in agitation and she tried to say something. Bending close, Catherine reassured her, 'I'm here, don't fret.'

For a moment Kate's eyes flickered open and gave a flash of recognition. Her hand groped out to hers. Catherine took it and held it. Kate's fingers grasped hers weakly.

'Forgive me, lass,' Kate rasped, her breathing ragged.

Catherine leant over and tenderly kissed her forehead.

'God bless you, Kitty,' she murmured and closed her eyes again.

Catherine sat holding her mother's hand as the clock ticked on towards midday. It was Bill pushing open the door, padding into the room and whimpering at the bed that alerted her to the sudden stillness. Kate was gone.

For a moment Catherine was filled with a sudden sense of peace, of relief. Kate lay there looking so calm and untroubled, a much younger woman. Catherine felt a pang of loss. She wished she could have known that Kate – the one with whom Alexander had fallen in love. Rising, Catherine leant over her mother and kissed her cooling cheek.

'It's over,' she whispered. 'All your struggling's over, Mam.'

Tears flooded her eyes as she said the word – the name she had never been able to utter when Kate was alive, Mam. She went to the French windows and threw them open, letting the autumn breeze sweep into the room. With Bill at her heels, Catherine escaped into the garden to weep.

Chapter 52

The time following Kate's death was like a strange limbo for Catherine. She alternately rejoiced in her freedom from her overbearing mother and mourned her passing. Right at the very end, she had come closer to her mother than at any time in her life, only to lose her just as she was getting to understand her.

Kate's going seemed to sever her ties with Tyneside, cutting Catherine off from the source of her inspiration. She began to realise just how important Kate had been to her writing; she had been the life-blood to her stories, their stormy relationship the spur to her creativity.

It was Tom who suggested she write about Kate directly.

'Get her out of your system, Kitty,' he encouraged. 'Write about her if you can't write about anything else.'

Catherine tried. Over the next few years she attempted to make sense of her childhood and her seesawing emotions over Kate. At times it was too brutal, too unforgiving, and Catherine abandoned the project. It was too personal, stirring up raw feelings she had tried for years to bury. But having given up on the idea, she found a renewed creativity in her fiction.

By the end of the decade, she was making a name for herself as a popular writer, a number of her novels being adapted into films. Some people found it strange that she could write so vividly about the north country when she had lived away for more than half her life.

She ventured back on occasional research trips, and even rarer visits to her few remaining relatives. Tom encouraged these and liked to go with her. But after a day or two she was always homesick for their house in Hastings and could not wait to get back.

'Maybe we'll end up living in the north,' Tom once suggested, 'when I retire.'

Catherine had laughed at such an idea. 'Like elephants going home to die, you mean?' she snorted. 'You can go, Tom, I'm staying here.'

Then, one day, quite out of the blue, a visitor appeared on their doorstep.

Catherine stared at the middle-aged woman in the neat coat and hat, clutching a handbag.

'Hello, Kitty,' she said nervously. 'Or should I say, Mrs Catherine Cookson?'

Something about her joky singsong voice made Catherine's heart twist.

'Lily Hearn?' she gasped. 'It's never you!'

The woman grinned and nodded. 'I'm on a coach tour. Knew you lived round here. Wasn't ganin' to come, but one of the lasses said to get mesel' along and give you a fright.'

Catherine laughed and rushed forward, hugging her long-lost friend in delight.

'Eeh, Lily, I'm so glad you did. Come in, come in and meet Tom. We're having tea in the garden.'

'Listen to you,' Lily teased, 'tea in the garden. You always did have fancy ideas, Kitty. And, by heck, you've made them come true. Just look at this place.'

She gazed around in awe as Catherine showed her through the house to the sheltered garden. Proudly Catherine introduced Tom to Lily.

'Lily was my best friend from Jarrow.'

'Till we fell out,' Lily said bluntly.

Catherine blushed to remember their painful parting. 'I was daft to let that happen. Always too quick to take offence in those days. I thought you'd told that terrible old Atter about me having no da.'

Lily was indignant. 'No, I never! Is that why you never kept in touch? I thought you'd just got too grand for the likes of me. I would never have dropped you in it, Kitty.'

'I know you wouldn't,' Catherine assured her quickly. 'Atter must've worked it out herself – she was that nosy. By the time I stopped being angry, it seemed too late to make amends. I'm sorry.' She slipped her arm through Lily's as if they were girls again. 'It's so good to see you.'

They spent the afternoon catching up on what each had done. Lily had married a local man, had two children and still lived in Shields. They talked non-stop, regaling Tom with stories from their past. Tom watched in astonishment; he had not seen Catherine look so young or light-hearted in years. The two friends giggled and teased each other mercilessly. Why had she never mentioned this Lily Hearn before?

Catherine urged her to stay for dinner, but Lily refused.

'My Matt'll think I've run off.'

'Your husband's here too?' Catherine exclaimed. 'Why didn't you bring him?'

Lily's look was sardonic. 'Said he wouldn't know what to say to a lady that writes books. I told him you were just a lass from Jarrow, but he wouldn't have it.'

Catherine flushed. Once she would have given anything to hear people from Jarrow call her a lady, but now it just made her feel empty.

'I'm pleased for you,' Lily said generously. 'You deserve it, Kitty.'

Catherine felt overcome. 'Come and visit again,' she pleaded. 'Next time come for a holiday and bring Matt and the family.'

Lily shrugged. 'Maybes we'll see you up our way some time?' When Catherine did not answer, she added, 'You better come quick or you won't recognise the place. They're pulling down the New Buildings.'

Catherine was unexpectedly upset by the news. After Lily had gone, she could not settle. Tom spoke her thoughts out loud.

'You should go, Kitty, before it's too late. You should return to Jarrow.'

On a blustery spring day, Catherine stood with Tom and Lily on the half-demolished site in East Jarrow. William Black Street was already a pile of rubble, only the end gable still standing where Catherine had once played shops. She could almost hear the chants of the children at play, the beat of a skipping rope, a mother's voice calling for a child to come home.

The Jarrow she knew was almost unrecognisable, the shipyards gone and new blocks of flats pushing towards the sky instead of cranes and gantries. Yet the past was still there all around her – the blackened outline of St Paul's and its ruined monastery, the oily Slake, the pit wheels of South Shields and the restless River Tyne.

Catherine held Tom's hand.

'Do you still want to live in a place like this?' she challenged.

Tom smiled at her fondly. 'Only if you're there with me.'

Catherine's eyes smarted as she gazed at the bulldozed bricks of her former home. She heard Kate's promise ringing in her ears: *You'll see your day with them – get your own back. By God, you will!*

Suddenly Catherine realised it no longer mattered. She did not need to prove herself to her old community, did not want to get her own back at them for the slights and cruelties of her childhood. More than anything else, she yearned to be accepted back. The restless, impetuous

Kitty McMullen who had run away all those years ago wanted to come home.

Perhaps one day soon, she and Tom would come back for good. Catherine was surprised by the warm feeling the idea gave her.

She turned to Lily and smiled. 'Any chance of a cup of tea?'

'Aye,' Lily grinned, 'and some of Mam's scones – the ones you like. She's been waiting for you to call for over thirty years.'

Catherine laughed, linking her arms through Lily's and Tom's. How she loved them both. Together they set off down the bank from the New Buildings into Shields one last time.